HEART
OF
THORNS

HEART OF Thorns

BREE BARTON

 KATHERINE TEGEN BOOKS
An Imprint of HarperCollins Publishers

Katherine Tegen Books is an imprint of HarperCollins Publishers.

Library of Congress Cataloging-in-Publication Number: 2017955884
ISBN 978-0-06-244768-5

Typography by Joel Tippie
18 19 20 21 22   PC/LSCH   10 9 8 7 6 5 4 3 2 1
❖
First Edition

For Carli Christina Cat,
the original BA

One of the ancient maps of the world
is heart-shaped, carefully drawn
and once washed with bright colors,
though the colors have faded
as you might expect feelings to fade
from a fragile old heart, the brown map
of a life. But feeling is indelible,
and longing infinite, a starburst compass
pointing in all the directions
two lovers might go, a fresh breeze
swelling their sails, the future uncharted,
still far from the edge
where the sea pours into the stars.

Fidacteu zeu biqhotz limarya eu naj.

Trust your heart, even if it kills you.

Prologue

Once upon a time, in a castle carved of stone, a girl plotted murder.

PART ONE

Flesh

Chapter 1

PORCELAIN BOSOM

ON THE EVE OF her wedding to the prince, Mia Rose ought to have been sitting at her cherrywood dresser, primping her auburn curls and lacing her whalebone corset. She should have been fussing with the train of her gown, a piece of oyster silk that unfurled behind her like a snow-kissed boulevard.

Mia was doing none of those things.

She paced her bridal chambers with a pouch of boar's blood gripped between her fingers. For weeks she'd done meticulous research, filching various cuts of meat from the castle kitchens—duck, goose, venison—but the boar emerged victorious. The blood would dry like human blood: a dark crusted brown.

She had purloined one of her sister's gowns so she could

shred it alongside her wedding dress, leaving them both behind in bloodied ribbons. The plan was simple. She would stage the scene in the tunnels beneath the castle, with only one logical conclusion to be drawn: Mia, the prince's intended bride, had been brutally attacked, abducted, and most likely killed, along with her younger sister, Angelyne. The poor little Rose girls, taken before their time.

While the king's guards scoured the castle grounds for the vile murderer, Mia would lead Angie to freedom.

It was admittedly not her finest plan. The problem was, it was her *only* plan. And there was one additional, fairly significant hitch:

She hadn't told her sister.

"Mi? Are you nearly ready?"

Angelyne swept into Mia's chambers, her satin slippers gliding over the floor. "I came to see if you needed . . ." She stopped short. "Why are you wearing a rope?"

Mia had fed a thick rope through her trouser loops for their descent into the castle's subterranean bowels. She opened her mouth to explain, but no words came out. The beginning of a headache was scratching at her temples.

Angie frowned. "You do know the final feast is about to begin."

"I am aware."

"And you are gownless and gloveless."

"True."

"And your hair looks like a poodle died on your head."

"I've always enjoyed the company of poodles."

"Is that blood?" Angelyne snatched the leather pouch out of Mia's hands, sniffed, and grimaced. "I don't care what you were about to do; I'll tell you what you're doing now." She gestured toward the cherry dresser, nudging a stack of books and a stubby wax candle aside. "Sit. I'm going to pin your hair."

Mia flumped into the chair, irritated. The headache was clawing at her skull. Why was she unable to tell her sister about the plan? It wasn't as if the stakes weren't treacherously high: one month ago, their father, Griffin, had promised the king a bride for his son. At seventeen, Mia was the obvious choice. But fifteen-year-old Angie was a close second.

Mia had tried desperately to dissuade her father. Girls in the river kingdom were rarely given a say in the men they married, yet Mia had naively assumed she would be different. Under her father's tutelage, she had trained as a Huntress for the past three years. Surely he wouldn't pawn her off to the highest bidder. But no matter how much she pleaded, he never wavered.

He had condemned her to a lifelong prison sentence, annihilating all chance of love or happiness. Her own father, who knew better than anyone the power of love. Fortunately Mia had no intention of wedding and bedding Prince Quin. She had work to do. A sister to save . . . and a murderous Gwyrach to find.

"Angie? I need to—"

"Sit still? You're absolutely right." Angelyne rummaged through her basket of hairpins and alarmingly sharp objects. It was Mia's fault she was in the castle at all. When the queen had tried to furnish Mia with a lady-in-waiting to help with gowns, gems, and skin greases, the whole idea made her nervous (what was the lady waiting *for*?). So she had requested that Angie stay in Kaer Killian, the royal castle, during the engagement.

Most days she regretted it. The drafty castle had only exacerbated her sister's many mysterious illnesses. The Kaer was an ancient citadel, carved from a mountain of ice and frozen rock. It was miserably cold. Not to mention Angie had been attracting the attention of the young duke, which was troubling. Ange was lithe and slender, with a pale heart-shaped face, rose-petal lips, and wavy hair the color of summer strawberries ripening on the vine.

"Mia Rose," Angie muttered, "Princess of Chaos, Destroyer of Nice Things."

Ange let out a short, sharp cough before swiftly regaining her composure. She yanked a bone comb through Mia's tangles hard enough to make her gasp.

"Angelyne Rose, Mistress of Pain, Wielder of Torture Tools." Mia massaged her temples. "My head was killing me *before* you started this torment. I don't know why I'm suddenly getting these atrocious headaches."

Angie paused. "Where does it hurt, exactly?"

"Here." She pointed to the back of her skull. "The occiput. And here." She dug her fingertips into the bridge of her nose. "The sphenoid bone. It's like my whole cerebrum is on fire."

"Human words, please. Not all of us speak anatomy."

"Even my mandible is throbbing." Mia massaged her jaw.

"You mean you have a toothache."

6

"Teeth. All of them."

"How can all your teeth ache at once?" Her sister smothered another cough. "Here. I have just the thing."

Angie fished a dented tin of peppermint salve out of her basket. When she tried to twist off the lid, she fumbled. They both stared at her gloved hands. The lamb slinkskin was a soft, pale pink.

"It's all right," Mia said. "You can take them off. I won't tell Father."

Slowly, carefully, Angie pinched the lambskin at her pinkie, then her ring finger, then her pointer. She inched the glove off her hand and laid it neatly on the dresser. Her complexion was smooth and peachy, so different from Mia's ivory skin and copper freckles.

"Just think," Ange said quietly. "After tomorrow, you'll never have to wear them again."

How easy it was to forget.

With the exception of the royal family, all girls were required to wear gloves as a precautionary measure. Any woman might be Gwyrach; hence every woman was a threat. The Gwyrach were women who, through the simple act of touch, could manipulate flesh, bone, breath, and blood.

Not women, Mia reminded herself. *Demons*. They were half god, half human—the wrath and power of a god mixed with the petty jealousies and grudges of human beings. The Gwyrach could fracture bones and freeze breath. They could starve limbs of oxygen, enthrall a heart with false desire, and make blood boil and skin crawl. They could even stop a heart. How effortless, this act of murder: a palm pressed to a chest, and a life snuffed out forever. Mia had seen proof.

A Gwyrach had destroyed their lives—and Mia was going to find her. *Heart for a heart, life for a life.* But first, she and Angelyne had to escape.

In the mirror, she saw a shadow flicker over her sister's face. Then it was gone. Angie rubbed the peppermint salve into Mia's jaw and quickly slid the glove back over her hand. Her wrists were so thin they made Mia's chest ache. Birdlike. There was a reason their mother had called Angie her little swan.

Before she knew what was happening, her sister was lifting Mia's linen tunic up over her head and fitting the whalebone corset around her rib cage.

"Four hells, Angie!"

"What? You look like a princess!" She stared admiringly at Mia's reflection. "Will there be candlelight in the prince's chambers? Because it does wonders for your bone structure. Your clavicle throws the most beautiful shadows. . . ."

"I doubt it's my *clavicle* he'll be looking at," Mia said darkly. Between the whalebone corset pushing up and the gown's neckline plunging down, she had never seen so much of her own flesh.

"You have Mother's figure." Angie sighed. "What I wouldn't give to have a porcelain swell of breast."

Mia caught her sister's eye in the polished glass, and despite everything—or maybe because of it—they both burst into laughter. It was always like this: they could be bickering one moment and shrieking in unabashed delight the next.

"You've been reading your dreadful novels again, I see."

"You have so little faith in fate. There's nothing wrong with wanting to fall in love! To be swept up in something bigger than yourself—to find a handsome partner in the dance of destiny."

"Like Mother and Father."

Angie touched the moonstone pendant at her throat. It had belonged to their mother. "Yes," she said, her voice feathery soft. "Like that."

They were wasting precious time. It was now or never. "I need you to listen, Ange. What I'm about to tell you is important."

"Oh?" Her sister seized a long hairpin and plunged it into the smoldering candle, then took a strand of Mia's dark-red hair and coiled it around the warm, waxy pin. When she let go, it snaked into a perfect corkscrew. In the torchlight Mia couldn't help but think her curls gleamed the color of wet blood.

"Angelyne." Her voice was deadly quiet. "We are getting out of here. You and I. I have everything arranged, so you don't have to do anything but trust me."

Angie set the pin slowly on the dresser. Her blue eyes flashed in the mirror.

"I know what you've been plotting, Mi. I've seen you with your maps, packing your secret satchels. I know you're running away. And I'm not coming."

Mia was stunned. "I—I'm not leaving you behind."

"Maybe I want to be left behind. Have you considered that? Maybe this life you're so determined to hate—living in a castle, married to a prince—isn't such a bad life."

"To be trapped forever in this frozen tomb?" She reached up and pressed a palm to her sister's forehead. "Are you febrile? The fever is stealing your sense."

Angie shrugged her off. "*I'm* the one who's being sensible! You treat me like a victim. Poor sick little Angie, always in need of someone to save her. But I don't need saving. Go. Flee the castle. Run off to have your adventures."

"My *adventures*? You speak as if I'm going on holiday. You know I have to find her, Angie. If Father won't, I will. *Heart for a heart, life for a life.*"

"Yes, well. You Hunters all think you're exacting justice when really you're just adding weight to one side of the scale. More bodies. More loss."

The conversation was twisting too quickly for Mia to grab hold of. "Why would you choose a loveless marriage? What about the 'dance of destiny'? Think of the way Mother looked at Father . . ."

"I try *not* to think of her," Angie snapped. "Though you seem intent on reminding me."

"Is that really what you want? To be bound by sacred vow to a boy who doesn't love you? All so you can twirl around the castle in a pretty gown?"

"You don't get to tell me what I want!"

All the blood drained from Angelyne's face. She staggered forward, clutching the bedpost, her slim body racked by coughs. Instantly Mia was by her side.

"The dizzy spells again?"

"They come out of nowhere. Everything is fine and then the world goes white."

"Maybe you should lie down."

"Maybe I should." Mia helped ease her onto the canopy bed, plumping the vermilion silk pillows under her head. She watched her sister's chest rise and fall, a delicate paper lantern. Guilt roiled in her belly.

Mia didn't feel so well herself. An inexplicable heat poured over her, as scorching as if she'd leaned over a fire, orange flames licking her freckled flesh. She felt the sweat gathering damply beneath her arms, pooling in the scoop of her lower back. Reason number six hundred and twelve she wouldn't make a very good princess: princesses did not have sweat stains blooming on their fine silken gowns.

Angie's smile was sad. "Look at me. Not even strong enough to have a proper fight. I really am a heroine from one of my novels." She reached for Mia's hand, her skin sweltering. "Go, Mi. If you want to run, run. I'll only slow you down."

Mia's heart plummeted. Her sister couldn't go more than five minutes without succumbing to one of her unexplained ailments—fevers, coughing fits, dizzy spells, monstrous headaches. Sometimes Ange stumbled forward, her feet gone suddenly limp, her toes numb. Mia had searched all her books on physiology, exhausted every tome on maladies and infections. She always came up short.

To escape, they would need to slip stealthily through an endless maze of tunnels, flee the castle, make it through the village undetected, commandeer a boat, and sail the Natha River east to Fojo Karação. Fojo was where her mother had first fallen in love—and where she had made enemies. The journey would take days. Weeks.

Angie would never make it. In her heart of hearts, Mia had always known.

The truth seeped into her with sickening certitude.

She would never find the murderous Gwyrach.

She would never leave the castle.

She would marry the prince.

Mia tried valiantly to mask her despair. If she couldn't save her sister, at least she could make her smile.

"You're stuck with me, I'm afraid. Even if you'd rather have a handsome boy to admire the swell of your porcelain bosom."

She heard footsteps in the castle corridor. Two harsh knocks echoed through her chambers.

"Lady Mia?" It was the prince, his voice icy. "I've some news."

Chapter 2

INSTRUMENTS OF WAR

PRINCE QUIN STOOD AT the threshold, arms crossed. He bore a striking resemblance to her favorite human-anatomy sketch: his body long and lean, his face perfectly symmetrical. Not that she'd noticed.

"You can call me Mia. I've told you a thousand times, no 'lady' required."

"Until you are my princess, you will remain my lady," he said in his oddly formal way. He stared at her bare arms and flinched.

"My apologies, Your Grace." The last thing she needed was the prince to report her. "I was performing my ablutions," she lied.

She seized the velvety gray gloves off her dresser and slid them over her hands. While most girls in the river kingdom wore coarse bullock and deer hide, Mia and Angelyne enjoyed gloves of lamb slinkskin, soft and buttery. There were perks to being the daughters of an assassin. Especially when that assassin led the Circle of the Hunt, the king's dedicated tribe of Gwyrach Hunters.

Quin cleared his throat. "I've come to tell you the final feast has been postponed."

"Oh? To what do we owe this tragic turn of events?"

"Something about a burnt duck. We will reconvene in one hour."

Mia wondered why Quin hadn't sent one of his myriad servants to impart this news. The Kaer was swarming with them, all young, all female. Was there something else he wanted?

They stood angled toward one another in the doorway, studiously avoiding eye contact. He fidgeted with a gold button on the sleeve of his smart green jacket. Quin was wearing the colors of Clan Killian: seasick emerald and scintillating gold.

He cleared his throat again. "I trust you won't be late?"

"Of course not."

"Unlike last night."

"Last night was an anomaly."

"And the night before."

So that's what he wanted: to mock her. She glared at his glittering green eyes, framed by high chiseled cheekbones and a light smattering of freckles across sandy skin. His gold mane of hair curled over his ears in a perpetual state of touslement. Yes, Quin was beautiful. He was also cold and arrogant and completely unknowable. More than anything, Mia wanted to know and be known.

He was right about her being late to dinner; she'd spent the last few evenings mapping the tunnels, preparing for her and Angelyne's escape. Had she actually fooled herself into thinking she could evade her fate?

She looked at Quin with new and heavy understanding: this would be her husband. Her lifelong mate. Mia had logged very little time with him—too little to know what kind of boy he was—but she knew exactly what kind of man King Ronan was. Clan Killian had ruled Glas Ddir for centuries, glutted on power and the abuses of it. It seemed only natural the prince would take after his father.

Fear sank its teeth into her stomach and she swayed on her feet.

"Are you—" Quin reached out to steady her, then quickly withdrew his hand from her gloved arm. "You're not going to faint, are you?"

She exhaled. "I've never fainted in my life. I'm not that kind of girl."

What she didn't say was that his touch had pierced the slinkskin like a dagger. Was it always this unpleasant to be touched by a boy? She didn't have much personal experience. While other girls were sneaking into empty market stalls to shyly touch their lips to someone else's, Mia was throwing blades into tree stumps and studying the number of bones it was possible to break in a Gwyrach's neck.

Quin gestured toward the bed, where Angelyne's tiny feet peeked out from under the canopy. "Is that your sister?"

"She's resting."

"Make sure you wake her within the hour, or she'll be late, too."

"Why the sudden interest in punctuality, Your Grace?"

He shifted his weight. "My father demands it."

A chill snowflaked under Mia's skin, as if someone were sliding an ice cube along the nape of her neck. The *inside* of her neck. She did not care for King Ronan. Didn't care for the way he spoke to his servant girls or looked at her sister. Nor did she care for the pleasure he took in torturing the Gwyrach who'd been captured and brought back to Glas Ddir. She had seen his Hall of Hands.

Mia straightened. "We'll be in the Gallery in one hour. Worry not."

Was it her imagination, or did an inch of tension melt from his shoulders?

"Good. My father will be pleased. My mother is already furious at the cooks for ruining the duck—I'd rather not give her one more reason to whine."

Mia felt the gut punch she always felt when people spoke of their mothers, especially with such obvious disdain. She wanted to grab Quin by the shoulders and shake some sense into his cerebral cortex. Remind him how lucky he was.

"The Hunters are here as well," he said. "They will join us at the final feast, to ensure we are protected. But you are not to speak to them."

Anger flared in her chest. She had every right to speak to the Hunters if it pleased her. She had, after all, been training with the Circle for the past three years, poised to take the sacred oath on her eighteenth birthday and pledge her life to tracking and eliminating Gwyrach. The clean logic of the Hunters' Creed appealed to her: *Heart for a heart, life for a life.* Though she had never killed a Gwyrach—her father had strictly forbidden it—Mia knew she would not hesitate when it was time.

And then her father had summarily dismissed her from the Circle and announced her wedding plans.

"I will take it under advisement, Your Grace."

She studied him. When Mia first arrived at the castle, she'd nursed a wild hypothesis that, underneath his ice-cold exterior, Quin might actually have a red beating heart. She searched his green eyes for it—a spark of joy, a terrible secret, a tiny fissure in his veneer. Something. *Anything.* But if this were a mask, it was permanently frozen to his face, the secrets frozen with it.

The prince lingered in the doorway. What was he still doing there?

"Your buckles," Quin said.

"My buckles?"

He nodded toward the decorative buckles on her boots.

"They're very shiny."

"Thank you?"

The silence was excruciating. They each cast about for something to say.

"Your buckles are shiny, too," she blurted.

"Thanks much."

If this were the sort of conversation that would fuel the next fifty years of marriage, she was tempted to take the buckles and stab herself.

"I've got to—"

"I should be—"

"Yes," they said in unison. Without another word, Quin strode down the corridor on his long legs, his reflection flashing off the black onyx walls. He really did look like Wound Man, the lanky male figure on her favorite anatomical plate, minus the various weapons sticking out of his body.

Mia's fingers thickened, blood crawling through her veins. It was not the first time Quin had left a trail of frostbite in his wake. She couldn't account for the sluggishness of her hands or the kiss of cold against her cheek. Was this how it felt to be hated? Like sinking into a snowdrift, naked and exposed?

She banished the notion. Hatred wasn't cold, any more than love was hot. To start assigning meaning to bodily sensations was a dangerous game. The Gwyrach trafficked in sensations, and as long as they roamed free, touch was a battlefield, bodies the instruments of war. For Mia, the casualties had been devastating.

She brushed past her sister, sound asleep. Angelyne could fall asleep faster than anyone she knew. She'd always been that way.

Mia rubbed her hands until the blood was pumping through them once more. She plucked a bundle of sulfyr sticks from her dresser and retrieved the satchel from its hiding place under the bed. Then she stooped over the stone fireplace and brushed aside the mound of ashes. Under the ashes was an iron grate, and beneath it, a trapdoor.

She lifted the grate quietly so as not to wake her sister, then lowered herself into the darkness.

She would pay her mother a visit.

Chapter 3

BONES AND DUST

MIA SCRAPED A PINEWOOD sulfyr stick against the coarse rock of the tunnel wall. The sticks, thick as thumbs, were a gift from her father, his latest spoils from Pembuk, the glass kingdom to the west. They were clearly his attempt to worm his way back into her good graces. It hadn't worked, but she'd taken them anyway.

Griffin Rose traversed the four kingdoms hunting Gwyrach, and his pockets were always full of exotic gifts. Mia still remembered how, when she was a little girl hungry for adventure, he would unroll crinkling scrolls of parchment paper on the kitchen table, letting her trace her tiny finger over his travels.

"This is the known world," he'd told her, "carved into four kingdoms."

"River, Glass, Snow, and Fire!" she'd cried, eager to please.

"Very good, little rose." Her father had pulled a peppery-spiced chocolate from his pocket, though for Mia the greater reward was always the way he nodded with pleasure when she answered a question correctly. "Now name them in their native tongues."

Languages came easily to Mia, in the same way mathematics and sciences came easily to her. A language was simply a system of grammar and rules. It was, at least in its early stages, about sticking variables into equations. Mia liked equations. She loved having the right answer.

"Glas Ddir, Pembuk, Luumia, and Fojo Karação," she'd said proudly.

"Your pronunciation could be better," her father had said.

The green flame flickered out as dark shapes swam before Mia's eyes. She struck the stick against the tunnel wall and the fire winked back to life, flooding the corridor with the sour pinch of eggs. Like magic, sulfyr sticks manifested flame.

Not magic. Chemistry. Strike pinewood sulfyr against a rough surface, add a dose of friction, mingle the escaping gases, and green flame nips at your fingertips. She'd learned this from her father during Huntress training. "Sometimes science masquerades as magic," he'd told her. "But never forget: science requires a cool head. Magic relies on a cruel, unruly heart."

She clenched the sulfyr stick. Ever since her father auctioned her off to the royals, Mia's heart had grown increasingly unruly and dangerously cruel. She cupped the tender flame in one palm and reached into her satchel, extracting a hand-drawn map and the compass her father had brought back from Luumia in the south. The sulfyr stick smeared green light into the corridors as she edged forward, the iron needle of the compass spinning left and right on the watery corkboard. Her headache vanished like a teardrop on the sand.

Then it came howling back as she recalled the prince's words. *The Hunters are here, but you are not to speak to them. Until you are my princess, you will remain my lady.* Even the "my" soured her stomach. As if she were a pretty bauble or a fluffy spaniel at Quin's feet, waiting to have her ears scratched.

Chattel in a silken dress.

Trinket in a golden noose.

Of course, outside the fortified walls of the Kaer, girls all over Glas Ddir were prodded into marriages "for safekeeping." Some unions were violent. Even when they weren't, the women were relegated to a lifetime of cooking and cleaning, birthing children and feeding them, like good-natured housecats purring in the sun. Had she really thought she was immune?

The Gwyrach were wicked, but the king was wicked, too. He had built his kingdom on the bones of fear and terror. The Gwyrach looked like normal women. When that comely girl in the market brushed against your arm, it was impossible to know if her touch was an innocent blunder or the last sensation you would ever feel. In the copious brothels encircling Kaer Killian like a corset, men might feel a spike in their pulse or a quick stiffening of their other parts, then suddenly collapse onto the soft feathered floors, their hearts overgorged with blood.

In the absence of obvious signifiers distinguishing Gwyrach from non-Gwyrach, *all* women were closely watched. Their own husbands and children feared them. Even in the safety of their homes, they were forbidden to remove their gloves. King Ronan issued law after law to restrict their movements. "We are committed to keeping the *good* women of the river kingdom safe," said the royal decree. "We are acting out of duty and love."

Mia wasn't sure when love had come to mean a cage.

She'd made a wrong turn.

The passageway dead-ended into a small circular chamber, so low she had to hunch. She hadn't been here before. Overhead, a rusted iron door was wedged into the low ceiling. She unlatched the chain and gave the handle a hard tug, releasing a shower of dust.

She hoisted herself halfway through the hole. Folds of purple velvet obscured her view; she gathered the lush cloth and pushed it aside, inhaling the earthy scent of lilacs and tallow. Rows of candles in thin brass flutes illuminated a small octagonal room. This was the Sacristy, annexed to the Royal Chapel. Mia could see into the Chapel, too, a room she had intentionally avoided. Impish fat-bottomed angels peered down from vaulted, gold-limned ceilings, aiming their love arrows at the altar—the very altar where she and Quin were to be married the following eve.

She heard a loud metallic crack and ducked back into her hiding place just as Tristan, the duke, strode into the Sacristy. Tristan was twenty, Quin's second cousin, son to some long-dead cousin of the king. He was broad-shouldered and muscular, with fierce white skin and day-old scruff cutting dark shadows across his cheeks. Angie found him attractive, but Mia thought him brutish. The duke was studying to become a clerig, a vocation that seemed strikingly at odds with his temperament. Despite his youth and inexperience, the king had agreed to let him perform the royal wedding ceremony, much to Mia's chagrin.

At the moment, however, Tristan was swinging a pewter candlestick in a wide arc, using it to bludgeon each thin brass flute. With every crack, another candle went skittering across the checkered marble floors.

"We have come here today"—*crack*—"by royal decree of Ronan, son of Clan Killian, uncontested king of Glas Ddir"—*crack*—"to witness this most hallowed union." *Crack, crack.*

So he was practicing the wedding vows. While also creating a mess for the servant girls to clean up, destruction for the sheer sake of destruction. Charming.

Mia dropped lightly back into the tunnel. She pulled the door shut overhead and latched the chain. Then she retraced her steps, murky light leaking through her fingers and painting moss-green shapes on the walls. A story told in shadows.

The crypt was empty. It always was. No one else in Kaer Killian seemed interested in roving the catacombs.

Moonlight dripped in from some unseen crack, etching a pearly white strip on the tombs. Mia walked among them, trailing her fingers over the vaults and sepulchers, until she found the name she wanted. *Wynna Rose.*

"Hello, Mother." She knelt quietly beside her mother's tomb, pressing her palms into the cool gray stone. "I've come to see you before my wedding day."

The silence was all consuming. It stole into the hollows of Mia's heart.

Her mother's vault was unadorned but lovely, a far cry from the ornate mausoleums around it. Her father had commissioned a mason to carve a simple image of a plum tree on his wife's tomb. Delicately Mia traced the grooves, drawing her fingers up the slender trunk, then over the serpentine boughs. Her mother had always loved trees, and snow plums were her favorite.

The part of the carving Mia loved best, however, was something most people missed: a solitary bird perched on a branch, staring up at a round moon. A touch of life on a cold, dead stone.

This was the one good thing about being confined to the castle for the last few weeks: Mia had been able to spend time with her mother. When Wynna died three years earlier, the king had demanded her body stay in the crypt of Kaer Killian, making her the only non-royal in the catacombs—and adding to the mysterious circumstances surrounding her death.

When Mia shut her eyes, she could still see her mother's body, luminous red hair strewn over the cottage floor. Gloves snarled beside her, the moonstone askew at her throat. Eyes open and forever black.

Killed without a single scratch.

When Mia thought of the Gwyrach who had done this, her

blood turned to black oil in her veins. She wanted more than anything to find her. To make her pay.

Hatred will only lead you astray. Sometimes love is the stronger choice.

The last words her mother spoke, engraved like an epitaph in Mia's mind.

"Little rose."

She gave a start as her father emerged from the shadows.

"What are you doing here, my little rose?"

He looked tired. She noted the stoop of his shoulders and the deep grooves in his face, a face that was an older, wearier version of her own: same thin nose, fair cheeks, and thirsty gray eyes. When she was a little girl, he would kiss her on each eyelid before tucking her in at night. "Two dark ships bearing secrets," he'd say. "Batten the hatches, bring down the sails."

"I came to see Mother," Mia said.

"Your mother isn't here." He held her gaze, and for a moment she thought she saw something ignite behind his eyes. Then he looked away. "A body without a soul is simply bones and dust."

Precious bones, she thought. Precious dust.

He offered her his arm. "Come. Walk with me."

"Where?" The word singed her tongue. "Down the aisle to my betrothed?"

"I have something for you. Something I think you'll want." When she didn't take his arm, he reached out and took her compass, dropping it in his pocket so casually it infuriated her. "This won't do you any good. But what I have might."

Chapter 4

BLANK

THE CATACOMBS TAPERED INTO a small square room, then a long corridor, and Mia's father led the way, no map required. His beard was salted white, but he was still light on his feet. No matter how fervently she trained in the practical skills of hunting—tracking, mapping, survival—her father was still the master. Griffin Rose was the greatest Hunter the river kingdom had ever known.

"Lightly, now," he said. "This path is unforgiving."

They were walking underneath the grove of snow plum trees. Through a fissure in the stone, Mia saw them bending to the wind. There were one thousand trees, a personal gift to King Ronan from the queen of the snow kingdom. They blossomed only after the first frost, when their silver branches grew thick and heavy with succulent purple snow plums.

Mia stumbled into her father's back as the tunnel dumped them out onto a narrow ledge outside the castle. The icy night wind bit into her skin.

"You're cold." He dropped his thick cloak over her shoulders before she could object. "Funny, isn't it? For all our study of human physiology, we cannot master the simple act of insulating our own bodies against the cold."

He gestured for her to sit on the edge of the cliff. He wasn't the kind of parent to yank his children back from a precipice— she'd always appreciated that about him. Though at the moment she was firmly committed to her outrage.

"The *Gwyrach* can warm anyone they want," she said pertly. "They can set fire to human flesh if they're so inclined."

She sat roughly and he sat beside her. In the yellow moonlight, she could see Killian Village, the cottages, taverns, shops, and brothels flanking the Natha River. In the old language, *Natha* meant "snake," and the name fit; the river coiled through the kingdom like a nest of vipers, slippery and black. The tributaries of the Natha stitched a hundred isolated villages together. *Glas Ddir* meant "land of rivers."

If Mia squinted, she could just make out the snow-dusted peaks and verdant groves of Ilwysion to the east, the alpine woods where she'd grown up. Beyond it, the river curved to the southeast and climbed into Foraois Swyn, the Twisted Forest.

Her father followed her gaze. "I should have taken you to see it. The Twisted Forest is a marvel to behold."

She almost laughed. Girls were not permitted to wander in Foraois Swyn, where both water and wood broke the natural laws. The Natha forked into a thousand smaller serpents coursing *up* the mountain instead of down, and the misshapen swyn trees bowed uniformly to the north, then braided themselves together under a canopy of blue needles. No one knew why the trees bent or why the water flowed upward, but girls were strictly forbidden to enter the forest, for fear they would be tainted by this most unnatural magic.

Mia's father pointed to the craggy peak a short way above them. To her surprise, a dusty bronze carriage hung from a parapet, bobbing slightly in the breeze. "That's the old laghdú. When I was a child, they used it for royal weddings. See the cable?" He pointed to a streak of black stretched across the sky. "They would drape the bride in heavy silks, saddle her with jewels, and lower her down the cable over the village, inch by inch. A glittering tableau of wealth and power."

In which the bride played the part of sparkly ornament, Mia thought.

"They called it the *Bridalaghdú*," he said. "In the old language it means 'flight of the bride.'"

"*Fall* of the bride, actually." She couldn't help but feel a swell of pride. For once, she knew more than her father.

He smiled. "Your mind is dazzling, little rose."

"Why did they stop doing the ceremony?" She hadn't meant to engage, but she was too curious not to. Her father was good at dangling the right bait.

"A bride fell. She was shrouded in so many pounds of cloth and precious stones, she tipped right out of the carriage in a puff of velvet and splintered bones. The next day, instead of a royal wedding, the Chapel held a royal funeral."

Mia shivered. In Glas Ddir, girls were expendable. She wondered how long the royal family had waited before scrounging up another bride.

"The Bridalaghdú was one of the first rituals Bronwynis revoked when she became queen." Her father sounded wistful. "She found it archaic and demeaning."

Mia had heard plenty about Queen Bronwynis. Nearly twenty years before, when Glas Ddir was poised on the shimmering cusp of progress, Mia's father and mother had stood shoulder to shoulder in a crush of people outside Kaer Killian, some laughing, some weeping, on the day Bronwynis was crowned queen. Not in all of recorded history had a woman ever sat on the river throne.

Her reign was brief. The Gwyrach killed Bronwynis shortly before Mia was born, and her younger brother inherited the throne. Her brother was, of course, Ronan. The first thing he'd done as king was reinstate the old laws to ensure only men had the right of succession.

Mia's father sighed. "I've taught you a great many things, have I not?"

"Let's see." Mia ticked them off on her fingers. "Hunting Gwyrach. Catching Gwyrach. Never letting my body be controlled by anyone. Oh, and surrendering my body to a boy I don't even know, all because my father told me to."

He was silent a moment. "I know you've been mapping the tunnels. Always my little explorer. But I also know you would never leave your sister behind."

Her face burned hot. So he'd known all along. The gentle affection with which he said "my little explorer" stung—as if she were a curious child with a spyglass and a weathered pocket map. She'd been that girl long ago, back when the world was still a rosy plum waiting to be plucked. Her mother and father had told her she could craft whatever future she wanted, but that she'd have to leave Glas Ddir to do it. Mia remembered the ripe sense of longing, how she ached to sail the other three kingdoms, drinking in the colors, scents, and flavors her father brought back in glass vials and crisp brown packages.

That dream had died with her mother. Almost overnight, Mia traded in her geographical maps for another kind of map: an atlas of the human body. She spent every waking hour poring over her anatomy books and plates, examining the vulnerability of heart valves, tracing blue tributaries of veins, studying her Wound Man diagram for a better grasp of wound theory. If she could reduce the body to a system of cohesive parts, she could master it—and fortify hers against the Gwyrach.

But there was another reason. Mia couldn't shake the feeling that, if she'd known more about the body—if she had understood the way blood flowed through the vena arteriosa to the heart's left chamber, or known how to invoke the subtle rhythm of the cardiac systole—she might have saved her mother's life.

"You said you had something for me," she said to her father, struggling to keep her voice even.

He pulled a thin parcel from his cloak and handed it to her. The paper crinkled as she untied the waxy twine, lifting a small leather book from its trappings.

It was no larger than her hand, full to bursting with ivory pages and bound together by a scarlet stone clasp. The brown leather had gone soft with age, worn clean through in spots like the knees of a well-loved pair of trousers.

She ran her fingers down the book's cracked veins. Slashed into the cover were the initials W.M., two bundles of white scars. *Wynna Merth.* Her mother's name before she married Griffin and joined Clan Rose.

Mia's heart pounded against her rib cage. "Mother's journal."

How many times had she seen her mother curled up in the window seat of their cottage, scribbling furiously? Wynna often looked peaceful as she gazed out into the forest, watching the birds flit through the plum trees and blackthorn brambles. But her face would darken as she turned back to the journal, ink spilling onto the page, sometimes tears spilling along with it.

Mia still remembered the time she mustered enough courage to ask her mother if it caused her pain, the things she wrote about. "Oh yes," she'd said. "I write about the most painful thing of all." When Mia asked what it was, she answered simply, "Myself."

"Your mother wanted you to have it," her father said. "When you were ready. I believe you are ready."

Mia pressed the journal to her chest. Her mother's history had always been enshrouded in mystery, a heavy veil drawn across some unspoken horror of the past. What secrets had she buried in these pages?

A half-formed memory flashed through Mia's mind. "There was a key."

"Yes." Her father drew a carved red stone out of his pocket. It was small and winged, head cocked slightly and beak open as if in song. A ruby wren. Mia had studied the species with great interest: native to the snow kingdom, the ruby wren was the only bird known to hibernate in winter, when the females built domed, tightly woven nests in the branches of the snow plum trees. Mia's mother had always loved them. She was destined to: in the old language, *Wynna* meant "wren."

"The little ruby wren," her father said, pressing the stone into Mia's palm. She felt an instant flutter, as if the bird had melted through her skin and spread wings inside her chest, desperate to escape.

Again Mia heard her mother's voice, calling her birdlings home to roost. *Mia, my red raven. Angie, my little swan.*

The memory was too tender, so she pushed it aside. Her fingers worried the red stone. More vitreous than carmine quartz, luster almost like glass; brittle tenacity with imperfect cleavage. She'd studied the physical properties of dozens of minerals, but her mother had never let her study this one.

"Do you know the stone?" her father asked, watching her closely.

"Is this a test?"

He nodded. "Perhaps the most important one you'll ever take."

She paused, thumbing through her mental catalog.

"Fojuen," her father said.

"If you had just given me a second!" she snapped. The only thing she hated more than not knowing the answer was when her father answered for her.

She had read about the fojuen craters in the fire kingdom to the east. Fojo Karação was where her parents had met as students: an archipelago of islands forged from the molten magma of volqanoes, spewed out centuries ago and hardened into dazzling red rock. Thanks to her father's language lessons, she knew *fojuen* meant "fire-forged." Fojuen was also the official language of Fojo. How interesting to think of language as a kind of volqanic glass, a history told in the remnants of what once was.

Mia knew something else about fojuen: once cut and polished, it was deadly sharp. Her mother, who had studied medicine in Fojo, had told her how physicians in the fire kingdom carved the red stone into swords and arrowheads. Surgeons performed surgery with fojuen scalpel blades. The glass made clean, minuscule incisions, barely visible to the human eye.

"Don't make me do this, Father." She closed her fingers around the bird, its sharp beak digging into the soft flesh of her palm. She felt both dizzy and ferocious, closer to her mother than she'd felt in years. Braver, too. "Don't make me marry Quin."

He wouldn't look at her. "I'm protecting you, little rose."

"From *what*? I know your life has no value since Mother died. But my life does. I want to fight with the Circle. I want to find her killer. The father I knew would never hand me off like this, a pretty princess for a petty prince."

"Perhaps your union with the prince will surprise you."

"I don't want to marry him! I don't want to marry anyone. But if I someday choose marriage—of my own volition—I want what you and Mother had." Her parents' love had exploded like a shower of sparks in the sky, casting off cosmic dust that still glimmered. It had also led to misery and grief. Wynna's death left a gaping crater no one could ever fill.

Her father stood stiffly. "I have promised a daughter to the royal family. Perhaps it should be Angelyne. The royal family will ensure she receives the very best of care."

"*No.* Don't put this on her." Mia drew herself up. "It has to be me."

"Very well then." He clasped her gently by the shoulders. His hands were blocks of ice searing through the cloak. "The bridal feast awaits the bride."

He disappeared into the tunnel, leaving her alone.

Mia refused to cry. She hadn't cried since the day she held her mother's lifeless body. Tears were mercurial and untrustworthy. Feelings of any kind made a person vulnerable, weak. Sometimes she wondered if her body even remembered *how* to cry. Did she have whole mines of unwept salt stored up inside her? Maybe someday, like a pillar, she would crumble to the earth.

What was the good of loving anyone if they'd only be taken from you? If loss were bound up in love, perhaps it was easier to seal her heart to both.

And yet Mia's love for her sister welled up inside her, like salt water, like bile. The illogic of love infuriated her. What was love if not a rippling bunch of nerves and valves misfiring? An equation with no known variables? An incalculable contraction of the heart?

Saving Angelyne meant sacrificing herself. Was love a willing sacrifice?

Sometimes love is the stronger choice.

Mia had never missed her mother more. She was starved for comfort. Perhaps her mother's words would soothe her soul.

She slid the ruby wren into the lock and turned the key. The book whiffled open.

She sucked in her breath.

The pages were blank.

Chapter 5

A COMMON ENEMY

"LADY MIA. HOW KIND of you to join us."

King Ronan had a way of injecting every word with simmering menace. One look at him lording over the feasting table and Mia's headache came raging back. His skin had a grayish pallor, his gaunt form swathed in plush robes of lynx and ermine. Ronan's plate was piled high with roast duck, boar fritters, cream of almond, green goose jelly, venison paste—and he hadn't touched a morsel. His steely blue eyes bored into Mia so savagely that for a moment she worried she had forgotten her gloves. She dragged her fingers over her wrist, confirming the slinkskin was still in place.

"My apologies, Your Grace. After all these weeks, I still find myself dizzied by the intricate corridors. The Kaer is beautiful but bewitching."

Immediately she regretted her choice of words. *Bewitch* was not a term to be used lightly. She watched the king's face harden.

"We wondered what tragedy had befallen you." Queen Rowena's lips curled into a smile so cultured, Mia expected a string of pearls to pop out. The queen was beautiful but brittle, with silvery blond hair thinning at the temples, eggshell skin, and haunted violet eyes. There was no love lost between Rowena and Ronan—if passion had ever spiced the air between them, it had long since cooled.

The queen motioned toward the feasting table, gesturing to the chair at the prince's side. "My son has been so anxious."

Quin didn't look anxious. He looked annoyed.

"Four gods! Let the girl be." Princess Karri, Quin's older sister, raised her pint of stonemalt and winked. "You've missed nothing but mindless prattle, Mia. Drink! Be merry! You're just in time for the stoneberry flambé."

Mia sank into her chair, grateful to the princess for intervening. She thought, not for the first time, that Karri would make an excellent queen. She was both proud and unassuming, and she seemed older than nineteen, a bold, spirited girl who could eat, drink, and fight with the best of them. Many Glasddirans considered her blunt and impolitic (including her own mother), but Mia was in awe of her. Karri's fair skin was reliably sunburnt; she dyed her hair bright white and kept it clipped short, wore unadorned tunics and trousers, and could easily command a room.

But despite being a year older than Quin—and infinitely more qualified—Karri would never rule the river kingdom. Ronan had seen to that.

Mia stared at the prince. He was currently hard at work spearing a fresh green pea on the end of his fork. This was the heir apparent.

"Perhaps," Quin said, keeping his voice low, "instead of a ring, I should give you a pocket watch."

A servant fluttered a cloth napkin in Mia's lap and set a goblet of blackthorn wine before her. She took a not-very-ladylike gulp and shut her eyes, hoping it would dissolve the knot of pain inside her head. Perhaps it would make Quin disappear, too.

She opened her eyes. He was still there.

"Some good it would do me," she muttered, "since I don't have a single pocket in these doll clothes your mother insists I wear."

The prince swiveled in his chair. "Wulf!" he called. "Beo!" His two dogs trotted eagerly to the feasting table, and he bent down to scratch their ears. Their dusty fur was Killian gold, or—if you preferred—the color of Quin's mop of curls.

Wulf rested his chin on Mia's knee and stared up at her with doleful brown eyes. "They like you," Quin said. "And they don't like anyone."

She might have smiled, if not for the tiny monsters lighting sulfyr sticks inside her skull. Perhaps the Grand Gallery was to blame. It boasted two gigantic stone hearths on either end, and the walls, floors, and ceiling were all lustrous black. The onyx didn't just reflect the fires and people; it magnified them, giving Mia the distinct feeling she was trapped in a giant black die.

She pressed her hand to her chest and felt the fojuen wren. After leaving her father, she'd made a brief stop in her chambers to stash the journal, slip on a velvet gown, and tuck the key into her corset. She wasn't sure why, but it gave her comfort to have her mother's ruby wren so close to her heart.

Mia noted thirteen familiar faces at the far end of the Gallery. The twelve Hunters—and one Huntress—were clustered around a gray slab table, eating in tense silence. They had quivers of arrows slung over their shoulders and daggers tucked beneath their plates. Any good Hunter knew to keep his weapons close. Spot a Gwyrach from across the room and you might stand a chance. But if she were close enough to touch you, you were close enough to die.

Mia's eyes came to rest on Domeniq du Zol, her childhood friend. Dom had started training with the Circle around the same time she did. They shared a common wound: the Gwyrach had killed his father. Yet even in the wake of that earth-shattering loss, Dom's wide, crooked smile could light up a room.

He was smiling now, laughing at something one of the other Hunters had said, the firelight warming his dark, mellow-brown skin. Mia's gaze fell to the silver dagger at his fingertips. The blade was serrated, the scabbard limned in pale-green stone. Was it aventurine? Jade? What other surprises had Dom dug up while she was trapped in the castle playing damsel-in-distress?

Mia was flooded by longing. She didn't crave Dom; she craved the life he was about to live. She was meant to be with them, on the cusp of a great adventure, soon to bring her mother's killer to justice. She should have been at that table with a pack of Hunters by her side, not Prince Quin forking peas.

In her periphery she saw the prince staring at the Hunters. Had he ever seen them before? Unlikely. They were an unsavory lot of criminals and assassins, men with less-than-sterling reputations and a keen ability to wield a blade.

When Quin realized she'd caught him looking, he quickly turned away.

Mia's mind kept snagging on the journal. It didn't make sense—she'd seen her mother write in that book a hundred times. Had her father replaced the inked pages with blank ones? She stole a glance at him. Even he wasn't *that* cruel.

And then she was worried about something else entirely: the fact that cousin Tristan was leaning wolfishly close to her sister. He whispered something in Angie's ear that made her blush. Mia watched uneasily as the duke tore into his duck with bloody abandon. He had clearly worked up an appetite cudgeling innocent candles and who knew what else.

Tristan looked straight at her, a smirk pinned to his face. "Perhaps you can enlighten us, Lady Mia. We were just discussing the efficacy of your father's Hunters." He brandished his fork toward the Circle. "They take the sacred oath to eradicate magic across all four kingdoms. But is it not true that the more Gwyrach they kill, the more there seem to be?"

"All the more reason the Circle must keep up their numbers and their strength," Mia said tartly.

"It seems to me the Gwyrach have become like the ancient Máiywffan. Cut off one head, and ten more rise from the bloody stump."

"Four kings." Karri's cheeks were flushed, her eyes sparkling. "You believe in mythical sea monsters now, do you, Cousin?"

A loud pop echoed from across the Gallery as a servant tossed another log onto the fire. The flames raged and crackled beneath Mia's skin.

A scullery maid knocked into her shoulder with the flambé.

"Forgive me, Your Grace." The maid's thin eyes flashed, her tawny amber skin gone a few shades paler. Servants were whipped for less clumsy acts than this.

"It's all right," Mia said quickly. "You're all right."

The girl ducked her head. "Thank you, Your Grace."

"Incompetent fool," Rowena hissed. She turned to Ronan. "But then, you don't employ them for their *scullery* talents, do you, my love?"

If the king injected his words with menace, the queen had a gift for filling hers with venom. Mia's head was beyond aching— she felt as if her medulla had come loose in her skull. On a good day she couldn't stand the royals, but tonight they were even worse than usual. The dogs were the most decent people there.

King Ronan ignored his wife and fixed Mia's father with a penetrating stare.

"One does have to wonder, Griffin. You've brought us pitifully few Gwyrach in recent months. My Hall of Hands is hungry."

A gust of cold brushed over Mia. The monsters in her head

were carrying pitchforks now, gleefully jabbing her in the temporal bones. What in four hells was happening? Her body had become a foreign instrument, fine-tuned to a symphony she couldn't hear. Crash and crescendo, freeze and burn.

Princess Karri spoke first. "Your methods are barbaric, Father. The Gwyrach are merely women. Some of them have children. Many are but girls themselves."

Ronan turned on her with cold, calculated fury. "If you believe this, you are no daughter of mine. Why do you persist in seeing goodness where there is only wickedness and perversion? They are bastards descended from the union of gods and ruined women. They are not *people*. They are half-breeds who seek to do us harm."

"They also have the power to heal. They can stanch the flow of blood and knit flesh back together with merely a touch of their hand."

This was true: Mia had read about it in her books. In olden times, the Gwyrach were simply Gwyddon. *Creatures.* Beautiful and young, they were treated with curiosity and affection, even wonder. The Gwyddon were thought to be blessed by the four gods. But their fledgling magic soon warped into something dark, a way to exert power over the innocent and weak.

"You know it wasn't always like this," Karri continued, gaining steam. "Magic ebbs and flows—the only thing that changes is our response to it. When your sister sat on the river throne, she encouraged the study of magic. She invited scholars and scientists from all four kingdoms to come to Glas Ddir. Before you closed the borders—"

"Your father had every right to close them," Tristan said coolly. "Our neighbors were permitting unnatural perversions to flourish."

King Ronan nodded, clearly pleased. "My nephew has more sense than the rest of you put together. The other kingdoms created a breeding ground for magic. They let this filth infect their populations over many years. I promised my people a triumphant return to a better time."

"Yes, Father." Karri's voice sizzled. "I read the decree. Did you know it was one of the first texts my tutor gave me when I was learning to read? 'A triumphant return to the greatness of old, when Glas Ddir was both respected and feared.'"

Princess Karri could always be depended on to speak her mind. Even so, Mia couldn't believe how brash she was being, especially with such a large audience. The stonemalt had loosened her lips. Karri's conviction was unnerving; it snaked through Mia's head with the uncomfortable aura of truth.

But she couldn't accept it. Though it turned her stomach, she had to side with the king, at least on this. Gwyrach were born, not bred. Their troubled ancestry was legend: after the gods mated with human women centuries ago, the early Gwyddon birthed daughters, those daughters birthed daughters, and the lineage continued. But some of these daughters were no human girls. They were demons, each generation more wicked than the last.

Mia was a scientist, not a mystic. She'd always had her doubts about the origin myths. But the empirical evidence was irrefutable. She had spent three years studying every heinous act the Gwyrach had committed, and the list was long. They held grudges, and they never forgot. They melted skin off bones, swamped lungs with phlegm and fluid, burned whole hearts out of innocent people's chests. The Gwyrach no longer used their power to heal: only to enthrall, wound, and kill.

"Every living being has the capacity for both good and evil," Karri said. "Something you, Father, have never understood. Queen Bronwynis believed the more we understand magic, the better we can harness its power for good."

The color was high in the king's sallow face. "Do not *ever* speak her name."

A hush fell over the Gallery. In the kitchens, a cup clattered to the ground.

Mia's body was behaving strangely. Her humerus bones hummed at the elbow joints, arm muscles clenching and unclenching of their own accord. She could feel her ribs pricking the hollows of her chest—and it wasn't just the corset. She clutched the table to keep herself from keeling into her flambé.

"If I have a foolish daughter by blood, perhaps I will acquire a better one by marriage." The king's ice-blue eyes sliced into Mia. "The floor is yours, Lady Mia. Give us a rousing toast."

The breath scraped through her chest. She was acutely aware of the ruby wren beneath her dress, red-hot, a smoking coal against her heart. Mia felt all eyes on her as she reached for her goblet. For once she was grateful for the slinkskin; it hid her trembling fingers.

Heart for a heart, she reminded herself. *Life for a life.*

"A toast," she said, trying to smooth out the quaver in her

44

voice. "To the Circle of the Hunt: the true heroes of this feast. They are the warriors who purge the four kingdoms of magic. The brave souls who risk their lives to keep us safe."

She looked at her father, whose face was inscrutable. A burst of anger flowered in her sternum. It was his fault she would never search the four kingdoms for her mother's killer. But why wasn't *he* searching? Why had he given up? Mia would have stopped at nothing to avenge her mother—even if it cost her life.

An idea was weaving itself together in her mind. If she were barred from seeking justice for her mother, she could at least empower the Hunters to do so in her place.

She hefted her goblet a touch higher, her words gaining vigor. "When I am princess, I will do everything in my power to make sure the Hunters have everything they need. Today the Circle numbers thirteen. Someday they will be ten times that. May my presence in the Kaer strike fear into the heart of every living Gwyrach."

For a moment, the Gallery was choked with silence. Out of the corner of her eye, Mia thought she saw the scullery maid shrinking back into the kitchens. Her father was squeezing the life out of his dinner napkin, his expression pained. And were those tears on Angie's cheeks?

Mia's gaze fell on Prince Quin. His mouth was twisted into an almost smile, a mixture of admiration and concern. But no sooner had their eyes met than he looked away. He busied himself scratching his dogs behind the ears, their fur shining like burnished bronze in the firelight.

It was Tristan who broke the silence.

"Brazen words from a not yet princess." He wiped the sneer off his face before turning to the king. "But let's be sensible, Your Grace. If we're going to talk politics, isn't it time the ladies retire?"

Outside the Gallery, Angelyne stalked past without a word. She bristled when Mia touched her arm.

"I'm tired. I'm going to bed."

"What's wrong? Are you angry with me?"

"Not angry. Just tired."

Angie spun out of her reach and disappeared down the corridor, leaving Mia perplexed. "Batten the hatches," she murmured, "bring down the sails." But her sister was already gone.

The queen had retired to her chambers, so Mia and Karri stood alone—quite uncomfortably, in light of their positions on the subject of Gwyrach. The princess's fingers tapped absently against her broad leather belt as if itching for her sword.

"I'm sorry, Your Grace," Mia began. "I didn't mean to—"

Karri waved her off. "You are entitled to your own opinion. The day we forfeit our opinions, we are truly lost. But as I will soon be your sister, may I offer one small piece of advice?"

Mia nodded.

"Be wary of my father, Mia. You may share a common enemy, but he is not your friend."

Chapter 6

PAINFULLY SMALL

It was impossible to avoid the Hands.

The Hall of Hands was nestled in the central corridor of the Kaer's stony heart, a proud showpiece for foreign dignitaries. Never mind the flow of dignitaries had trickled to a standstill after King Ronan sealed the borders—there were still plenty of servants and courtiers to shudder at the Hands.

Or in Mia's case: reluctant brides.

Usually she hurried through the Hall, but tonight, as she wound her way back to her chambers, she slowed her gait.

The room was cavernous, more sanctuary than hall, and always strangely warm. The air was fragrant with the smell of vinegar and moldering meat. Clasped in iron manacles on every wall were cream-colored candles bathing the Hall in soft light. A servant kept watch from the shadows to ensure the fires never went out.

And in the flickering candlelight were the Hands.

For every Gwyrach captured, King Ronan took her left hand. He sawed it off while she was still alive and kept it as a trophy. A few days earlier, Mia had wandered into a restricted part of the castle and heard screaming. *Demon screams*, she'd told herself as she swiftly retreated. But they sounded human.

Eight carpal bones in the wrist: the hamate, capitate, scaphoid, pisiform, lunate, triquetral, trapezoid, and trapezium. Five metacarpals. Three tendons. Countless aponeuroses and ligaments. The ulnar and radial arteries, shunting blood through the sturdy arm bones to the joints and sutures. Mia couldn't help but wonder how long it took, cutting through all that blood and bone.

Once removed, the Hands were placed in an earthenware pot with salt, vinegar, and powder of zimat. After seven days of pickling they were baked in the sun. The servants made a candle from the corpse's fat, mixing the tallow with rosewater. Thus with every new Hand, new light poured into the Hall.

The Hands themselves were gray and brown and black, the fresher ones a bruised purple. Often the finger bones poked through the rotted flesh. Some were displayed in glass cases, artfully arranged on crimson velvet pillows. Others were strung from the rafters by long leather straps. When Mia walked past them, they twirled in silent pirouettes.

Someday, when they found the Gwyrach who had killed her mother, her Hand would join the others. Wasn't that what Mia wanted?

A servant girl stood quietly in the shadows, watching. She was wide-eyed and coltish, her thick hair woven into a long yellow braid that hung down her back. She raised her gloved hand in a tentative wave, and Mia tipped her head. When she did, her eyes fell on a fresh Hand encased in a glass box. The skin was caked with grime, nails torn to shreds and still rimmed with blood. Surely this Hand had belonged to the Gwyrach she heard screaming.

It troubled her how thin the wrist was, how frail. Child size. Mia saw the angry fingernail grooves in the palm where she had clenched her little fist.

Demon hand, she thought as she picked up her pace. *Demon flesh.*

But for the Hand of a demon, it was painfully small.

Chapter 7

SMOLDERING

MIA WAS ALMOST THROUGH the Hall when she heard music. A fragile, haunting melody, one she was sure she'd heard before. She followed it.

The notes led her down the castle's glossy black corridors, past the buttery and the watching chamber, through the sunken indoor gardens with their twisting vines and blooms. At every turn Mia saw herself reflected in the glassy walls.

She came to a halt outside the library. It was her favorite room in the Kaer; she'd spent many hours there, happily ensconced in books. The library boasted an impressive collection of anatomy plates and medical journals, with far more volumes than the Roses kept in their mountain cottage.

Now she peered in from the corridor. In the eastern alcove, the prince sat at a satiny black piano. She'd never even noticed there *was* a piano in the library—but then, her head was always in a book.

Quin's head was bent over the keys, Beo and Wulf curled around the pedals at his feet. He was singing softly.

"Under the plums, if it's meant to be. You'll come to me, under the snow plum tree."

He had a beautiful voice, light and pure. She'd never seen him look so peaceful. Though he had lit no torches, a shaft of silver moonlight threaded through the narrow loop window, and his hair glinted like spun gold.

She recognized the song. Once, when she was a child in the forests of Ilwysion, a troupe of traveling musicians from Luumia had performed a play in the village square. This was the ballad the knight sang to his fair maiden. For months afterward, Mia and Angelyne donned their mother's fancy lavender and lemon-yellow gowns and whirled through the cottage, belting out the words to "Under the Snow Plum Tree" and making proclamations of undying love. Back then, Mia had been happy to read dreamy novels and play dress-up with her sister. It was only after their mother died that she decided she had no use for fairy tales.

Now, as she stared at the prince, her mind wandered back to those stories. Quin was as handsome as any knight. A few years ago, she might have swooned over his flawless face. If he had even a kernel of warmth, the smallest spark of passion, perhaps it could be coaxed into a flame, the flame into a fire. But all she had ever felt from Quin was ice. How was one supposed to kindle heat from an iceberg?

As she stood in the doorway, ruminating over this impossible alchemy, the dogs gave her away.

Wulf and Beo loped toward her, happy to press their noses into her knees. They must have picked up her scent.

The music ceased abruptly as the prince rose from the bench.

"I didn't hear you come in."

"I didn't mean to startle you, Your Grace. I thought you were in the Gallery discussing politics." How had he managed to bypass the Hall of Hands without her seeing him? She answered her own question: because he'd lived in the castle his whole life. He knew the labyrinth passageways far better than she did.

"I've never cared much for politicking," he said.

Mia stifled a groan. He caught it.

"Have I said something to amuse you?"

"Nothing. It's just . . ." She hesitated, wondering how much to say.

"Speak your mind."

"Of course you're not interested in politics. Politics is about power, and yours has never been in dispute."

To her surprise, he didn't contest the point. "You think I'm a spoiled brat."

"I think you've been coddled. Your Grace," she added quickly. She hadn't meant to be quite so surly. But then, she had no interest in being charming, either. To charm someone was just a watered-down version of enthralling them.

Second only to murder, enthrallment was the form of magic Mia feared most. The Gwyrach could entrance a victim's heart with passion, spike his blood with desire, and—most unsettling— strip him of his consent. She could hear her father's voice in her head: *To enthrall someone is to enslave them, little rose. You've stripped them of their consent, robbed them of their choice. And without choice, what are we?*

She stooped to pet Beo. "Do your dogs like the music?"

Silence. Then, "Beo does. Like any woman, she has excellent taste. Her brother is a wholly different matter, the uncivilized beast. Wulf prefers the clavichord."

Was he making a joke? His face was unreadable. Prince Quin, master of deadpan. Who'd have thought?

She waited for him to say something else, then realized he was waiting for *her* to say something. Her mind was as blank as the pages in her mother's book.

"Well then. I'll leave you in peace." She turned to go.

"Wait."

He looked different, standing there at the piano, with Wulf at his feet whining to be petted. The top buttons of his emerald jacket were unbuttoned, revealing a triangle of smooth golden skin. She forced her eyes back to the bookshelves.

"Do you agree with my sister?" he said. "About magic?"

Her internal organs were listing again, a fleet of ships canting against her bones. Even if she *had* agreed with Karri—which she didn't—she would never confess it to Quin. To disagree with King Ronan was tantamount to treason.

53

"Your father understands the import of the Hunters," she said. "For that I am very grateful."

It was difficult to see in the moonlight, but she thought she detected disappointment on Quin's face. He stiffened.

"I know you want nothing to do with me. You'd rather join your father's merry band of assassins and go hunt Gwyrach for sport."

"You think we hunt for *sport*?"

"You should know I'm not pleased about this marriage, either. Not that my father cares one whit about what *I* want. Not that he'd ever take my personal desires into account. Our union is an alliance between powerful houses. If magic roils and bubbles under the meniscus of assent, your father will find it and choke it out. You offer a constant reminder that, for a Gwyrach, death is never far behind."

She'd never heard the prince speak so many consecutive words. *Meniscus of assent.* Who talked like that outside of books?

Pretentious coddled princes, that was who.

Her anger was a soft tapping from a distant room. So the prince would never love her. Fine. She would never love the prince. Love was a gambit, and a bad one at that. The only love she trusted was her love for Angelyne. For her sister, she would die a thousand deaths. To save her sister, she was about to.

"On this we are agreed," she said. "Our union is purely transactional. An unfortunate symptom of our parentage, nothing more." She marched briskly to the piano and extended her gloved hand. "Are we of accord?"

For a moment, Quin paused. Then he reached out and shook her hand.

Heat poured over her like honey. Steamy, sticky warmth, spilling across the soft skin of her arms and shoulders. Her fingers were ten bars of chocolate, slowly melting into paste. Good enough to eat.

"Mia?" The prince's voice was soft, curious. He wasn't where she remembered. When had he stepped behind her? She could feel his breath against the nape of her neck. Slowly he reached forward and drew his thumb across her collarbone, gooseflesh rising up to meet him. Then he took her gently by the shoulders and turned her around to face him. His eyes bore a distant, golden glaze. He brushed a curl from her cheek and her zygomatic bones thrummed in their sockets.

"Your Grace." Her breath was a knotted ribbon in her throat. "This is most irregular."

He froze. His hand was suspended in midair, curved sweetly, as if he'd been about to cup her chin in his palm. A bead of sweat glistened on his brow, and his breathing was choppy, a staccato rhythm pulsing through his chest.

And then the moment dissolved. She watched as Quin's face slipped back into its familiar furrows of disdain. He whistled for his dogs.

Mia's mind was in tatters. She didn't understand what had just transpired between them, or why her body was still swathed in tender heat. The prince was no longer rime and hoarfrost: he was fire and ember. He was not what she'd assumed.

And something was wrong. Very wrong.

"We meet on the morrow, Lady Mia," he said brusquely.

"On the morrow," she echoed numbly as he strode past, the dogs nipping at his heels.

All night, as the castle creaked and slumbered, she traced the trail of goose bumps across her smoldering flesh.

Chapter 8

BLACKMAIL

MIA WOKE WITH A start. She lay in her bedchambers amidst scarlet satin pillows wreathed in black lace. Had the royals intentionally draped the canopy bed in the colors of Clan Rose? It seemed a trifle overeager.

She'd been dreaming of Quin's eyes. His irises were concentric circles, one pale green, one a deeper viridescent. How had she never noticed that before? She saw soft light pooling in them the moment he'd reached out to touch her, and she saw it leaking out just as quickly.

Why did he hate her? She didn't want to marry him, either, but she didn't blame *him* for the arrangement. From the sounds of it, he was just another pawn in his father's master plan.

The minutes inched by, then an hour, then more. Perhaps a book would lull her back to sleep. She dug out from under her barricade of lacy pillows, put on silk slippers, threw a sable shawl over her nightgown, and stole through the shadowy castle corridors.

Mia was halfway to the library when she heard voices seeping out of the north wing. Angry voices. If she wasn't mistaken, the prince's chambers were in the northern section of the Kaer, just beyond the drawing room.

She changed directions, slipping quietly down a different passageway and dodging two guards along the way. In her black shawl she blended in beautifully with the onyx walls. She tiptoed into the northern wing as far as she dared and made it to the prince's drawing room, complete with a golden clavichord, a smattering of sculptures, and a small wooden stage framed by thick brocaded curtains. She had just tucked herself behind the green velvet when she heard Quin's indignant voice.

". . . could have thought to warn me?"

"It behooves us to keep her close." Mia recognized King Ronan's signature growl. "Despite your utter lack of statesmanship, surely you understand that."

Queen Rowena's cool voice cut through the quiet. "You will be perfectly safe, my love. We don't intend to let any harm come to you."

"But she is dangerous. You won't deny it."

"The Circle is not what it once was," said Ronan. "We suspect her father's allegiances may have shifted. As long as she is in the Kaer, we can exert a certain . . . *leverage*."

The words wrapped around Mia's throat. They were talking about *her*.

Quin said, "I know what this is really about. You'll never stop punishing me. This is simply the latest in my ongoing penance."

"Be grateful," the king spat. "I have been far more munificent than you deserve."

Silence. Then the queen said smoothly, "Sleep long, sleep sweet, my darling."

Mia's heartbeat thrummed in her ears. The quarrel was over, and now Ronan and Rowena were leaving. In moments they would find her eavesdropping from the drawing room, slippered feet poking out from beneath the velvet curtain.

She willed her legs to move. Swiftly she slid away from the prince's chambers and back down the corridor, but not before she heard Quin's voice, cold and flat.

"Ah, yes. Thank you, Father. Thank you so very much for my blackmail bride."

Chapter 9

LOVE IS A LODESTONE

ANGELYNE HAD A GIFT for embellishment. While Mia had spent the last three years drawing anatomically correct sketches of the pleurae binding the mediastinal membranes, Angie had been working in far prettier mediums.

She stood behind Mia at the cherrywood dresser, applying one tincture after another. "Rosewort for your cheeks. Crushed lullablu petals for your eyes. Tansy and snow plum paste for your lips. Oh, and I know you hate skin greases, but can I daub on just a dash? It really will make you glow."

"Daub as much as you like," Mia said. What better way to herald the complete dissolution of her life than by daubing an animal's entrails on her face?

She hadn't slept a wink after her late-night wander. Over and over, she heard Quin's voice intermingling with his parents'. What did they mean, her father's allegiances had shifted? Griffin had never been anything but loyal to Clan Killian.

She tried in vain to patch together the rest of the conversation from the snippets she'd overheard. In the library, Quin had told Mia their union was an alliance between powerful houses. But that was before his parents paid him a midnight visit. Their marriage was still about leverage . . . just not the kind he'd thought.

Now Quin had even more reason to hate her. *My blackmail bride.*

Did they really think she was dangerous? Some unspoken truth nibbled at the fringes of her consciousness. She pushed it aside.

"You won't even recognize yourself," Angie said, "once I've worked my magic on your face. You're absolutely stunning, Mi, but it wouldn't hurt you to embrace a little embellishment every once in a while!"

Her sister was chattering more than usual. Mia was grateful; it kept her from having to talk. She gazed sullenly at her reflection, her mind blurred with dread and confusion as Angie pinched and painted her into the shape of a princess.

She stayed silent as her sister led her to the wardrobe and deftly laced her into the whalebone corset, then the oyster silk wedding gown. With nimble fingers, Angie threaded the train into the back drapery. Mia despised the train. It was absurdly large—you could hide whole worlds in there—crimped and creased into a froth of cumbersome ruffles. She was trussed up like a birthing cow.

Angie stepped back to admire her handiwork. "You're so lovely, Mi. At least there is something beautiful amidst so much sadness. I wish Mother were here to see." She touched the moonstone at her throat and squeezed her eyes shut.

"Do you need to rest?" Mia said, worried. Her sister had gone vaguely green.

"I'm all right. I was just thinking of Mother. Sometimes it's all too much."

Mia ached to tell Ange about the journal. In a night of cruel mysteries, the journal was the one that hurt the most. But her sister was devastated by anything that had belonged to their mother. Other than the moonstone, she'd kept nothing; the smallest knickknack could bring on a torrent of memories that put her in bed for days. After Wynna died, Griffin and Angie wanted to burn all her things, whereas Mia wanted to keep everything she had ever touched. It wasn't sentimental. She was combing every artifact for clues: a strand of hair, an unfamiliar fragrance. Even the tiniest trace might illuminate the path to her mother's killer.

"You look like a princess from a fairy tale." Angelyne leaned against the bedpost, her long lashes dewed with tears. "Mia Morwynna, Daughter of Clan Rose, Princess of the River Kingdom."

Mia didn't know whether to laugh or cry.

She startled at a sharp rap on the door. Her father was standing on the threshold.

"They await you, little rose."

This time, when he offered her his arm, she took it.

The sun sank in the west as Mia and her father proceeded down the castle corridors, a cavalcade of guards and servants keeping pace a short distance behind them. She wore a new pair of lambskin gloves for the occasion, milky white studded with black and red buttons. After the ceremony, she would be free of them forever. Small consolation for the price she had to pay.

She longed to tell her father what she'd overheard, to ask him what it all meant. She wanted desperately to believe he had done what he'd done for good reason. Perhaps he really was trying to protect her.

"Father," she began, but the words died on her lips. Her whole life she had trusted him fully and implicitly, as only a child can do. But trust took a lifetime to build and only a few short weeks to destroy.

He was keeping secrets. Something her mother said came back to her: *Secrets are just another way people lie to one another.* Mia wanted her father to tell her everything, but she couldn't trust a word he said.

They were almost at the Chapel when he did the most peculiar thing. He dropped her arm and pressed his hand into her back, firm and urgent. When he spoke, his words were gruff.

"Your mother loved you more than anything. Never have I seen such a heart. A love like that has power. Love is a lodestone, a force so powerful nothing can stop it, not even death. You, too, bear this love. Run to it, little rose. Run fast and free."

She felt her soul lift its weary head, tilting toward this

sun-drenched promise. The corridors were dark but she felt lighter. Perhaps her mother was there—in the air, in Mia's reflection on the onyx stone. Perhaps she was not alone.

She was sure she saw her father work his mouth around *forgive me* when the wedding trumpets blew.

Chapter 10

PROMISE ME

MIA STOOD AT THE golden altar to marry her true love.

Only, it wasn't true and it wasn't love. The altar wasn't even really golden, more of a tarnished bronze. She was drowning in oyster silk, and the air was redolent of rotting lilacs. The prince was an icicle with perfect curls.

"We have come here today," Duke Tristan intoned, "by royal decree of Ronan, Son of Clan Killian, Uncontested King of Glas Ddir, to witness this most hallowed union . . ."

He wasn't walloping candles this time, but he might as well have been. Mia felt every word shiver through her with a resounding *crack*.

Five hundred pairs of eyes bored into her back—servants,

courtiers, dignitaries, and the ominous guards. In her periphery she glimpsed the Hunters, their hands resting on the grips of their swords and bows.

Overhead, a colossal pipe organ jutted out of the balcony like a skeleton with jagged bones. Statues of deities lined the walls, emaciated male figures in funereal robes presiding over mausoleums harboring the early kings of Clan Killian, now piles of sacred human dust. Beneath the vault of smirking angels, a giant ring of candles was suspended from the ceiling, dripping wax. The Royal Chapel was gargantuan and gloomy, a cathedral more befitting a funeral than a wedding.

"It is the obligation of all those present to honor this most perfect union," said Tristan, "marking an alliance between two great houses . . ."

She snuck a glance over her shoulder to where her family sat in the balcony. Angie braved a smile, but her father's face was drawn shut like a curtain. Why had he spoken of her mother? In the moment it had given her courage, but in hindsight it seemed almost cruel, taunting her with a lesson on love before she embarked on a loveless marriage.

The prince raked his fingers through his blond curls. He wouldn't look at her. She thought of the honeyed warmth when he touched her in the library, compared to the icy stab of his words to the king and queen. *She is dangerous. My blackmail bride.*

"If any man has cause for objection," Tristan said, "sound belief these two should not be wed, let him speak now or forever hold his peace."

Always the man, Mia thought darkly. Gods forbid a woman have cause for objection. Gods forbid a woman ever express a "sound belief." Girls destined to be Huntresses were expected to waltz happily into marriages with boys they hardly knew. Magnificent princesses were forced to watch churlish little brothers inherit whole kingdoms when they themselves were far more qualified.

Mia had always harbored a hope that maybe someday, if the Hunters could eliminate magic, King Ronan would deem Glas Ddir safe. This was another reason she labored over her anatomy texts: surely there was some way to neutralize magic, to figure out *how* Gwyrach could control another person's body, and put an end to it. Girls would no longer be monitored and confined, but free to live out their destinies.

It was a wild dream and a sweet one; it had pulsed through her every day of Huntress training. Why shouldn't women get to craft the lives they wanted? Messy, complicated, vibrant lives full of adventure? That sort of freedom had always been her dream—not just for her, but for all Glasddirans.

Now that she had spent the last few weeks in close proximity to the king, she realized what a child she'd been. Ronan thrived on power and violence. He saw the Gwyrach as an assemblage of demon body parts to be dismantled and strung up—but he didn't treat his human subjects much better. There would be no freedom for the women of the river kingdom. Mia would bury her dream in a shallow grave.

Quin fidgeted with the gold buttons of his bridegroom jacket.

As usual, wintry squalls were rolling off him, prickling her skin. How was it possible that, only hours before, his touch had ignited her flesh? She closed her eyes to clear her head.

But it didn't clear. A strange thing was happening. Her mind conjured a vision of a place she couldn't quite see, all hues and textures, no distinct shapes. She closed her eyes and let the colors dance across her lids, vivid sea blues and igneous reds, alive with movement and vibration. She wanted to drink it down. Had she been to this place, or only dreamed it? She couldn't grasp hold of any one image, but she heard music trilling at the edges, mingled with the rich, raucous laughter of girls.

What was this sumptuous delusion? She wanted to believe, to inhabit its colors and feel its truth in her bones. This was a place where she would never be forced into a marriage arranged by men, a place where she could roam free, owned by no one, loved by none. Only in a life without love could you ever be truly free.

Her eyes shot open, drunk on what the world could be. She meant to look past Quin, but she looked right at him.

He was looking back. His eyes were two sulfyr sticks, a scintillating green.

"No objections, then," Tristan said.

Mia objected. A moment ago she'd been safely ensconced in her own fantasy world. Now she was stripped to the nubbins, raw and vulnerable and bare. She had no theories as to why her whole body popped and rattled, a whirl of feelings without logic, thoughts skittering, slamming, crashing into one another.

It was not a pleasant feeling.

"You will now speak your vows in unison," said the duke. "Take one another's hands and swear your sacred oath."

Quin took her gloved hands in his. Did she imagine it, or were his fingers trembling? The rest of the Chapel flickered and dissolved in a cloud of smoke, leaving only them. The candles braided themselves into a tapestry of light.

"Flesh of my flesh, bone of my bone.
I give you my body, my spirit, my home."

The words rolled effortlessly off her tongue. After weeks of not sparing her a second glance, Quin wouldn't *stop* looking. She watched his chest rise and fall as he pressed his lips together. His gaze tore into her flesh and knit it back together, building a whole history of fire and frost and ashes beneath her skin.

"Come illness, suffering, e'en death,
Until my final breath I will be yours."

His upper lip bowed in the middle; his lower lip was plump and full. She felt the integrity of her patellae turn to paste. So this was how it felt to go weak at the knees. Their vows reverberated through the Chapel, a hum of consonants, an aria of vowels.

"Till the ice melts on the southern cliffs,
Till the glass cities sink into the western sands."

She had the distinct feeling there were two heartbeats woven together in her chest, two lovers interlacing hands.

"Till the eastern isles burn to ash,
Till the northern peaks crumble."

This was madness. Mia felt as if she were being torn apart. She had no idea what was happening—and she couldn't trust what she couldn't know. The prince leaned forward and encircled her wrist with his fingers.

"Promise me, O promise me.
You will be mine."

"I will," Quin said.

I will, she said, but the words stopped somewhere in her throat.

She had to run. It wasn't logical, but to hell with logic. The urge was primal, tearing through her like a snarling beast. She had to get out of there.

She shook his hand off her arm and lunged backward. She started to turn, but Quin was faster. His hands were on her waist, soft yet firm, spinning her around to face him, stepping into the space where she'd stood, incinerating her momentum, cradling her face in his hands—and then falling, falling, falling into her arms.

His face was too close, too heavy. His body had gone limp.

Pandemonium erupted in the Chapel. What was happening?

She tried to hold Quin up, struggling to support his weight, and that's when she felt it. The shaft of an arrow plunged deep into his back.

Mia's hand was slick with blood as the prince slumped to the Chapel floor.

Chapter 11

GWYRACH

CHAOS. SHOUTING. MURDEROUS HEAT from every direction, liquid and thick, like the churning vortex of a volqano.

Mia crouched over Quin's crumpled body. She thought she heard Queen Rowena scream, followed by a clash of steel, but it was impossible to sort one sound from the next. A panicked man rushed the altar and swiftly found himself on the wrong end of a guard's blade.

She couldn't see her family—the balcony was bedlam. Her eyes blurred as she stared down at Quin, blood pooling in a dark circle beneath him. So much blood she could see her own face in the stain.

The prince convulsed, flecks of spittle on his lips. He was alive.

But not for long once he was trampled, his skull crushed. Why hadn't the king's guards swooped in to protect him?

As the Chapel roiled around her, she realized two things. First: if no one else was going to help, it was up to her to get the prince to safety.

Second: the archer who'd tried to kill him was almost certainly still there.

She wrapped her arms around Quin's chest and, staying low to the ground, dragged him into the Sacristy. Her head was raging, but her hands were steady. She silently thanked her father: she had inherited, among other things, his cool head in times of crisis.

The Sacristy was exactly as she remembered it: a small table in the corner, skirted with purple velvet folds. She snatched a candle off its surface, shoved the cloth aside, and crawled under, pulling Quin in behind her.

He moaned. She couldn't lay him on his back—the archer had made sure of that—so she propped him on his side.

"You're going to be all right," she said, though she had not the faintest inkling how. The arrow had gone in deep, and the wound was gushing.

The wedding guests had gone feral, the turmoil from the Chapel threatening to spill into the Sacristy at any moment. A new thought struck with horror. What if it was one of the guards who had tried to kill the prince? She had to act quickly.

Mia dug at the edges of the trapdoor, wood splintering beneath her fingernails. The thin chain snapped easily as she pried open the door and pitched herself through. Standing in the corridor below, she looped her arms around Quin and half dragged, half fell with him into the tunnel. The train of her dress collapsed on top of them like an overcooked soufflé.

Quin cried out. He'd fallen on his back, propelling the arrow more deeply into his chest. She cursed herself for her carelessness. She grabbed the candle from the floor above and pulled the door shut over their heads.

"Quin, look at me. I need you to look at me." His eyes wouldn't focus.

She had to get the arrow out. She didn't have the right equipment—most brides didn't bring surgical knives and dwayle to the altar—but she had to try.

She held the candle close, the flame dancing wildly, battered by her uneven breath. The arrow had gone in above his left scapula and sliced all the way through his chest; she could see the sinister red tip cresting the skin above his clavicle. The arrow had missed his lungs and heart by a hair's breadth. He was lucky to be alive.

She flipped him over onto his stomach and applied pressure to the bony ridge of his shoulder blade, holding him steady. It was a common misconception that an arrow, once lodged in the body, should be pushed all the way through. This was bad science. If forced through the chest, the vanes in the back of the shaft could cause more tearing and internal bleeding. If the arrow had made a clean incision, then the means of egress was ready-made: the arrow could be pulled out the way it came in—as long as you proceeded very, very carefully.

She closed her eyes and conjured up the image of Wound Man:

a tall, lean figure pierced by all manner of arrows, daggers, spears, darts, and swords. Macabre, yes, but there was a reason it was her favorite anatomical plate. Next to every wound site was a neat caption with a description of the injury, recommended treatment, and the likelihood of recovery. It had brought Mia tremendous relief that even wounds could be categorized and solved. She had memorized every word.

From what she'd seen of the arrowhead, it appeared to be a clean stone blade, not barbed or jutted. Barbed heads were problematic—they could tear vital organs upon extraction—so all things being equal, she was in an objectively good position. What better time to rip an entire arrow out of a man's chest?

"Take a deep breath," she said. "This will only hurt a moment."

She was quick. With one hand pressed firmly into his scapula, she gripped the wooden shaft in her other hand, took a breath, and wrenched the arrow out in one solid piece.

She tossed it aside, pleased. She'd gotten all of it, including the arrowhead: a perfect extraction. But her satisfaction was short-lived. Quin rolled onto his back as fresh blood spurted from the wound. He howled in pain, then lost consciousness. She'd done something wrong. She must have nicked the carotid artery—there was too much blood.

Mia tried not to panic. Why had her father never let her study wound theory in practicum? A surgeon was only ever as good as his cadavers. But although the other Hunters often practiced extracting arrows from the corpses of Gwyrach, her father had forbidden her from attending these gruesome training sessions.

The prince groaned, his pallid lips moving soundlessly. He was trying to speak. She felt his forehead: simmering hot.

"Under the plums," he whispered. *"If it's meant to be. You'll come to me, under the snow plum tree."*

With a pang she thought of Angelyne and felt a searing sense of shame. In the Chapel, Mia had tried to run away. She had promised to protect her sister, but in the end, her baser instincts had won, proving that instincts were never to be trusted.

Where was Angie now? Was she safe? It was an insipid question, considering someone had just shot an arrow into the prince's back. Were the Gwyrach to blame? That theory didn't hold up— the Gwyrach had no need for bows and arrows when they could stop a man's heart. Was the Kaer under siege? Had one of the other kingdoms decided to attack?

Suddenly Quin sat ramrod straight, startling her. "We only wanted . . . she was lying there on the stone . . . so still . . . so cold . . ."

A chill swept down Mia's spine. "Who was lying there?"

"We didn't mean for him to find us. I never meant to . . ."

"Who? Who found you?"

He sank into her arms, mumbling nonsense. Was this febrile delirium or a last confession? When he coughed his lips were streaked with blood. Mia knew enough about anatomy to know this wasn't a good thing.

She ripped open his bridegroom jacket and then his shirt, popping off several gold buttons in the process. His chest was smooth and hairless, a clean slate for the blood leaching from the gash.

She'd never seen so much blood. It was everywhere. The white oyster silk of her dress was soaked a deep, pulsing red.

What bitter irony. Here she was, in the tunnels beneath Kaer Killian, holding a bloodied wedding gown. She was living out a grotesque parody of the very escape she'd plotted for herself and her sister. How naive she'd been, hatching schemes of boar's blood and faked murder. Real murder was a different thing entirely.

She stared down at the prince's ashen face, his shirt torn asunder, golden curls mashed to his forehead with sweat. He'd never looked so young or innocent. Hard to be an incorrigible ass when you were dying, even for someone as gifted at assery as the prince.

"Stay with me, Quin."

In seventeen years she'd only seen one dead body, and it was eerily neat and sterile, her mother's flesh unmarred by any visible wound. Until now, Mia hadn't known a person could hold so much blood. Reading about the ten pints in a human body was one thing; marinating in them was another.

She was accustomed to having the right answer, but she didn't have it now. This was a test she was going to fail. Barring a miracle, he would die in her arms.

The candle flame winked and twirled, then sputtered out, shrouding them in black.

Mia was bone tired. She couldn't give up. Not now. Not like this. In her mind she paged through every book she had ever read: all the anatomical sketches she'd drawn as a Huntress, the physiology lessons from her father, her mother's medical skills. Maybe she could stanch the flow of blood. Maybe it wasn't too late.

Instinctively she tore off her gloves and flung them aside, pressing her hands to Quin's chest. For once she felt no cold rolling off the prince; only sickly heat. The trick was to apply pressure. The trick was to let him know he was not alone. The trick was to do everything in her power to make sure he didn't die here in this dark tunnel, without his family, without his dogs.

"Stay with me. Please."

To her surprise, her voice was cracking. She'd never felt more alone.

Her body was a wrung-out cloth. In her mind she watched all her hope and strength swirl down a giant porcelain drain. A crush of feet and metal sounded from above. Either the guards would find her with the prince dead in her arms, or the assassin would drop down into the tunnel and kill them both.

Was there wind in the tunnels? It suctioned her skin, siphoning the air from the corridor. She wanted desperately to sleep. She started to drift off, then jolted back awake. How could her body mutiny at a time like this? She fought to maintain control. But her fingertips were numb and heavy on the prince's chest. Her eyes stung, her eyelids were leaden.

Mia's head drooped, her limp curls brushing Quin's face.

She pressed her ear to Quin's chest, listening frantically for a heartbeat. Nothing.

She'd lost him. It was over.

"Tickles."

Mia's eyes flew open. Had he just spoken?

"Your hair." His voice was a fuzzy murmur, as if he were lying at the bottom of a long chute. In the dark she felt him lift a shaky hand and part the curtain of ringlets splicing the air between them. "It's everywhere."

She sat upright. Heart racing, she squinted into the fathomless black. But it *wasn't* fathomless: hazy light seeped in from some unseen cleft in the rock. Quin's cheeks were tinged with color. His iridescent eyes were clear and open—and also baffled.

Mia was baffled herself. How was the color flooding back into his face?

He sat up, then sank back onto his elbows, woozy. "What happened? We were in the Chapel, saying our vows. The last thing I remember . . ."

Quin stared at the arrow on the ground. Then he looked at his wound.

"You shouldn't—" she started to say, but it was too late: he touched the hole in his chest. Mia winced, waiting for him to cry out. But he didn't even flinch. He simply stared at his fingertips, dazed.

There was no hole.

In the weak light, she saw the impossible: the flesh had stitched itself back together, stanching the flow of blood. The gash was no longer oozing; it was white with notched pink ridges, already a fish-bone scar.

"Four gods," he said.

Mia's mind was reeling. He should have died. She stared at her hands, still wet with his blood.

"You healed me," the prince said quietly.

No. It wasn't possible. She had spent three years studying the human body. A wound of that depth and severity did not vanish from a simple touch.

Unless.

Unless.

"You're a Gwyrach," Quin said.

Chapter 12

TIMES OF UNIMAGINABLE DURESS

MIA HEARD THE WORDS Quin was saying, but she couldn't comprehend them.

"I—I'm not a Gwyrach," she stammered. "I can't be a Gwyrach."

"You healed me with your touch." He poked gingerly at his wound. "It doesn't even hurt. Like it never happened." His eyes narrowed. "In the Chapel, during the ceremony . . . you were enthralling me, weren't you?"

Mia's stomach pitched. Molten lava popped and boiled inside her chest; she swallowed hard to stop the rising bile. Everything she had ever known, every hard-won truth: gone.

"I wouldn't—I can't—I would never do that."

The words came out mangled. Even as she said it, she knew

it was a lie. Now she saw the wedding ceremony in a new light: the honeyed heat, the fiery sparks boring into her skin. She had enthralled him. She must have enthralled him in the library, too. What she had naively mistaken for budding attraction was her own dark magic.

How could she be so obtuse? She had studied it in a hundred books, knew the signs, the symptoms. She had touched his hand in the library and again in the Chapel. Both times Quin had been sweating and breathing heavily, his heart beating so loudly she'd felt it thrum beneath her own skin. She had, unwittingly, spiked his blood with desire. She had made him want her.

But hadn't she been wearing gloves?

To enthrall someone is to enslave them, little rose. You've stripped them of consent, robbed them of their choice. And without choice, what are we?

The king's guards slammed through the Sacristy overhead. Joined by the Hunters, no doubt. A grisly truth settled into the pit of her stomach.

She was a Gwyrach. If they found her, they would kill her.

Quin wobbled to his feet. "We have to run."

She blinked. "I'm not sure I—"

"Someone clearly wants me dead. And once they discover you're a Gwyrach . . ." His face was grim. "Your Hand will be the latest addition to my father's Hall."

Fear thrashed in her chest. "You would reveal me?"

"No, Mia. I'm not as evil as you seem to believe." He gestured at his wound. "But it's a little obvious, don't you think?"

He was right. The regrown flesh was an unnatural perversion;

it could only be a product of magic. They were both doomed.

Yelling broke out overhead, then a crash of steel and brass. A wild notion flashed through Mia's mind. It was completely illogical, wholly unreasonable, something she would never have cooked up in a million years . . . and it just might work.

She summoned all her strength and stood.

"I know a way out," she said. "Follow me."

She'd spent days agonizing over her carefully inked map of the tunnels, but in the end it wasn't the map that saved her. As she led Quin through the corridors, she invoked her father's swift, sure footfall the night before. His parting gift.

Moments later, they were standing in the castle crypt.

Mia ached to press her cheek into her mother's tomb. In the dim light she saw the elegant plum tree carved into the cold gray stone, the little bird on its lonely perch, peering up at the moon. *Good-bye, Mother.* It seemed she would never get the chance to say a proper farewell—not three years ago, and not today.

"Why are we in the crypt?" Quin said, uneasy.

"You'll see."

She had never known exhaustion like this. Her body was an empty vessel, subject to the whims of a force greater than her own. The prince was light-headed, too, she could tell. She circled an arm around his waist and together they staggered shakily along the passageway feeding out of the crypt.

"The path is unforgiving," she said, echoing her father. "Watch your step."

She was grateful for her strong legs and hips as they lumbered forward on four legs. They stumbled onto the precipice outside the castle, the bitter wind whisking Mia's hair into a fine cherry mousse, the moon a glowing stone in the sky.

And there it was, a shimmering beacon twenty feet above them on the cliff side.

The laghdú.

The carriage that had once carted princes and princesses across the quarry, now empty, bobbing on a long, taut cable—the very cable that connected Kaer Killian with the village far below.

Run, little rose. Run fast and free.

Had her father known?

She didn't have time to wonder. She helped the prince up the bluff and packed him into the carriage in his shreds of bloody shirt.

"Mia?" Quin's voice was uncertain. "What exactly are we about to do?"

"You have to trust me."

A bold proposition, considering how the wedding gown tangled around her ankles, nearly catapulting her into the abyss. This pretty trifle would be the death of her—she had tripped on it for the last time. She dug her fingers into the train and ripped it out, tossing it onto the rocks in a wad of grimy silk.

Something skittered out of the cloth.

It was small and stout, teetering precariously on the edge of the yawning chasm. She scrambled forward and scooped the something off the rock.

It was her mother's journal, the little ruby wren fitted into the lock.

Who had put it there? Her father? Angelyne? She hadn't felt anyone slip the book into her train. But then, the train was practically its own sentient being, and she'd been reasonably preoccupied with other things, including but not limited to: botched marriage, attempted assassination, dark magic, et cetera.

Perhaps the real question was not who, but *why*. The journal was a useless brick of blank pages and nostalgia. She pinched the wren's wings, twisting the lock. A breeze fluttered the pages, and a glimmer of black ink caught her eye.

Mia's heart unfolded.

Most of the pages were still blank, but the first one no longer was. Her mouth went chalk dry as her fingers traced the inscription in her mother's elegant script:

Should this book become lost, the writer humbly requests that she who finds it make all reasonable efforts to return it to its rightful home.

Should the finder of this book become lost, the writer humbly suggests that she consider a journey in the same direction.

The path to safe haven will reveal itself to she who seeks it.

All you seek will be revealed.

W. M.

Under the words, in a smudged cluster of curves and coils, was a map.

Mia didn't have time to question it. Shouts clamored through the tunnels. The guards were plowing toward them, all fealty and righteous fury. Were the Hunters with them? If so, Mia's breaths were numbered.

She tucked the book back into the balled-up train for an added layer of protection and stuffed the bundle beside the prince. Then she hoisted herself into the carriage.

Quin's face was flushed. "Might I suggest this is a momentously bad idea?"

"Do you have a better one?" She ran her hands over the inside of the carriage, looking for a sharp blade. With no one at the crankshaft, she'd have to cut the rope that held the carriage to the cable, launching them into free fall down the copper wire. *Bridalaghdú: fall of the bride.*

"What are you looking for?"

"I need a knife."

He blanched. "A knife?"

"I'm not going to stab you, Quin. I just saved your life, remember?"

He stared at her for a long moment. Too long. The tunnels were preparing to belch out a lethal mix of guards and assassins; she could feel it in her blood.

Quin extracted a leather scabbard from his boot and unsheathed a thin silver blade. He held it out to her. Now it was Mia's turn to blanch.

"Do I want to know why you brought a sheath knife to our wedding?"

His smile was rueful. "Always wise to carry a weapon in times of unimaginable duress."

Perhaps the prince was not what he seemed. Perhaps he *did* have secrets.

Mia took the knife and held it high, silver moonlight glinting off the blade. She stared at herself in the reflection. A demon in oyster silk stared back.

And yet, in spite of everything—even as she stood amidst the charred cinders of her life—she felt freer than she had in ages. Powerful.

Run, little rose. Run fast and free.

"Where are we going, Mia? Where is there to hide?"

She didn't answer. In one swift motion, she hacked the cord cleaving them to the black rock. The rope snapped and the carriage heaved, free from its bindings after so many years.

Together, they flew.

PART TWO

Bone

Chapter 13

HOW TO ESCAPE SUCCESSFULLY IN EIGHT SIMPLE STEPS

1. Survive five-hundred-foot drop* in a potentially fatal machine.
2. After renegotiating relationship with solid ground, ransack laghdú hut for provisions. Find nothing but moth-eaten smocks and trousers.
3. Don moth-eaten smocks and trousers and tailor them with available materials. "Available materials" being: a ball of moldy twine.
4. Forge makeshift satchel out of bloody wedding gown.
5. Pack sheath knife in satchel.
6. Do not waste time wondering why your betrothed had a sheath knife in his boot.

7. Steal through Killian Village without attracting attention.
8. Consult mysteriously appearing map and make for the fork in the river.

For future escapes, consider alternate method.

Chapter 14

A BRIEF AND BLOODY END

MIA AND QUIN'S DEATH-DEFYING plummet had bought them limited time. Other than free fall by laghdú, there was only one way in or out of the Kaer: the steep road hewn from the east-facing mountainside. Mia's feet were still struggling to find purchase when she spotted the throng of guards darkening the eastern road.

"They'll be in the village within the hour," Quin said. "My father's men are fast."

"Then we'll be faster."

She was still in a state of shock, but at least her flavor of shock was mobilizing. They slipped quickly through the back alleys of Killian Village, darting between huts and lean-tos. The houses were mostly still, cocooned in the night quiet, but the taverns and brothels were simmering with debauchery. As they hurried by one such structure, a man stumbled down the front steps and vomited a stream of bile onto the ground, narrowly missing the prince's boots.

"Lovely," Quin muttered.

Having not spent much time in the village, Mia was surprised how ramshackle it was. She had expected crisp, clean cottages like the ones in Ilwysion; instead she saw shabby huts and thatched hovels, muck shoveled into brown heaps on the streets and attended by swarms of flies. The people were thinner than she remembered, their clothes ragged and their faces smudged with soot and dirt. She counted at least five rats scurrying across the cobblestones.

"Glas Ddir has not prospered under my father's reign," Quin said as they leaned against a blacksmith's forge to catch their breath. "Bronwynis encouraged free trade and commerce to flourish. But after my aunt was murdered and my father seized the throne, our fine kingdom has watched its imports vanish and its exports turn to ash."

Mia arched an eyebrow. "I thought you didn't care for politicking."

"I don't care to sit around smoking cigars with bloated braggadocios. Politicking is one thing. Politics is another."

He was right about the river kingdom. For as long as Mia could remember, Glasddirans had subsisted on their own meager wares: linen and wool, timber, salty meats, soft cheeses, and seemingly unlimited barrels of blackthorn wine, which she had always found rather watery. Glas Ddir had sunk into rawboned poverty, and nowhere was that more evident than in Killian Village.

"We should keep moving," she said as they ducked out of the alley and hastened down another filthy avenue of cobblestones. They weren't moving as fast as Mia would have liked. "You have to keep up."

"I'm trying," Quin huffed. "Turns out nearly dying is pretty exhausting."

"So is saving your life. Turns out."

A girl with a torn linen dress and large, hungry eyes staggered past. Was she coming from the brothels? She was much too young. Mia's stomach tightened like a fist. She wished she had a pouch of silver coins to give the girl, or food, or gemstones from the castle—anything to deliver a dose of hope.

Quin shook his head. "I don't go into the village often, but when I do, I am always reminded of the true cost of my father's *policies*. I do what I can to help."

Mia was surprised by the prince's candor. In the library she'd called him coddled, when in fact he'd been out making mercy visits to impoverished Glasddirans. Her mother had done this, too; for years Wynna traveled to various alpine villages and river towns on the banks of the Natha River, even all the way to Killian Village, to administer medicine to people who were sick. What had Mia spent the last few years doing? Reading anatomy books in the rarified air of Ilwysion.

Mia cringed. *She* was the coddled one.

"Excuse me, miss?"

She whirled around to see a boy about Quin's age, though his back had the stoop of an old man. He didn't look Glasddiran; his dark freckles spilled like specks of ink across his cool bronze skin, and beneath his tangle of black hair, there was something fragile about him, a dull glaze in his thin silvery eyes. Though he addressed her as "miss," his voice had the strains of nobility.

He nodded toward her and the prince. Mia felt Quin bristle beside her.

"Do you seek a place to stay?"

She wanted nothing more than to sleep in a warm bed. Her limbs were thick with fatigue. But if they stayed in the village, they would be discovered by the guards, or worse: the Hunters.

The boy read her hesitance correctly. "Nourishment, then. For your journey. I don't have much to offer you, but I have this." He held out a small loaf of bread and a pouch of snow plums. Mia noticed his right hand was missing two fingers.

"At what cost?" she said. For all she knew, the boy was one of the king's spies, men stationed at village brothels to report suspicious activity. There were spies everywhere, hungry men desperate for the reward money Ronan offered for turning over any girl suspected of practicing magic.

"No cost, miss." He paused. "You remind me of my sister, is all."

Quin stared at the boy intently. "Where is your sister?"

"She's gone. Taken."

"By Gwyrach?"

"No, sir. By the king's men."

Mia's stomach twisted yet again. She had heard talk of girls no older than twelve or thirteen being rounded up by Ronan's guards and brought straight to Kaer Killian, bypassing the Circle of the Hunt. Some girls were deemed innocent and returned to their families. Some were never seen again.

She wanted to dismiss the rumors, but once, during her stay in the castle, she had seen a girl she'd known in Ilwysion, willowy and strong, with radiant olive skin and black hair so silky it fell like a sheet down her back. As a child, this girl had raced three boys up the mountain and won. But she was no longer a graceful, fleet-footed athlete. She was a living doll, heavily made up with skin greases, jewels, and feathers dipped in gold. She had been paraded through King Ronan's court with other favorites from the village brothel, and when Mia saw her, she'd felt sick.

Yet another way in which Mia was privileged: as the daughter of Griffin Rose, she had been spared a similar fate.

"We have to go," she said to Quin. They were already risking detection. If the boy recognized the prince, he would be all the more inclined to point the guards in the right direction.

"Please." The boy took a step forward, and Mia noticed a hitch in his gait. He held out the provisions. "A gift."

He was staring relentlessly at her arms. She wasn't wearing gloves—she'd left them behind in the tunnels, she realized. The boy would report them for sure. Mia felt a wave of nausea: he *should* report her. She was a Gwyrach.

"We must go *now*," she whispered fiercely in Quin's ear.

As she turned to go, she saw the prince reach out to accept the food, his fingers lingering for an extra moment on the boy's palm. If Quin were a woman, that touch would have cost him his hand.

"Be well, Your Grace," the boy said softly as they slunk back into the shadows. So he had recognized Quin from the beginning.

Mia wondered how much they had just sacrificed for a bag of bread and plums.

Her mother's journal had magic. That much was clear. Normal ink in normal books did not suddenly appear on the page. As she squinted at the elegant handwriting, she felt a squirm of discomfort. She'd spent the last three years singularly focused on expunging magic in all forms. Now, without warning, she had become a magical creature holding a magical book.

Did that mean her mother was magical, too?

"It's hopeless." Quin was panting, his cheeks ruddy from exertion. They'd made it to the outskirts of the village and were nearing the river. "The guards have horses. And dogs. *My* dogs, who know my scent. We have four legs between us, and shaky legs at that. Unless you can *magic* your way out of this"—he wiggled his fingers in the air—"we don't stand a chance."

The thing about the color flooding back into his cheeks was that all his usual surliness was flooding back, too.

"Magic," she said, "is not a verb."

Or maybe it was. She clearly had a patchy understanding of what magic was and wasn't. It hit her all over again: she was a Gwyrach. Demon. *Murderer.*

98

Mia brushed the thought aside. She refocused her attention on the map.

Her mother had sketched the castle and Killian Village, but the landmasses to the west and south were conspicuously absent, blank space on a flaxen page. To the east she'd drawn the serpentine Natha River, with a mysterious crescent squiggle at the fork, and then the westernmost borders of the tall trees of Ilwysion. But the forest vanished long before it reached the Twisted Forest or the eastern coastline, where the Salted Sea connected the river kingdom to the islands of the fire kingdom. Almost as if Wynna had run out of ink.

So, Mia reasoned. If the ink had filled in to the east, they were right to be moving in that direction. She'd never been ruled by instinct—she wasn't the impetuous sort—but this time, her instincts had proven correct.

She scoffed at her own flawed logic. She was staring at a fanciful map rendered in fanciful ink, attempting to read meaning into an inscription that, for all she knew, was nothing more than one of her mother's riddles. *The path will reveal itself to she who seeks it. All you seek will be revealed.* Wynna had always had a poet's love for syllogism and a jester's sense of play.

Mia, on the other hand, had a habit of taking things too literally, something Domeniq du Zol liked to chide her for during their Hunter training sessions. "You take the world too seriously," he often said.

"I take the world at its purported value," Mia would correct him. "As anyone with common sense would do."

She didn't even have her beloved compass to help chart her

path. This was *not* the Mia Rose she knew.

She swallowed hard. The real Mia Rose was a Gwyrach. Which meant she had never really known herself at all.

"I hope whatever you're looking at in that book," Quin said, "is a blueprint for a river craft. Because unless you can summon a boat once we reach the Natha, this little expedition of ours will soon come to a brief and bloody end."

"Ye of trifling faith."

"Faith gets people killed. I'd rather worship at the altar of logic. A cold altar, but a rational one."

Funny, Mia thought. She'd always felt the same.

But now her logic was contorting into a wild hypothesis about the mysterious squiggle on her mother's map. It was nothing more than a scrap of a hangnail at the fork of the river, a half-moon bobbing on the Natha's inky surface, and yet she felt certain she knew what it was.

A boat.

Before Domeniq du Zol's father was killed by Gwyrach, he had captained a coracle: a small, oval-shaped boat. He collected silver coins at the fork of the Natha River and ferried passengers along its watery ventricles. The du Zols called the boat the *Sunbeam*, a tribute to their Fojuen heritage: *du Zol* meant "of the sun."

Maybe the boat was still there.

Never mind Dom's father had died three years ago. Or that the du Zols—with the exception of Dom, who had stayed in the river kingdom to train with the Hunters—had fled Glas Ddir and returned to Fojo Karaçäo shortly after his death. Or that boats tended not to stay in the same place for years on end. Boats moved. That was the point.

"We're close," she said, with more confidence than she felt.

"Close to what?"

She was almost certainly chasing the ghost of a boat. And still she moved doggedly toward the river as the earth grew soft and spongy underfoot. She could smell the wet scent of the Natha, the blackthorn brambles on the banks wicking sweet moisture from the mud. Centuries of erosion had pulverized the rocks, sugared them into glittering black sand.

Mia and Quin stepped into a small clearing. The Natha surged oily black past their feet. In the moonlight it looked like a forked tongue, one prong flowing west, the other east. She shuddered. The black tongue of a demon.

She heard dogs barking, followed by the harsh shouts of men.

Panic rose in her chest. But the map had not misled her: a small, dilapidated dock jutted out into the water. She recognized the smell of rotting wood. This was indeed where Dom's father had picked up his passengers in the *Sunbeam*.

Quin blinked. "Is there supposed to be a boat?"

"Shh." The hairs bristled on Mia's neck. "Someone's coming."

Chapter 15

SILVER BLADE

MIA HADN'T HEARD THEM; she'd *felt* them. Her ears were not as fine-tuned as her father's, but she'd felt an ominous prickling heat as blood pooled in her toes and fingers. Did her magic allow her to sense when someone was near?

"Tree," she said, shoving Quin toward the closest one. "Can you climb?"

"I'm not a kitten. I know how to climb a tree."

"So do kittens."

She scaled the tree, scrabbling up the trunk and wedging her hips between boughs. Quin swung himself up far more gracefully on his long limbs. He'd grown up in a castle, she in a forest, but he was right: he wasn't shabby at climbing trees.

I don't hear anyone, he mouthed.

She daggered a finger to his lips. *Stop talking.*

I'm not talking!

She clapped a hand over his mouth. His breath was warm against her fingers.

Twenty feet below them, Tuk and Lyman, two of her father's best Hunters, skulked into the glade.

The most seasoned Hunters knew how to tread lightly, their footsteps dew upon the earth. Despite the fact that Tuk was the size of an ox and Lyman never stopped running his mouth, they'd both mastered the art of the silent approach. If Mia hadn't felt them, she never would have heard them coming.

She didn't like Tuk or Lyman, not since overhearing them make jokes one day after a training session. "What did she expect?" Lyman had said. "The wife of an assassin will always have a target on her back. Should have thought of that before she married him!" Mia never forgave them for speaking so callously about her mother.

Now she clutched the tree limb, her skin tingling, peppered with a fine frost. Perhaps the boy from the village had sold them out. Or perhaps, said a dark little voice inside her, Tuk and Lyman had picked up her scent. Some Hunters claimed to be able to smell magic, to sniff out a Gwyrach in their midst. "The magical stench," Lyman called it. "Not very becoming on a lady. But then, we aren't dealing with ladies, are we?"

Tuk stooped beside the river and splashed water on his broad, russet-brown face. Then he sat and hefted his full weight against the trunk of an oak tree. Tuk pulled a flask of demon's dwayle from his rucksack and quaffed a long swig, smacking his lips in pleasure. Lyman paced nervously up and down the riverbank, his pinkish cheeks alive with movement, fingertips dancing on his palms.

"Be that as it may," Tuk was saying, "it doesn't mean she deserves to die." He swilled a mouthful of dwayle and belched, as if to prove his point.

"We don't decide who lives or dies."

"She saved the prince's life."

"And she'll kill him soon enough. You know as well as I do: that's what they *do*."

The air locked in Mia's throat. She felt a subtle change in Quin's breathing, too: a quick inhalation, followed by a tightening of his chest. Would he scream out? If he believed what Lyman was saying . . . if he thought she would try to kill him . . .

But he was silent. He let out his breath, the air fogging her fingers, hot and humid. She loosened her grip.

"She can't have gone far," Lyman said. "The girl is book smart, but she won't last a single night in the woods. She'll get scared. Come crawling back to Papa."

Mia knew the woods like the back of her hand—at least she would, once they reached Ilwysion. She was strong there. Competent. Lyman could choke on a plum pit.

"Have a swig and calm down, would you?" Tuk wagged the flask. "You're making me tense."

Lyman stopped moving. "Someone's here."

"You mean the king's herd of fools stampeding through the forest?"

Then Tuk went still, too.

Mia's stomach was a slab of ice sweating through her belly. The Hunters had sensed her. They knew.

Lyman lifted his head, his eyes grating over her like steel wool.

"*There* you are," he said, and then said nothing more, as a silver blade caught him in the throat.

Chapter 16

A RAVEN ON THE RIVER

MIA COULD PINPOINT THE exact moment Lyman died. She felt it in her own body, the agony whipping through her chest like a scourge: the fractured trachea, silencing his screams; the severed carotid artery, starving his brain of oxygen; the gasps and gurgles from his broken throat. He was drowning in his own blood. His heart writhed as red liquid spurted from his neck, drizzling the sliced knot of flesh and staining his tunic dark.

She didn't understand how she felt these things, but there was no doubt the collapse in Lyman's body resonated in her own flesh, her own bones, her own blood. Was this part of having magic, too? Feeling the sensations of a body that was not your own? She'd never read about it in any of her books. But it was very real, and very terrible. Hot bile seethed in her belly; she struggled to keep it down.

Tuk was already reaching for his sword. For such a large man, he was surprisingly light on his feet. With his free hand, he pulled a bone talisman from his pocket, kissed it, and tucked it under his belt.

"Show yourself!" he barked, but no assailant emerged from the forest.

Air burbled in Mia's throat. This time it was Quin who clapped a hand over her mouth so she wouldn't cry out. His fingers were glacial.

Who had thrown the dagger? Her mind was swimming in blood, but the blade looked familiar. That pale-green stone.

"Only a coward kills in darkness," Tuk growled. "Show yourself."

Domeniq du Zol stepped out of the trees.

Tuk's eyes widened, though not as wide as Mia's. *Dom* was the assassin? None of this made sense.

Tuk gave voice to the word bubbling up inside her: "Traitor."

Domeniq rubbed the back of his head, his coarse black hair cropped close. It was a tic she knew well: whenever he was uncomfortable, he rubbed his head and flashed that crooked smile. But he wasn't smiling now.

Dom bent and drew the serrated silver dagger from Lyman's throat, the sound of bisected bone and cartilage slurping off the metal. He stepped forward. The stone at his neck burned a deep midnight blue.

"I'm sorry, Tuk," he said.

Tuk brought his broadsword down hard, his aim straight and true. But Dom was quicker. He parried the blow, catching the side of the blade in one of the twisted ripples of his dagger, twisting his wrist and knocking the sword off course. Mia had never seen Dom move like this. She knew he was a gifted swordsman, but he'd been holding back in their training sessions: now he was all flash and lightning, powerful and stunningly precise.

One step and a feint was all it took: Dom fit his blade cleanly into the space between his opponent's ribs, impaling the heart in its bony cage.

Tuk sputtered, skewered like a pig on a spit. The cliff of his body crumbled and fell, his giant mound of a chest heaving with effort, his large brown eyes blinking back tears. His face twisted in shock. He had been betrayed.

Dom stooped beside the large man and put a steady hand on his shoulder. It was hard to see from her hiding spot, but Mia was almost certain his smooth brown face was creased with grief. He bowed his head.

"I'm sorry, brother. You didn't deserve this."

The moment Tuk's heart stopped, a shivering emptiness swept through Mia, like a gust of cold down a dark corridor.

She was tired. So tired. Fatigue bled from her pores. Should she try to heal them? All the animosity she'd felt toward Tuk and Lyman had evaporated the moment they fell. They didn't deserve to die. Not at the hand of their friend and brother in the Hunt.

But somehow she knew they were beyond saving. Their hearts

were silent. The men were gone.

The horror of what she'd witnessed shuddered through her, turning her limbs to jelly. She was losing her grip on the tree.

She felt Quin's hands firm around her waist. He held her to the bough, encircling her torso with his arms, holding her steady. His face was crushed into the back of her head, his nose buried in her hair, and she could feel his breath all the way down to her follicles. His slender hip bones pressed into her back, piercing the thin smocks that lay ruffled between them.

Wulf and Beo plowed into the clearing in a cacophony of yips and howls. Domeniq snapped his fingers and whistled. She felt Quin's body stiffen. If Dom hurt those dogs . . .

But he didn't hurt them. He placed a hand on each of their golden heads, scratching them behind the ears. They wagged their tails.

"Wulf! Beo!"

A magnificent white mare galloped into the glade, with Princess Karri astride.

"The dogs had the scent," she shouted.

Dom stood. "They must have lost it, Your Grace."

Karri looked fierce in the moonlight. Her short white hair stuck out in a dozen directions, and the gown she'd grudgingly worn for the wedding was filthy and torn. At her hip, instead of a bouquet of posies, she now wore a longsword. Mia thought it suited her much better than the posies.

Karri nodded toward the two dead men. "What's this?"

"My brothers in the Hunt." Dom nodded at the dagger

protruding from Tuk's mountain of a chest. "Wound's still fresh. Their attackers can't have gone far."

Mia was reeling. Dom had just killed them in cold blood, and now he was framing someone else?

Karri dismounted her horse and crouched to inspect the dagger. "Gwyrach?"

Dom shook his head. "Magicians have no need for blades."

"They do if they're attacking from a distance." She pressed a boot into Tuk's shoulder and tugged the blade out of the wet wound. "It's not Glasddiran." She tested the weight, tossing the knife from one hand to another, catching it neatly by the green hilt. "Steel is light. Winged on the tip."

"Pembuka," Dom said. "Look at the stone in the grip, Your Grace. It's aventurine. Nothing from around here. My money's on the glass tribes in the far west—they like their weapons with a thin blade. There must have been at least three men, maybe more, to take down two Hunters."

He stretched his arms overhead, showcasing the ropy sinews of his back. Dom had rippling muscles and a physique straight out of the novels Angelyne loved. Mia felt a pang. *Angie.*

"We find who killed these two," Dom said, "and we find your brother."

"And Mia, too?"

Mia was surprised, and more than a little pleased, that Karri cared about her safety. Dom cocked his head.

"Her too. Whoever killed these Hunters took both the prince and his winsome bride."

His winsome bride. If she ever got out of this alive, she made a mental note to slug Dom in his nether regions. Unless he killed her first.

Princess Karri furrowed her brow, weighing her options.

"Were there any Pembuka guests at the wedding?"

"There aren't many Pembuka left in Glas Ddir, Your Grace."

"Perhaps not. But there are some." She shook her head. "Yet another reason my father's bigotry will be the death of him. He thinks he has stemmed the flow of foreigners, but they are still here, and they hate us now more than ever."

She looked evenly at Dom. "If I were to rule this kingdom, all would be welcome. I would fling open every gate and crumble every wall."

Her words sent a thrill through Mia, reminding her why Princess Karri had all the makings of a great queen. Reopening the borders would unlock a world Mia had never known. A conversation with her mother came flooding back, one she had lost in the aftermath of her death. Wynna rarely spoke of her past, but there was one night, toward the end, when her cheeks had grown rosy from blackthorn wine, and Mia was able to nudge her into loose-lipped nostalgia.

"The world of the river kingdom is all you've ever known, Mia—a world of terror and restraint. The fire kingdom was different. I went to Fojo Karação to study medicine, but I learned so much more. Imagine a place where Pembuka, Luumi, Fojuen, and Glasddiran all live peacefully side by side. Imagine languages and cultures and histories blending together—not without tension, but with a spirit of curiosity and exchange. And magic. In Fojo, magic was not so different from love."

Mia arched a skeptical eyebrow.

"I know you don't believe me," her mother said, her words softened by the wine. "But magic was a way of bringing pleasure to the people you touched. You could love anyone you wanted, no judgment, no fear. Men could love men." A smile danced on her lips. "Women could love women."

Her laugh was a nip of spirits, the kind that burned the throat. "It might have been that way here, if Bronwynis were still alive."

"If Fojo was so perfect," Mia asked, "then why did you leave?"

Sadness flickered in her mother's eyes. "Mark my words, my raven girl: love can be a beautiful thing. But the people you love are the ones who hurt you most."

Now Mia saw the conversation in a different light. Perhaps her mother had loved a woman—a *Gwyrach*—who had once used magic to bring pleasure instead of pain.

If her mother had loved a Gwyrach in the fire kingdom . . . a former lover who bore a decades-long grudge . . . had this same Gwyrach slunk into the river kingdom three years ago, fueled by bloodlust and revenge?

The blade of an epiphany twisted in Mia's gut.

The people you love are the ones who hurt you most.

In the clearing, Princess Karri hoisted herself back onto her horse.

"Take these men back to the Circle and bury your dead," she said to Domeniq. "I'll tell the guards we're looking for a pack of Pembuka raiders—at least one archer and two men skilled with a blade. We'll follow the Natha west toward the glass kingdom."

Dom straightened. "Let the Hunters search the river. The glass tribes don't know the Natha like we do—we'll catch up to them within a day. And, Your Grace." He grinned. "You must admit your royal river craft is no match for ours."

"True, true. Our boats announce themselves like a pack of lumbering elephants. You Hunters do have a gift for stealth. Very well. You take the river. The guards and I will cut them off by land." She whistled at the dogs. "Beo! Wulf!"

"Your Grace." Dom rested one hand on the mare's flank. "We'll find your brother. If he were dead, we would have found him already. He has more value to them alive."

"My brother will one day be king." Mia couldn't read the emotion that swept over Karri's features. Was it pride? Envy? "Do not forget that, while he may have value alive, he also has great value dead."

She galloped out of the glade, the dogs trotting dutifully along behind.

Quin's shoulders sagged, his body heavy against Mia's. Could she blame him? What his sister said was true: as heir to the throne, someone would always want him dead. He was drooping, both their grips faltering on the tree. They were too weary. She didn't know how much longer they could hold on before they revealed themselves.

Dom was very still. He gazed across the river at nothing, deep in thought.

She wondered if he was thinking of his father. Just days before Mia's mother died, Dom had found his father's body on the banks of the Natha, long black braids steeped in mud and dark umber skin sapped of its color. There was no blood, no obvious wound. Dom didn't like to talk about it, but Mia had heard the Hunters discussing the details: when Dom had touched his father's face, he found his tongue frozen to his teeth, his mouth coated with frost despite the warmth clinging to the air. The Gwyrach had turned the breath in his body to ice.

Domeniq was left with his father's cerulean stone around his neck and fury in his heart. Judging by the two corpses bleeding out on the riverbank, more fury than Mia had known.

But why would he kill his own brothers in the Hunt? The men who were trying to *hunt* the Gwyrach who had murdered his father? She didn't know the answer. She hated not knowing.

Dom bent forward, picked up a smooth pebble, and skipped it across the black water of the Natha. The stone skimmed the river like a raven, elegant and light, landing with a soft crack against something wooden.

On the far shore, Mia saw a scoop of pale yellow, camouflaged so well behind a copse of white-bark birch trees she never would have seen it.

The *Sunbeam*.

Dom craned his neck, that lovely crooked smile lighting up his face. In the moonlight his teeth shone bright white against his warm ochre skin.

Was he staring up at her? His face twitched, and Mia's pulse slammed through her body as he turned on his heel and strode out of the clearing.

She could have sworn he winked.

Chapter 17

MERELY GIRLS

THEY WAITED FOR WHAT seemed like hours to drop down from their hiding spot, though it was probably only minutes. Stealthily they swam out to the boat, the cool river lapping at their flesh, and heaved themselves aboard.

Mia was grateful for the silence. Her thoughts, normally etched down one smooth line of logic, forked into channels and streams, eddies of unanswerable questions that only led back into themselves.

Dom had killed Tuk and Lyman but saved her. He had lied to Karri, thrown the guards off their trail, and fabricated a narrative to send the search party in the wrong direction. Not only that: he had led Mia directly to his father's boat.

But why?

If it was Domeniq who'd put an arrow in Quin's back in the Chapel, he could have easily finished the job in the forest with a mere flick of his wrist. No, Dom wasn't the assassin. But why had he helped them escape? There was something more at play. Something Mia wasn't seeing.

The Natha sluiced over the bow of the *Sunbeam*, slicking off the moss and dust that had accumulated after who knew how long. The coracle, shaped like half a walnut shell, was spliced together with split and interwoven wood—willow for the laths, hazel for the weave—then waterproofed with bullock hide and a thin layer of yellow tar. Coracles were perfect for rivers: their flat, keel-less bottom hardly disturbed the water, and one person could easily maneuver the craft.

Mia sat tall in the *Sunbeam*'s stern with an old, splintered oar, one insistent sliver digging into her palm. Despite her exhaustion, she felt invigorated by her new theory. If her mother's cryptic message was true—*All you seek will be revealed*—and what she sought most was Wynna's murderer, then she was finally on the right path.

"I'm tired." Quin was slumped against the *Sunbeam*'s starboard side. "Aren't you tired?"

"Extremely."

"Do you have any idea where we're going?"

"I know we're going east."

"The depth of your knowledge astounds me."

"Perhaps it's time you get some sleep."

Their exhaustion had made them ornery. Mia wasn't sure what had drained her more, healing the prince or watching Tuk and Lyman die, but she knew her body had never felt so ravaged. A bone-deep ache swelled up inside her, expanding in her ribs, hips, and shoulders. She'd felt like this once before: when she was blossoming into a woman. As if her skeleton were no longer large enough to contain her.

She had an unsettling thought: Was this what it felt like to "blossom" into a Gwyrach? She shut her eyes to quell another queasy wave. Her father had told her you were either born a Gwyrach or you weren't—there was no middle ground—but that sometimes the dark magic could lie dormant for many years, stewing and simmering until triggered under just the right conditions. He said this magic was most often coaxed out during fits of extreme passion: rage, terror, love. Mia wondered which one had caused her magic to reveal itself. Perhaps all three: rage at her father, terror of her impending marriage, and love for Angelyne.

Another, more unsettling, thought occurred to her: Had her father been telling the truth?

"Humor me on something," Quin said. "My demonology is rusty, but isn't a Gwyrach the child of a human and a god?"

"My mother did not lie with a god, if that's what you're asking."

"Not at all," he said evenly. "I don't believe in gods. Even if I did, it seems highly unlikely they would gallivant around the world with human . . . parts."

Mia flushed. She had zero desire to discuss the mechanics of lovemaking with Prince Quin.

She said, "You know the origin myths as well as I do. In olden times, when one of the four gods lay with a woman, she bore him a Gwyrach daughter, a demon with the wrath and power of a god mixed with the petty jealousies and wickedness of a human. The daughter had daughters, and those daughters had more daughters, and on it goes. Demons all the way down."

He was studying her. "What do *you* believe?"

She opened her mouth to fire off an answer but came up short. If she subscribed to the popular belief, then, yes: Mia was the descendant of a long-ago coupling between a woman and a god. Truth be told, the origin myth had always struck her as a little far-fetched, but she'd also never felt a burning need to question it. Of course, that was when she was *hunting* Gwyrach, not being one.

"If you believe the myths," Quin said, "then your mother was a Gwyrach, too."

She didn't want to accept it. *Couldn't* accept it. She knew her mother: she was grace and generosity and love. In no way did she resemble the depraved demons Mia had been studying for years.

"Let's talk about something else," she said.

"Let's." Quin didn't seem to need much persuading. "Did you know I have never been on a river? Not once."

"And you call yourself prince of the river kingdom." It came out more snippily than she'd intended.

"You know, in order for us to have a normal, civilized conversation, you might try acting normal or civilized."

I'm not normal, she wanted to scream. I'm a Gwyrach.

"After all," he said, "isn't civilized discourse what husbands and wives *do*?"

"I don't know. I've never had a husband. Or a wife," she added. "And I don't now."

He cocked his head. "Don't you?"

"Surely you don't call *that* debacle"—she gestured back toward the Kaer—"a success."

"Even a debacle of a wedding can be efficacious."

"Do you always use such big words?"

The river sucked greedily at the sides of the boat. Quin let out a long breath.

"You grew up here, didn't you? On the river?"

"In Ilwysion, yes. We're not quite at my part of the forest, but we'll be passing through shortly. But I never cared much for the water."

"Because of your hair?"

"What?"

"I was under the impression that ladies did not appreciate the water mussing their hair."

"Who told you that?"

He cleared his throat. "I suppose I read it in a book."

"Perhaps it's time to reexamine your reading selection."

She didn't like the water on account of how quickly it could change. Placid one minute, fatal the next: crystalline in some places and opaque in others. It unnerved her that, no matter where you were, whether camped by a fresh mountain stream or sailing the Opalen Sea, cup water in your hands and you could see right through it, a transparent shimmer slipping through your fingers.

She didn't like the idea that something invisible could kill you.

"I'm starving," Quin said. "We haven't eaten in hours."

For someone who had been so taciturn in the castle, the prince was awfully chatty out in the wild. She watched him extract the pouch of food the village boy had given them. He shook out one purple snow plum and poked at a fuzzy white spot on the surface. He sighed. "He gave us moldy plums. Of course he did."

Mia looked at him, curious. "Did you know that boy?"

"I've seen him in the village." He looked away. "Once or twice. A friend."

She felt a curious sensation, her pulse quickening as the sound of sloshing filled her ears, viscous liquid coursing through a valve.

"Would he poison you?"

"Gods, no! He's not that sort of friend." Quin thwacked the bread against the side of the *Sunbeam*, where it cracked like wood on wood. "Though I suppose he's not above giving us stale bread." He chucked the loaf overboard.

"There goes our only food."

"You weren't going to eat it anyway. You're more distrustful than I am."

"I'm careful," she said. "You could stand to be more careful yourself."

As if to spite her, he bit into one of the plums. She could see him squirm as the mold furred his tongue.

"Please do not spew boat on the bile," she said.

He grinned. Mia was so tired she wasn't speaking clearly. She

120

thought of asking Quin to take over so she could doze for a bit, but she didn't want to ask him for anything. She was steering the ship now—quite literally—and she liked it.

Besides, if he'd never been on a river, he'd never even held an oar.

Quin was asleep, his head lolling, when Mia heard a splash.

She saw them from a distance: two girls facing off beside a swampy inlet, their long skirts tucked up into their undergarments, corsets discarded on the riverbank. They were young, no older than twelve or thirteen, the moonlight painting both their heads a sapphire silver. They wore no gloves. Their bare hands gripped two birch-wood sticks whittled into makeshift blades, laced with kindling and lit on fire. In the darkness, they looked like blue demons wielding stars.

Mia felt a clutch of fear. Were they Gwyrach? Or merely girls?

She didn't know the answer, but she was drawn to them anyway.

Their faces were painted like warriors, though as the *Sunbeam* grew closer, Mia saw the war paint was mud and crushed blackthorn petals. The girls were fighting, rapturous as they roared and charged toward one another, brandishing their white torches in the air.

The taller girl took a bad step and fell sideways, landing in the sludge. When the other girl offered an arm to help her up, she took it—and wrenched her friend down with her. The bog gobbled them up greedily, and they sloshed around, giggling and filthy and glorious. In that moment, they were more than girls: they were creatures, wild and free.

The second they saw Mia, they went completely silent.

They watched each other as the boat slunk by, two mud-caked girls on the riverbank, one blood-caked girl in a boat. Mia softened. She had been like them once, out climbing trees and exploring Ilwysion under the cover of night. She and Angie had never sparred like this, though she would have liked to. Even before their mother died, Angelyne was always the fragile one, while Mia pushed the limits of herself and everyone around her.

She felt a twinge of shame. Of course she'd pushed the limits. She'd always had magic, and magic relied on a cruel, unruly heart.

As she passed the two girls on the riverbank, she feared for their safety. If the king's spies caught them tussling in the forest, gloveless and behaving like boys, they would be whisked off to the castle, where all manner of horrors awaited.

But as the *Sunbeam* glided silently past, Mia saw they didn't need her fear, and they didn't want her pity. Their faces were flushed and furious, their eyes full of something she had forgotten how to feel. It was only Mia who felt frightened and ashamed.

How sick a place Glas Ddir was to shame girls for being wild. King Ronan patted himself on the back for keeping them "safe," but it was all twisted lies. The ones he brought to the Kaer weren't safe. As for the other girls in the river kingdom: what good was safety at the expense of freedom? Glasddiran women were still trapped in cages, whether that cage was a pair of gloves or a wedding gown.

"Mia."

Quin's voice startled her. She turned and saw him in silhouette, the moonlight laying jagged yellow patches on the river behind him.

"I can row now. You should get some rest."

Had he seen the girls? She blinked and saw only blackness. The river had swallowed them whole.

"If you give me the oar," he said, "I'll man the boat."

She frowned. "You said you'd never manned a boat before."

"I said I'd never been on a river. In my royal bathtub hewn of gold, I steered small ships made of walnuts." She didn't laugh. He sighed. "I don't know where we're going, but as long as the river's current takes us in the opposite direction of my attempted murderer, you won't find me complaining. I'm no boatswain, but I know not to let us run aground."

She was too tired to argue. She handed him the oar and crawled forward, tucking herself into the *Sunbeam*'s bow.

The warrior girls stayed with her: their ferocious triumph and their unabashed defiance. Angelyne had looked at Mia with the same defiance when they fought in her bridal chambers. Was that really only yesterday? She had packed whole lifetimes into a single night. Where was Angie now? Was she safe?

Mia was struck by a sudden epiphany. A royal wedding required a royal groom. At the moment, that groom was sailing down the Natha at her side, farther from Kaer Killian by the minute. Angelyne was at no risk of being married to the prince—as long as the prince was with Mia, and alive.

A blissful contentment enveloped her. She hadn't abandoned her sister after all. She'd protected her.

The river vanished behind them like a line of disappearing ink. Mia felt, for a moment, happy. She reached for her wedding gown to ball it up into a pillow—and felt her mother's journal. So much had happened, she hadn't peeked at it in hours. She drew out the book, tracing the neat, straight grooves of the W.M. scars. For all her mother's luscious curves, her initials were strikingly angular.

On instinct, Mia fit the ruby wren into the lock. She pivoted away from Quin and quietly opened the journal. The first page was dappled with starlight, but the right side was no longer blank.

The map had revealed more.

Chapter 18

BAIT

MIA WOKE TO THE noonday sun. She covered her eyes, blinded by the harsh light. Where was she? The memory of the prior night came rushing back to her, reds and blacks and a pale-yellow boat. She sat up with a jolt.

Gwyrach. She was a Gwyrach.

The word was like an infection crawling through her body. She had read plenty about infection: microscopic animalcules that attacked blood and bone and tissue, killing a person from the inside out. Didn't magic do the same? There were Gwyrach who killed their victims in showy ways, of course—her father had told her about boils and blisters, rotted flesh, asphyxiated limbs—but they seemed to prefer the invisible kinds of murder, frozen breath and clotted, bloodless hearts.

A ray of hope glimmered in Mia's mind. She'd always had a hunch that Fojo Karação played a key role in her mother's secret past. Now the map had filled in with more ink, nudging her east. *The path will reveal itself to she who seeks it. All you seek will be revealed.*

She would find her mother's murderer in Fojo.

Mia wasn't running away from something, not anymore. She was running toward it.

"Good morning!" said the prince, startling her. She had forgotten he was there.

Quin sat tall in the stern, looking hale and rested, his shirt gaping at the chest. When they'd swum out to the boat, the water had rinsed him off nicely; there was no longer any dried blood spoiling his smooth, golden skin. His curls were wind-raked, ruffled by the breeze and really quite charming.

She rubbed her eyes. "How long was I sleeping?"

"A good while now. You sleep like the dead."

She squinted into the forest, keen to get her bearings. The chalky birch and silver plum trees stood in prim, sensible lines, a forest of neatly scrubbed bones. Behind them were the lofty spruce and elms, their luscious needle-gowns growing sparser as the peaks climbed and the air thinned. On the mountaintops, the trees stripped off their garments completely, standing brown and bare in the alpine wind.

They were in Ilwysion, the woods she grew up in. Mia couldn't help but smile. As a child she had greedily climbed every tree, dug up every rock. It was the perfect place for a girl who wanted to be an explorer, full of natural wonders and opportunities for adventure.

Mia sipped the air. She loved how fresh and clean it was, so different from the cold, stale air inside the Kaer or the foul odors of Killian Village. Ilwysion was a cornucopia of green: rain-worn stones slung with moss and lichen, young saplings sprouting from tree trunks, and ground shrubs laced into a thick, soft carpet, more comfortable than any shoe Mia had ever worn. Woodland creatures scampered into holes—her first friends— and giant white rocks were stacked on top of one another, some in tilting towers, others arranged in mysterious rings. Whimsical seven-year-old Mia liked to imagine the ancient gods playing a parlor game where the forest was the parlor and the boulders were the dice.

Practical seventeen-year-old Mia felt a stab of dread, thinking about the gods. Was she really the demon descendant of a deity? It struck her as increasingly ridiculous, even laughable. But then, if her father had told her a few days ago that she was a Gwyrach, she would have laughed at that, too. The knowledge of who she was—*what* she was—kept seizing her anew, shock and horror spilling over her like a vat of scalding oil.

Mia plucked at the crusty, sun-dried fabric of her smock, forcing her thoughts down a brighter path. She leaned over the edge of the *Sunbeam* and caught a glimpse of her reflection in the river. It was even worse than she'd expected. Her auburn curls were frizzed and matted like the nest of a wild bird; the skin greases

Angie had so carefully applied were now smudged ruins beneath her eyes. She had slept too long—she was grumpy and disoriented. She splashed water on her face.

"You look lovely," Quin said. "Really. Stained smock is your color."

She rolled her eyes. His smile was downright roguish.

"Are you hungry? I caught us some fish."

"You did what?"

He gestured toward the neat white cubes of meat lined up on one of the *Sunbeam*'s laths.

"Skalt," he said. "In case you were wondering."

She was astonished. "You caught, cleaned, and cut skalt while I was asleep?"

He shrugged. "I have many gifts."

She was suddenly famished. She reached for a piece of fish, then paused, her hand poised in midair.

"Shouldn't we boil it first?"

"Absolutely. Skalt is best when broiled, salted, and brushed with melted butter. Since you're a Gwyrach, I presume you can make air spontaneously combust?"

The prince was certainly in high spirits.

"Microscopic animalcule can be more lethal than poison," she said. "And there's a good chance you contaminated the meat when you cut it."

"I checked for skin lesions. And I cleaned the fish quite well. It may surprise you, but I've had some practice." He patted his stomach, which was lean and surprisingly toned; she caught a peek through the gap in his shirt. "I've eaten at least six skalt, and I feel superb."

He did look quite well: his cheeks were rosy, his green eyes reflecting motes of blue from the river. The brisk mountain air had rejuvenated him. His long body had uncoiled itself, and she thought he looked taller than he had in the castle, sitting comfortably on the transom, his face and hair as gold as the sun.

She ate a chunk of fish, then another. It was salty and wet, slimy raw hunks sliding down her throat, but after several bites, she felt her body gaining vigor.

"Have another," he said, pleased.

She wondered for a moment if she'd awoken in an alternate world, where Quin was not a pampered prince but a seasoned survivalist.

"Who taught you to fish?"

"I spent hours in the kitchens at Kaer Killian. It was the one place I knew my father would never go." He cleared his throat. "You slept through all the river towns. At least, I think that was all of them. I don't really know how many river towns there are."

"If I had a map, I could show you." The river towns of Ilwysion were the small villages clustered along the banks of the Natha. Mia knew them well. "There used to be at least twenty, depending on what you consider to be a town. There are far fewer now that the markets have all but disappeared."

"The river markets," Quin said wistfully. "I heard the castle cooks speak of them many times. They were apparently quite popular when my aunt was queen."

She nodded. "They were part market, part social gathering. The sort of thing people looked forward to every week. Or so I've heard."

Her mother had told her all about the markets, lively with traders, musicians playing lutes and psalteries, and mirthful dancers drinking and making merry. Merchants and apothecaries hawked their wares on the shores of the river: fur pelts; earthenware jugs and tankards; sumptuous indigo silks; dolls, combs, and dice carved from bone; glass curios; and all manner of ointments, elixirs, and essences with purported magical properties.

As Mia's mother explained it, before the steady stream of traders and visitors from the other three kingdoms dried up, they had brought with them many different opinions on magic. Glasddirans were a suspicious lot, but they were also curious. What if magic, in small doses, could smooth the lines out of their skin or add a touch of spice to their bedchambers? Mia herself had been curious about magic before her mother died: that was when her feelings on the subject abruptly changed course.

Mia forced herself back to the present. "My mother said it was her favorite part of the week. The air was rich with bouquets from all four kingdoms—melted cheese burbling and sizzling in terra-cotta pots, chopped cabbage pickled in brine, lime-mango chicken dipped in spicy ginger sauce and served on long silver spears."

Quin groaned. "Must you talk about all the delicious foods we do not have? My raw skalt is looking more pitiful by the minute."

She couldn't help but smile. When her mother had talked

about the river markets, Mia closed her eyes and tried to make the scenes spring to life. She had trouble imagining them. The picture Wynna painted was so different from the sparsely populated markets Mia had gone to as a child, somber affairs with flavorless food and free knife sharpening, where all women were required to have a father, husband, or brother present to ensure all was as it should be. Which was to say: boring.

"Look," she said. "There's what's left of one."

The boat was skirting the bank of the Natha where one of the old river markets had stood. Wood frames and beams, once draped with canvas tents, were now in shambles. There wasn't much left: looters had long since combed the flotsam for valuables. Mia did spot a few swatches of soiled linen crushed into the earth and stamped with muddy boot prints. It seemed impossible this empty space had ever held anything vibrant or alive.

"My father has made a royal mess of things," Quin said quietly. "In his efforts to restore the rich heritage of the river kingdom, he has stanched the flow of everything that might have made it rich. He promised a return to greatness and then stripped Glas Ddir of all the tastes and colors and cultures that made us great."

The sunlight shifted, shining on a copper scrap tucked amidst the ruins. Mia thought of Domeniq's mother, who had sold iron and copper cookware at the river markets before all female merchants were banned. Lauriel du Zol was a big woman, in both stature and heart, with ample flesh and a lush waterfall of tight black curls. Laughter came easily to her.

Lauriel was also Wynna's best friend. She had moved her

young family to the river kingdom from Fojo, following Mia's parents back to their homeland. Soon after, King Ronan sealed the borders, trapping them there. The du Zols found a cottage in Ilwysion, and Mia and Dom grew up together, thick as thieves. She could still picture their mothers on the balcony of the Roses' cottage, reminiscing about life in Fojo in hushed tones, the quiet murmur of their voices punctuated every few minutes by Lauriel's hearty belly laugh.

Mia missed that life. She had lost it all so quickly: Dom's father murdered by Gwyrach, then Mia's mother killed within a matter of days. Lauriel and the twins—Domeniq's nine-year-old sisters, Sach'a and Junay—left the river kingdom overnight, slipping through some secret channel back into the fire kingdom. Dom chose to stay behind to train with the Circle.

"May I ask what you're thinking about?" Quin asked.

"The river markets. Everything we've lost."

In fact she was thinking of Domeniq standing over the dead men in the glade. What would his mother say if she had seen him kill two men? Lauriel was skilled with her hands, too, but she used them to meld cookware out of iron and copper, not lance a man's heart with a dagger.

"Where did you live?" Quin said. "Before you came to the Kaer."

Mia's thoughts had spiraled into a dark place; she was grateful for the interruption. She pointed toward a snow-frosted peak in the distance. "Our cottage was halfway up that mountain."

"Did it get cold in the winter?"

"Miserably. We had to wear three layers of socks just to get out of bed. But I always liked the snow. My sister didn't." She paused, savoring a childhood memory. "Once I lured her outside by promising to make her fifty angels in the snow. A host of Angels for Angelyne."

"Did you keep your promise?"

"Absolutely not. I'd lost all sensation in my toes after Angel number nine."

Quin looked amused. He took a deep breath and sighed it out. "The air is so clean here. All these tall oaks and elms. It must have been nice to be lulled to sleep by the whisper of wind in the trees."

He wasn't wrong: she'd been happy as a child. But once her mother died, the things Mia loved seemed smaller. The cottage felt shrunken and suffocating. Her father had assured her she was not in danger, but it was impossible to feel safe.

She darkened. She'd spent three years hunting Gwyrach. Did that mean she'd been hunting herself all along?

"All my life I've wanted to leave the Kaer and the village beyond it." Quin shook out his curls. "It took nearly getting killed for me to do it."

She was surprised. "Why would you want to leave?"

"Didn't you?"

"That's different. Kaer Killian is your home. You belong there."

"The place you were born is not always the place you belong."

A squall of homesickness blew over her. Her mother had always been home for her, a calm, soothing presence. Mia winced, remembering the atrocious things she'd said to her the day she died, the grief writ large in Wynna's hazel eyes. A cruel trick of memory, the way certain words snaked constantly through Mia's mind, a serpent coiled and ready. Her mother's eyes were two giant canvases of feeling, ever-changing portraits of spark and shadow, but by that night, they were two black holes gone dark forever.

Mia had been fighting off the memory for three years, and once again she forced it away. How could you feel homesick when you no longer had a home?

"I owe you an apology," Quin said.

She raised one brow. "An apology for what?"

"I had to repurpose your wedding gown as a fishing line."

He nodded toward the line trawling on the boat's port side. She recognized the tangle of white silk on the floor of the coracle, no longer quite so white. By some small miracle, Quin had managed to slip the dress out from under Mia's head while she was sleeping, slice off strips with his sheath knife, and knot them together into one long rope.

He poked at his bridegroom jacket, now missing a few more gold buttons. "Did you know fish love shiny things? When you don't have a lure, a bright button works brilliantly as bait."

Mia hardly heard him. All her thoughts had boiled down to one: *the journal*.

Her mother's book was gone.

Chapter 19

TOO LOVELY

"Are you looking for this?"

Quin held up the soft brown book, the fojuen wren still fitted into the clasp. Her relief was palpable as she snatched it from his hand.

"You shouldn't have taken—"

"It's blank, Mia."

She could feel his eyes on her, watching. She shouldn't be keeping the key with the journal; that was careless. From now on she'd keep the ruby wren tucked into the neckline of her blouse, close to her heart at all times. Not that Quin couldn't rip open the book if he wanted to. It was leather and paper, nothing more.

Mia twisted the stone and the pages fluttered open. The book was most certainly not blank. Her mother's inscription and the map were still intact, and in fact the ink extended a touch farther; she saw the beginnings of the Twisted Forest, the Natha River winding up into the braided trees. She felt a strong tug to the east, as if her mother were pulling the boat gently toward Fojo Karação, dangling the bait of safe haven. Mia knew in her bones they were headed in the right direction.

In her *Gwyrach* bones. A firestorm of anger tore through her. She was hunting the Gwyrach who killed her mother, yet she *was* a Gwyrach. She couldn't hold the two things in her head. Every time she remembered she had magic, it decimated her; she oscillated from numb gray disbelief to scorching white fury. She hated that this was happening to her. It wasn't fair.

"It's your mother's, isn't it?" He hooked one arm around the oar and folded the other over his chest, studying her. "You called out for her in your sleep. You kept saying, 'I'm sorry, Mother. I'm sorry.'"

She wasn't surprised she'd apologized in her sleep; she had spent every day of the last three years apologizing silently for the awful things she'd said. But there was an edge to Quin's words she didn't understand.

"I don't trust your father," he said, apropos of nothing. "Neither does my father, for what it's worth. There has been a remarkable shortage of Gwyrach caught in recent years, though they seem to be reproducing beyond the walls of the Kaer just fine."

The conversation she'd overheard in the drawing room came

rushing back. She weighed the benefits of telling the prince she had been eavesdropping, but that was a delicate confession. She decided to bite her tongue.

"My father has been an invaluable resource to the crown. If not for him, the kingdom would be crawling with Gwyrach."

"The kingdom *is* crawling with Gwyrach. Yet another reason I don't trust the Hunters. The Circle has turned against us—and against each other, as we've seen."

She felt suddenly protective. "Domeniq du Zol is the only reason we're here right now. He saved our lives."

"By taking two others."

"Sometimes that's how it works. *Heart for a heart, life for a life.*"

"For someone so obsessed with justice," he said, "you sure do have a funny way of doing math."

Irritated, she held out her hand. "Oar."

He stood, gave a sardonic bow, and slapped the oar into her waiting palm.

"The lady wins."

As she passed him, his shoulder brushed against hers, and for a second, the boat tipped, uneasy from the weight of their two bodies. The coldness pouring off him was stippled with little sparks of warmth.

Then it was gone. He jerked away and leaned over the edge of the boat to twang the fishing line. Of course he didn't want to touch her—she had the power to take his life. But she'd also *saved* his life. Did he really think she was going to hurt him? What more did she have to do to prove her good intentions?

She'll kill him soon enough, Lyman had said. *That's what they* do.

No. They wouldn't. *She* wouldn't. She wasn't that kind of girl.

Mia revised. Wasn't that kind of *Gwyrach.*

When she put it that way, it sounded so ridiculous she almost laughed.

While a glowering Quin busied himself with the fishing line, Mia got to work. It was time to subject the journal to a series of experiments. She could see the writing and the prince couldn't: that much was clear. But how was the book doling out ink at its leisure? What made it tick?

She'd spent the last three years subjecting magic to careful scrutiny, treating it like she would a scientific theorem. Yes, magic was magic, but it also existed in the natural world: surely magic subscribed to its own set of laws. If she could crack the code and delineate those rules, maybe she could understand it, and if she could understand it, she could master it. For Mia mastery meant precisely one thing: a road to eradicating magic.

The book was as good a place as any to start.

She had several theories. A Gwyrach had clearly found a way to bewitch the book through some kind of mysterious ink-dispensing device. Was it magnetic? Did an internal lodestone siphon ink from a secret compartment in the book's spine? Or was it mechanical, a widget or a compass that activated the ink reserves?

Mia angled her body away from Quin. She was subtle, tilting the journal in all four cardinal directions to see if the ink revealed itself. It did not. She tapped the book gently against the boat's edge, in the hopes that she could dislodge the widget and shunt more ink onto the page. No luck.

She knew nothing. She *hated* not knowing. Her only grounded theory was that Gwyrach could see the ink and non-Gwyrach couldn't, though her sample size—herself and the prince—was woefully small.

And her mother, of course. An uneasy truth slithered through her thoughts. How could her mother write in Gwyrach ink unless she were a Gwyrach herself?

Quin let out an exaggerated sigh. "If you're following something you think you see in that book, then we truly are on a path to nowhere."

"Oh? And where would *you* have us go?"

He shifted in the boat but said nothing.

"Good, then. Lucky for you, I've always been good with maps."

"To be good with maps," he muttered, "one must actually have a map."

She shot him a withering glance. But he was right and she knew it. She was letting herself be tossed on an unpredictable tempest, biding her time until the magical map deigned to reveal the path to "safe haven." Mia Morwynna Rose was a rational thinker, a scientist, a Huntress—and apparently a lost little girl, twiddling her thumbs as she waited for invisible ink to appear.

Safe haven. What did that even mean? For a Gwyrach, nowhere was safe.

The rage was inching back into her sternum, a coil of crimson fire. Why was she so angry? And at whom? She didn't understand why her body now vacillated between extreme temperatures. In the lists of crimes committed by Gwyrach, she'd read about how they could conjure up diseases of the flesh that began with icy-cold sensations, followed by sharp, burning pain, then vesicles on the skin, topped off with putrescent limbs that eventually dropped off the body completely. She shut her eyes, not wanting to believe it. Magic really was an infection. For all she knew, her own magic was eating her alive.

How much farther to the Twisted Forest? The trees were beginning to slope to the east, a pinch of winter in the air. In light of her failure with the journal, she comforted herself that they were headed toward answers. No. Toward justice. *Heart for a heart, life for a life.*

"I didn't mean to be cruel," said the prince. He was more mercurial than the waters flowing beneath them. "I told you as long as we were headed in the opposite direction of the Kaer, I wouldn't complain. And I meant it."

She nodded. "Good. You needn't worry; I'm taking us somewhere safe."

He was watching her again. If he were aiming to unnerve her, two could play at that game. Her eyes scraped over his face, looking for flaws. What she found instead were long lashes, piercing green eyes, sharp cheekbones, a slightly upturned nose, bowed lips, a fine collarbone, sloping biceps, and the smooth plane of a chest tapering into lean stomach muscles. His shirt was gaping at the waist; she could see the top of his hip bones cutting a sharp V, like a bird taking flight.

She felt a flutter in her belly. Butterfly or dove, she didn't wait to see—she reached inside and strangled it.

They were silent a long time, day sinking slowly into night. The sunlight on the water was golden, then salmon pink, then dusky as the moon put on a white veil and walked the sable sky.

When the boat ran aground, Mia wasn't expecting it. The jolt wrenched the oar from her fingers, and she tumbled forward. Her arms were sore and swollen, her hands so numb she could no longer feel them. Quin caught her before she pitched over the side, his hands firm around the curved mounds of her shoulders.

"You should eat more skalt," he said, though she sensed he'd been about to say something else. Then he pulled his hands back sharply. For a moment he had forgotten the dangers of being skin to skin.

Mia stepped shakily onto the shore, willing her river legs steady. She stared up at the forest. The Natha dead-ended into a small cove where the *Sunbeam*'s bow was lodged on a bank of cracked gray rocks.

The prince massaged his neck. "I guess this is where the river ends."

But the river had not, in fact, ended. Above them was a sight that defied logic: the Natha burbled upward over the cascading boulders in an inverted waterfall. As she stared in awe, Mia realized she had never truly believed this place existed. But here was the proof, incontrovertible. Water running up instead of down.

She felt disquieted, curious, and—against all reason—hungry.

"Four hells," the prince murmured. "Would you look at that."

In the woods beyond, the crooked swyn trees clung to one another, swathed in a canopy of sultry blue.

The Twisted Forest beckoned, too lovely to be believed.

Chapter 20

AWFUL BLOODY WORK

THE NATHA FLOWED UP the mountain, more stream than river, forcing Mia and Quin to abandon the boat. They cut a path through Foraois Swyn, an apricot moon slipping long, eerie shadows between the braided trees.

The Twisted Forest was one of the great mysteries of Glas Ddir. The white-barked swyn trees leaned uniformly toward Fojo Karação in the east. The base of their trunks grew horizontally, flush with the ground, forming an easy, low seat. But after a few feet, the trunks shot up sharply at a right angle, like the elbow of an arm reaching toward the sun.

After that, the trees became even more interesting. Twenty feet off the forest floor, the swyn began entwining with other swyn—at least two or three at a time, often more. Creamy white branches twisted themselves around one another like broken fingers, their velvety blue needles forming a thick canopy overhead.

Since girls were not allowed in Foraois Swyn, Mia had never seen the trees before. But her mother, a lifelong lover of all kinds of trees, had drawn pictures for her daughters. "Lonely trees," Angie would say, tracing the braided limbs. Mia had always thought the opposite. No swyn ever grew alone.

The distinctive shape—the elbow bend and the braiding—had earned the Twisted Forest its nickname, and endless conjecture about why the trees grew in such a way. There were scientific hypotheses: ancient farmers had manipulated the young saplings for timber, or the trees were responding to some kind of magnetic shift in the Earth's core. But Glasddirans were by nature a suspicious lot, and most suspected magic. The demons of old were an excellent scapegoat. In the river kingdom, demons were blamed for everything.

Mia had always laughed at such ludicrous notions. Now, as she padded quietly along the soft bed of blue needles carpeting the forest floor, she wondered. What if these superstitions bore the seeds of truth, and the trees themselves once held magic? Did that make them wicked?

"As I contemplate who wants me dead," Quin said, "I keep thinking about the rules of succession."

"And?"

"If something happens to me, the throne would go to my cousin. Which seems fitting, considering Tristan is the son my father never had."

Mia detected more than a trace of bitterness.

"It should be Karri," he said. "My sister was always better than I was at everything—at least everything that mattered. Hunting, archery, swordplay, diplomacy, war games. I was off deboning fish in the kitchens while Karri was crushing our weapons master out on the castle grounds."

"Perhaps you can change the laws of succession when you're king."

"I don't *want* to be king."

"Then you're the only man in history who hasn't dreamed of sitting on the river throne."

"And yet I'm the one who must. Meanwhile, my sister, the most talented swordsman I've ever seen, the most gifted politician, the sharpest mind, and the noblest soul, will wither in the queen's gallery, getting drunk on stonemalt."

Mia studied him. "You have talents, too. You caught a dozen skalt with a button."

He laughed. "Ah, yes. Master of the button arts. That's me." He added ruefully, "Would that a dozen skalt would save my skin."

They fell back into companionable silence. After a while, Quin said, "I am good at other things besides catching fish, you know. I loved history. I excelled in theatrical studies—I have a gift for the pretending arts. And I took a particular shine to music."

"Yes," Mia said. "I've heard you play."

Was it her imagination, or had Quin's eyes gone hazy? "I had a music teacher. He was from Luumia, only a year older than I was—his parents were musicians in my father's court, so he lived in the castle with his sister. She was lovely. We used to take long walks through the grove of plum trees. Sometimes she and I would—"

"I don't need to hear what you and she would do," Mia interrupted.

Quin smiled. "Her brother was a musical prodigy. He was also my first true friend. We spent long hours together in the library, playing piano. He told me a pianist should touch the keys the same way he touched a woman: gently. But my father . . ."

He set his jaw in a hard line. Whatever he'd been about to say, he thought better of it. "My father decided the piano was not in my future after all."

"Quin." She stopped walking. "What if your father is grooming Tristan to be king? If he really does consider you unfit to rule, he could have hired an assassin to kill you."

Quin didn't seem half as delighted by her theory as she was.

"While I appreciate your keen eye for filicide, that does seem a touch extreme." He paused. "Though I suppose, if my father were looking to hire a skilled assassin, he wouldn't have to look far."

He looked at her pointedly.

"Oh. You mean *my* father."

She remembered her father's strange manner when he gave her the journal, and again when he escorted her to the Royal Chapel. Had King Ronan commissioned Griffin to kill his own son?

Or did Quin mean *her*?

Once again, his conversation with his parents came flooding back to her: he'd thought her dangerous, even then.

"The Hunters only kill magicians," she said. "That's the Creed. It's sacrosanct."

"You must admit you're being a touch fanatical about this, Mia. We just saw a Hunter break the Creed and kill two other Hunters. Everyone can be bought."

"Not my father."

"Fine, then. One of his men. They were the only people in the Chapel with bows and arrows."

"Except all the guards! I'm telling you, the Hunters only kill Gwyrach."

He stared at her, his green eyes reflecting the blue needles, the color of a shallow pool at the base of a waterfall.

"Why did you want to join the Circle? Seems like awful bloody work. For a girl, anyway." He jerked his head back toward the river. "Your Hunter friend is clearly good with a blade, but I can't imagine you—"

Mia bent, whipped the knife out of Quin's boot, clasped it lightly by the tang, and flung it at a swyn tree twenty feet ahead. It sailed through the air like a silver ribbon, slicing into the white trunk with flawless precision.

"Point taken," he said.

Mia retrieved the blade, using her smock to wipe off the soft white curls of birch bark before sliding it back into the sheath. The prince's mouth was smiling, but his eyes weren't.

"You know," he said. "I'm beginning to regret bringing that knife."

Chapter 27

UNKNOWABLE PARTS

THEY WOVE THEIR WAY through the Twisted Forest as the air thinned. Mia was tired, but the crisp alpine wind was invigorating. Though she carried no compass and no map save her mother's, she couldn't help but feel like an explorer, the very thing she had wanted more than anything to be.

The prince flumped down on a swyn trunk, effectively spoiling the silence.

"I'm hungry."

"But the fish—"

"Was hours ago. I am reliably always hungry." He stretched out his arms, catching the back of his head and staring up at the swyn needles. "Exquisite. It's like looking at two blue skies."

She sat down on her own tree trunk. She was hungry, too. Ravenous.

Discreetly she opened her mother's book. They were loosely following the Natha on its ascent: the river was the clearest strip of ink. She tried once again to rub the page gently with her finger, on the off chance she could court more ink. It was useless.

"I truly hope you are not charting our escape route with that book of nothing."

She snapped it shut. "Perhaps it's time for you to catch more fish."

He flourished a hand at the river. "It would appear the good fish of Glas Ddir are constitutionally unable to swim upstream."

He was right. No shimmery silver skalt had braved the uphill climb.

She chewed her lip. In light of her mother's capricious journal, it was hard to pin down an exact itinerary. When she closed her eyes, she conjured the non-magical maps she'd spent her childhood poring over. By her estimation, they would be hiking through the Twisted Forest for several days, maybe a full week. They had to climb the mountain and descend the other side to reach the Salted Sea, which connected Glas Ddir with Fojo Karação. Until then, the river would provide freshwater aplenty, but they needed food.

"You're the Huntress," he said. "Why don't you hunt us some game?"

"I don't hunt animals."

"Humans are animals."

"Gwyrach aren't human," she said.

"You look human to me." His smile faded. "How did you heal me, Mia?"

"I don't feel like giving you a primer in magic."

"You don't know how, do you?"

She could feel the flush creeping across her cheeks and neck; yet another example, she thought, of how your own flesh could betray you. Her words slammed through her. *Gwyrach aren't human.*

Did she really believe that? If so, then the blood shunting through her—the breath hissing through her trachea—the aortic valves contracting to keep her alive—were inhuman valves, inhuman breath, inhuman blood.

What made a creature human? Her brain? Her heart? Or was it some unknowable sum of unknowable parts?

"I'm not going to hurt you."

"How do you know? If you accidentally brush against me, I might drop dead."

"Is that why you told your parents I was dangerous?"

She'd revealed herself. He stared at her, unblinking. "What else did you hear when you were eavesdropping in my chambers?"

"That your parents mistrusted my father. And I was leverage. Your *blackmail bride.*"

He reddened. "That wasn't my fault. I knew my father intended our marriage to be an intimidation tactic—and I was right. But I'd assumed it was the people of Glas Ddir he wished to intimidate, when in fact it was your father."

He picked up a stick and jabbed it into the ground. "They

promised him they would keep you safe and unharmed . . . as long as he fulfilled his quota."

"His quota of Gwyrach."

"Yes." Quin stared hard at his stick. "For my father's Hall of Hands."

"And if my father did not comply?"

Quin's silence spoke volumes. Shelves. Libraries.

So her father hadn't lied to her: he really was trying to protect her. They had forced his hand. If Griffin refused the marriage, the king would have killed her.

Or worse.

She swallowed hard.

"But you didn't know I had magic. Even *I* didn't know. Why did you think I was dangerous, Quin?"

Mia's blood skulked through her veins. The prince turned away.

"Because," he said, his voice low and cold, "you are."

Chapter 22

THAWING

As THE NIGHT WORE on, the air grew colder, and for once Mia didn't think the ice prince was to blame. A northern wind nipped at her nose and fingertips.

She heard a crack of twigs and whirled around.

"Quin?"

They hadn't spoken for hours, but his voice was soft. "I'm here."

"I thought I heard something." She sniffed the air but smelled only damp, loamy earth.

"Probably just the sound of my empty stomach. I'm going to forage for purslane."

"Purslane is an excellent plan."

She had no idea what purslane was, but she wasn't about to admit it.

Quin began rummaging around the forest floor, plucking handfuls of green, until finally he dropped a clump of fleshy leaves into her lap. "Surprisingly nutritious, for a weed."

"It's edible?"

"Yes, Mia. I'm not trying to poison you."

The purslane tasted like paper, but she wasn't complaining. While she discreetly picked the fibrous strings from her teeth, she stared up at the trees.

From her mother's sketches, Mia had failed to grasp how sensual swyn were: their supple, graceful curves; the long limbs intertwining, interlocking. The moon shone against the creamy white bark like candlelight on naked skin.

"What are you thinking about?" Quin asked.

Embarrassed, she looked away. "That we should make camp." She had been thinking nothing of the sort. "If we stretch the gown between trees . . ."

And thus began her embarrassing attempt at shelter making. First she tried tucking the wedding dress between plaits of swyn, but there wasn't enough fabric left, thanks to Quin's fishing efforts. So she resolved to build a lean-to. She made a simple frame by driving two forked sticks into the ground and lashing them together with what was left of the gown and train. But she needed a stronger pole or at very least more robust branches: every time she tried to brace it, a chilly gust of wind collapsed the whole mishmash.

Quin watched her in silence, munching his purslane.

"Don't feel like you have to help," she said.

"Oh, I won't." He spat out a piece of bark. "I did see a cave a ways back."

Mia could have pummeled him.

"I've changed my mind," she said. "We don't need covering. We'll sleep out in the open. The sky is perfectly clear."

No sooner had she said it than a crack of thunder pealed overhead. The first drops of rain misted the tops of the swyn.

Quin folded his arms and leaned back into the tree, infuriatingly smug.

"You were saying?"

Mia shivered at the mouth of the cave. Rain fell in rivulets from the ledge above, reminding her of pale ribbons streaming off silk, or her sister's silver tears.

She hugged her legs to her chest, chin resting on her kneecaps, and let herself be soothed by the susurrating rain. She had wrapped herself in the tattered remains of the wedding dress: not very insulating.

Mia was busy knitting together her own rules of magic—*real* magic, not the faulty information populating her books. Her wildly fluctuating body temperatures were clearly a symptom, as were the sudden pains that split her head apart like fractured glass. She had been taught that a Gwyrach manipulated her victim's body, controlling his bones and blood, breath and flesh. But she had come to suspect the true physiological transaction was far more complicated. What her books had failed to mention was that the Gwyrach's *own body* was also affected.

Mia's body was a sensitive instrument fine-tuned to the people around her. The headaches had lessened significantly after leaving the castle, supporting her theory that they only occurred when she was suffering from a kind of sensory overload: dozens of bodies with their own delicate chemistries jostling against hers. Healing felt like being wrenched and drained. Watching someone die was emptiness.

And then there were the sensations she'd felt when enthralling Quin: honeyed heat, supple limbs, flesh like melted chocolate.

If her body were calibrated to the bodies of those around her, it made sense that her internal temperature would mirror theirs. Magician and non-magician were yoked together by this strange alchemy. Specific emotions registered at specific climates.

Enthrallment felt warm. That made sense: desire was hot.

She stole another glance at Quin.

Hatred, apparently, was cold.

He was curled into the back wall of the cave. Mia had the impression he would fold himself up like a pair of trousers if it meant keeping her at a distance. Earlier, when she'd leaned a little too close, he'd spun away, the air around them crackling into black frost.

It hurt more than she cared to admit. She'd caught herself enjoying Quin's dry wit, and she could feel her own dislike thawing. She had mistakenly believed his was thawing, too.

She couldn't get warm or comfortable on the rocky cave floor.

The rain rasped through the Twisted Forest, drumming lightly on the swyn, as Mia's teeth began to chatter.

Quin stirred behind her. Something soft and heavy swept past her cheek. She caught a glimpse of green and then felt a weight, her body cocooned in thick, warm fabric.

The prince had dropped his bridegroom jacket over her shoulders.

Every time she thought she had the prince figured out, he surprised her.

She stayed awake until she heard the soft, steady rhythm of his breathing. Then she stood in the mouth of the cave, feeling protective for reasons she didn't understand. Above her the blue needles wept and whispered. Through the gray fog of rain, she could just make out a slice of river far below. She thought she saw a blotch of green and gold.

She rubbed her eyes. They were not to be trusted. When she blinked, the blotch was gone.

Mia curled up on the rocks and hugged Quin's jacket close. It smelled of fish and metal. She closed her eyes and conjured up the scent of orange peels sizzling on fresh-caught trout, baking bread, sweet milky cheeses, and hot coffee in a copper pot—the memory of pleasant childhood mornings when the Rose family piled into the du Zols' cozy kitchen for tasty, steaming breakfasts. Small comforts, from a life that no longer seemed like hers.

Her hands made bony pillows as the clouds of sleep rolled in.

Chapter 23

A PIPING HOT MUG OF BUTTERFEL

THEY WERE HUNGRY, AND they were cold.

Mia had witnessed three sunrises since they'd left the river, maybe four. It was hard to keep track. The farther into the mountains she and Quin climbed, the more the days and nights bled into one another, a mélange of whites and blues.

The rain had turned to sleet, then snow, clumping onto the azure swyn branches like hand-whipped cream. Mia padded the inside of their boots with dry moss and needles. Every day she and Quin refreshed the padding, though it was getting harder and harder to find any dry brush. They foraged what food they could—weeds and shrubs and berries—and when they grew weak, they dipped scalloped bark into the stream burbling up the mountain and let the icy water slake their thirst. Though the blood in their veins slowed and thickened, the Natha did not freeze.

"Where are we going, Mia?" Quin asked. "Where are you leading us?"

"To safe haven," she said. She saw the question in his eyes, the suspicion, but on some level they both understood he had nowhere else to go.

They were getting closer. Mia's frozen fingers hurt when she pried open the book, but every day more ink shimmered on the page. In the east, the isles of Fojo Karação had begun to reveal themselves, a cluster of landmasses bobbing on the Salted Sea.

Pace by pace, Mia and Quin climbed higher through the Twisted Forest. Once they summited the peak, they could begin their descent on the other side—if they survived long enough to get there.

She was determined to survive.

Even without her trusted sulfyr sticks, she'd had some luck striking the back of the sheath knife against a hunk of coarse jasper until it sparked. She coaxed an orange flame from the kindling, and once it caught, she shoved it under larger, thicker branches. On one fortuitous evening, Quin managed to boil a soupçon of water in a hollow stone to make chokecherry tea. It was the most pungent, sour, delicious thing Mia had ever tasted.

"We need more sustenance," Quin said.

She nodded. Her lips were so cracked it was painful to speak.

Her tendons quivered, her legs straining as the slopes plunged down into canyons and up tall cliffs. Mia had scratches on her arms from the twigs and branches. When the brush grew too thick, she took Quin's sheath knife and hacked an improvised trail.

Silence stretched between them like a frozen black lake. Mia started inventing sounds to fill it. Her grip on sanity was fraying: one night she was sure she heard a hound baying at the lemon moon.

To keep her brain alert, she worried the fojuen wren between her fingers, mentally reciting everything she knew about ruby wrens. They were the only birds that hibernated in winter. They were indigenous to the snow kingdom. Their anatomy was unique: like mammals, they had a four-chambered heart. But whereas humans had two pulmonary veins, wrens had four, a more efficient circulatory system that allowed them to fly. The wren's heart beat more quickly, too—its resting heartbeat was seven times that of a human—but when it went into hibernation, it could still its own heart for months on end.

Sometimes, when Mia held the ruby wren to her cheek, she thought she could hear her mother calling her home. *My red raven. My little swan.*

Every time Mia thought about her sister, a nameless fear gnawed at her chest. The Kaer was not a safe place, not with King Ronan, not with Tristan.

Perhaps the fear was not so nameless after all.

Quin kept pace by her side. He no longer sat sulking while she

159

did all the work; he dug fire pits and lashed branches together. They each found ways to relieve themselves without drawing attention to it, little coded expressions they came to understand: "I'm going to forage for berries." "Look, a stoat."

But the less they ate, the less they needed to relieve themselves. They saw ermine and cwningen and majestic white stag, beautiful animals, probably very tasty. But every time Mia reached for her knife, her fingers were thick, her hands heavy.

As dusk fell on their fourth, possibly fifth night in the forest, Quin asked a question.

"If you could eat anything right now," he said, teeth clacking against the cold, "what would it be?"

Was he a sadist? Mia's stomach creaked and grumbled, an empty ship on a stormy sea.

"I'll go first," he said. "Black truffles. Succulent black truffles in crempog sauce with a little shaved friedhelm on top."

Mia said, "A potato cake."

"One potato cake?"

A memory came unbidden: a meal she'd shared with her family before her mother died. They'd gathered at their simple square table, laughing and swapping stories, tearing off chunks of warm potato cake and dipping them into a puckered tin of sweet brown mustard. Her mother had kissed her father that night, really kissed him. When Mia and Angelyne heckled her for it, she'd raised her pint of stonemalt and made a toast:

"To my kind and clever birdlings: may you both find the sort of love your father and I are lucky to have found ourselves."

Mia shook her head to clear it. "I stand by my potato cake. With sweet mustard for dunking."

"I see your potato cake and raise you a rabbit stew. And a piping hot mug of butterfel. And honey cake with caramel sauce and raspberry jam. And—"

The prince stopped short.

They'd come to a small dell where the rocks leveled out and the pale trees wreathed themselves into a circle of ghostly nymphs.

In the center of the glade, arranged neatly on the unblemished snow, was a hare.

A *dead* hare.

As if it had been left just for them.

Chapter 24

DANGEROUSLY WARM

A LINE OF SWEAT beaded on Mia's forehead as Quin let out a war cry and pounced on the meat.

"It's a fresh kill," he said. "Some owl or wolf must have caught our scent and ran off. This is unbelievably lucky. I'll make us a whole stew!"

The skin on her neck was prickling. "This doesn't feel right, Quin."

"Has the cold frozen your brain? This is the first real nourishment we've had in days. The hare doesn't have much fat, as far as woodland creatures go, but it's a million times better than all the purslane and tree nuts we've been eating."

She took a closer look. "What killed it? I don't see a wound."

Exasperated, Quin picked the hare up by its ears, inspecting the length of it. "There." He pointed to a mark on its neck, triumphant. "Something got it in the neck."

"That's a clean cut. It doesn't look like the work of a predator."

"You're really going to quibble with how it died? It died! Now we can eat it. Knife, please."

She drew the sheath knife from her boot, then hesitated before handing it over.

"I'm not sure we—"

"Four gods, Mia." He plucked the knife out of her hand. "At least *one* of us should take an interest in keeping us alive."

In the sun's waning light, Quin was a flurry of activity. After days of creeping along at a glacial pace, he came alive: he found a piece of old rope in the satchel and cut off a swatch, stringing the hare up by its hind legs. With his sheath knife he cut around each ankle, slitting up the inside of first the left leg, then the right. With a flourish, he made a long cut from the vent up the abdomen. Mia watched him carefully peel back the skin.

"I didn't take you for a butcher," she said.

"Perhaps you could get a fire started? Make yourself useful?"

How the tables had turned. She would have found it amusing, if a sense of impending doom wasn't playing her spinal column like a harp.

"I'll make us a soup hole," Quin murmured to himself. "Use the bones to get some nice broth simmering. Flavor it with wild leeks and a handful of chokecherries."

She walked a few paces to scavenge for wood and stopped dead in her tracks.

"Firewood," she said.

"Yes, well, I can't do everything, can I? You'll have to—"

"No, I mean, here's a stack of firewood."

Quin lowered his knife.

A bundle of logs sat at the edge of the clearing. They weren't ax-hewn, exactly—they were mostly tree branches, swyn and spruce—but the timber was bone dry, clearly gathered and stacked by a creature with more agency than an owl or wolf.

Quin raked a hand through his curls. "Curious. Maybe someone lives in the forest? I still think this is a brilliant stroke of luck."

But he no longer sounded quite so certain.

They worked in silence, Mia tense and on edge, Quin humming to himself, perhaps to cover the fact that he, too, was tense and on edge. But he didn't seem it. She marveled at his abilities with a knife. He extracted the hare's innards, trembly loops of pink and red, palming them as casually as if they were hair ribbons. He used his blade to free the hide from the body in the places where it became stuck, without puncturing any organs. He pulled out all manner of small fleshy parts—the liver, kidneys, and heart—and laid them out neatly on a rock.

"You're alarmingly good at that."

"I told you. I spent scads of time in the kitchens."

"The cooks let the little prince eviscerate rabbits for supper?"

"The cooks were honored I took an interest in their work. My sister was always out on the hunt—she never set foot in the kitchens, but they were my favorite part of the castle."

Thanks to the dryness of the mysterious wood, Mia had a fire crackling in no time. She followed Quin's instructions and stacked three large stones over the flames, then used a stick to scoop a hole in the ground, lining it with fresh hide and packing it with melted snow. Once the stones were sizzling hot, she added them to the packed snow and watched it melt into broth.

"Heat a few more stones," said the prince. "The broth has to be boiling hot to cook the meat."

She nodded and set to work. Once the broth was heated to Quin's satisfaction, he dropped in hunks of raw flesh and a smattering of small bones. He slit one large bone open, slurping out the liquid.

"Four hells, this is good." He held it out to her. "Marrow. It's rich in minerals. Very nourishing."

She sucked out the rest of the marrow and licked her lips.

Mia was struck by the changes in the prince. In one short week, he'd gone from a sniveling brat to a competent woodsman, someone who could deftly carve up a hare for supper. She wouldn't have thought watching a boy butcher meat would be attractive, but seeing Quin's hands flick over the viscera, separating fat from bone, was, in a word, appealing.

Despite the cold, Quin was perspiring; he kept brushing the curls off his forehead with the back of his hand. The firelight bathed him in a ruddy orange glow. A flame of heat curled through Mia's belly.

She sensed a quiet thumping in her chest, a feeling of all not being as it should be. Did someone leave the firewood for them? Had they arranged the hare so she and Quin would find it?

Her gut feeling told her something was wrong. But since when had she trusted her gut feelings? Mia wasn't the sort of person to make decisions based on what she felt; she based them on logic and hard evidence.

They were going to be fine. The meal would give them the fuel they needed to make it to their destination—an odd thing to say, perhaps, considering she didn't know where their destination was. *The path to safe haven will reveal itself to she who seeks it.*

There wasn't much page left for the map to spill onto. They had to be nearing the end.

They devoured the stew, slurping hot broth out of hollow stones. The meat was rich and mouthwatering; Mia didn't think she'd ever had such good stew. When she said as much to Quin, he grinned.

"I can make the leftover meat last, too. I'll smoke it, maybe dry a few strips in the sun tomorrow morning. Better for traveling that way. Excellent source of protein."

The soup was warming her, dissolving the knot of tension between her shoulders. She was being paranoid. She had no good reason to be uneasy; beavers and other animals gathered driftwood, and a dead hare was no cause for alarm.

"I'm sorry I've been disagreeable," Quin said, surprising her. "I know I can be odious when hungry, and I've been hungry for days."

He reached out and touched her wrist. His fingers weren't cold, not even a little.

"More marrow?"

She nodded. He let his fingertips linger on her skin a moment, and she felt her pulse trill to meet them before he retracted his hand.

Her heart was throbbing somewhere in her glottal region. She cast a sideways glance at Quin, but he was staring hard into the hare carcass. Either he enjoyed looking at intestines or he was avoiding her eyes.

Mia inhaled deeply to steady her breathing. The sour pinch of eggs filled her nostrils. She froze. Had someone lit a sulfyr stick?

Quin started to say something, then stopped.

"Is it just me, or do you smell—"

"Sulfyr." She was on her feet, stepping forward, but she lost the scent. When she moved in the other direction, the smell grew stronger. The unease she'd felt earlier was back, a whole orchestra pounding on her vertebrae.

He started moving toward the odor.

"Quin? I don't think we ought to—"

But he was already pushing out of the glade, his energy replenished from the stew. She had no choice but to follow. He was fleet, graceful on uneven terrain, while she felt dizzy and not at all sure-footed. The firelight quickly faded, and she found herself stumbling over swyn trunks. Her stomach had shrunk on their meager sylvan diet; it sloshed with undigested meat.

Quin was a ways ahead when he shouted, "Mia! *Mia!*"

Her blood congealed. She couldn't read the emotion in his voice. Surprise? Terror?

She ran faster to close the gap between them. Seconds later she charged full tilt into a small clearing—and nearly knocked Quin into the hot spring bubbling at his feet.

"Look what I found."

Before Mia could respond, he was peeling off his jacket and the shirt beneath it. She wondered if she should look away as he removed his trousers, but he'd discarded them before she had time to think. Her eyes tripped over his smooth golden body as he leapt into the water.

Her viscera were liquefying inside her body, bones dissolving into bonemeal. It was a familiar feeling, and dangerously warm.

Chapter 25

UNDERGARMENTS

"You're coming in, aren't you?"

Quin patted the water beside him. Steam coiled off the surface. The spring was phosphorescent, spirals of sulfyric scurf mingling with starlight so green it shimmered.

"Come on, Mia. It's insensible not to warm yourself."

Mia wanted nothing more. The pool was perfect, a natural tub of hot water carved out of the mountainside, an indicator of subterranean volqanic activity. She would have happily jumped in, if not for one little problem.

Heat.

She was still hammering out her theory of magic and body temperatures—complicated by infinite unknown variables—but both times she had enthralled the prince, heat was a constant. As a Huntress, she'd come at it from the opposite angle, studying the symptoms of an enthrall. Elevated pulse, sweaty palms, dilated pupils: these were the signs of physical attraction. They were also the body's natural response to warmth.

What if the only reason she hadn't inadvertently enthralled Quin in the forest was because they were too cold?

And if that were the case, what would happen in a thermal spring?

Not unrelatedly, was he still wearing undergarments, or had he stripped those off, too? On a scale of one to ten, how naked was the prince under all those bubbles?

"I thought I was too *dangerous*," she said. To her surprise, it came out sounding rather coy.

His eyebrows had a fine arch, especially when he raised one. "I've never been afraid of a girl in undergarments. Though I must admit I've had limited experience."

In the game of being coy, Quin was winning.

He grew suddenly serious. "We're teetering on the edge of frostbite, Mia. This could save your life."

She sat on the edge. The snow crunched beneath her as she tugged the boots off her swollen feet. Cautiously she dipped one toe in the water. Paradise.

"If you stay on your side," Quin reasoned, "we'll manage just fine."

Her toes felt delectable. Quin was right, she could control herself. If rage, love, and terror triggered magic, then she would make sure she didn't feel rage, love, or terror. Easy enough. And in the event that she began feeling the sensations of an enthrall, she would simply climb out. Most important, she would not touch him, no matter how much she might want to.

Mia slipped the smock over her head, slithered out of her trousers, and eased herself over the ledge with barely a splash.

The water didn't just feel good. It felt like cinnamon and chocolate, like someone had thrust a hand into her heart and made it beat again. She sank deeper, the warm water swirling in around her neck and shoulders, caressing her wind-roughed skin. Everything that had been frozen inside her was thawing, every dead part shivering back to life.

Quin let out a long, contented sigh. "Perfection, isn't it?"

She submerged her head lower until only her eyes peeked above water.

"Careful of the meniscus," he said. "There's some kind of sulfyric film."

She lifted her mouth. "The 'meniscus of assent,' was it?"

His face went blank for a moment. Had she offended him? Then his eyes sparked with the memory.

"Ah. That. I suppose I can be a bit pretentious."

"A bit. But passably intelligent."

"Passably." A smile tugged at the corners of his mouth.

She dunked her whole head underwater and ran her fingers over her hair. The grime came off in clumps. She'd had no idea how dirty she was. The water felt inhumanly delicious as it licked off layers of filth. How had she ever been suspicious of heat? It was glorious.

She heard Quin's garbled voice and bobbed back up.

". . . cold is that I haven't smelled my own sweat." He took a whiff and grimaced. "Until now."

"Hard to tell with all the sulfyr."

"You can come a little closer," he said. "If you want."

"I'm just fine over here, thanks."

She went under again and rubbed furiously at her face, wondering how much dirt was ground into her skin. The unease she'd felt over supper melted into the foam. The only unease she felt now was how good she felt, bubbly warm down to her core.

Bubbly was not good. Warm was not good, either.

The prince was speaking again. She only caught the end of it.

". . . married?"

She sputtered. "What?"

"Are we married? In your humble opinion."

"No," she said.

"We said the sacred vows."

"I didn't. Not the last one."

"You're right. I promised-you-O-promised-you I would be yours. But you did not O-promise you would be mine." He tilted his head, thoughtful. "And Tristan did not pronounce us man and wife."

She burbled water. "I've always hated that part of the vows. Just once I'd like to hear 'woman and husband.'"

"You probably won't hear it from dear cousin Tristan. He's rather old-fashioned that way. Just like my father."

"*Old-fashioned* is one word for it."

"You'd prefer *odious*?"

"I'm quite partial to *vile*."

They shared a smile. Then Quin cleared his throat. "You should know I meant what I said about having limited experience with girls in undergarments. My father fills the Kaer with beautiful women, but it never felt right to—"

"You don't have to say it," she said hastily.

"You once told me my power had never been in dispute. You were right. Even if I had honest intentions, there was always an imbalance of power. I saw my father abuse that power daily . . . and I swore I would never be like him."

Mia felt unreasonably happy. She had assumed the prince treated women the way his father did, but she'd been wrong.

"That's quite lovely, Quin. And wise."

"Haven't you heard? I'm passably intelligent."

Mia slid two clicks closer. Not close enough to touch—just to hear him better. She was in complete control, fully in command of her faculties. She was a Gwyrach, yes, but she was stronger now, smarter. Magic was not the reason she felt so tantalizingly warm. She was completely . . . almost . . . mostly certain.

"The water in a hot spring percolates through a reservoir of magma and rises through the Earth's crust," she said, because she didn't know what else to say.

"Is it a requirement for Huntresses to know an insufferable amount about everything?"

"You underestimate me. I know everything about an insufferable number of things."

He flourished a bow. "The lady wins."

She edged closer, still mostly submerged, combing through her ringlets underwater. She could feel her locks floating on the surface of the water, vermilion silk. Quin was still smiling.

Mia was only a few inches away now. Close enough to see the blond scruff on his face, just a hint around the mouth. To note the silver starlight caught in his curls.

He was gorgeous. Even after a harrowing week in the woods. Even after nearly dying. Mia's body hummed with sensation. The perfection of Quin's face pulped her internal organs.

He looked at her looking, and he looked back.

Mia's fingers ached to touch him. His eyes shone greener than ever, maybe from the spring, maybe because they burned with feeling. Was she inventing fictions or deducing truth? His breathing was different, that was a fact. Frankly, so was hers.

This was dangerous. She knew she should climb out of the hot spring immediately. What if her magic was exerting a subtle influence, stirring his blood and subverting his desire? Impossible. She hadn't touched him. Of course, if Quin were looking at her because he truly wanted her . . . that was something else entirely.

She stood, her gaze meeting his. The water dripped off her curves, her undergarments clinging to her warm, wet skin. Quin parted his lips ever so slightly. Her eyes swept over them, down the perfect curve of his jaw, the sharp ridges of his collarbone, and then snagged on a torn piece of red skin above his heart. She stared at the angry, jagged mark, inflamed and oozing black pus.

The breath jammed in her throat.

The arrow.

Chapter 26

A MAGICAL HONEYMOON

QUIN DUNKED HIMSELF BENEATH the water. Only his face resurfaced, now drenched and dewed.

"Don't look at me like that. It's nothing."

It was most definitely something. She'd seen the lesion, the sinister purple tendrils around the fishbone scar, and most damning: the sliver of red arrowhead protruding from the skin.

"I didn't get it all," she said.

Her own failure walloped her in the face. She'd been cocksure, absolutely certain she'd extracted all pieces of the arrowhead, but how closely had she looked? Not closely enough. She'd tossed the arrow aside in the tunnels and never given it a second thought.

Mia knew enough about wound theory to recognize the

warning signs. A fragment of the arrowhead had broken off in Quin's chest, lodged in the tender tissue above his heart. The body, in an attempt to fight off microscopic animalcule, triggered an inflammatory response. But over the last week, infection had crept in. The wound had gone septic.

Dread sank its hooks. Quin's body would turn on itself, waging war on his organs, collapsing the pressure of his blood, and ultimately ravaging his brain.

If the sepsis was not treated, he would die.

"It's fine," he said brusquely. "I'm fine."

Sulfyr was a natural antiseptic. Quin's soak in the hot spring might have been curative, but Mia feared it was too late: once the infection had spread into his bloodstream, any cursory cleaning of the wound site was futile, like tying a green blade of grass around a shattered bone.

Gingerly she grazed the wound with her fingertips. He gasped in pain—and ducked out of reach.

"We have to get it out, Quin."

"I know you're trying to help, but you might kill me instead."

She opened her mouth to voice an objection, but none was forthcoming. He was right.

"To be perfectly honest," he went on, "I think you may have been enthralling me just now."

"All I've been thinking about was how *not* to enthrall you. I haven't touched you once."

"Maybe we've been wrong about magic. Maybe it's not bound to touch." He combed his fingers through his wet curls. "Just now, the way you were looking at me . . . my body was behaving strangely."

"So was mine. We are divested of our garments in a hot spring, Quin. I think 'strange' is a matter of perspective." She sighed. "I don't ever want to make you do anything you don't want to do. But you can't go blaming my magic every time you *feel* something."

And yet, hadn't she been doing exactly that? Blaming her magic for every spike or drop in body temperature, every flash of cold or spark of desire?

"It isn't fair you have this power."

"What's fair about any of this? I don't want to control you. I want you to feel the way you're feeling because you feel it. Because it's real. And right now I want to get that arrow out, before—"

"Mia."

"I do!"

"*Mia.*"

He'd gone stark white. She felt the blood thrumming down her backbone a moment too late, as a shadow unfurled behind her.

"A supper of vermin and a dip in a bubbly tub." The voice was rough, familiar. "What a magical honeymoon."

Cousin Tristan, flanked by two giant white hounds and three of the king's guards, stepped out of the Twisted Forest.

Chapter 27

BECAUSE A KING CAN

"FANCY SEEING YOU HERE, Cousin."

Quin had reverted to his cold, formal tone, the one he used in Kaer Killian. Mia hadn't realized how much his voice had changed in the woods; he had abandoned his haughty cadence for a warm, lower register.

Tristan's hounds chomped their massive jaws.

"You can drop the pleasantries." The duke motioned to his men. "Seize them."

The wiriest of the three guards came toward Mia. With his lean frame, blazing white skin, and bright shock of ginger hair, he reminded her of a maple tree in autumn, the kind that might snap in a ferocious storm.

But he was stronger and meaner than any maple, and wearing coarse bullock gloves. He grabbed Mia under her arms and dragged her across the ground. She felt painfully vulnerable as she was wrenched from the water, her soaked undergarments like an oozing second skin. The boiling headache, which had granted her clemency over the last week, was back with a vengeance, roasting the tender bones of her skull.

The other two guards wrestled Quin to the ground. He was wearing undergarments after all. He was also furious.

"Unhand her," he spat. "I command you let us go."

Tristan crouched, pinching Mia's dirty smock between his fingers with obvious disgust. He flung it aside. He had grown a week's worth of scruff, but it was patchy and uneven, dark-brown stubble carving jagged lines across his pasty skin. His blue irises had vanished completely, and his pupils were dilated to an unnatural degree, painting his eyes an eerie, solid black.

"Here's the thing, Cousin. You're dead. Or so the rest of the river kingdom believes. And a dead man can't very well give commands, can he?" He turned to the guards. "Tie them to the swyn."

Mia reached for her trousers, but one of Tristan's hounds snapped at her hand.

"Can I please get dressed?"

"Why?" The duke was droll. "Must you be dressed to die?"

"This is absurd." Quin's voice was cool with disdain. "I'm not dead. Good news all around. I'm sure my father will be happy to see me alive and well, along with my wife."

Wife. The word jarred. Mia knew what Quin was doing,

though she wasn't sure how effective it would be. Safe to say the duke didn't have much invested in their nuptials.

The guards bound Mia to a tree, lashing Quin to a trunk a few feet away. She was intimately aware of his body, the breath in his lungs, the blood in his limbs. The cold blew off him barbed and brittle, giving credence to her theory: hate was cold.

She felt Tristan's eyes scratch over her bare skin. "I've never seen you in the flesh before. A pity to execute a thing so pretty."

"She's not a *thing*," Quin growled.

"A demon, then."

They both froze. Tristan looked pleased.

"Did you take me for a fool? There's enough blood in the tunnels for a virgin sacrifice. But *virgin* isn't exactly the right word, is it?" He kicked the tree the prince was bound to. Mia felt Quin flinch. "It seems you have unsavory tastes, Cousin. Your wife is a Gwyrach."

The duke scraped a knife from his scabbard and crouched in front of the prince. "You do know what happens to men who marry demons, don't you?"

Quin roared. The sensation ricocheted through Mia's body; Tristan had pierced the infected arrow wound with his blade. Cutting down the line of the scar, snapping the thin threads of cartilage. Quin gasped, and though she couldn't see him, she could feel his jaw clench, his teeth grit against the pain. Whatever bond her magic had woven between them, she felt his body as her own.

But Tristan didn't plunge the blade deep. Mia heard the knife slide back into the scabbard.

"So close to the heart," said the duke. "I do believe your little demon saved your life."

He stood. "I've been tracking you for days. My hounds had no trouble finding your scent." He tossed two large beef bones to his dogs and smiled as they tore into them with bloodthirsty ferocity, red chunks of flesh flecking their white fur.

"We left you a hare. Did you enjoy it? Some nice crisp fire-wood, too. It seemed the least we could do; a last supper fit for a king." He laughed. "It was disappointingly easy. Like luring two starving animals into a cage."

Mia cursed herself. All her instincts—the splash of gold in the river, the hound baying at the moon, even her hunch about the hare—had been spot-on. Why hadn't she listened? Perhaps because never in her life had she done anything "on a hunch." She was not a hunch kind of girl.

If she made it out of this alive, she resolved to be better at listening to her intuition. Though it seemed unlikely she would make it out of this alive.

The prince was inhaling and exhaling in short, sharp bursts, trying to regulate his breathing. The colors of his suffering painted themselves across Mia's mind in too-bright strokes.

If they had any chance of getting out of this alive, she needed to keep Tristan talking. She lifted her chin.

"So this was always your plan? Kill your cousin and comman-deer the throne?"

Tristan stared at her for a long, hard beat. Why were his eyes so black? There was violence in them. She remembered the way he'd swung the pewter candlestick in the Sacristy, how he so clearly derived pleasure from breaking anything breakable. She felt him fighting the urge to wrap his hands around her neck.

"Pretty demon," he said, "but stupid. I had nothing to do with the assassination. Though thanks to a spectacular twist of fate, I will now get everything I want."

When he crouched in front of her, she saw it. Through the cleft in his shirt, a silver chain hung around his neck, a pendant swinging at his heart. The stone was pearly white, delicate and orbed. A moonstone.

Panic blanked out Mia's mind.

"Where is she? What have you done to her?"

"Nothing."

"You've hurt her. She would never give you that stone. Not willingly. Not unless . . ."

"Your sister is a special girl." His lips curled. "You needn't worry; she'll be well cared for. I, unlike you, will keep Angelyne safe. I want only the best for my bride."

Mia's chest seized. She saw everything with sickening clarity: the duke, always with an eye for personal advancement, had seen his opportunity and pounced. He didn't merely lust for the river throne: he lusted for her sister. And now he would get everything he wanted.

His crown, his queen.

She feared Angelyne was too weak to resist him. Hadn't she said she wanted to live in a castle and marry a prince? But even if Angie were frivolous enough at fifteen to believe a royal marriage was what she wanted, Mia knew her better. The misery would creep into her heart like a cold, wet fog.

Angie was moonlight and music and swannish grace. She didn't deserve death in a gilded cage.

A spike of ice skewered Mia's skull. Hate, hate, hate—Tristan's or hers, she didn't know. With her body so closely attuned to everyone else's, how could she tell which feelings were her own and which had taken her hostage?

He leaned closer. "Don't you have anything to say?" He raised his knife and she winced, waiting for the sting of metal. Instead he traced the blade over her clavicle and flicked it lightly over her breasts. *Porcelain bosom,* Mia thought, and the memory nearly broke her heart.

She felt Tristan grow aroused, trailing the knife down her stomach, and her heart withered in her chest. So this was it, then. This was the end. He would kill her, or worse, rape and kill her. She would die at the hand of the duke, violated and diminished, unable to ever protect her sister again.

Her heart punched a hole through her chest.

She had magic.

Mia didn't need a blade to kill a man. She could stop his heart. She didn't know exactly *how* to stop his heart, but if she summoned love, rage, and terror, she might be able to channel her magic, and at the moment, all three were alive and well. If not kill, then she could at least enthrall him—and buy herself a chance of escape.

Magic was wrong, wicked, evil. She knew all those things. But this was life or death.

183

She had to convince Tristan to touch her. "Your Grace," she murmured in what she hoped was a breathy, sultry voice. She knew the duke was a regular at the brothels in Killian Village, a place where pretty girls pet his ego and pretended to enjoy his company. "I've wanted you to touch me for as long as I can remember."

"Do you think me a fool?"

Mia sensed his hesitation—his suspicion mingled with his lust. He drew the back of his knife blade slowly up her thigh, then her stomach, then her neck. Though she tasted acrid bile in her mouth, she let out a low moan.

"Yes," she said. "Like that. Now let me feel you, flesh to flesh."

"You aren't wearing gloves. You aren't wearing much of anything." He pressed the tip of the knife into her bottom lip, his touch light, but even so she felt a tiny bead of blood bubble up to the surface.

"Such a pity," he said, "that I can't even give you a good-bye kiss."

He wasn't going to touch her.

Her mind spun in desperate circles. What was it Quin had said in the hot spring? That perhaps magic didn't always require touch?

It was her only hope, and she hurled herself toward it. She let her feelings course through her unchecked, fury flowing upward from her belly to her brain. She loosened her logic, held her reason under the roiling surface of her thoughts until it sputtered and drowned. She stacked everything into a bundle—terror, rage, love—and lit it on fire.

Nothing happened.

"Tristan. Cousin." Quin's voice was a dry croak in his throat.

The duke's arm tensed, the knife poised at Mia's neck.

"I owe you an apology." Quin wheezed. "I owe you many apologies."

"I'm not interested in your apologies."

"I know you're not. You do what you must. We're as good as dead anyway. I only mean to say . . ." He trailed off. When he spoke again, his voice was choked with emotion. "I've underestimated you. My whole life I've underestimated you. And for that I am sorry. I see now what a mistake that was. I can't ask anything of you . . . I deserve nothing of you . . . but if you would hear me out, I have but one final request."

They all waited. Tristan's hounds pricked their ears, and even the three guards leaned forward. Mia couldn't believe these were the same men who had sworn to protect her only a week before. Now they would stand idly by while she bled out on the snow.

"One last toast," Quin said. "One last drink together. That's all I ask."

Tristan's eyes narrowed. "Why would I grant you this?"

"Because you are the man who will be king. You're more of a man than I ever was. You understand power and influence—you won my father's favor in a way I never could." His voice wavered again. "I was never fit to be king. I knew it, you knew it, and my father knew it most of all. In a way you do me a great service, releasing me from this burden. I am a dead man. I've always been a dead man. But you, Cousin; someday, you will be king."

He cleared his throat and swallowed. "A king grants a dead man his last request, because a king can."

The duke hesitated. Mia could see him turning the proposal over in his mind. A dark smile stretched from his shadowed cheeks to his cold black eyes.

"Very well." Tristan sheathed the knife in its scabbard. "Because a king can."

Chapter 28

BROKEN

THE DEMON'S DWAYLE WENT down like a tube of pig's grease, thick and rancid.

Mia hadn't wanted to drink it, but Quin insisted.

They were gathered in Tristan's camp around a crackling fire made by one of the guards. Mia had watched the man tie his long black beard into a knot at his chin and take a knife to a stick of softwood, using sharp, short strokes to shave a fuzzy mop of curls. He sparked a rock and lit the shavings, and soon the campfire was christening his satiny taupe skin with soft flecks of ash. When he'd seen her watching, he'd said, "It's all in the wrist," and given her an almost paternal wink.

It was a strange thing, envying a man's fire-making abilities minutes before your execution.

"It's good to drink together," Quin said, clinking his flask to Tristan's. He waved the guards over. "Them too. Them too."

He had convinced the duke he deserved to toast his successes ("because you got what you came for, did you not?"), that the drink should be hot ("there can be no demon in demon's dwayle without a red flame!"), and that they should all raise a glass ("the man who drinks alone is cold as stone"). He'd even managed to cajole his way out of his shackles, though they'd kept Mia's ropes tied. The men had prodded her forward with sticks, careful to avoid touching her skin.

Quin had talked a blue streak and gotten Tristan to agree to all sorts of things. Unfortunately, none of them included sparing their lives.

The prince raised his flask.

"To Tristan, Son of Clan Killian, uncontested Prince of Glas Ddir. Here's to you, Cousin, for letting a man warm his bones before the cold final slumber."

Surely this was some kind of ruse. If it were genuinely a last hurrah, the whole production struck Mia as downright bizarre, drinking chummily with the men about to take your life. That was just like a man, she thought, to embrace a senseless archaic ritual.

The duke raised his demon's dwayle. Quin clinked flasks and glugged his dwayle, and Tristan and the other men followed suit. They grunted, nodding in approval, wiping their mouths on their sleeves.

The wiry, ginger-haired guard quaffed another swig. "It's better 'an the dross Spence cooks up for us." He glowered at the third guard, a graying man whose hairy hand rested on his paunch.

"*You* try cooking for four in the woods, Talbyt, you ol' crab."

Mia had never tasted dwayle before, and she didn't understand how anyone could like it. She took another sip. Like sucking down goose fat.

Was Quin concocting some kind of plan? She kept trying to catch his eye, but he steadfastly refused to look at her.

Mia's head was a block of ice sweating into her brain. The thought of her sister walking down the aisle of the Royal Chapel, forced into marriage, trapped forever in that stone prison . . .

She had to save her. The ropes chafed at Mia's wrists as she tried to break free. She eyed the hounds, threads of drool dangling from their jowls, gums red and wet against their razor teeth. Even if by some miracle she could work magic on all four men at once, she couldn't subdue two dogs.

"How do you like it, Mia?" Quin was staring at her. "The dwayle?"

"I hate it," she said.

"Good." He nodded. "Because yours was different from the rest."

The wiry guard brought a hand to his throat.

It happened fast: Tristan sprang to his feet, then pitched forward, nearly staggering into the fire. He shouted, but the words came out as spittle and yellow froth. He was trying to give a command to the dogs. They couldn't understand it, but they were picking up on his distress, growling and pawing at the snow.

Spence was on all fours, retching mustard-colored bile onto the ground. Talbyt clutched his stomach, his face bone white, while the fire-building guard frantically shoveled snow into his mouth. They were clawing at their chests, heaving the contents of their stomach into the earth.

Quin was on his feet. Mia watched in bewilderment as he pulled a white slice of tree bark from his mouth and spat it out onto the ground.

"Swyn," he said. "Very absorbent. A natural antidote to poison."

Quin spun through the camp, grabbing their piles of clothes and shoving everything into the cook's satchel. He sawed through the ropes around Mia's wrists and took her by the hand.

They turned, ready to run—and there were the dogs.

Tristan's hounds were ready to tear them apart. Their eyes rolled back into their skulls, leaving two white moons; their tails were taut, their teeth bared.

"Mia," Quin said, "can you enchant the dogs?"

"I—don't think—"

"Can you try?"

They had no other choice. She sank to her knees.

She willed herself to think gentle, calming thoughts. A dog in and of itself was not a threat. They were loyal creatures, submissive to their masters, eager for a kind word or a greasy treat. She conjured Quin's dogs, those gentle golden beasts, with their firelit fur and soft snouts, the way they always looked like they were smiling. A half-forgotten memory tapped at the corner of her mind.

She had no idea what she was doing. How was she supposed to

turn two attack dogs into docile puppies? Mia shut her eyes, her fingers quivering. She extended her hands.

Something happened.

She felt clean and buoyant, as if her insides had been scooped out and replaced with goose down. Her head was light, and her fingers, which had been trembling only a moment before, were now bloodless, ten lily pads floating on a cloud of hot steam.

She felt something warm and wet. She was sure the dogs had sunk their teeth into her hands, blood spurting from the wounds.

But when she opened her eyes, she saw the liquid was saliva, the something warm a tongue. The bigger dog was licking her palm. The smaller one wagged his tail.

Mia watched, astonished, as the hounds plopped down on the snow. They whimpered and rolled onto their backs, offering up pink bellies to be rubbed.

Five cold fingers wrapped around Mia's ankle. Tristan lay prostrate on the ground, face contorted, a smeared mess of vomit and saliva, but somehow his grip was ironclad.

Her bones jittered in their sockets. She heard a sharp, dry crack, and Tristan shrieked in pain. He let go of her ankle. She looked down and saw the impossible: his fingers bent backward, the bones fractured at the middle joints. His pale face had gone sallow.

Mia kicked his broken hand away, locked her fingers into Quin's, and ran.

Chapter 29

IMPERFECT CLEAVAGE

THE MOON WAS A white scar in the sky, gray clouds oozing from the puncture. A light snow dusted the swyn as Mia and Quin raced up the mountain. They were breathless, running without looking, worrying the same unspoken question: How soon would the magic wear off the hounds?

Mia Morwynna Rose, Knower of All Things, Mistress of Theories, was a blank slate. She didn't know what she'd done to the dogs or how she'd done it. What she did know was that Quin had most certainly saved their lives. He was a culinary genius—and a better assassin than she was.

She could still hear Tristan's fingers breaking. She'd felt the telltale twitch of magic in her fingers, the mirrored reflection of his body in her own. She had splintered his bones without meaning to. Had Quin seen her do it? She eyed him in her periphery. This probably wouldn't allay his concerns about her ability to control her magic.

Thin air whistled through her nostrils and into her aching lungs. She was grateful Quin had thought to grab their smocks and trousers—the snow was falling faster by the minute. But the clothes weren't enough. She banged her hands together to keep warm.

"How did you know Tristan would say yes to a last drink?"

"I didn't. I just hoped. He's always been fond of dwayle."

"'Because a king can.' Brilliant."

He looked thoughtful. "My cousin has always been vain. I knew if I could play on his vanity, we might survive."

"And you said you were never any good at war games."

"No. I told you my sister was better. I've always had a knack for the pretending arts." His smile was sad. "Vanity looks like strength, but is almost always weakness."

"And you exploited it beautifully. You're a tremendous actor. Pure genius."

"Passably genius."

"What did you put in the brew?"

"Remember our chokecherry tea?"

She nodded.

"The berries aren't poisonous. But the pits are." He shook the snow out of his curls. "Chokecherry brew, with a dash of extra choke."

Mia was impressed. "You saved the pits?"

"You can't take enough precautions. Not in this fugitive life we're living."

There was no sound but the snow crisping underfoot, the muted hush as it fell around them. Their pace had slackened. They were beginning to feel safe—more dangerous, Mia thought, than when they felt hunted.

"Is it odd that I believe him?" Quin said. "I don't think Tristan was behind the assassination—at least not the mastermind. He's just taking advantage of it. My cousin can be violent, but he doesn't have the acuity to execute a complex plan. He's the sort of person who waits for destiny to arrange itself pleasingly on his plate before reaching for the knife."

"He must have been working with someone." She didn't have to say, *Probably your father or my father.* They were both thinking it.

"Is it a horrible way to die? The chokecherry?"

"Oh, they won't die. They'll be wretchedly sick for a few days. Their stomachs will be properly ravaged. But they shouldn't die." His brow furrowed. "I don't think. I tried not to put in enough to . . ."

He trailed off. "It's hard to get the quantities right. It's like all cooking: trial and error. A dash of knowledge and a pinch of intuition." He paused. "Not that killing is like cooking."

"But cooking *is* often killing, isn't it? Before we eat the meat, we must slaughter it."

"Cooking is an act of love. To cook is to care for someone. It isn't . . ."

He stumbled forward.

"Quin?"

His cheeks were too pink. He tripped again, then hooked his arm around a tree branch. Woozy, he sank into the snow, clutching his left shoulder.

The arrow. She had once again forgotten. How many times would she forget? She was reckless, asinine, an absolute travesty of a—

"Help me," he said, and then collapsed.

Mia fell to her knees and ripped open his shirt.

The wound was festering. Tristan had made it angry; now it oozed with white and yellow pus. Quin's whole shoulder was inflamed and distended. When she touched the swollen skin, he moaned.

Could she heal infected blood? She didn't know how far her powers extended. She had mended Quin's arrow wound, goaded the tissue along its natural path of repair and recovery, but that was a single site of aggravated trauma. She had knit skin back together, not repaired an entire system of flagging organs. Quin's body was rallying against him. His brain. His heart.

"I'm going to lay you down," she said. He was still unconscious, but maybe he would be comforted by the sound of her voice. She eased him onto his back and hastily arranged a pile of soft needles under his head.

She tore open the satchel. In their hasty retreat, Quin had thrown a handful of things into the bag, but the sheath knife wasn't among them. Gone was the smooth, sleek blade; instead they'd inherited the cook's corroded chopping knife. It might as well have been a rusted tent spike, not to mention crusted with animalcule from years of carving up raw meat. If Quin's blood weren't infected already, it surely would be.

She pushed the thought from her mind. She had two tasks:

Extract the fragment of the arrow.

Heal the infection.

Quin had saved her life; now she would save his.

His face shone beneath a patina of sickly sweat. He slipped in and out of consciousness, mumbling the same song: "*Under the plums, if it's meant to be. You'll come to me, under the snow plum tree.*"

"Shh. Save your strength."

Mia took a breath, resurrecting the Wound Man plate in her mind. She felt a wash of sudden calm—after all, she'd done this before. This time she'd do it better. She braced her hand against his sternum and eased the rusty knife into the wound.

His body jerked, an instinctual reaction. She kept digging. The blunt chopper made precise movements impossible, so when the incision was big enough, she slipped a finger beneath the skin. His flesh was warm and spongy, and she felt the stone immediately, tiny and ice cold.

As she extracted the last shiver of arrowhead, Quin's body shuddered and went still.

Mia pressed both hands to the wound. She could feel it—his blood clotting, slowing, thickening. She felt her own blood thicken in response. Her body tingled, her fingers losing sensation.

Fatigue drew a shroud over her eyes.

This time it was harder. She could feel the animalcules screaming through his veins. She was furious that his blood was battling hers—that his body would kill itself in an absurd plot to save itself. Were human beings really so flawed? So defective?

Mia bit her lip so hard she tasted copper. Back in the tunnels, she wanted for the prince not to die. This time, she wanted him to live.

His heart raged in an explosive frenzy, and hers raged, too, contraction for contraction, expansion for expansion. She heard her father: *Magic relies on a cruel, unruly heart.* She didn't care. Quin's body hummed a song that she recognized. The tremendous hurt he'd suffered at the hands of his family. His fury over being trapped in a life he didn't want. A deep, perplexing shame.

How was she feeling Quin's feelings? She was so tired. She was the heaviest mountain. She was weightless, a skip of air.

And then it was over. Her hands slid off his chest, skidding into the pillow of swyn needles. She collapsed on top of him, spent, his body smooth beneath her, his chest warm. Her curls were strewn over his face, and she worried she was crushing him, but she didn't want to leave. Not until she felt him breathing.

He inhaled sharply, and she wanted to shout for joy. His hands moved over her arms, smooth and steady, sending little vibrations up her spine. His chest and stomach were taut as he pressed himself into her hips, and a shiver trembled through her, starting in the pit of her belly and flowing outward in rippled waves, like silk unspooling.

His lips were soft against her neck.

"The lady wins," he murmured.

Mia was woozy. Was it possible to fall when you were already lying down? Quin shifted beneath her, and she felt the hard cut of his hip bones, then his strong hands at her waist. His body heat spread through her. She had him pinioned to the earth, but from the way he ran his fingertips up her skin, singeing her flesh, she didn't think he minded.

But she was wrong about that, too, because suddenly she was being pushed aside. She realized what he was doing and scrambled off him, embarrassed. He lifted himself to a seat and pressed his long back into a tree. She crouched on her heels.

"I'm sorry," he said weakly. "I don't mean to be ungrateful. It's just . . ."

"You don't want me to accidentally kill you."

"That, among other things."

His face was a stormlit sky, streaked with indecipherable emotions, like a book written in a language she couldn't read.

"What do you mean, *other things*?"

"Can I ask you a question?"

She nodded.

"What happened to your mother?"

"She . . . she was killed by a Gwyrach."

"And did you find this Gwyrach?"

"Not yet. But I will."

Instinctually she touched her chest, but the ruby wren wasn't there. Mia was stricken. The journal and the key were back at their camp, sitting by the abandoned stew. She ached to retrace her steps and go back for it, but that would take hours, and who knew when the dogs would snap out of their enchantment? The last fragment of her mother was lost to her forever.

How would Mia know where to go? The fire kingdom was an archipelago of hundreds of islands. Without the map, she was truly lost.

"How do you know your father didn't do it?" Quin said.

"I told you, my father is not a killer. He's a Hunter. He only hunts—"

"Gwyrach. Yes, I know." He looked at her pointedly. "Isn't it obvious, Mia? Your mother was a Gwyrach, just like you."

"I won't believe that. I *can't* believe it. My mother was good. She was the kindest, warmest, gentlest woman I knew. She would never—"

"Use magic to heal someone?" He gestured toward his shoulder. "The way you've used yours to heal me *twice*? How truly atrocious, you saving my life."

Mia shook her head sharply, unable to accept it. Her father had woven a dark web of lies, but her mother was no better, with her veiled secrets. Was Wynna a Gwyrach? Even if she were, Griffin had not killed her with a sword or arrow. Mia had seen and held her mother's lifeless body: no blood, no bruises, no broken bones.

She shuddered, remembering the dry pop of Tristan's fingers.

"Mia." Quin touched her chin lightly with his fingertips. She felt a rush of cold, but his face was free of hatred. "All I'm saying is that I don't think you're as wicked as you think."

He smiled faintly. "And I'm in a unique position to say so, as someone you've ensorcelled."

Ensorcelled. Who used words like that outside of books? A smile lifted the corners of her mouth.

But the smile faded as quickly as it had come. A dog howled in the distance. Two dogs.

Quin rose unsteadily. Mia stood, too . . . and would have fallen flat on her face if he hadn't caught her by the arm.

"I'm exhausted from healing you. I don't think I have any magic left."

"We need a weapon."

She sank to her knees and scrabbled through the snow until she found the tip of the arrowhead she'd dug out of Quin's chest. The shard was still plenty sharp; when she pinched it between thumb and forefinger, it pricked the skin and drew blood. But it was too small. She threw it onto the snow, where it arched crimson like a wren's wing.

Something about the color caught her eye.

She picked up the stone again, more carefully this time, and wiped it across her trousers. The blood swabbed off, but the stone was still red. Vitreous, brittle tenacity, imperfect cleavage. A luster like glass. She recognized it instantly.

Fojuen.

A stone that did not exist in Glas Ddir.

A stone manufactured by the volqanoes of Fojo Karaçào.

The same stone her mother used to lock her little book of secrets.

If Wynna's killer hailed from Fojo, was it mere coincidence that Quin's assassin was Fojuen, too?

She dropped the arrowhead into her pocket. The "safe haven" they were careening toward looked more and more like a den of murderers.

"The dogs, Mia." Quin was very pale. "They're here."

Chapter 30

MONSTER

MIA SPRINTED UP THE mountain with Quin beside her, batting away the overgrown foliage. She ran until her heart was bursting, until her calf muscles were raging flames and her breath rasped through her lungs. They charged up the mountain as if their very lives depended on it.

She heard Quin panting. How much longer could they run? She didn't know if minutes or hours had passed, but suddenly they weren't climbing the peak anymore; they were coming down it. The rocks were uneven as they sloped and spilled onto a footpath. To Mia's surprise, the stones were worn, scuffed by centuries of feet and hooves—proof that even after Ronan sealed the borders, there were still ways to escape.

The trail zigzagged down the mountain, hugging the side of

a dramatic white cliff. Beyond it, Mia saw a trembling gray body of water.

They'd made it to the Salted Sea.

Mia's blood tilted forward in her veins. She didn't need her mother's map—something called to her, some unseen force tugging on the iron in her blood. Was this how the Natha snaked up the mountain? Was there a giant lodestone, calling it forth? It shattered every theory, every scientific principle she had ever learned, to think an invisible force could summon blood and water. But then her hard-won theories were being shattered left and right.

A shower of pebbles clattered down from overhead. The dogs were kicking rocks from the path above. They were close.

Quin's pulse intertwined with hers, an echo of his heartbeat resonating in her own, as they skidded to the edge of the cliff. One minute the path was chugging along; the next, it vanished.

She heard a monstrous, thundering roar.

At their feet was a waterfall.

Water poured off the cliff like a wedding veil, white and terrifying. She had never heard water hit with so much force. The mist made it impossible to see down into the chasm, obfuscating everything below. Surely they couldn't survive the fall; at this height, the water would fracture their bones like glass.

Again she saw the unnatural bend of Tristan's fingers, the crushed phalanges, fractured from the metacarpal bones. A body was weak, an assemblage of breakable parts. What broke more easily? A person's bones or a person's heart?

Mia's brain was silent. But her heart was screaming.

"We have to jump," she said.

"*What?*"

In seconds they would feel the hot breath of the hounds against their necks, teeth tearing into skin.

But it wasn't just that. The little voice inside her that had beckoned ever since she'd left the castle, coaxing her forth, asking her to trust it; she could no longer ignore the call. She didn't know what would happen the moment they hit the water—after that, her future was a blank page. But she knew she had to fill it.

"We have to jump."

Mia had never put much stock in fate. But now she felt it, the siren song of destiny. She was exactly where she was supposed to be. She was doing exactly what she was supposed to be doing— for maybe the first time in her life.

The dogs were a few short bounds away. Mia held out her hand. Quin took it.

All the air whipped out of her throat.

Stone and earth, then emptiness.

Free fall.

Ice air.

Skin scourge.

A froth of white and spun gold. The prince's golden curls. He pitched through the air like a bolt of lightning.

Mia closed her eyes.

The water reached hungrily for their soft bodies, a monster draped in white, as death rose up to greet them.

PART THREE

Breath

Chapter 31

FIRE AND AIR

QUIN'S BODY STRUCK FIRST. Hers a moment after.

The surface was a thin plate of glass, and they punched through it, the water rupturing beneath them. The world went white, then black, then blue. Mia waited for a million shards to slice into her skin.

But the water was warm.

She felt herself being shoved down, her head held underwater by the falls. Despite the tremendous force, she kicked violently, propelling herself up. Her face broke the surface, and she gasped for air. She swam out of the roaring mist, paddling hard until she found herself beneath a lighter trickle, the water anointing her head and gluing her curls to her face. A lick of softness and warmth, not the cold bludgeon she'd expected.

In the distance, she saw looming rock formations, a cinnamon brick red. A few feet away, Quin's golden curls bobbed in the water. She couldn't tell if he was coughing or laughing. Maybe both.

Are you—?

Did we just—?

The falls were pounding too loud for them to hear each other, but they didn't need words. They were alive. They had survived.

In the east, the sun was rising, a thin pink wafer on the horizon. They craned their necks to stare up at the cliff. Two tiny spots squirmed on the ridge, their howls drowned out by the waterfall. The dogs were nothing more than specks of white pepper on the scarp.

How had she and Quin survived that jump?

The pool at the base of the waterfalls was a deep bluish green, but a little farther out, the water grew hazy. Mia cupped a handful of water and brought it to her mouth. The salt stung her lips.

She paddled away from the falls, water lapping over her skin. She squinted at the strange red rocks. She wanted to swim out to them, but she hesitated. Could the prince swim? When would he have learned, cloistered in a castle?

But he was swimming beautifully, his strokes long and smooth. He clasped his hands behind his head and floated serenely on his back, as if he were born for the ocean.

They swam out to the red rocks. More sunlight spilled across the ocean, casting long tendrils of rust and peach. The pink wafer on the horizon was now a gold crown rising from the sea.

Mia was tired when she reached the rocks, in a good way, her muscles soft as paste. She followed the cliff's natural curve, running her hands along the porous surface as the water slurped at her shoulders. The rock wall led her to a shallow cove, where she crawled out on her knees, feeling the crumble of red sand beneath her hands, the muddled sunshine warm against her back.

Quin climbed out and stood facing her, shaking the salt water out of his curls. His hair was a more muted gold when wet, the color of fire-roasted wheat. He was trembling.

Mia felt not a modicum of cold. In her body, the seasons had changed from winter to summer. The salt water trickled off her hair, pooling in the nooks of her clavicle. Her skin was soft and glowing, dewy to the touch, and she felt soft inside, too. Luscious.

Quin reached out to touch her. He pressed a fingertip to the scoop of her collarbone, then brought his finger to his mouth.

There were a million things she wanted to say, and none of them sayable. He'd trusted her, and they'd survived. She'd trusted *herself*, and they'd survived. It flew in the face of everything she knew in her head, but confirmed the quiet whisper of her heart. For once, she had listened.

"Thank you, Mia," he said softly. "For saving my life."

His voice echoed off the red walls. He traced her jawbone with the tip of his thumb, leaving a trail of heat so smoky it reduced her chin to cinder.

He took a step toward her, and her stomach clenched.

Behind him was a hot air balloon.

The balloon was gigantic, winged and painted red.

They approached cautiously, unsure if they'd discovered a treasure or a trap. The balloon was tethered to a rock; it bumped gently in the breeze as they ran their hands over the bronze bucket, scalloped and grooved, a narrow wooden bench snugged inside.

Overhead a giant tube was welded to the metal with a simple crank on one end and wads of dry kindling stuffed inside the other. A strip of coarse rock was nailed beneath it, and swinging from a rope was the biggest sulfyr stick Mia had ever seen.

The sun, now a sphere balanced happily on the horizon, warmed the balloon like a red coal.

"Have you seen one of these before?" Quin asked.

"Only in books."

She knew the basic mechanics: capture hot air in an envelope and the balloon would float higher than the cold air around it. This was the law of buoyancy. The rider need only fire up the burner to reheat the air and float higher; to descend, lay off the burner and let the air cool to make the balloon sink back to Earth.

Mia climbed into the bronze bucket, testing the primitive metal rudder—the only way to steer the balloon once it was airborne—and saw the words engraved on the red wing:

If you have found your way thus far,
You don't have far to travel.

Ride fire and air to Refúj, where
All your troubles will unravel.

Unravel in a good way or a bad way? It was one of those words she didn't trust; a word that meant one thing but could also mean the opposite.

Her mind was busy turning over *Refúj*. The word meant "sanctuary" in Fojuen. Safe haven.

The path to safe haven will reveal itself to she who seeks it.

So her mother's cryptic message had not been cryptic after all. She was leading her daughter to Safe Haven, an actual geographical place. *Refúj.* Refuge with a capital *R*.

Mia felt a flush of triumph. Even without her mother's book, she had found her way. Perhaps she had always known the way—she simply had to listen.

Quin stood poised with one hand on the bucket of the balloon. She could feel the conflicting currents rolling off him, cold and piping hot.

"I can't promise you'll be safe," she said. The sliver of the fojuen arrowhead burned hot in the pocket of her trousers.

"I'm not safe anywhere," he said, and clambered into the bucket by her side.

Mia scraped the giant sulfyr stick against the rock, and it spat and sparkled. When she kissed the kindling with the fiery end, the torches roared to life. Instead of the greenish light of the sulfyr stick, they burned a bright golden red, the color of molten lava.

Mia's hands were steady as she reached for the rudder.

"Do you think . . . ," Quin began.

She knew what he was going to say. Did she think someone had left this balloon here for them? That they were expected in Refúj?

She did.

Because they were.

Chapter 32

FIVE SMALL CRATERS

As THE HOT AIR balloon lifted them into the sky, Mia saw her mother.

She saw the tumble of her hair in the red slopes and hills; the curve of her hips as the Salted Sea curled into the sunrise. This place held the very shape of Wynna, and Mia saw her mother's spirit in the vibrant bath of colors—the sanguine rock, the cerulean ocean.

She hoisted them higher, the hiss and gurgle of fire puffing hot air into the balloon. She felt the same tilt in her blood. A gentle tug—or was it a nudge?—and an almost magnetic force pushing her gently toward something, or pulling her in.

It was a jerky ride, not for the weak of stomach. But Mia wasn't queasy; she crooked her fingers over the metal rudder and breathed it all in. She felt warm and sad and alive. She thought of her mother coming to Fojo Karação as a girl, her heart rising to meet the beauty of this place, the fire kingdom that had called so deeply to her soul. It even smelled like her, a little sweet and a little wild, like fresh-cut flowers and wood smoke. Mia had to remind herself her mother wasn't waiting for her in Refúj. Her mother wasn't waiting for her anywhere.

She cranked the torch and the balloon sipped a mouthful of air. The sun had turned a simmering orange as it hung suspended above the ocean, and Mia felt birdlike, a winged creature suspended between worlds.

"We're always crossing a boundary, aren't we?" said Quin. "The laghdú, the boat, the balloon. We're always in some liminal state, moving toward something or away from something else."

She supposed he was right. The balloon rose above a ridge, and they both gasped.

There was a perfect blue jewel of a lake scooped out of the rock. The reflection was stunningly clear, a flawless replica of the sky. The water glistened in the morning sun, and in its center: a tiny red island set in the bezel of blue. Red ringed with blue ringed with red.

"I've never seen water that blue." Quin coughed. "The air smells like smoke." He ran his hand along the edge of the bronze bucket. His fingertips came back smudged gray. "Is that ash?"

Mia stared hard at the crater of the lake. When she took a closer look at the dazzling red peaks around them, she saw they weren't peaks at all; the tops were dipped like spoons. In the distance, black smoke coiled from one such ladle.

"It *is* ash," she said. "And the reason you've never seen a lake that blue is that you've never seen one that deep. It's called a *qaldera* in Fojuen. 'Boiling pot.'"

"Does that mean what I think it means?"

"We're in the crater of a volqano."

Mia had only read about volqanoes, never seen them in real life. Excitement whiffled through her. She was exploring the four kingdoms at last, fulfilling her childhood dreams. She was free.

She felt a sharp stab of guilt. She wasn't here to explore; she was here to find the Gwyrach who had killed her mother.

"When I was little," Quin began, "there was a scholar who came to the Kaer."

He rolled the ash between his fingers into a small kernel. "He taught us about the four ancient gods—four brothers—who warred with one another. How they each sulked off to their own corner of the world, hence the four kingdoms. But the Glasddiran god loved his brothers most, so he wept the hardest. That's why the river kingdom has so many rivers."

"Every child knows this story. It's our creation myth."

"My father made a big show of believing the myths—'restoring the kingdom to its former glory,' all that—but he never liked the part about the god of the river kingdom. He said a real god wouldn't weep."

Quin roughed up his curls. "The thing is, Glas Ddir never seemed like some epic place where gods wept and warred. It was a cold, wet kingdom, and Glasddirans weren't descended from

215

greatness—they were sad, hungry people my father abused. But this . . ." He gestured at the striking scenery around them. "This place *looks* like it was made by the gods. 'The river god wept water, but the fire god breathed fire.'"

"I thought you didn't believe in gods."

He shrugged. "The myths seemed unreasonable, but I secretly hoped they were true. Don't we all want to believe in something bigger than ourselves?"

Mia wasn't sure. Her magic was bigger than herself, and she didn't like it. If something grew too big you could no longer control it.

But wasn't magic the reason Quin was alive? Wasn't it why they had *both* survived?

No, she concluded. They survived because she'd listened to her instinct and intuition, not her magic.

What if they were one and the same?

Quin smiled. "According to legend, you're descended from a god. Don't tell me you haven't thought about how much untapped power you have inside of you."

"Power is useless unless you know how to control it."

"You *do* know how." He cupped his hand over hers.

She stared at his bare skin against her bare skin. In seventeen years, she had never held a boy's hand. In Glas Ddir such a thing was treason. Her body thrilled to his touch. Was it because her skin had always been sheathed in gloves? Or was there something special about Quin's flesh against hers, some alchemy of chemistry and desire?

His fingertips were warm.

"You don't hate me anymore," she said.

"I've never hated you. Not even for a second."

A sulfyr stick winked to life in her brain. She'd guessed—correctly—that her body was intimately attuned to the bodies of others. The prince's chilly fingers, his frozen gales.

Quin's words to his parents the night before the wedding came back to her: *She is dangerous. You won't deny it.*

She had correlated the temperature to the wrong emotion. The constant frostbite she'd felt in Quin's presence wasn't hatred.

It was fear.

"You've been afraid of me," she said slowly.

"Yes. But not anymore."

He brought her hand to his lips. His mouth was both soft and scorching as he kissed each fingertip. She wondered if, when he removed his hand, he would leave five small craters.

"I've wanted to do this forever," he murmured. "Ever since you came to the Kaer. I dreamed about peeling off your gloves. I was dying to know what your hands looked like. They're even more beautiful than I imagined."

Mia went cold with fear. Was she enthralling him?

She pulled back. "How do you know I'm not . . ."

Before she could finish her thought, her eyes caught movement beneath them.

A village spilled onto the uneven red rocks, shapes and colors bustling on the shores of the blue lake.

They had made it to Refúj.

Chapter 33

A LITTLE HEAD MAGIC

THE FIRST THING MIA noticed when the balloon touched down was that the earth was softer than she'd imagined. A good thing, too, since her landing skills left much to be desired.

The balloon smashed into the ground, the bucket tipping, and Quin slammed into her, the two of them nearly pitching over the side as they clutched whatever they could get their hands on, which happened to be each other.

Mia realized they were not alone.

A group of girls stood in a circle, watching them.

Their hair was coiled into intricate puffs and twists, their skin fawn and mahogany and black as onyx, their arms gloveless. Some wore long, loose-fitting linens dyed white and tan; others wore smart trousers cropped at the shin.

"Tie her up," said an older woman with glossy black hair wrapped in a brilliant purple scarf. Mia flinched as a curvy girl with jewels in her nose stepped forward. But the girl reached for the balloon, not Mia. She grabbed the rope and tethered it to a metal hoop in the ground. The balloon listed once more, then stilled.

The girls did not offer to help as Quin and Mia disembarked. They hefted themselves out of the bucket and onto the ground, their feet sinking pleasingly into the earth. The igneous rock of the volqano had been crushed and pulverized, a million years of chaos resulting in a bank of soft red sand.

"Bhenvenj Refúj." The woman's voice was richly accented as she waved them forward. "Come, come. Please make yourself a home."

Mia had never been greeted in such a way. *Please make yourself a home.*

The woman in purple didn't seem particularly interested in them. She was already instructing the girls to repack the torches with kindling.

"I'm sorry," Mia said. "We're not quite sure where to . . ."

"Refúj."

"But shouldn't we . . ."

The woman muttered something in a language Mia didn't understand. She gestured to the right. "The merqad! Go, go."

She seemed eager to get rid of them. Mia and Quin, bewildered, plodded off in the direction she had pointed.

Strange-looking trees flanked the path, a genus Mia didn't recognize. Unlike the graceful swyn, these were shorter, gnarled, and dappled with gray spots, like the hands of an old witch.

Mia heard the low hum of voices ahead. They'd seen movement on the lakeshore as they descended, a diorama of commotion and wheeling dots of color. Now she spotted a yellow tent flap rippling in the breeze.

"My Fojuen is abysmal," Quin said, "but I take it *merqad* means 'market'?"

Mia nodded. As the footpath opened onto a small sandy circle ringed with food stalls, she expected to see something akin to the dull river markets she was used to—and she found nothing of the sort.

The merqad was an explosion of scents and colors. Roasted meat, sweet wine, tangy fruit juices, bitter teas, and freshly baked bread spiced the air. Rows of orange and yellow tents leaned into one another, stalls cobbled together out of tarps and timber, as girls in bright leggings, trousers, and long flowing skirts spun down the avenues. A girl of twelve or thirteen sped by in a three-wheeled wicker chair, racing a group of her friends. She laughed as she shot past them, her brown forehead shining from exertion as she twisted the hand crank, her dark umber skin luminous with sweat and happiness.

A brood of fat chickens burst out of a tent, clucking as they scampered across Mia's feet. She jumped back, startled, and knocked into a trio of older girls who had gathered a few feet away. They giggled and whispered something to each other. Were they looking at Quin?

He was looking at them, too. Mia felt a twinge of jealousy.

"Come on." She grabbed his arm, sticky-warm heat radiating off his skin. That was one emotion she knew she had correlated correctly: desire was hot.

"Look at that." Quin licked his lips. "Is that not the most beautiful thing you've ever seen?"

The prince was staring at a gigantic bird leg roasting on a spit.

Mia was experiencing her own kind of hunger. She was still tired from healing the prince, bone weary from her run up the mountain, and faint from her leap into the waterfall—or at least, she *should* have been these things. But ever since she'd drawn herself out of the Salted Sea, a warm bliss had cocooned her. She couldn't explain it. For once, she didn't want to.

Mia the Scientist slapped Mia the Gwyrach on the cheek. Warm bliss was treacherous. So was not being able to explain a bodily sensation. And wasn't it all a little too good to be true? Her mother's map led them to exactly the right Fojuen island, where a red balloon led them to safe haven, otherwise known as Refúj. If she still had any good sense, she'd say they were being lured into a trap.

But it didn't feel like a trap. That was the thing. This didn't make her skin crawl the way she'd felt as they wandered into Tristan's lair in the forest.

It felt like coming home.

"Quin?" She'd lost him. "Quin!"

She spotted him a ways down the avenue, moving slowly toward the turkey leg. A circle of women knitting yarn in dazzling colors clucked as he walked past. The prince was definitely attracting attention, and Mia wasn't sure how concerned she should be. Was he safe here? Was *she*?

"Quin!" she hissed, but he either didn't hear or pretended not to. At every stall he passed, girls stopped and stared. Mia had a revelation.

She'd yet to see a single man.

Was that possible? In the river markets she'd been to with her mother, Glasddiran women were always escorted by a man. "To keep the good women of the river kingdom safe," claimed King Ronan.

But the merqad in Refúj was only girls and women, and everyone seemed perfectly safe. Mia's instincts were warring with her reason, blood pooling in her toes, leading her to something, or someone, she was sure of it.

"Veraktu."

She felt a sharp tug and spun around. A stooped older woman had Mia's shirt balled up in her bare fist. Her puffy silver twists were gathered into a knot, her skin a rich, weathered sepia, creased like a piece of parchment paper lovingly folded and unfolded over many years. Her face told a story.

The old woman was agitated. "T'eu veraktu," she said.

T'eu meant "you are" in Fojuen, but Mia didn't recognize the other word. She'd always excelled at language studies; she hated not knowing the answer.

"Nanu!" The girl who had won the race wheeled up to them, maneuvering her low, triangular wicker chair with a mechanical hand crank. The victory sweat had furled her fine black curls into a puffed halo at her hairline; she reached up to smooth the edges. The girl's large brown eyes regarded the old woman with both love and frustration.

"You slipped away from me again, Nanu. Are you causing trouble?"

She began prying the woman's fingers from Mia's shirt. "I'm sorry. This happens sometimes—my grandmother gets agitated. I promise she doesn't mean anything by it."

The girl peered up at Mia for the first time. A smile broke over her face.

"Mia Rose!"

She couldn't believe it. This was Sach'a, Dom's baby sister. Mia hadn't seen the twins since they were nine years old, not since their mother packed them up and fled the river kingdom overnight.

Mia was astonished by how much the girl had grown in three years. She was virtually unrecognizable. Sach'a carried herself with the poise and gravitas of a young woman.

"Mamãe is going to be so happy to see you . . ."

Nanu wheezed and mumbled incoherent words. Sach'a sighed. "Forgive me, Mia. This will only take a minute." She pulled her grandmother's face down close to hers and cupped her hands around the old woman's skull, digging her thumbs into the cavities of her brow bone.

The air around them rippled. Mia felt two pocks of pressure behind her own brow; an echo of the girls' thumbprints on her ethmoid, the bone bridging nose and cranium.

When Mia found her breath, she gaped at Nanu. The woman was serene, her mouth still, a faint smile on her lips. She uncrooked her back and patted her granddaughter affectionately on the head.

Sach'a nodded, pleased. "Sorry about that," she said to Mia. "She just gets confused. But once I calm the nerves in her brain, she's the sweetest thing in the world."

Mia's world was spinning. "How did you do that?"

"That? It's just a little head magic. Unblooding for the brain. Mamãe says no Dujia my age can do it." She sat a little taller in her chair. "But I can."

Since when did Sach'a have magic?

"Mia!" Quin reappeared holding two roasted bird legs. He held one out to her. "Hungry?"

"How did you get those?"

"I bartered."

"With what? Don't say gold buttons."

From the look on his face, the answer was definitely gold buttons.

Sach'a looked up at Quin, then Mia, then back at Quin. She dipped her head respectfully. "Your Grace."

Even disheveled and half frostbitten after a week in the woods, bereft of his gold buttons and regal pout, Quin looked every bit a prince.

"Are we safe here, Sach'a?" Mia asked.

"*You* are," she said to Mia. She sized up Quin, started to say something, then stopped. "It's just, you're the first Glasddiran man I've seen in three years, Your Grace. We're not exactly . . ."

She fiddled with the crank on her chair, then sighed. "Why don't you both come with me? I'll take you to Mamãe."

Chapter 34

FORBIDDEN

WITH HER GRANDMOTHER SHUFFLING alongside them, Sach'a led them through the merqad, where Mia saw all the things she'd missed.

She saw a fair-skinned woman in a crisp, unstained apron, wheat-colored hair swept into a loose bun. The woman drew a bird from a wooden crate and placed it on a butcher block. Instead of wringing its neck, she laid her pale, unfreckled hands over its heart. Without a sound or a single flap of its wings, the bird stilled.

She saw a little girl with thin beaded braids crying over a skinned knee, the blood oozing dark from the fresh wound, until a stout woman with mellow gold skin and a kind face placed a hand on the girl's kneecap and her sobs turned to hiccups. When the woman wiped off the old blood, the girl didn't even wince. Her knee was healed, copper skin glowing warm and unbroken, as if kissed by a forgiving sun.

Was *everyone* here a Gwyrach?

Mia oscillated wildly between euphoria and shock. Years of lies—*Gwyrach never use their powers to heal, Gwyrach are demons who enjoy causing suffering and pain*—were toppled in an instant. The merqad was flooded with light and laughter and music. In the distance, Mia heard the airy strand of a viol blending with a girl's silvery voice. Everyone seemed happy and joyous, with the exception of the woman who had killed the bird. Her face was solemn and respectful.

The more women Mia saw, the more she felt she somehow knew them, as if an invisible thread bound them all together. She saw mothers, daughters, sisters, lovers, and friends, as vibrant as they were different—young and old, fat and skinny, beautiful and ugly, and a hundred variations in between.

But what struck her most were their hands.

Growing up in Glas Ddir, she had only ever seen three pairs of hands without gloves: her mother's, her sister's, and her own. Here in Refúj, every woman's hands were bare. Mia saw a profusion of freckles, moles, birthmarks, and scars set against backdrops of warm russet brown, milky white, pale bronze, and glimmering ebony. She saw long, curling fingernails and nails trimmed short; palms thatched with lines and creases; light ink etched on dark skin, dark ink etched on light skin. She saw women with their

227

fingers laced together or their arms linked, and in one corner stall, two girls stood with their bodies pressed close, raking hungry hands through each other's sleek raven tresses as they kissed.

And it wasn't just the hands. Women sported silky straight locks, coarse black plaits, blond ringlets, and shaved heads—an abundance of hair coiffed, curled, and shorn. Everyone was draped in a dizzying array of fabrics, cuts and styles Mia had never seen in Glas Ddir, and as she pushed through throngs of girls, her ears drank in the sweet cacophony of languages.

"I dreamed of a place like this," she said, remembering. During the wedding, Mia had stood in the Royal Chapel and seen these colors, heard these sounds, inhabited this place. She'd just never expected it to be filled with Gwyrach.

"I couldn't have dreamed up a place like this in a million years," Quin said. "And I have an active imagination."

Mia knew what he meant. She had never imagined so many rich cultures melding together in one place. For the first time she understood the true cost of King Ronan's policies: he had drained the river kingdom of the energy and life that once flowed through it, like a body drained of blood.

"When your father closed the borders," she said, "he didn't just erase these places from our maps. He erased them from our minds."

The sound of singing grew louder. At the end of the avenue, they passed a flapping flag with a midnight-blue bird rising from red flames. *Phénix Blu*, it said. "The Blue Phoenix." Behind the flag stood a hearty three-walled tavern where women sat in chairs and reclined in the scarlet sand. The patrons sang heartily around a roaring fire, holding pints and squat glasses of a drink Mia couldn't identify, an amber liquid speckled red. They all seemed to know the song by heart, even as the words slurred together. Intermingled with the women were three men and a couple of boys; the first males Mia had seen in Refúj. She found it jarring.

She almost laughed. How was it the presence of *men* jarred her, but not the Gwyrach? Amazing how quickly she had adjusted. Alarming too. And yet, if she stayed grounded in her body, she felt no alarm. Only curiosity—and a quiet giddiness building slowly in her sternum.

"But I don't understand," Mia asked Sach'a. "Do all these women have magic?"

"Most of them, yes. The ones who don't have magic came here with someone who did."

"What about the men?"

Sach'a laughed. "Men are not prohibited in Refúj. But they must come here with their Dujia mothers or sisters or wives. They must be deemed safe."

"Dujia is what you call Gwyrach?"

"*Shh!*" Sach'a lowered her voice. "You can't say that word. We're not demons. Not here."

Mia made a mental note. "But what does that mean for Quin? He's not strictly my husband, and . . ." She turned and blinked at the empty space beside her. She'd lost him again.

"Quin?"

She pivoted and saw him peering into the Blue Phoenix,

229

transfixed, holding a forgotten bird leg in each hand. When he saw her, he straightened.

"Sorry," he said, rushing to catch up. For a boy surrounded by a village of Gwyrach, he was remarkably unruffled. Before she could ask what he'd been so mesmerized by in the tavern, he said to Sach'a, "This meat is delicious. I think it's the best I've ever had."

She smiled with pleasure. "It ought to be. When you kill an animal with violence, the fear toughens and spoils the flesh. A terrified beast will always produce inferior meat. A creature killed with magic dies a peaceable death. It never feels fear."

Mia had trouble parsing her words. Magic as an act of mercy? Yet another lie debunked: her books had failed to mention a Gwyrach could use magic as a way to make death *less* painful.

"Here. You should eat." Quin tried again to give her the second roasted leg, and this time she accepted. She took a small bite and had to agree; the meat was succulent and sweet.

"I didn't know turkey could taste this good."

"Actually," Sach'a said, "it's swan."

Mia choked. All she could see was her sister's angelic face as their mother braided her strawberry hair. *Angie, my little swan.*

"You know, I'm not actually that hungry," she said. Quin happily swooped in to take the bird.

And then, for the first time since arriving in Refúj, Mia saw something that scared her.

A girl was throwing a tantrum. She was no older than four, with flaxen pigtails, porcelain rose skin, and cherry-pout lips. She stood behind a stall stacked high with iced loaves and teacakes, tugging at her mother's skirts and screaming so loudly flecks of spit flew from her mouth. The woman shouted something in a language Mia didn't understand. Then she snatched her daughter up by the wrist. Instantly the girl went quiet.

Uneasy, Mia turned to Sach'a. "What did that woman just do?"

"What woman? I didn't see."

"She took that little girl's wrist and . . ." Mia stopped. "I don't know. She got very quiet."

"Probably just unblooded her," Sach'a said breezily. "It's not *strictly* forbidden—it doesn't quite break any of the Three Laws, though you could make a case for it. My mother does it to my sister sometimes. It's the only way to calm her down when she goes feral."

"You said that word earlier: *unblood*. What does it mean?"

"Exactly what you think." She wheeled her chair a little faster. "Mamãe will explain everything far better than I can, I promise."

Despite the buttery sunshine on her arms and shoulders, Mia shivered. She shot a glance at Quin and felt a chill growing beneath her skin. Despite his apparent nonchalance, maybe he *was* afraid. He was, after all, gifted in the art of pretending.

She dropped a short distance behind Sach'a and said to Quin, "Everything all right?"

"The swan is excellent. Very toothsome."

"Are you frightened?"

He shrugged. "No."

She heard a strange sound, almost like a whoosh of water.

231

She'd heard that sound before. Quin's blood was pressing against his arterial walls with greater force. This time she could intuit what it meant.

"You're lying," she said.

He reddened. "I'm not."

"You are." She heard the slosh again. "I can *hear* you."

"That's impressive," Sach'a said over her shoulder. "It takes most Dujia years to be able to hear a lie. I can't do it myself. I wish I could."

Pride flashed in Mia's chest. She could do advanced magic. She had talent. But no sooner had she thought it than she felt a tremor of shame. Being in this strange, beautiful place—it was eroding her logic. She forced herself to remember what the mother had done to her little girl. A Gwyrach could silence and subdue another human being. That kind of power was not something to be proud of.

"Here we are," Sach'a said. "Home at last."

She had led them to a row of cottages dotting the edge of the lake. Mia could see the red island in the middle of the water, humpbacked like a living creature, pulsing with energy. She felt drawn to it in a way she couldn't explain. But it felt forbidden, too, a ripe red apple lacquered with poison.

"That one's us." Sach'a nodded toward a cottage the exact color of the lake, as if the water had sloshed over the sides of the crater and slathered the walls blue.

And there, in the doorway, stood Lauriel du Zol. Her mother's best friend.

Lauriel had always had a tremendous presence, large in both voice and stature, a boundless fount of energy as big as her glorious crown of black corkscrew curls that danced every time she laughed. It hurt Mia to see her. The du Zols had been a fixture of her childhood in Ilwysion, their cozy kitchen and warm, easy jokes. Seeing Lauriel brought back a happier time, before everything went wrong. Just days after Mia's mother had vanished from her life, Lauriel had vanished, too.

"Mia. Darling one." Mia felt comforted by the way Lauriel said her name, the soft-mouthed *M* and honeyed vowels. The big woman bundled her into a crushing hug and kissed first one cheek, then the other.

"Bhenvenj. You are most welcome here. Vuqa. Come, come." When she finally released her, Mia saw her eyes were shining. Lauriel wiped a tear off her glistening brown cheek. "Your mother would be so happy. She used to dream you would come to Fojo Karação someday and see the world she had fallen in love with. I only wish she could be here to see it."

The truth coiling through Mia for days finally settled in the pit of her stomach. She knew the answer before she even asked the question, but only now did it materialize in clear strokes, like ink drying on a page.

She took a breath. "Did my mother have magic?"

"Oh, darling. Your mother had mountains of magic. In our sisterhood, she was a powerful Dujia, a gifted Dujia." Lauriel touched her cheek. "As are you."

Chapter 35

MURDEROUS ANGELS

MIA SAT AT A small wood table with Lauriel, Quin, and the twins, devouring a savory breakfast. She ached for the journal—she wanted to wrap her arms around it, squeeze out every last drop of truth her mother had concealed for so many years. She understood nothing: about her mother, about magic, about the world.

But the kitchen was warm. Days of fear and exhaustion melted from her pores. In spite of everything, she could feel her heart opening like a flower to the sun. If she closed her eyes, gave herself over to the clank of forks and aromas of fire-cooked food, she could pretend she was at home, sitting around their kitchen table, her father stealing kisses from her mother while the bread dough rose. The one benefit of her raging headache was that it obliterated all possibility of scientific conjecture. She was forced to live in her body, to let the morning wash over her, a medley of simple pleasures, not least among them: eating real food again.

"How's the minha zopa?" Lauriel asked.

Mia nudged her bowl forward, and Lauriel smiled and spooned out another generous helping. "A Fojuen classic. Pork chouriço, grilled onions, roasted tomatoes, and straw-fried potatoes seasoned with garlic and wine."

Lauriel had prepared them a magnificent feast: in addition to the minha zopa, there was crusty bread hot from the oven, pats of yellow butter and zanaba jam, soft crumbling cheeses, fresh-grilled cod with green chilies and tiger milk, sautéed mustard greens, peppery chicken baked in hot ash, and a sweet liquid made from roasted corn. Lauriel proudly named the dishes as she set them on the table, hot steam snaking up from each plate.

Mia's taste buds were in ecstasy. A rawboned hunger poured through her, and with every bite she took, she felt her body replenish. Her mother had tried many times to cook her favorite Fojuen recipes for their family, but she could never get them quite right. It was next to impossible to find the right ingredients and spices in Glas Ddir, she said, after King Ronan closed the borders.

Now, sitting in Lauriel's cozy kitchen, Mia knew she was eating authentic Fojuen cuisine for the first time. The tangs and flavors flooded her mouth. She thought of all the mornings she had spent with the du Zols, comfortably ensconced in their sunny kitchen in Ilwysion, her mother looking as happy as she ever had.

"There's more of everything, darling," Lauriel said, tapping a scooped spoon against a giant saucepan. Above the stove, long ropes of garlic swung from the wood beams, next to iron and copper pots forged by Lauriel's own hand. Beneath them a row of orange baked-earth pots sprouted robust plants and herbs. There were no walls in the kitchen; it opened onto the rest of the modest cottage. Through the back door, Mia spotted plump red tomatoes growing on a vine.

"Do you like the fish, Your Grace?" Sach'a stared hopefully at the prince. "I helped make it."

Mia waited for Quin to express his usual food euphoria, but he'd been quiet and withdrawn ever since arriving at the cottage.

"He loves it," she answered for him. "Quin adores fish."

"Good," Lauriel said. "We haul a fresh catch from the lake every morning."

Junay rolled her eyes. "If I have to eat one more fish, I will bury its carcass in a part of this house none of you will ever find."

Junay, the other twin, had retained every bit of fire Mia remembered from three years ago. Sach'a was charming and poised, with a carefully controlled maturity; Junay was volatile and righteous. The girls shared their father's dark umber complexion—Dom favored their mother, with his warm ochre skin—but that was where the resemblance stopped. Even the twins' hair was a testament to their warring personalities: thick, spirited corkscrews bounced off Junay's shoulders, while her sister sat primly in her wicker chair, smoothing sweet almond oil into her scalp.

"If you buried a fish in your own house," Sach'a said calmly, "then you would have to smell it, too."

"Thank you," Junay snapped. "I'm so glad I have a sister who knows everything." She turned her attention to Mia. "How come you didn't know your mother was a Dujia?"

"Duj!" Lauriel scolded. "Junay!"

"What, Mamãe? I want to know." She turned back to Mia, undeterred. "Weren't there signs? Things that didn't add up? Surely you wondered."

Mia was taken aback. "She never talked about her past, I guess. I knew she had secrets, but I never thought . . ." She trailed off, feeling like a failure of a daughter to miss such an obvious part of her mother's life. Not to mention a bad scientist: she had ignored every clue.

"I . . . I knew she'd studied medicine in Fojo Karação. That she traveled to the river towns in Ilwysion and Killian Village to help people who were sick or dying."

Junay groaned. "She didn't come here to study medicine! She came to study magic. Did you never wonder why so many of those sick people recovered?"

Mia opened her mouth but no words came out. Her mother had healed people with magic. Of course she had. A twelve-year-old knew more than she did.

"Junay." Lauriel placed a firm hand on the table. "You are being relentless. Mia has just arrived after a long journey. Can you leave her in peace?"

"Fine." She folded her arms, then unfolded them. "You really didn't know? That just seems hard to believe."

"My father led the Circle of the Hunt! How could my mother have had magic? The Gwyrach were demons. They were ruthless and inhuman."

She saw Lauriel glance at both her daughters.

"I'm sorry," Mia said quickly. "I didn't mean . . ."

Lauriel waved a hand. "I imagine you've had many surprises on your journey, and not all of them pleasant."

"Including when Nanu grabbed her in the merqad and called her a veraktu," Sach'a said. They all turned to look at the old woman, who was now knitting passively, no threat to anyone. She wheezed.

Lauriel turned to Junay. "It was your day to watch her, Jun."

"I watched her yesterday!"

"And I watched her the five days before that," Sach'a said quietly. "Did you give her her medicine?"

"She didn't need it," Junay fumed. "She's *fine.*"

"Her medicine is for when she gets confused?" Mia asked.

Lauriel shook her head. She stood and began plucking leaves from the herb pots. "Our bodies and minds fail us as we age, even Dujia. *Especially* Dujia. It's as if our magic erodes our shells more quickly." She stuffed the leaves into a speckled stone mortar and ground them with a pestle. "Nanu's mind disturbs her, but her lungs give her trouble, too. They are not what they once were. Sometimes the air becomes trapped and she has trouble breathing."

Lauriel sprinkled the herb powder into a dented copper cup

and poured in a stream of steaming purple liquid. When Nanu wheezed again, she fitted the cup into her wrinkled brown hands.

"Drink, Mamãe. This will smooth your breath."

As the old woman sipped at the broth, Mia said, "Why can't you use magic to heal her lungs?"

Lauriel smiled. "It's not as if we lay our hands on someone and heal all their ailments forever. We heal them in small ways every day. But magic is reactive, not preventative. By the time we are forced to use magic to intervene, it is often too late." She patted her mother's knee. "So we take what precautions we can. And when it becomes necessary to use our magic, we do so."

"I used head magic on Nanu today," Sach'a said proudly, "after she called Mia a veraktu."

"What is a veraktu?" Mia asked.

"It's nothing," Junay sniffed. "Just a Dujia who's in denial. A Dujia who's ashamed of being Dujia because she's been fed lies her whole life and sucked them down like jelly." She smiled brightly. "Can I do something with your hair?"

Helpless against the girl's mood swings, Mia nodded. Junay clapped her hands and bounded off to the loft upstairs.

"Forgive her," Lauriel said. "She hasn't bloomed yet. Her sister has, and . . . well. As you might imagine, this house is something of a war zone. To have one Dujia daughter and her unbloomed twin is a nightmare no parent should have to endure."

Mia had so many questions. What did it mean to "bloom"? Was that when the dormant magic in a Gwyrach's body manifested? And where was Domeniq? She tried to imagine masculine, strapping Dom in a village overflowing with demon women. The thought amused her. She supposed he'd had good training for it, growing up in a house with three women.

Considering the way all the girls in the merqad had gaped at the prince, Dom was probably very popular.

Mia snuck a peek at Quin. He was chasing a piece of cheese around the plate with his fork. He felt her eyes on him, looked up, and tried to force a smile. She knew she should ask Lauriel if the prince was safe. But if the answer was no, did that mean she'd have to leave Refúj? Selfishly, she didn't want to. Sitting here with Lauriel, learning about magic, she felt closer to her mother than she had in years.

"Does *Dujia* mean 'demon' in Fojuen?" she asked.

"Duj, no! A Dujia is a creature of the divine. The Dujia are a sisterhood."

"So here in Fojo, Gwyrach are creatures of the divine?"

"My darling, *everywhere* we are creatures of the divine. Duj katt," she swore. "Did your mother teach you nothing?"

Mia switched into translation mode. "*Duj katt* means 'four gods'?"

Lauriel tipped her head back and let out a full, throaty laugh, her black curls dancing merrily. "Heavens no. *Duj* means goddess! Not god. Never god. We are Dujia, descendants of the goddesses. In the river kingdom, they call us demons, but here in the fire kingdom, we go by our true name." Her eyes glittered. "We are angels. A sisterhood of angels descended from the Four Great Goddesses who gave birth to the four lands."

"She won't say four *king*doms," Sach'a explained, "because she doesn't believe in kings."

"Kings are just men in paper hats." Lauriel gestured toward the prince. "It just so happens that sometimes the paper is made of gold."

"Gold crowns can be perfectly lovely," Sach'a added, smiling shyly at Quin.

From upstairs Junay yelled, "Not when they're worn by the king of Glas Ddir!"

Quin shifted uncomfortably in his chair.

Seeing him like this, taciturn and reserved, reminded Mia of the prince she'd known in the castle. She felt more at home with the du Zols than she'd felt in ages, but she imagined he felt the opposite. As unhappy as he was in Kaer Killian, he did have power there; in Refúj he was powerless. Was he frightened? She listened for the rhythm of his pulse, but she couldn't hear it.

Come to think of it, she couldn't hear *anyone's* pulse. Not even her own.

The absence of sensation unsettled her. She'd only been aware of her magic for a week, but already it had animated her blood and made it sing. The headaches were atrocious—she could do without those—but she had swiftly acclimated to the symphony of other heartbeats, the sweet harmony or discordant notes. Not hearing them now, engulfed in silence; it was lonely.

"I can't feel anything," she said.

"Of course you can't." Junay bounded back in holding a comb with heavy iron teeth. Mia flinched as Jun reached out her hand—other than her mother and sister, no woman had ever touched her hair without wearing gloves.

"For someone with curly hair," Junay said, "you should really take better care of it." She yanked the comb through her tangles so hard Mia cried out.

"Duj! Junay!" her mother reprimanded.

"What? You always told us sometimes beauty hurts." She inflicted more brutalities on Mia's scalp. "You can't feel our pulse because of the uzoolion."

She pointed at the doorway, and for the first time Mia noticed the border of blue stones: the same cerulean stone Dom wore around his neck. They continued past the doorframe and onto the floor, where they ringed the entire cottage in an unbroken line. There must have been thousands of stones pressed into the earth.

"It's a boundary," Sach'a explained. "To keep us safe."

Mia got up from her chair—to the consternation of Junay—and stooped over the uzoolion. She ran a finger down the line of smooth blue stones and felt nothing. But that was just it. She felt *nothing*. Every time she'd touched her mother's ruby wren, it ignited her blood, shook her to life. But when her fingers grazed the uzoolion, it was as if her blood had struck a wall.

"*Uzool* means 'water,'" Mia murmured. She was stitching together a new theory: fojuen catalyzed magic, while uzoolion impeded it.

"We have a family rule," Lauriel said. "No magic in the house. That way we can trust our own bodies, our own hearts."

242

"Which means if someone is being obnoxious in this house," Sach'a said, "it's because they're obnoxious." She looked pointedly at her sister.

"Certain stones come with certain potencies," Lauriel went on. "They can enhance or diminish magic. Some stones can even store it up. Fojuen is born in the vibrant, thrashing heart of a volqano. When Dujia wear the red glass, it amplifies their magic. It makes the heart pump faster and the blood flow quicker. If a Dujia has not yet bloomed, fojuen can usher the magic in more swiftly."

So Mia's theory was correct. Now she understood why, when she pressed the ruby wren to her chest, she'd experienced all manner of side effects, from headaches to heart palpitations to full-on fainting. It was no coincidence she had first enthralled Quin the same night she received her mother's book—and the fojuen key that went with it. The little ruby wren was powerful.

"And uzoolion does the opposite," Mia murmured.

Lauriel nodded. "Uzoolion weakens a Dujia's magic. With enough of it"—she gestured to the stones trimming the cottage floor—"you can block magic entirely. If we wear uzoolion, we cannot be controlled by any Dujia who would seek to hurt us. Even a man who wears the stone can sense the presence of magic. A quiet *tap, tap, tap.*"

"I'm guessing this is why Dom wears uzoolion around his neck."

"We all do." Lauriel pulled a blue amulet from her blouse. "It keeps us safe."

"Lauriel?" Mia's voice was small. "Why wasn't my mother wearing uzoolion the day she died?"

The room went very still. Even Junay was quiet.

"Darling, I don't know." Lauriel's shoulders sagged. "I've asked myself that many times. If Wynna was with someone she trusted . . . someone whose magic brought her pleasure . . . someone she *wanted* to touch her . . ."

"Someone she loved," Mia finished.

Lauriel wouldn't meet her eye. Mia thought of all the evenings her mother had spent with Lauriel on the balcony of their cottage, talking, laughing, sipping blackthorn wine, and taking nips of the stronger spirits they smuggled in from Fojo. For the first time, a smoky coil of doubt ringed itself around her thoughts. She knew Wynna and Lauriel were best friends, but what if their relationship was something more?

"I did love your mother," Lauriel said, as if she could read Mia's thoughts. "But only as a friend. I was not the angel Wynna loved."

Mia's heart beat so hard it threatened to crack her sternum. The theory she'd hatched in the Twisted Forest was rekindling. "But you're saying she did love someone. Someone who had magic."

Lauriel stood and wiped her hands on her apron. Her curls were no longer dancing. "I've said too much."

"Lauriel. Please. I've been searching for the Gwyr . . . the *Dujia* who killed my mother for the last three years. The journal was spurring me onward, leading me to this place. That can't be a coincidence. If the woman who killed her is here . . . if she's in Refúj . . ."

They stared at each other. Mia didn't like not being able to sense the people around her; she couldn't tell if Lauriel was lying. She couldn't tell what *anyone* was feeling, not even herself.

"Duj katt." Junay pinched the cod by the bony tail, lifted it into the air, and dropped it onto the plate with a slimy slap. "Who needs to hide a dead fish? The secrets in this house already stink."

Lauriel shot her a warning look. "*Junay.*"

"*Mamãe,*" she mimicked. "She deserves to know! If *you* died, wouldn't I deserve to know who killed you?"

She turned back to Mia. "I don't know who did it, but I know who will. Ask Zaga. She knows everything. She probably has a whole roster of murderous angels in her secret cave." Off Mia's blank look, she added, "Go find my brother down at the lake. He'd be happy to take you to Zaga."

"Why are you doing this, Jun?" Sach'a murmured.

Junay smiled beatifically at her twin. "Watch out for those obnoxious ones, Sach. We're even more obnoxious when we tell the truth."

Chapter 36

MEANT FOR YOU

THE PATH TO THE lake was a carpet of soft red sand, studded with low, dry brush. Mia felt better once she was beyond the reach of the uzoolion. As the sun sweated in the morning sky, her blood was making music inside her again.

Lauriel had pleaded with her not to go—"not yet, not until you're ready"—but the moment Junay had given her a destination, they all knew there would be no debate. Mia had pushed her chair back from the table and left without another word.

"Mia?" Quin easily caught up to her on his long legs. "Do you really think this is a good choice?"

"Good or not, it's the choice I'm making."

"Where's the logical girl I met in the woods? The one who

needs a theory for everything? I've never known you to be so . . . instinctual."

"You've never really known me at all."

He stepped in front of her, blocking the path. "Can we at least talk about this? You're not just putting your own life in jeopardy . . ."

"Move."

". . . you're risking mine."

She felt the icy blade of his fear, but she shoved it aside. He wasn't going to ruin this for her. She had not worked this hard and come this far to have the prince stand in her way.

"I said, *move.*"

She pushed him aside and walked on.

The lake was a pebble in the pocket of a volqano, the water as still and silent as a blue plate. As Mia approached the shoreline, her skin tingled, a fibrous heat pulsing through her. Her theory was that it had something to do with the red island. The fojuen stone was spiking heat and sensation in her blood, summoning her forward in a silent incantation.

"Can I see what's in your pocket?" Quin called out from behind her. When she didn't move, he added, "I know you saved the arrowhead you pulled out of my chest."

She kept underestimating the prince; he was shrewder than she gave him credit for. Grudgingly she extracted the sliver and handed it over.

"Interesting." He held the stone high, framing it against the volqanoes in the distance. Then he bent and scooped up a handful of red sand, letting it sieve through his fingers. "Considering I've never seen this volqanic rock in Glas Ddir, it would appear my would-be assassin is also from Fojo. The safe haven you promised might not actually be all that safe."

"There are hundreds of islands in the Salted Sea," Mia shot back. "The chances that your assassin is from this island are exceedingly slim."

"So were the chances that I'd survive an arrow in the chest. Or that we'd survive the jump from the waterfall. Or that I've been in Refúj for hours and no one's tried to kill me yet." He tapped the arrowhead against his palm. "You and I seem to do well with exceedingly slim."

Quin ran a hand through his tousled golden curls. "I understand those are your friends back there, and they seem like lovely people. But how well do *you* know them? Did you know they had magic?"

He had a point.

"She said kings are just men with paper crowns," he went on. "And in a funny way, I think she's right. Maybe she's right about the Dujia part, too."

Mia folded her arms over her chest, amused. "You don't believe in gods, but now you believe in goddesses?"

"All I'm saying is that I don't blame them for mistrusting my family. My father treats magicians as less than human. But I'm not my father. I told you as long as we were headed in the opposite direction of my assassin, I wouldn't complain. But if we are in fact moving *toward* my assassin . . ." He sighed. "I know you want to find who killed your mother. If my mother died, I'd want the same. But if I'm about to walk the plank, I'd at least like to know if you're with me or against me."

"With you," she said instinctively. She meant it.

"Well, look at that," said a sharp voice behind them. "If it isn't the royals."

Mia whirled around to see a girl with her arms folded tightly across her chest. Her face was bold, her jaw angular, and though she was short, her body was compact and ready to spring. She looked oddly familiar. She was about Mia's age, maybe a year or two older, and there was something similar about their faces, though this girl had darker skin, a tawny amber Mia had rarely seen in Glas Ddir. She wore her jet-black hair cut sharply at the chin, and her eyes were brown instead of gray—thinner than Mia's, but just as thirsty.

Mia noticed something else, too: the quiver of arrows strapped to her back.

"Dom!" the girl called over her shoulder. "Your friend is here."

Domeniq du Zol heaved a small fishing boat onto the shore. He jogged up to them, brushed the sand off his trousers, and flashed his crooked smile.

"Mia! You made it!" He wrapped her up in a bear hug, much like his mother. When he finally let her go, he held her at arm's length. "Took you long enough. I would have expected a little better showing from my sparring partner."

Dom always knew how to push Mia's buttons; he'd been there

all of five seconds and already her competitive spirit was flaring.

"How long have *you* been here?" she said.

"Days! I gave you the boat—you're welcome—but I couldn't row it for you." He tipped his head toward the prince and grinned. "Your Grace."

The girl was eyeing them. "Mia Rose, the girl who hunts Dujia. The girl who *is* a Dujia." Casually she pulled an arrow out of her quiver and used the tip of the arrowhead to clean the dirt from under her fingernails. "Seems like a conflict of interest to me."

Dom groaned. "You are awful at meeting new people." He turned to Quin and Mia. "This is Pilar. She doesn't do well with failure, which is why she's not keen on seeing the two of you."

"I prefer to air my own foul laundry, thanks," Pilar snapped.

Mia stared at the arrow in the girl's hand. The arrowhead was bright red. *Fojuen.* Her stomach squeezed to the size of a choke-cherry. Quin followed her eyes.

"It was you," he said slowly. "*You* shot me at the wedding."

Pilar didn't answer. She kicked at a rock and sent it splashing into the lake. Mia felt a cacophony of feelings and temperatures, visceral sensations so powerful she took a step back.

"That arrow was never meant for you, all right?" Pilar turned to Mia. "I was aiming for *you.*"

Chapter 37

SHIMMERING AND SLICED

Mia blinked in astonishment.

"Why in four hells would you want to kill *me*?"

Pilar slipped the arrow back into its quiver with an exaggerated sigh. "Do you really have to ask, Rose?"

"I'm asking, aren't I?"

"We couldn't let you marry the prince. You hated magicians. You wanted to purge dirty, dirty magic from the kingdom at all costs."

Pilar stooped down to pick up a smooth pebble and sent it skittering across the surface of the lake. It cut an elegant line of cones.

"You were going to be queen someday. We had it on good authority that you, Griffin Rose's daughter, would empower the

Circle of the Hunt to expand their campaign of hate. Thanks to your sorry excuse for a king, the Dujia still in Glas Ddir are constantly in danger. The last thing we need is a vengeful queen sitting on the river throne."

Mia turned to Dom. "Did you know about this?"

"I told them not to do it. I didn't think you deserved to die."

"Just like Tuk and Lyman didn't deserve to die?"

Her words hit their mark; Dom grew quiet. He lowered his eyes.

"They weren't bad men," he said. "They weren't good men, but they weren't bad."

"And yet you killed them."

"They knew who you were! I was trying to protect you."

"After your little friend here had already tried to kill me?" Mia fought to keep her voice calm. For years Dom had been playing both sides, pretending to be a Hunter while his true loyalty was to the Dujia. "I've known you my entire life!"

"Let's go back a moment," Quin said, "to where *you*"—he pointed at Pilar—"were trying to shoot *her*"—then at Mia—"and shot me instead."

Pilar groaned. "Not my fault! You did a funny little dance move and twirled her around. You got in the way. I wouldn't have missed otherwise. I'm a very good shot."

"Clearly you are not!" Quin pointed furiously at the scar above his heart. "I nearly died. *Twice.*"

"Well then. Aren't you lucky wifey had magic?"

Dom looked at Mia, then Pilar, then Quin. He ran a hand over the back of his head, rubbing his close-cropped hair.

"This is tense."

Mia turned to Pilar. "What do you mean, you 'had it on good authority'? *Whose* authority?"

She shrugged. "We had a spy in the castle. There were details— things you said about all Gwyrach being wicked demons, how evil and depraved we were. They said you twirled through the Hall of Hands, laughing and cursing all Gwyrach to the same gruesome fate."

"Who said that?" Mia's face was hot. "Your spy was wrong. I felt nothing but horror in the Hall of Hands. And I only wanted revenge on the Gwyrach who killed my mother. *Heart for a heart, life—*"

"I know the Hunters' Creed. But you wanted to empower the Circle to kill more of us. Can you deny it?" She cupped a hand- ful of air and lifted it high, miming a toast. "'To the Hunters! The true heroes of this feast! When I'm princess I'll give them coins and weapons and anything they need so they can kill every Gwyrach they find!' And so on."

Mia felt a crush of shame. She had said those words. The final feast in the Grand Gallery came rushing back, one moment in particular: the maid knocking into her shoulder, the correspond- ing dizziness and heat.

"*That's* how I know you. You're the clumsy scullery maid."

Mia saw the feast with new eyes. She assumed the dreadful royals were what had overwhelmed her senses, but Pilar had brushed up against her—Pilar who was preparing to kill her the next day. The heat Mia felt was a kindling of rage and murderous intent, magnified by the red ruby wren tucked close to her heart.

She drew herself up. It wasn't difficult to look down on Pilar; Mia was half a head taller.

"Since it seems you haven't done us any favors," Mia said, "by first trying unsuccessfully to kill me, then almost successfully killing the prince, I'd say you owe us a debt."

Pilar shook her head. "Typical. The princess leaves her castle, travels to a foreign land, and decides we humble slaves owe *her* a debt."

She exchanged knowing looks with Dom, who laughed. Annoyance flared in Mia's chest. The two of them were clearly in on some joke she didn't get.

"I want to see Zaga," she said.

"All right then," Dom said. "I'll take any excuse to do a little rowing. Pil?" He clapped Pilar on the back. "Let's take her to Zaga."

"She's not *ready* for Zaga."

"I bet Zaga will be the judge of that."

The ride to the island was smooth, the lake a flawless blue sheet until Pilar and Dom sank their oars into its invisible seams. The fishing boat held all four of them, albeit uncomfortably. Mia had told Quin he didn't need to come—that this was something she needed to do on her own—but he had insisted. Even if he was no longer dodging an assassin, she had a hunch he wasn't keen on being left behind with a coven of Dujia who might punish him for his father's sins.

"Swans," Quin said, pointing to a whole herd of them, gliding in formation on the surface of the lake. "They look different from the ones back home."

It was true: the swans' white feathers were accented in hues of strawberry and tangerine. They were somehow even more elegant than the swans in Glas Ddir, with long necks, crystalline blue eyes, and bills the pink of fresh-bloomed roses.

Mia closed her eyes and let the memory wash over her: the day their mother took her and Angelyne to a pond in Ilwysion to feed the ducks and swans. They had brought a loaf of brown bread and pinched off crumbs, throwing them to the hungry birds. Angie was only four, and she had wandered a little too close, hand outstretched with a piece of soft crust sitting on her palm. The swan had pecked her, hard, and she immediately burst into tears.

The bite left a mark, though only a small one. What Mia remembered most was the look of betrayal on her sister's face. Angie had trusted the swan implicitly, as if a creature that beautiful could never do her harm.

"Are those the same swans you eat?" It was Quin asking. Naturally.

"Some of them, yes," Dom said. "Refúj is rich in natural resources, but we're limited to what we can grow, hunt, or make. You're a fan of swan meat?"

"I had some in the merqad. I've never tasted meat that tender."

"Come with me to the merqad next time, Your Grace. I know

which vendor has the best cut of meat, tenderized and flavored to perfection."

"You act as if you've lived here forever, du Zol," Pilar muttered. "Keep in mind you are newly arrived yourself."

That effectively ended all conversation, so they rode the rest of the way in silence. Mia didn't mind. As the boat lurched forward on every oar stroke, excitement hummed through her. She was going to meet Zaga, the woman who knew everything, including who killed her mother. She was moving toward answers at last.

"Last stop, the Biqhotz," Dom said, as if there had been any other stops. "Here's your Fojuen lesson for the day, free of charge: *biqhotz* means 'heart.'"

She knew that already, of course, but the name fit. The rock formations were more intricate than they appeared from the shores of Refúj, with red caverns and lava tubes, a gleaming network of subclavian arteries and brachiocephalic veins extending from the arch of the aorta.

Mia's head was pounding. She pressed the heel of her hand into her brow.

Pil laid the oar across her knees. "The headaches are fierce at first, but you'll adjust."

Was Pilar being nice to her? Before Mia could cobble together a response, Dom stripped off his shirt and leapt into the shallow water, the muscles in his back ropy as he hefted the boat onshore. Flanked on all sides by volqanic rock, his reddish-brown skin glowed like a summer sunset, a pleasing contrast to the hard ridges of his scapulae. There was no denying Dom was handsome, with his broad shoulders, lopsided smile, and the ever-present flicker of mischief in his deep-brown eyes. If Quin were water, mysterious and changeable, Dom was fire and heat and explosive energy. Seeing him in the heart of a volqano felt exactly right.

Quin took off his shirt and jumped out to assist Domeniq. Mia couldn't help but think the prince looked like a blade of yellow grass against the rutted brown cliff of Dom's torso.

"Why don't I go in first?" said Pilar. "You can keep our guests occupied, Dom. Maybe give them the grand tour?"

Dom looked stricken. "I only just got here! You said so yourself."

"You'll be fine. It's ashes and dead people, what's so hard about that?"

She ducked behind a pillar of red rock and vanished.

"So that's it then. She's gone and here we are. Ashes and dead people." Dom rubbed the back of his head. "Easy, right?"

With that he began to show them around.

There was an early settlement of some sort—at least, there had been, before an ancient volqano had her way with it. Dom walked Mia and Quin through rows of crumbling rocks, held together with a crude mix of clay and calcined lime, primitive walls that partitioned the space into squares.

"These were the houses, I guess. Our ancestors lived here. Ancestresses, my mother would say."

"The bones of civilization." Quin's face was awash in awe. "I love history."

Dom raised an eyebrow. "Why, Your Grace?"

"I was just saying to Mia how back home I never felt like the myths could be real. But I'm getting chills just standing here. The origin myths begin to make sense." He flourished his hand and recited in a deep voice, "'The fire god was the angriest.'"

"'He breathed fire,'" Dom and Quin said together.

The prince smiled. "You know, not many people know this, but I played the fire god in a modest production at the Kaer. I played all *four* gods, actually. It was a masterpiece of theater, directed, written, performed, and attended by me, me, me, and me."

That made Dom laugh. "My mother would tell you they were never gods at all. There were only ever the Four Great Goddesses: four angel sisters who broke each other's hearts. Watching the way my sisters behave toward one another, I believe it."

"Just when I thought I had a firm grasp on demonology," Quin said, "turns out I should have been brushing up on my angelology all along."

Mia was thrilled Quin and Domeniq were getting along so famously, but at the moment she had more pressing concerns. Her body was raging with the heat, her thoughts a fraying thread that might snap at any moment.

"I thought I was going to meet Zaga," she said.

"Patience never was your strong suit, was it, Mia?" Sensing he'd found a more willing audience in the prince, Dom led him down a corridor, with Mia following reluctantly behind.

The hallway opened into a gigantic room with vaulted ceilings and magnificent archways, all carved from glittering vermilion.

Then she saw them: the strange shapes lying twisted on the floor. Human shapes.

"Those are our forebears," Dom said. "Buried in ash and perfectly preserved."

This wasn't a sanctuary. It was a crypt.

Mia knelt beside one corpse. It was a girl—she could tell from the soft curve of her young breasts, the lines of her dress frilled at the ankles. She was tucked into the fetal position, her arms shielding her head.

Quin crouched beside her. "I don't understand how they're preserved so well."

"I read about this," Mia said quietly. "In the last pyroclastic surge from a volqano, fine ash rains down and encases people's bodies. The shell is porous, so as their bodies start to decay, the soft tissues leach through. But by then the ash is already hard as rock, so not only are their skeletons still inside, their shape is permanently preserved. They're captured in their final postures—exactly the way they were when they died."

She shuddered. How awful, to be trapped forever in this moment of death.

Dom said, "If you'd rather see something else, Your Grace . . ."

"You don't have to call me that, you know. 'Your Grace.'"

Mia's head raged with heat and pressure. She felt as if the volqano had resurrected its fiery ash and brimstone inside her skull.

"Could we maybe not stay in this room of preserved dead people?"

"We're standing in the cradle of civilization," Quin said, "and you want to leave?"

"You don't have magic stabbing you in the head."

She heard footsteps and wheeled around. Pilar was standing beneath a carmine arch.

"She's ready for you now, Rose."

Mia was happy for the interruption. The boys would be fine on their own—Quin seemed enraptured with the history lesson, and Dom was all too pleased to give it.

As she followed Pilar into the mouth of a lava tube, Mia's capillaries felt plucked and ripe, ready to burst. The inside of the tube was duller than the outside, coarse gray and brown rock, and darker, too. Pilar struck a torch against the stone and it roared to life as they slipped through a labyrinth of passageways.

"Here."

Pilar stopped in front of two giant doors hewn from the rock, buffed and polished to a fine glint. Mia saw her reflection, carved into pieces by the volqanic glass, her body shimmering and sliced.

She reached for the doorknobs—two carved talons—and hesitated.

"You're not coming?"

Pilar shook her head.

Mia's skin was tingling. She felt the same rightness she'd felt at the waterfall and again in the hot air balloon, a sense of inevitability nudging her forward. She grabbed the talons and pushed.

The doors swung open onto a gargantuan room lit with candles and torches from floor to domed ceiling. Mia half expected a pipe organ to strike up an orchestral fugue. On the far wall, a tiny waterfall burbled into a silver basin, identical to the one she and Quin had jumped into, only in miniature. Beside it, a red hot air balloon puffed up and down on a piece of twine.

She inhaled sharply as the doors closed behind her. She wasn't interested in the waterfall or the balloon; it was what graced the other three walls that held her attention. This room wasn't an empty cave. It was her favorite thing in the world.

A library.

Chapter 38

BARE

LEGIONS OF BOOKS LINED every wall.

They were grouped by color: crimsons bleeding into rusts, rusts to roses, roses to creams. They easily numbered in the tens of thousands. The shelves were sculpted into strange shapes, and the books themselves became the art: swooping in concentric circles, extending into tiered wings, sweeping into spiral staircases. There were stacks that looked like pyramids and a tall ship with billowing book sails.

Mia had grown up with a respectable collection—and the library at Kaer Killian was nothing to sniff at—but she'd never seen anything like this.

She was in bliss. Her headache faded as she walked the

perimeter of the room. She ran her finger down spines, devouring titles like sugared fruit. *What a Witch Was. Mythologies of Magic. The Anatomy of Desire: An Introduction.*

There were titles in Pembuka and Luumi and dialects she couldn't even begin to guess. And of course books in Fojuen abounded. One caught her eye: *Zu Livru Dujia (The Book of Magic).* Maybe the truths in *this* book would actually be true.

Carefully she slid the tome off the shelf. It was very old, the pages rough and weathered at the edges, the spine clinging by a few thin threads. She traced the words on the cover, merlot against vanilla custard.

"So you have chosen."

Mia startled and dropped the book. It was a woman's voice, low and haggard with the consonants bitten off at the ends. The accent she couldn't quite place.

Mia blinked into the dark recesses of the room, the places where the candlelight could not reach.

"I can't see you," she said.

"Why do you assume you need to see?"

Mia stooped to get the book.

"Leave it," the voice said.

"But I—"

"You chose this book, why?"

"Because I want to learn the truth about magic."

"*Your* magic?"

"Yes. Well, all magic." She swallowed. "Are you Zaga?"

The woman didn't answer. When she spoke again, her voice

had shifted subtly; it seemed to be coming from a different corner of the room.

"You do not want to learn magic. You want to control it."

Mia wasn't sure what to say.

"You, Mia Morwynna Rose, do not read books to learn the lessons therein. You read them to master them."

Her cheeks burned. "How do you know who I am?"

"I know a great deal about you. I know where you come from and why you have come. I know you are not a true student of magic."

"How can I be a true student of magic? I've never studied it!"

"Yet you want to."

She hesitated. The strange voice was right; the moment Mia walked into the library, she had forgotten all about her mother's murderer. All she'd wanted was to curl up with a good book and throw open the windows in her mind.

"I'd like to debunk the lies I've been told my whole life, yes. But that's not why I'm here."

"That itself is a lie. You lie to yourself. You are desperate to learn about magic."

Mia shielded her eyes with her hand, thinking she saw a shape materialize by the toy waterfall. But there was no one.

"You're Zaga, aren't you?" Silence. "Why can't I see you?"

"And still you think you need to see. You are unable to trust things your eyes cannot behold, truths your mind cannot parse for instant meaning. Yet you think you are ready to learn magic."

This was maddening. Mia didn't want to talk in circles with an invisible woman. She needed answers, not more questions.

She took a breath. "Who murdered my mother?"

"One more answer you are eager to claim as your own. You covet knowledge the way others covet power or wealth. You seek a prize to be worn around your neck. Knowledge is something to be stalked and subdued, then displayed like a trophy."

"If that means finding my mother's murderer," Mia said sharply, "then yes. I'll stalk all four kingdoms to find her. *Heart for a heart, life for a—*"

"Life. Yes, I know. If you want answers, maybe you should read your book."

Mia stooped, picked up the book, and pried it open to the very first page. Scarlet ink curled and beaded at her fingertips.

The First Law of the Dujia
The practice of magic shall never be used by Dujia to consciously inflict pain, suffering, or death on her fellow sister, unless the Dujia's own life is in danger.

The Second Law of the Dujia
The practice of magic shall never be used by Dujia to consciously inflict pain, suffering, or death on herself.

The Third Law of the Dujia
In situations wherein the practice of magic is necessary, it is at the discretion of the Dujia to determine the most equitable balance of power and act accordingly.

Mia felt a glimmer of hope; even magicians subscribed to laws. Perhaps magic was not so different from science after all. Science was knowable. Science she could understand.

But when she flipped to the next page, it was blank.

She licked her thumb and leafed through the book. One empty page after another.

"The book is not what you imagined," Zaga said.

Mia yanked another book off the shelf and began thumbing through it, but it was empty, too. She pulled another book, then another, riffling through the pages, searching for ink. The papers were rich and varied—papyrus, hemp, linen, cotton, wood pulp— but they all had one thing in common: they were bare. It was uncomfortably familiar.

"Your mood has changed," said the disembodied voice.

"Yes, well. I'm angry."

"Good. Angry at what?"

"At you!"

"Not at the book? The failure you perceive is a failure of ink and paper. Is it not logical to be angry at the book?"

"What is this? Some kind of cruel joke? Fill a library with blank books and lure me into it?"

"The books are not blank. They are only empty to those who try to read them with their eyes, instead of with their hearts."

Mia wanted to laugh. The thought of reading a book with your heart was preposterous. But then, her mother's journal had been empty, too, until the ink seeped across the page. Was that the book's secret? You had to *feel* something to see the words?

Something her mother had said during their last fight came back to her. *Whatever you're feeling—fear, anger, love—let yourself feel it.*

Mia let out her breath. When she spoke again, her voice was steady.

"You speak as if it's arrogant to seek knowledge. I think it's the opposite. It takes great humility to admit you know nothing, and that you want to learn."

"This is uncomfortable for you, not knowing."

"I hate it more than anything in the world."

Zaga inhaled, and Mia caught the faintest hitch in her breath. "Good. Then you are ready."

And so began Mia's first magic lesson, a student with an unseen teacher, two voices touching and colliding in the dark.

Chapter 39

AN EXCELLENT STEW

—WHAT IS LOVE, MIA?

—Love?

—Surely you are familiar with the concept.

—I know what love is! I just . . . no one's ever asked me to define it before.

—What is love?

—It's a commitment. A sacrifice.

—A sacrifice of what?

—Of yourself. Giving up the things you want for someone else.

—That is not love. That is martyrdom.

—What's the difference?

—What is *true* love?

— . . .

—You are thinking about your parents.

—What do *you* know about my parents?

—This is where your mind fails you, Mia. For you the world is split into two halves: what you know and what you do not. But your logic is reductive. Some things do not fall cleanly on either side.

—You either know something or you don't.

—Not all true things can be known. Your mind is not sufficient for the task. Only the heart can lead you. Your heart knows what your mind cannot.

—That's not physiologically possible.

—Is magic physiologically possible? Is an enthrallment? A healing? What about this seems physiologically possible to you?

— . . .

—Until you learn to feel with your mind and think with your heart, you will never be a Dujia. You are no sister of ours.

—What is marriage, Mia?

—A pact of lies. Something you do because you have to, not because you want to.

—That is a rather cynical view on marriage.

—Then I'm a cynic.

—Was your parents' marriage a farce?

—A *farce*?

—Surely you have wondered how this came to be: your father, the great magic Hunter, married to a Dujia.

—My father stopped eating after she died. He didn't speak for days. It decimated him. I've never seen grief like that.

—Then would you concede that marriage can be a happy union?

—I would concede that marriage ends in misery, one way or another.

—What is the greatest gift of an inquisitive mind, Mia?

—Always asking questions. Thirsting for knowledge. Being agile, quick to adapt, ready to question.

—Wrong. The greatest gift of an inquisitive mind is its ability to silence its own inquisitions.

—What?

—You disagree?

—Why would I want to silence my mind? It's my greatest asset!

—A matter of opinion.

—A matter of *your* opinion, perhaps!

—You are angry.

—I'm insulted.

—A former teacher told you your mind is dazzling. Congratulated you on your exceptionally big and brilliant brain. Who rewarded you for asking questions?

—My father.

—What would you ask him, if he were here right now?

— . . .

—If I'm so bad at magic, how was I able to heal Quin?

—Magic is powerful, even in its inchoate form.

—I healed him twice. I enthralled him.

—You are proud of this?

—You talk to me like I'm a child.

—You are a child.

—I may be naive when it comes to magic, but I am not a child.

—You are correct. Children are impulsive. They have not yet learned to silence their feelings. In this way, you are not a child. A child is far more sophisticated. There is an ocean of distance between your head and your heart.

—Why can't I see you, Zaga?

—Because sight is an illusion of the mind.

—Sight isn't an illusion. It's science. It's the mind interpreting messages from the eyes.

—The mind, the eyes—you speak of these things as if they are sacrosanct. Why should you privilege either? Your eyes play cruel tricks. Your mind is the greatest liar.

—What is that supposed to mean?

—Perhaps it will surprise you to learn I agree with your father. You have an exceptional mind. Nimble. Quick. And this is why you cannot control your magic. Your mind is overdeveloped at the expense of your heart.

—I don't know what you want me to do. I can't change who I am.

—I want you to stop asking what I want you to do. Listen. Feel. Cease being my student, and be a student unto yourself. To learn the answer to your question, you must start with another. You must ask what magic is, and who your mother was.

—Fine, then! What is magic? Who was my mother? I can't learn if you don't teach me!

—I *am* teaching you. But you don't want to be taught. You want to know.

—What is brilliance, Mia?

—Someone is brilliant when her mind works more quickly than other minds.

—No. Brilliance has to do with light.

—Why do you ask me questions when you already know the answer you want to hear?

—You are opposed to my manner of questioning?

—I just wish you wouldn't ask open-ended questions that aren't actually open-ended.

—What is brilliance?

—You said it had something to do with light.

—In the old language, the word means shining. Brilliance is a brightness to the eye.

—You said I shouldn't trust what my eyes see. Is that why you hide in a dark cave?

—I said sight is an illusion of the mind.

—That's exactly what I said!

—You are frustrated.

—I don't know what you want me to see in all of this.

—I do not want you to "see" at all.

—Is there anyone you love, Mia?

— . . .

—The question is difficult for you?

—No. I just want to give a careful answer. Not that you'll like what I say.

—I promise to let you speak.

—I love my sister. I love my father—or I did love him. I don't know if I love him anymore. I feel . . . angry.

—Does anger run contradictory to love?

—No. I suppose not. The day my mother . . .

—Yes?

—Never mind. It's not important.

—You feel angry with your mother?

—No.

—Did you—?

—My mother is dead.

— . . .

—Say something, Zaga. It's too quiet when you don't talk.

—Perhaps anger is deeply tied to love. Perhaps you feel angriest at the people you love the most. Perhaps the love makes it safe to feel angry.

—Perhaps.

—And Quin? Do you love the prince?

— . . .

—You want to give a careful answer?

—My head hurts. Can I leave?

—No. Not yet.

—Follow the candlelight, Mia, to the silver basin beneath the waterfall. Do you see it?

—I see it. Wait—is this a trick? You said sight is an illusion.

—This time I want to know if you see it with your eyes.

—I do.

—Do you see the pink fish in the basin?

—Yes.

—Kill it.

—What?

—You said you know how to use your magic. Show me.

—I . . .

—As a Dujia, you have the power to take a life. Still the fish's heart.

—I don't want to.

—You are afraid of your own power.

—I don't want to take a life. Even a small one.

—Yet you have spent the last three years honing your ability to do exactly that. You have polished your ambition like a stone. You live to kill the Dujia who killed your mother. A heart for a heart, life for a life.

— . . .

—Is this not true?

— . . .

—Am I not correct?

—I don't know what you want me to say.

—What is hate?

—Hate is the antithesis of love.

—No. Hate is the perversion of love. It is love twisted in on itself, the feeling that floods the place where love once grew. If you saw her right now, here in this room, the Dujia who killed your mother . . . would you kill her?

—I . . .

—Every day for three years, you have thought of nothing else. It has commandeered your dreams and fueled your every step. It is what brought you here, to this village, to my island. If you hesitate, then why are you here at all?

—I'm so tired, Zaga. I only want to sleep.

—What is brilliance?

—I don't know.

—What is seeing?

—I don't know.

—What is love?

—I don't know.

—What is hate?

—I don't know.

—What do you feel?

—Confused. Exhausted. Angry.

—Good. You may take your leave. Tomorrow we commence your real lessons.

—My . . . real . . .

—If you want to face the Dujia who killed your mother, you must first learn how to be a Dujia yourself.

—But I . . .

—Go eat something, Mia. I hear the Blue Phoenix serves an excellent stew.

Chapter 40

RIVER RATS

MIA WAS IN SHAMBLES. She'd spent the better part of the day in the Biqhotz, and when she emerged, the sky was purple and salted with stars.

Now she sat at the Blue Phoenix, brooding, her chair drawn a short distance from the toasty fire. She'd hardly touched her stew. For the first time in her life, she had performed poorly on a test. Her mind was tied in knots. For someone who claimed not to trust logic, Zaga had introduced one paradox after another, fraying ropes and securing new ones, then leaving Mia alone to unravel the snarl.

Refúj: where all your troubles will unravel.

Mia was not amused.

It didn't help that Domeniq, Pilar, and Quin sat in a cozy circle around the fire pit, drinking libations and roasting shmardas: sugary egg pillows rimed in pink salt. Mia couldn't get over how at ease the prince seemed, even in a den of Dujia. But why not? He no longer had a target on his back. He was safe.

But he wasn't. Not really. Mia hadn't chosen her faraway seat just to sulk; it afforded her the opportunity to listen in on the conversations unfolding around the tavern. In the corner closest, two women were speaking in low voices, casting furtive scowls at the prince.

"I've said it for years: we're too close to the border," said the woman with a tuft of stark-white hair and bronze skin, a loose tunic tied around her waist with a brilliant purple sash. "It was only a matter of time before their hatred and bigotry crossed the Salted Sea."

Her companion, an older woman with a shaved head and rings of blue ink around her white arms and neck, nodded vehemently. "He shouldn't be here. The river rats are snakes."

"As shifty and treacherous as the rivers beneath them," the first woman agreed. "The royals worst of all."

Glasddirans weren't exactly beloved, Mia was learning. She, too, was a river rat.

"Truce?"

Pilar stood before her, holding a glass of murky liquid freckled red.

"A gift from my failed assassin," Mia said dryly. "Trying to poison me now?"

"If I wanted you dead, I wouldn't need poison."

"You might, given your success rate with an arrow." She sniffed. "I don't drink demon's dwayle."

It was true. The lady barkeep at the Blue Phoenix had looked at Mia strangely when she'd asked for a cup of tea, but she didn't care. Her head was foggy enough without adding strange spirits to the mix. Not half an hour earlier, she'd watched Dom slam back a dram of muddy brown liquid with a sqorpion inside.

"This isn't dwayle," Pilar said. "It's *rai rouj,* a Fojuen specialty. We're not in the river kingdom anymore, Rose, with your diluted excuse for spirits."

Mia accepted the glass, took a cautious nip, and nearly fell out of her chair.

Pilar laughed. "There's a reason they call it red rage. You shave off flakes of fojuen into the liquor and let it souse. Nothing like a good punch to the throat to wake your inner Dujia."

"I just drank *glass?*"

"It's ground to a fine powder. No need to call the cavalry."

Mia resolved to drink very slowly and keep her wits about her. She did not want to give this girl any leeway to punch her in the throat, literally or metaphorically.

"You should see what they drink in Luumia," Pilar said. "That's where my father is from. It's so cold they drop slabs of butter into their spirits to keep up their strength. The Luumi drink three glasses of *vaalkä* every night: butter and fire."

"Did your father come here with your mother?" Mia asked, genuinely curious.

"My father isn't in Refúj." Pilar's face hardened. "Mind your own, Rose."

She stomped back to the fire pit and settled into the chair beside Quin. She said something to him in a low voice, and—to Mia's surprise—he laughed.

Then Dom was scraping his chair toward Mia, blocking Quin and Pilar from view. "Mind if I sit down?"

Before she could answer, he plunked the chair down next to her.

"I didn't say yes."

"I know. But you were about to."

Dom was as cocky as ever. She'd almost missed it.

He brandished his clay tankard in her direction. "Care for a drink?"

"I don't drink with murderers," she said, "or the people who aid and abet murderers. Now that I know you were perfectly content to let me take an arrow in the heart."

He rubbed his head. In the firelight, she saw his coarse black hair was shaved into intricate shapes at the back of his neck, a row of whorls and interconnected diamonds.

"I tried, Mia. I really did. I'm the one who first guessed you were a Dujia." He touched the uzoolion charm at his neck. "I felt your magic tapping at my stone in the Grand Gallery the night of the final feast. I told Pilar they were wrong about you; that you were a Dujia. But by then the plan was already in motion."

"How do you even know Pilar? You grew up in Glas Ddir."

"I guess my mother knew her mother when they were younger.

279

And I got to know Pil a bit when she was disguised as a scullery maid in the Kaer. She's loyal to a fault—as long as you're on her side." He swigged from his tankard. "I never wanted any harm to come to you. But you know I'd do anything to protect my sisters."

Mia softened. When they were younger, she'd watched Dom defend his sisters, especially when the other children were cruel to Sach'a on account of her legs.

"You're a good brother," she said. "I feel the same about Angelyne. I would do anything to protect her."

And yet, Mia thought, she's back in the Kaer while I sit around watching a bunch of strangers roast shmardas.

"What happened in the Chapel, Dom? After Pilar shot the arrow. You were there—you must have seen Angie."

"I didn't see anyone. I left the Kaer faster than you. I had to make sure I got to you before Lyman and Tuk. I led you to the boat. I even looped back around to Tristan's camp, but you were already gone. All I found were two dead men."

Mia sat up. "*Two?*"

"Two guards, dead in their own sick. The prince did admirable work with that chokecherry brew. I do love a man who knows his poisons."

Mia's mouth had gone as dry as bonemeal. "What about Tristan? Where was the duke?"

"No sign of him. But there were tracks in the snow."

She staggered to her feet, her one swallow of rai rouj rushing to her head. How had it not occurred to her? Quin said the poison was temporary, that it would wear off in a few days. And if that were true . . .

"I have to go back. If there's even a *chance* Tristan has made it back to Kaer Killian . . . if he tells the king Quin is dead and that he should be prince, and then demands Angelyne as his princess . . ."

"Relax, Mia. These things take time. Just yesterday Tristan was rolling in his own vomit in the Twisted Forest. It would take him at *least* five days to get back to the castle, and that's if he were at peak health. It's not like they're going to schedule a royal wedding the following day. They'd have to mourn the prince."

She sank back into her chair, mollified, at least for the moment.

"The best thing you can do for Angelyne," Dom said, "is to learn how to harness your magic. If you want to keep her safe from the duke, stop fighting your magic and embrace it. Even the most powerful men can be felled by an enthrall." He eyed Quin over his tankard. "Have you two been fully yoked?"

"Like with an egg?"

Dom looked amused. "*Yoked*, Mia. You've been in the woods for days, eating together . . . *sleeping* together . . ."

"Not like that, we haven't."

"That's a pity." His eyes slid over the prince's slender form. "I would not miss an opportunity to exchange body heat with a boy that beautiful."

Mia stared at him. It had never occurred to her Dom might be interested in boys. She had, in her more arrogant moments, thought Dom might be interested in *her*. But when she saw the way he was watching Quin, with both shyness and longing, she realized he had probably always loved boys, and she'd just been too naive to notice.

"You really didn't know, did you? I wanted to tell you a hundred times. Now you know why you were never my type."

Mia felt sad. How much had her friend suffered in the river kingdom, longing for boys he knew he couldn't have? And why did this kind of love threaten King Ronan so deeply? Queen Bronwynis had envisioned Glas Ddir as a place where all loves could flourish. How far they had fallen.

"Four gods, Dom. All those years . . ."

"It wasn't easy, that's for sure. At least here I can be who I am." He laughed. "Sort of. There are forty-six men in all of Refúj. At least half of them are grandfathers. To say pickings are slim would be like saying volqanoes are hot."

Mia barely heard him. She was distracted by Pilar, who was now inching closer to Quin, her body canting toward him. She'd given him his own glass of rai rouj, and his cheeks were flushed and ruddy as he grew jollier by the second.

Pilar punched him playfully on the shoulder, and he burst into laughter.

"Quin." Mia stood. "You know you shouldn't let her touch you. She could be enthralling you."

"She can't," Dom said. He stood and kicked the loose dirt over the threshold of the tavern. For the first time Mia noticed the border of blue uzoolion. "That keeps the bar brawls from getting ugly. Magic and liquor: not a great mix."

Pilar stood with arms akimbo. "I didn't enthrall your precious husband, Rose."

There was a sudden hush in the tavern chatter. The two women who had been discussing the river rats leaned forward. Mia got the impression the patrons of the Blue Phoenix wouldn't mind if Pilar punched her in the face.

"All I'm saying," Mia said, taking a more measured tack, "is that you shouldn't abuse your power."

"*I* shouldn't abuse *my* power?" Pilar clenched and unclenched her fists. "Come with me, Rose. You're getting your first real magic lesson whether you like it or not."

Chapter 41

WILDER

THEY CLUSTERED TOGETHER IN an empty market stall, Domeniq and Pilar on one side, Quin and Mia on the other. Pil had drawn a line in the sand—a literal line in the literal sand—separating the Dujia and Dujia-adjacent from the river rats.

Pilar held out her hand. "Uzoolion," she commanded, and Dom unlatched the blue stone around his neck and placed it in her palm.

In one swift movement, Pilar jammed her thumb into the crook of his elbow, where the humerus met the radius and ulna. Mia watched his dark skin blanch, then turn a crude purple. His fingers twitched violently and went sickly white, and right as Mia was about to wrench him safely out of harm's way, Pilar let go.

"Faqtan!" Dom swore. He picked his arm up by the wrist and let it fall, his hand slapping lifelessly against his side, dead weight. Then he grinned. "You're getting faster."

Pilar grinned back. "I know."

Mia was horrified. She might not know much about magic, but she knew human physiology.

"You're starving the muscles of oxygen. That's neqrosis."

"Very good, Rose. High marks for effort. You've got the name wrong, though: it's called unblooding."

"Wrong. It's called neqrosis. Do you know what neqrosis means? *Corpse.* If you cut off the circulation for long enough, it isn't just your muscles that go numb—your tissue will die and your bones will collapse. You'd never be able to use your hand again, Dom."

Pilar shook her head. Her face was painted with an emotion Mia couldn't read. Anger? Sadness? Or was it, of all things, pity?

"There's so much you don't know," Pilar said. "And you're trying so hard to know everything. Can you think of any other situations where it might be useful to unblood someone? An assailant, perhaps?"

Mia said nothing.

"Or what about the history of magic?" Pilar prodded. "Can you tell me how or why it evolved the way it did?"

Every answer that landed on the tip of Mia's tongue was wrong. She would only be reciting what she had learned in books— books her father had given all the Hunters. Books inked with lies.

"Let me tell you a story," Pilar said. "When she was young, my grandmother was coming home from a hat shop with a new pink hat. Four men appeared from the shadows. They crushed her hat, put their hands around her throat, and ripped off her skirt. A fifth man came out of a nearby shop. She begged for him to help her, to show mercy. 'I'll show you mercy,' he said. He unbuttoned his trousers."

A thick, heavy silence fell over them. Pilar looked away.

"You think we exist on the margins of society because of our magic. That we have been hunted and killed as punishment for being Dujia. But you've got it backward. We were hunted and killed for thousands of years, long before we had magic. We are magicians *because* of our suffering. A woman's body can survive only so much abuse before our very blood and bones rise up in revolt.

"Magic is born in the margins. It is nurtured among the vulnerable and broken. It is our bodies crying out for justice, seeking to right centuries of wrongs."

Pilar had transformed into a gifted orator, eloquent and fierce.

Quin had noticed, too. Mia felt his body enliven.

"And that's what you don't understand about magic," Pil said. "It isn't evil—it's a way of *combating* evil. Magic is a way to topple the power structures that have held women captive for thousands of years. Why do you think we have the gift of enthrallment? Because sometimes the only way to escape a guard who has imprisoned you, or a husband who has forced himself upon you, or an executioner knotting the noose around your neck because you loved someone you weren't supposed to love . . . was to entrance his heart with passion, and then make your escape.

286

"And if a man was about to hurt you, to violate you, he needed *less* blood in certain areas. Say a king was about to make you his new favorite doll. You could funnel the blood away from his hands when he touched you, or his arms when he pinned you down. You could coax the blood out of the parts of his body he found most pleasurable. Drain him of his power to harm you. Slow the assault and buy yourself time. That's how unblooding was born."

Mia knew every word Pilar said was true; she heard no telltale whoosh, no agitation in her blood. Which meant *Mia* was the ignorant one. She hadn't known how much she hadn't known.

Pilar turned to Quin. "Your father has perpetuated the lie that we are wicked and depraved. That we are monsters, not people." She turned to Mia. "Your father has only made it worse. These men are threatened by our power. But that's nothing new. Our sisterhood has always been under threat. For the entirety of human history, weak men have been afraid of powerful women."

The moonlight anointed Pilar's black hair with a blazing blue halo. She reminded Mia of a phoenix rising from the ashes. Had the Dujia her mother loved also stood like this in the merqad, brave and beautiful, hair shimmering beneath the moon?

And then she saw this same woman reaching forward to touch Wynna on the last day of her life, death cloaked in a loving caress.

"If this is all true," Mia said, "if magic is a way for women to protect themselves against the men who would seek to hurt them . . . then why is my mother dead? Why would a Dujia turn on one of her own?"

The fire in Pilar's face flickered and went dark. "I don't know."

Mia closed her eyes and listened, straining—hoping—to hear the slosh of lies. But Pilar's blood was quiet.

When she opened her eyes, Pilar was watching her with something akin to pity.

"Sorry, Rose. I'm telling the truth."

Mia sat on the lakeshore, her knees tucked into her chest. Her feet were bare. She dug her heels into the earth, scooping up soft red sand in her hands and sifting it through her fingers. At night, the lake was stained a deep indigo, a swatch of smooth silk in the crater of a volqano.

She was thinking about her parents. The way they were physically drawn toward one another; how easily her mother's cheek found the smooth plane of her father's shoulder, or how his hand rested perfectly on the curve of her back. One of Zaga's questions had filled Mia with doubt: *Was your parents' marriage a farce?*

She ached for her mother's journal. Surely it held the answers. But it was buried under a heap of snow in the Twisted Forest, surrendering its secrets to humus and decay?

Mia should have gone back for it. She cursed herself for leaving behind her most precious possession. It was the last surviving link to her mother. In a way, losing the journal meant losing her mother all over again.

Mia heard footsteps and looked up to see Quin standing quietly on the sandy path.

"Can I join you?" he said.

"Yes."

They sat staring out at the lake. The water pitched the corn-flower moon back up to the sky, perfect and whole.

Quin raked his hands through the coarse red sand. "Do you think everything they've told us is true?"

"I can hear when someone is lying."

"You really are a marvel."

She didn't feel like a marvel. She felt like a fraud. No longer a Huntress, but not quite a Dujia, either.

"But you can't hear them if they lie in the cottage, right?" Quin said. "Or in the tavern? For a place where people purport to trust each other, there sure is a lot of uzoolion around."

She hadn't thought about it, but he made a decent point.

"Is that an active volqano?" Quin pointed to a molten cone of orange in the distance. It glowed incandescent, sending coils of gray smoke into the sky.

"I don't know."

He nudged her arm. "I thought you knew everything about an insufferable number of things."

"I don't know anything anymore."

Quin took her hand and a spark ignited in her belly. That was one thing she knew: the cold she'd once felt slinking off the prince had been replaced by the warm melt of desire. She tried to focus on the stars overhead, but they were hazy, trapped under a net of ash and smoke. Heat was pouring off her, or pouring off Quin, or maybe there wasn't any difference.

With his free hand, he reached out and delicately lifted one of her curls. "Your hair is wilder here than in the castle."

"I'm wilder, too."

"I know," he said. "I like it."

The heat moved into her mouth so suddenly she was at risk of garbling her words.

"I think Tristan is still alive. Dom found two bodies in the Twisted Forest. Two of the guards."

Quin's hand stiffened. "They're dead? He's certain?"

"It's not the dead ones I'm worried about. If Tristan is trekking through the forest, crawling back to the Kaer . . ."

"Then it's only a matter of time before he reaches your sister."

Mia's impulses were at war. A full day had passed, which put the duke one day closer to the castle and Angelyne. What was she still doing in Fojo?

"I'll go with you, " Quin said, "if you want to go back."

"You can't go back," said a dulcet voice behind them.

Mia turned to see Lauriel, a nubby pink shawl drawn over her shoulders. She was cradling something in her hands. "You shouldn't leave Refúj. At least not until you've read this."

Mia's heart leapt.

Lauriel was holding her mother's journal.

Chapter 42

THE BLOOD BENEATH

IT TOOK EVERYTHING IN Mia not to pounce on the book.

"Quin, darling." Lauriel smiled at the prince. "Dom and Pilar were asking for you in the tavern. Perhaps you could join them for a drink?"

He looked at Mia. "Go," she said. "I know where to find you."

Quin tipped his head toward Lauriel and disappeared into the night, taking his warmth with him.

Lauriel sat heavily on the bank of sand. Mia reached for the journal, but a smiling Lauriel tucked it beneath her arm.

"You don't get it right away," she said. "You have to talk to me first."

"About what?"

"About everything, darling. Everything you're thinking and feeling."

Mia exhaled. It was going to be a long night.

"How did you find the journal?"

"Dom brought it back from the Twisted Forest. He knew I'd given it to your mother, so he returned it to me."

"You gave it to her?"

"Yes. So that no matter how much she had to lie from day to day, there was one place she could speak true. She wanted so much to tell you about magic, Mia. Your mother believed magic was the body's response to a broken heart."

Mia thought of her own magic, blooming when she found herself on the cusp of a marriage she didn't want.

"How much do you know about magic?" Lauriel asked.

"A little." Mia conjured up Pilar's words in the merqad. "To be honest, not very much."

"For centuries," Lauriel began, "men have found ever-new ways of oppressing women. Our bodies have been receptacles, both container and contained; our wombs soft and pliant for the children we were meant to bear our husbands, whether we wanted to or not. We have been restricted, silenced, and confined. This has been called many things—'protection,' 'progress,' even 'love.'"

She tucked a stray curl behind Mia's ear.

"We Dujia have concealed our magic since the beginning of time, passed it down as a secret from one generation to the next, ever since the Four Great Goddesses were born in the heart of a volqano. The four sisters blessed us with the gift of touch, a gift that lives in our flesh, blood, breath, and bones."

Mia thought for a moment. "If Sach'a has magic, why can't she use her magic to heal her legs? Or why can't you?"

Lauriel smiled. "Not everything can be healed, darling. And not everything needs to be."

"Do *all* women have magic?"

"Not all. Many, but not all. Some have magic but fight against it. They are ashamed of who they are. They think Dujia are dirty creatures, a stain upon the earth, and that the world is better run by the men who have sworn to keep us safe."

"*Veraktu,*" Mia said.

"Yes. In Fojuen it means 'to silence the truth.'" Lauriel sighed. "You were always a truth-seeker, even as a child. Your mother hated lying to you. But she knew telling you the truth would put you at grave risk. Especially with your father."

"I thought he was a hero. That he was abolishing magic so science and reason would win." Mia thought of his never-ending drills and lessons and rebukes, the rewards he meted out for knowing the right answer. He had urged her to privilege her mind above all things, certainly over the insensible yearnings of the heart.

The irony stung. Science was about exploring new terrain, pushing boundaries, and above all else, asking questions. But in the river kingdom, questions could get you killed.

"Did your mother ever tell you about Queen Bronwynis?"

"She said she and Father were there for her coronation."

"That's all she told you? Bronwynis was the real hero. She was a symbol of the times, a shimmering beacon for the rest of us. In all four kingdoms, women were shedding their gowns and stepping into positions of power. Ship captains, merchants . . . even politicians."

"Like you selling copper pots."

Lauriel laughed her deep belly laugh, tight black curls bouncing mirthfully over her shoulders. "Yes, darling. I suppose my copper pots were a small part of the revolution. Your mother liked to say that progress is one little bird, pecking at a kernel. One bird will bring another, and another after that, until there's a whole flock. A flock of birds can be dangerous. Ask any farmer."

Lauriel reclined on the sand. "Bronwynis broke all the rules. Under her reign, five women sat on the Council of the Kaer, and only three men. She even offered a seat to a peasant woman. She said, 'If we do not invite the peasants to sit at the table, how will we learn what they eat?'"

Mia thought of Princess Karri. This sounded like something she might say.

"The Dujia didn't kill Bronwynis, did they?"

Lauriel shook her head. "Of course they didn't. She was murdered by King Ronan in her sleep."

"Her own brother." She felt a starburst of anger. "If not for Ronan's policies, we could have learned how to use our magic for good. Instead we all go around with fear in our hearts and gloves on our hands."

Lauriel howled with laughter. "That is the biggest lie of all!

Gloves cannot dampen our magic. They can briefly weaken our powers of touch, perhaps. But they cannot disarm it. Do you really think the Four Great Goddesses would be thwarted by a scrap of cloth?"

Now Mia understood why she'd been able to enthrall Quin in the castle library.

Lauriel spoke to the sky. "Ronan is an evil man, I will not deny it. He has ensured that suspicion trumps curiosity and hate trumps love. But those are simply new melodies to an ancient song."

Mia drew her knees to her chest. The history of magic was so different from the one she'd been spoon-fed by her father. Mia had accepted that Gwyrach were evil, men were strong, and women were weak—*she* wasn't, of course, but she was the exception to the rule, the courageous warrior girl who would bring her mother's killer to justice, then beat back magic and free all the poor damsels in Glas Ddir. She had internalized the idea that women needed to be protected.

She had done something else, too. She had confused women who were nurturing—those who privileged gentleness and compassion—for those who were weak.

She had called her mother weak the day she died.

"Why do Dujia turn against each other, Lauriel?"

"Why do humans turn against each other? Dujia are human, after all. Divine but also human. This is why hatred is the most dangerous of poisons: it turns us against the other, yes, but in the end, it turns us against ourselves."

Her voice softened. "Refúj is a sacred place where our sisters can seek refuge. We are not on any map. The balloon is the only way in or out, and no one from Glas Ddir has ever found it. But I will not lie to you. Our limited resources are a constant strain. In Luumia the Dujia do not live in exile. In the snow kingdom they are treated as queens."

"Then why don't you go to Luumia?"

"I was waiting for you, darling. Before she died, she told me you would come here. She left you her journal to make sure of it."

The journal. Mia had nearly forgotten. She saw it now, tucked loosely under the dimpled flesh of Lauriel's arm. How much longer until she could read it?

"Your mother talked often of going to Luumia. She had a troubled past here on this island." Lauriel's brown eyes had a faraway glimmer. "The Luumi have flourished where we have not, in part because they do not have to expend all their energy fighting their oppressors. They have made many advancements in alchemy and mechanics. The Luumi are interested in the ways magic and science interweave. So they study magic extensively—the effects, the advantages, the risks. They have learned how to bewitch metals and breathe life into stones. They have even found a way to still the heart inside a bird and bring it back to life."

Mia cocked her head. "If you mean the ruby wren, those birds still their own hearts. That's how they hibernate."

"I don't know what kind of bird, darling. Your mother was the one who loved birds." She stretched, lifted herself to an easy seat, and nodded at the cobalt moon. "In Fojo, we have a saying.

296

Lloira vuqateu: 'Come to the moon.' The moon can mend a broken body and heal a broken mind. The lloira stone draws its power from the moon's pull on the Earth. This is why it is a healing stone."

"Is that why my mother wore the moonstone?"

"Yes. She was a gifted healer without it, but the lloira stored up her gifts and made her stronger. I've never told you this, you or anyone, but I saw your mother the day she died."

Mia sat up straighter. Lauriel looked down at her hands.

"I was in a dark place after losing my husband. I knew I should stay alive for my daughters, but I didn't want to. I came to see your mother, begged her to heal my mind, to take away the darkness. And she did. I would have given up if not for her." She wiped the wetness from her eyes. "By that night, she was gone."

Sorrow fell like a mantle over Mia's shoulders.

"That's just like her, to save your life on the day she lost hers."

Mia thought of her sister. Angie had worn the moonstone for the past three years never knowing it had magic. But she had only grown sicker since the day she clasped the pendant around her neck. Whatever healing powers the lloira stone once stored up for their mother, those powers had died the moment she did.

"The Hunters were right about one thing," Lauriel said. "Our sisters bloom in moments of intense emotions, flashes of fear and anger and love. The same emotions that coax out the ink of the sangflur blossom."

She laid the journal gently on Mia's knees. "Sangflur is the ink your mother used. Visible only to a fellow Dujia."

Mia's pulse quickened. She drew her thumb down the initials scored into the soft leather. *W. M.*

"I have subjected you to my prattling long enough." Lauriel brushed an auburn curl from Mia's cheek, the way her mother used to do. "You look so much like your mother, darling. You have waited so long to meet her, and now it is time."

Lauriel heaved herself to her feet and headed back toward the cottage, leaving her comforting warmth behind on the lakeside. But Mia no longer felt alone. She opened the book and watched the ink pour onto the pages. Somehow she knew it would. She didn't need fear or anger to read it now. She had love.

Mia. My Mia.

If you are reading this, then you know.

The pages singed her hands like ashes, like fire.

This book and its map and its inscription were not arbitrary or random. They had always been meant for her.

Her eyes strained in the dim starlight. Every word hurt, yet every stroke of ink drew her in further. All her life she had inhabited a glass house of lies, and those lies were about to shatter. The book was the wound, but it was also the salve.

She would peel back the secrets to see the blood beneath.

She would meet her mother.

Breathless, Mia began to read.

Chapter 43

MORE THAN YOU WILL EVER KNOW

Mia. My Mia.

If you are reading this, then you know.

You are not yet born; I feel you writhe inside me. You kick and swim and kick. But I know you are my daughter, not my son. Don't ask me how I know. I am a Dujia; I know things.

The ink culled from the sangflur blossoms is special: it reveals itself only to Dujia, and in its own due time. The words will appear as you learn to channel the magic from your heart. When you are old enough, I will give this book to you, and when you are ready, you will know who I am.

The words I write here, the secrets I reveal, are my last bastion of truth amidst a life of fabrication. This book is the final fragment of my true self.

I am married to a man I do not love. That man is your father.

It is not so simple as you might believe.

Love is a twisty thing, serpentine, quicksilver in the palm of your hand. It is fluid in the heart of a volcano: hot one minute, cold the next.

I do not love my husband, and I have wronged him in ways too numerous to count. But I love the women I am bound to, my family of choice, my sisters. To them I am Wynna Merth, daughter of the Four Great Goddesses, Dujia.

I am not, nor will I ever be, a Rose.

*

Let me tell you a story.

I had come to Fojo Karaçāo to study medicine, but I learned so much more than that. The sensations in my body, the splitting headaches, my strange and powerful gift for healing—this was my magic. What I found in Fojo was a community of women who fed and nurtured me, who showed me my magic was a gift.

I also found a girl.

She was everything—funny, mischievous, cocky, sweet. She had magic, much stronger than mine, and I felt dizzy in her presence. My blood hummed when she walked into a room.

I'm not enthralling you, she said. But I can teach you about desire.

And so it began. I learned how to unlock a world of sensory pleasures—to turn flesh to cinder, tease blood into a frenzy. My body was a tuning fork, and she was the song.

She taught me other things, too, darker things. She showed me how to enthrall a man, how to make him delirious with wanting. She taught me how to wield power like a blade.

We practiced on your father.

Even this was not enough for her. She was insatiable, drawn to dangerous extremes. The Second Law had always needled her. So she turned her magic on herself, began stilling the blood in her own veins, quieting her heart. The more she explored this dark strand of magic, the more I begged her to stop—and the harder she practiced.

We quarreled over that. At the end, we quarreled over everything.

I was angry. I went too far. I did an awful thing, an unforgivable thing. The people we love are always the ones we hurt the most.

She said there was only one way I could atone for what I'd done. Only one way to prove myself to my sisters and fully commit to the cause.

So here I sit. Married to a man I do not love. Doing my penance, my retribution a kind of daily death. Day in and day out, I enthrall your father, leader of the Circle of the Hunt. I am a vessel for his deepest secrets, secrets I spill and pour into the night. Secrets that save Dujia lives.

When we first met, he was a student, bright and curious about the world. Yet even then, the royal family was courting him, preparing him for what he would someday be. He was hungry for the praise, the rewards, the validation. Your father has always taken great pride in being the best at everything he does.

I sleep beside a killer. I pretend to love a monster, and worse: I make him love me. Who is the monster now?

*

Lauriel writes me letters, telling me about the girl I loved: that she has grown old overnight, hardened with bitterness, and now has a baby. A little girl. I couldn't believe it. Last I checked, a baby requires a coupling with a boy, and unlike me, she never had any interest in boys. Lauriel says the father is long gone.

Soon I too will have a daughter, and we will be bound together by this thread, even as the other threads have severed. Life can be so strange.

*

I swore I would always live from my heart. And what have I done? Turned my heart against another human being, stripped him of his power. I've robbed him of his own heart and sealed mine in a tomb.

I want so many things for you, little bird. I want ferocity and love and space to breathe. I want a world where women are free to live and study, explore and be.

I want you to never have to pretend to love a man you hate.

*

Every day I make a choice to lie. There is no lonelier place in this world than in the heart of a liar.

I am afraid, Mia. What if I can't love you the way you deserve? Can true love be born out of a lie?

*

What is true love?

I used to know the answer, or at least I thought I did. Love was a feeling. Love was an action. Love was a partnership, a fiery union of body, mind, and soul.

Now I think I was a misguided child. Is there such a thing as "true love"? Love is nothing but a patchwork of fiery sensations, an explosion of light and heat, a bursting. Love is a volcano. A volcano is beautiful, but it kills.

*

Griffin cuts down lives with an unrelenting scythe, while I try desperately to glean them. He lies to my face, and I hear him lying, the vile rush of blood beneath his skin.

Men have always been threatened by the power of women. But the king has taken this to new heights. He aims to keep Dujia vulnerable and frightened, and your father is leading the charge.

At night, while he lies beside me with the blood of my innocent sisters ground into his palms, I dream of revolution. What if we women joined forces and rose up against our rapists, our deniers, our abusers? What if we toppled the old world?

There is a saying in Fojuen: *Fidacteu zeu biqhotz limarya eu naj.* "Trust your heart, even if it kills you." If I am saving my sisters so that they may one day rise up, it is worth it. To save one life, one single *Dujia*, I will die a thousand deaths.

Lauriel tells me I have saved far more than one. She writes to me of the *Dujia* from *Glas Ddir* who receive my warnings and flee to safe haven by the dozens. She tells me of the little lakeside refuge, flooded with women who without my work would be mutilated or lost or dead.

I hope she is right. I have to believe that love is the stronger choice—that love will always triumph over hate.

What cruel irony, to manufacture love out of hate, and hate out of love.

*

In every marriage, passions cool. But my marriage is different. In my marriage, I use magic to stoke the fire, fan the flames of desire.

My husband tells me he loves me. He kisses my eyelids and calls them two moons.

How can any Dujia trust the way her lover looks at her? How can I trust anything anymore?

All I trust is you, my daughter, growing in my womb. Waiting. Waiting.

*

Another sister dead today, another Dujia body broken. My heart broken along with it. When will the hatred cease?

*

Tonight your father heated pots of water over an orange flame and poured me a bath. He lit candles, crushed peony petals and sweet lullablus into the suds. For a moment I saw a life where I was a woman in love with her husband. I hate him most

307

when he is kind, because these are the times it is hardest to hate him.

We argued today, over your name. We both love Mia—we've always loved it—but your father wants to give you a strong Glasddiran middle name, and I want something lyrical and feminine. A name is a funny thing, isn't it? You will bear it for the rest of your life, but you get no say in the matter, and there is no way to know whether that small word will be a burden or a gift.

We settled on Morwynna. In the old language, Wynna means "wren." So you see, a piece of me will be with you always.

We wrens lay down our lives for the people we love.

*

Here is what I do not understand: the long-term effects of an enthrall. I can feel my blood aligning with your father's, my heart in harmony with his.

The thing about going to bed with a monster

night after night is that, in the cool light of morning, he no longer looks like a monster.

*

Today you were born into the world.

A tiny slip of a thing: purple lips, hair fojuen-red like mine, gray eyes like your father's. I held you, and I wept. I did not know a human heart could be so full.

Every ounce of love I feel is real. It is a relief, to feel love with no doubt, no shadow.

You are mine and you are his and you are all your own.

You are Mia Morwynna Rose, my daughter.

I love you more than you will ever know.

This was where the ink stopped. There were more pages, but they were pale as bone—if not blank forever, then at least blank for now. Not all the love pouring out of her was enough to fill them.

Mia closed the book and laid it gently on the sand. She pressed the red stone wren to her chest. Her shoulders trembled, and the pillar of salt inside her crumbled. She felt her heart splitting open, without a blade, without magic.

The moon pitched itself through the sky as Mia cried and cried.

Chapter 44

BEAUTIFUL VESSELS

THE NEXT MORNING, MIA paddled the boat herself.

She waited until dawn, but only just. She had spent a sleepless night on the lakeshore, checking the journal every few minutes to see if more ink would appear. Her face was puffy, her eyes red from three years' worth of tears.

When she arrived at the Biqhotz, she stormed into the library.

"Zaga!" she shouted. "I know you're here."

For a moment, the room was quiet. Then the voice rasped.

"You have returned angry."

"I know it was you. You're the woman my mother loved. You killed her, didn't you? You smuggled yourself into Glas Ddir. She let you into our house, let you touch her. She trusted you—and she died for it."

All Mia's theories were clicking into place: Zaga loved her mother. Zaga hated her mother. She practiced dark magic—the sort of magic a Dujia could use against her own kind.

"I haven't touched your mother in many years."

"That's right. Three years." Mia's fists were clenched so tightly her knuckles ached through the skin. "Why did you do it? I have to know."

"Still obsessed with the knowing. Still treating love as a text to be analyzed. You treat books as human and humans as books."

Mia forced herself to breathe, biding her time. She would only kill Zaga if she could confirm Zaga was guilty. Then she would act swiftly, without regret. Yes, Mia was Dujia, but she'd been a Huntress for longer.

Heart for a heart, life for a life.

"I need to know, Zaga. I need to hear you say it."

Silence. Then, "I did not kill your mother, Mia. Your mother tried to kill me."

"*Lies.*"

But she couldn't be sure. Despite the walls of fojuen fomenting her magic from all sides, trying to read Zaga's emotions was like hitting a stone rampart. Mia couldn't tell if she was lying.

"You do not know what your mother was capable of."

"You're right, I don't. But I'm done with secrets and riddles and lies."

A shadow passed across the miniature waterfall. Mia whirled around.

"Why do you hide in the dark? What are you so afraid of?"

Zaga stepped into the light.

Mia reached for the knife she'd hidden in her boot. She had purloined it from a drunk Dujia stumbling out of the Blue Phoenix in the wee hours of the morning. It was an inferior blade, but it would suffice. She had spent three years planning, dreaming, breathing, living for this very moment.

But when she saw Zaga, she stopped cold.

Zaga was emaciated. She had the look of someone who had been ill a long time. Her coloring was Fojuen or perhaps native Luumi, her skin tawny and olive-hued—or at least it had been. Now it was pale and moth-eaten, her once-lustrous black hair missing in clumps. She was tall but stooped, thin as a willow reed, with a severe face and harsh, dark eyes under deep lids. Her left arm hung limply at her side, fingers curled into her palms.

"Your mother left her mark on all of us," Zaga said.

Mia's hand tightened on her knife. But when Zaga took a step closer, letting the torchlight bathe the left side of her body, her stomach twisted. She saw Zaga's withered arm, her fingernails yellow and decayed. The tributaries of veins snaking up her wrist were clotted black instead of blue.

"You would kill me before you knew the truth. Before you saw your mother's handiwork."

Mia recognized the symptoms of neqrosis. The tissue had been starved of blood for too long, causing the muscles to atrophy, the bones to collapse.

"My mother would never do that."

"I assure you, she did."

"She didn't hurt people. She healed them."

"Are they so different? Both require a manipulation of another person's body. Whether you hurt or heal them, you assume control over their flesh."

"They are *not* the same."

"Your mother was tempestuous. Unpredictable. She made mistakes."

"Is that why you sold her off to my father? Forced her into a miserable, empty marriage so she could 'atone' for what she'd done?"

"Do you know the most effective way for a Dujia to kill another Dujia, Mia? It is not to touch her heart. This is what the Hunters think: that we clasp our hands over a man's chest to still his heart forever. We have this power, yes. But a Dujia is most vulnerable at the wrist, not the sternum."

Zaga drew her right fingers up her left wrist, tracing the black veins, then up over the bony olecranon on the tip of the elbow, all the way to her chest. "If you want to kill a Dujia, touch her wrist when you are angry. The veins in our wrist are delicate but direct, and they make beautiful vessels for rage. If you touch the soft skin of her wrist, you will shunt your rage directly into her heart."

Mia felt uneasy. She knew these veins well; she had studied them in her books and anatomy plates. She had traced them up her own arms, a map of cephalic and basilic and cubital veins, blue irrigation systems. But now the map chilled, the tributaries slowing. A premonition.

"Your mother tried to stop my heart," Zaga said.

Mia saw now why she couldn't read Zaga's emotions: she was

wearing not just one piece of uzoolion, but an entire breastplate. Her chest was encircled in a corset of blue stone. You only wore that much protection, Mia thought, when someone had hurt you.

An awful thing, her mother had written in her journal. *An unforgivable thing.* Mia couldn't reconcile this with what she knew of her mother, her gentleness. Was it possible Wynna's big messy heart had led her to be passionate and reckless, even cruel?

Zaga limped back into the shadows, and Mia cursed herself. Three years she had been preparing for this moment: when she came face-to-face with her mother's murderer. And she had failed to enact justice.

But what if Zaga was telling the truth?

Mia heard a telltale catch in Zaga's breathing, then a deep cough. She had read about neqrosis of the pulmonary tissue, where abscesses filled with fluid and neqrotic debris led to gangrene of the lungs. A victim might die quickly, but they might also live a long, painful life.

"Anger is a weapon," Zaga said. "But like all weapons, it is useless unless you know how to wield it. Learn to harness it, and rage can prove a clean and silent blade. If you do not learn how to control it, it can destroy you."

"Mother?"

The voice made Mia jump. Pilar was standing just inside the library doors, her face in shadow, fists bundled at her sides. She was fully clothed and dripping wet, lake water pooling on the red rock at her feet, her shiny black hair glued to the sides of her head like a silken helmet.

"You shouldn't be here," Zaga said sharply to Pilar. "Go back to the tavern with your little friends, drink yourself into oblivion."

"It's morning. And they're not little. They're just my friends." Mia heard the pain in Pilar's voice. "And this is my home, too."

Of course Pilar was Zaga's daughter. Now that they stood side by side, Mia could see the resemblance: same sharp chins and thin, dark eyes. That explained her natural air of authority, the easy confidence that came from being the daughter of someone with power. Mia knew it well, having been such a daughter herself.

"Is my mother asking you a million questions, Rose? Without answering any of yours?" Pilar let out the kind of exasperated sigh only a daughter could make. "She's very good at that."

Mia was struggling to stay afloat. She had fled the river kingdom, followed a map that promised answers, trekked through a frozen forest, and escaped death, all so she could find her mother's killer and avenge her. Every step had brought her here: to the place where her mother fell in love . . . the place where she made enemies. After all that, had Mia really stumbled into a dead end?

"If *you* didn't kill her, then who did?"

Silence.

"Are you sure you don't already know who killed your mother?" Pilar said. "Your father leads the Circle of the Hunt. Surely you've considered what he would have done if he'd discovered his wife was a Dujia."

"Of course I've considered it," Mia snapped. "But I *saw* her. I saw her body. There were no wounds, no broken bones. My mother was killed by magic."

"All right then. It was worth a try." Pilar gestured toward her soaking wet clothes. "After you stole the boat, I was forced to swim the lake to deliver a message. The prince is in dire need of your assistance."

The breath locked in Mia's throat. "Why? Is he all right?"

"He's perfectly fine. Though for some reason, he seems to be in love with you." She shrugged. "He's making breakfast and humbly asks that you attend."

Chapter 45

CHOKING

As Pilar paddled the boat across the lake, Mia traced the words into her arm. *Love.*

What was love? She'd once postulated that a rippling bunch of misfired nerves were the symptom of a malfunctioning heart. Now she simplified her definition: love was a lie. Her parents, who had appeared to be very much in love, were liars. Their marriage was founded on enthrallment, not love.

If Mia was born of this union, did that make her a liar, too?

Her entire life had been built on lies, an infinite bundle of them, the pyre stacked high. She imagined it would take a lifetime to burn them down to truth.

Mia stopped tracing meaningless words onto her flesh. Love had no meaning, not in a land of lies.

Pilar left her on the stoop outside the du Zols' cottage. "I'll be back," she said. "I'm going to get Dom."

"Where is he?"

"Who knows? Probably off with some boy. But he'll come back for breakfast. He's got quite an appetite."

Mia stood on the front stoop watching Pilar go. She heard the clang and clatter of pots inside the cottage, and a chorus of giggles. From the sounds of it, Quin had help in the kitchen, either from one or both of the twins.

A sudden wave of homesickness spilled over her.

Mia sank heavily on the stoop and pressed her back into the wood beam, her sleepless night catching up to her. On a whim she opened the journal to see if her sadness had coaxed more sangflur onto the page. When she saw the ink, her heart lurched toward it.

Mia, my Mia.

My sharp-eyed raven, my little love. You are still small, but you are so smart, so dangerously clever. I urge you to listen to your heart, to let empathy and compassion guide your choices, but your father lavishes praise on your intellect, your logic.

Logic is insufficient. Love will always expose its flaws. It is good to have a mind, but it is better to have a heart.

*

Today we went to the merqad, you on your father's shoulders, our little family of three. Only, it isn't a merqad here, it's a market. There is no music, no laughter, no touch. The market becomes a coffin: full of bodies with no life in them. It seems laughable that we bring our knives to be sharpened in a place so dull.

*

You asked me if the things I wrote about in this little book caused me pain. I told you I wrote about myself, the most painful thing of all. I could see how much it hurt you that I was hurting. In moments like this I see the woman blossoming inside you. A wise, kind woman with gray eyes and a brave, loving heart. You will be better than I am, stronger.

Will you promise me you will always keep the Three Laws? They are beautiful in their simplicity: Do not harm another Dujia. Do not harm yourself. Do not abuse the power you have inside you. Three simple rules for a life worth living.

I have broken the Third Law, Mia. I break it every day with your father. And I have broken the First Law, to my eternal shame. But I have always kept the Second. Small recompense, perhaps, for the mistakes I have made.

Mia frowned. Twice now her mother had referenced hurting a fellow Dujia. *An awful thing, an unforgivable thing.*

It would appear Zaga was telling the truth.

Mia didn't want to believe her mother had ever been cruel. Wynna was perfectly preserved in her mind, her sweeping beauty and gentle heart.

People were flawed. Mia knew that. But had her mother really tried to stop Zaga's heart? *Why?*

The Hunters say we are demons, bodies with no souls. They say we feel no remorse. They say we feel nothing at all.

Lies! All I do is feel. It is relentless. To be a Dujia is to feel, feel, feel.

Have you learned to use your magic, little raven, now that you have bloomed? Have our sisters taught you how to channel your gifts for good? It is good to feel your feelings, and it is also good to learn to calm them before they take

you places you do not wish to go.

I will give you a short lesson. The next time your breathing becomes quick and irregular when you are frightened or upset, sit in a chair and plant your feet firmly on the ground. Press your left hand to your heart and your right hand just beneath your ribs, until you feel your belly rise and fall. Then close your eyes and imagine the wind coursing through the trees of Ilwysion before a rainstorm. Recall it whipping through the oaks and maples, the whispering leaves. Let the memory pool in your fingertips as your breath becomes the wind. Your lungs will soften, and your breathing will slow.

In the old language, the word for breath was the word for life. The ancients believed our breath was the seat of our spirit. I agree. Every time we take a breath, the goddesses breathe through us, their daughters.

We are not demons, Mia. We are the goddesses' greatest gift to the world.

"HELP! HELP US!"

Mia's blood curdled. It was Junay's voice.

322

She leapt up from the stoop and flung the door open, stepping over the uzoolion border with her mother's book clutched to her chest.

Quin stood motionless in the kitchen, holding a copper spoon. Junay's face was frozen in panic. At their feet, Nanu lay face-up on the ground. Choking on air.

Chapter 46

SISTER OF MINE

NANU CLAWED AT HER throat as she writhed on the cottage floor. She coughed and wheezed, her tiny gnarled fist pounding against her chest, a film of sweat on her forehead.

"Mia!" Junay cried. She took Mia's arm and pulled her to her grandmother's side. "I don't know what happened, she just stopped breathing. . . ."

"Where's your mother?"

"She's at the merqad with Sach'a." Junay was terrified. "Please help her, Mia. I can't help her. I don't have magic."

Mia sank to her knees. Nanu's puffy twists had broken free of their knot and were thrashing like silver snakes around her head.

"We have to get her out of here," Mia said. "Away from the uzoolion."

Quin sprang into action. He grabbed hold of Nanu's frail ankles while Mia took her beneath the arms, her head lolling on her neck as they lifted her off the ground.

"The door," Mia said.

Junay charged toward the back door and kicked it open. Mia and Quin hefted Nanu onto a soft patch of earth by the vegetable garden.

"Can you do something?" Jun whimpered. "Can you help her?"

"I'll try," Mia said.

Healing an arrow wound was a world apart from healing a chronic condition. She'd never tried to mend someone's lungs, to coax the air through them, calming the inflamed tissue and smoothing the breath.

Remember the wind . . . Let the memory pool in your fingertips. Your lungs will soften, and your breathing will slow.

Tears pricked her eyes. Her mother had given her exactly the lesson she needed at exactly the right time. As if she'd *known*.

Mia slid one hand over Nanu's heart and the other over her belly. She closed her eyes and conjured up the wind in Ilwysion, the steady, rhythmic whisper of the trees.

She did something else, too. Instead of shoving the feelings away, she let love wash over her—love for the mountains, love for her childhood among tall trees, love for her mother. She summoned the crisp fall day her mother wrapped a toddling Angelyne to her chest with a thick wool shawl and asked five-year-old Mia if she wanted to climb a mountain. They had climbed together, step-by-step, until they stood on the peak, looking down at the leaves in all their autumnal glory, a billowing canopy of rusts and golds and siennas. "Let's take off our gloves," her mother had said, and when Mia hesitated, she'd said, "You're safe here, little bird."

Mia could still remember how it felt to stand on the summit holding her mother's bare hand: the fizzy hum that rushed up her arm and swept down her spine, comforting and warm, like sitting by a crackling fire with a cup of cocoa.

Had that been magic? Was her mother giving her a small, secret gift?

"Mia," Quin whispered. "You've done it."

She opened her eyes.

Beneath her, Nanu's breathing was even, her chest rising and falling with no strain. The old woman stared up at her and blinked. Quin took her arm and helped her up until she was sitting on the softly caked earth. Nanu's hand was steady as she collected her long silver coils into a bundle at the nape of her neck.

"Nanu!" Junay threw herself into her grandmother's arms, nearly knocking her down again. Tears were streaming down her cheeks, no trace of the proud, impudent girl from the day before. "You're all right. You're all right!"

As Nanu hugged her granddaughter, a smile spread across her weathered brown face, crinkling the soft skin around her eyes.

"Yes, Junie. I'm all right."

Over the quivering crown of Junay's curls, Nanu fixed Mia

with a calm, knowing look, her eyes as clear as Mia had seen them.

She didn't say *veraktu.*

She said, "Sister."

Quin had made them a magnificent feast. The table was lined with all kinds of Glasddiran delicacies, modified to accommodate the available ingredients: thin-sliced potatoes with cheese curds, corn fritters and goose gravy, buttermilk pudding, cinnamon bread dumplings dusted with nutmeg, and warm drinking chocolate dotted with shmarda cubes.

But the food was all but forgotten once Lauriel and Sach'a returned from the merqad and Junay told them what had happened.

Lauriel kissed Mia on the forehead and both cheeks. "Angel," she said. "Today you are my angel." Sach'a rolled her chair to her grandmother's side, stroking and squeezing her hand, as if she needed reassurance that Nanu was still there.

Mia was numb but grateful. Breath magic, Lauriel had told her. "Not an easy kind of magic to do, darling. I think you have your mother's gift for healing." Mia felt contentment swirling through her. Her mother felt so close.

A memory stirred. Dom had told her his father died when the Gwyrach froze the air in his lungs.

"When you lost your husband . . ." Mia trailed off. She didn't want to bring up any painful memories.

But Lauriel smiled. "It's good to talk about him. It helps keep him alive. It was your father's men who killed him—he was trying to protect us from the Hunters. We knew our days in Glas

Ddir were numbered, that we had to flee before we were exposed. The Hunters lied and said the Gwyrach had turned his breath to ice, and I told Dom to lie, too. Anything to keep the girls safe. And then your mother died days later . . . two unconscionable losses, one right after the other."

She pressed her hands to her chest. "They stabbed him in the heart. They didn't even let us keep his body; they took it to the Kaer."

A cough from the kitchen made Mia turn around.

Quin was lingering uncomfortably behind the table, apart from the others. He hovered over the food, trying to cover the dishes with iron lids to keep them hot, but steam leaked out anyway. It broke Mia's heart how hard he was trying. But she couldn't shake the feeling he didn't belong here. This was not his world.

"I shouldn't have left," Sach'a said to her mother. "I told you, Mamãe. It's too dangerous to leave Jun alone with her. If Nanu has another attack . . ."

"But it won't be dangerous," Junay insisted, "once I bloom."

Her mother sighed. "Yes, Jun. But we don't know when that will be. And until then . . ."

"I don't understand why *she* bloomed before I did." Junay turned on her sister. "You don't feel anything. You just sit in that chair, all prim and proper, passing judgment on everyone else."

Sach'a spoke very slowly. "You have no idea what I am feeling."

"I know you hardly even *have* emotions. What could have possibly triggered your magic? You don't even—"

"How *dare* you." Sach'a slammed her fist on the table so hard the room went silent. "You think it doesn't hurt me to see the way you run and skip and play? How I sit in this chair while you take everything for granted? You are selfish and reckless—you don't care about anyone but yourself. If you haven't bloomed, it's because you don't deserve the gift. You don't deserve *anything*. Someday you may be a Dujia, but you are no sister of mine."

The words were trembling cold.

Tears shimmered in Junay's brown eyes. Even Lauriel seemed surprised by the outburst. Sach'a was normally so mature and composed. But perhaps the composure was carefully constructed. Mia felt as if she'd seen the crack in the veneer.

"Mia?" Quin lilted her name into a question. "Would you care to accompany me to the Blue Phoenix?"

She stared at the untouched plates of food. "What about breakfast?"

"I'm not feeling particularly hungry at the moment."

She wasn't, either. She squinted out the window. A screen of volqanic ash clung to the air, diffusing the harsh morning light. The clouds were divided into rosy furrows, long rows of blushing pink crops, as if the sun had tilled the sky.

"Isn't it a little early for the Phoenix?" she said.

"It's never too early for a drink."

Chapter 47

HOLLOWS

As THEY WALKED TO the Blue Phoenix, Mia found herself think-ing of Angelyne. They'd had their fair share of sisterly squabbles, but they always ended the same way: with apologies and small gifts. Mia would bring Angie pleasant-smelling salves and striped hair ribbons from the market, and Angie brought her maps and knives. They each knew what the other liked. When the fight subsided, neither of them truly wanted to hurt the other.

But the way Junay harangued her sister, or how coolly Sach'a had sliced into Jun? Mia had never taken a bite out of Angelyne, not like that. What was it Zaga said? *Learn to harness it, and rage can prove a clean and silent blade.*

Something about that made Mia uncomfortable.

"Are you all right?" Quin asked.

"I was just thinking about my sister."

"Ah, yes. I suppose it's true what they say: girls will be girls."

She glared at him. "I hope you don't truly believe something so asinine."

He held up his hands in surrender. "Point taken. I'm beginning to think no one girl is like any other."

When he spoke again, his voice was tinged with sadness. "I wonder if my sister is even looking for me anymore, or if my father has poisoned her against me."

"You speak as if your father hates you."

"What gave you the impression he didn't? He can hardly bear to look at me. He finds me repulsive." His voice wavered, but only for a moment. "Considering his fetish for severed hands, I find him repulsive, too."

The fragment of a memory dashed through her mind: the night she hid in the drawing room, Quin had accused his father of punishing him for some unspoken crime. *I have been far more munificent*, the king had said, *than you deserve.*

"Why does your father hate you, Quin?"

Was it her imagination, or did his jaw tighten?

"No particular reason," he said. "You've met my father. That's just who he is."

She heard liquid dripping, then rushing, then slowing to a drip again. Her ears were fine-tuned to the sound of lying, but this wasn't quite the surge of pressure she'd heard before; it was more nuanced. Not quite a lie, perhaps, but not quite a truth, either.

Quin seemed eager to change the subject. "I don't imagine my cousin was lying, at least not about everyone thinking and hoping I'm dead. My father would be thrilled to get rid of me. Tristan was the son he always wanted."

Dread curled into Mia's stomach. How could she keep forgetting? Tristan was one day closer to the castle, which meant one day closer to Angelyne.

She had to get out of Refúj.

"I have to go, Quin. I can't let Tristan make it back to the Kaer."

"We'll go together. But how comfortable do you feel using magic as a weapon? Because if we're going up against my father and a legion of trained guards, it would be reassuring to know we had more than our four fists."

She knew he was right. If only the book would reveal more. So far a single magic lesson from her mother had proven far more useful than Zaga's meandering sessions on nothing.

"Let's have a drink first, at least," Quin said. "Before we go charging into a battle we are unlikely to win. Then we can make a plan."

She assessed him. A week ago, she would never have thought it possible that the prince would be her ally, her friend. But was that all he was? *He seems to be in love with you.* Was it true? Did love mean standing by someone even when they were making what probably amounted to a terrible decision?

The sadness gripped her again. Her father had *seemed* to be in love with her mother. Her mother *seemed* to be in love with him.

If love only came attached to seeming, safe to say it wasn't love.

Besides. The prince had lied to her before, and judging by the clever way he'd shifted the conversation only moments before, he was *still* lying. Mia felt the familiar walls rise inside her.

They'd made it to the Blue Phoenix. Mia heard music plucked on a cacophony of sheep-gut strings, jovial laughter pouring out onto the sandy avenues of the merqad.

"Hear that?" Quin smiled. "That's the sound of people enjoying themselves."

She hesitated. She saw Dom and Pilar in the tavern—they had clearly been sidetracked on their way to breakfast, not that breakfast happened anyway. They were carousing and having a fine time, but something about their happiness made Mia lonely.

"Actually," she said. "I think I'll sit out here for a little while."

He appraised her. "You're not going to run off to Glas Ddir without me, are you?"

"I just want to collect my thoughts. It's been a strange morning."

He nodded. "Is there anything I can do?"

It struck her that the only time people asked "Is there anything I can do?" was when there was nothing *anyone* could do.

"I know where to find you." She wanted—needed—him to leave. She didn't want to trust him, not if he was only going to lie to her. Sometimes when she looked at Quin, she could feel her reason cracking, her heart swelling between her ribs. She didn't want to feel anything. It wasn't *safe* to feel anything: not gratitude, not vulnerability, and certainly not love.

But if she didn't feel anything, how could she read her mother's words inscribed in sangflur ink?

Once **Quin** ducked inside the tavern, she searched for a secluded spot in the merqad. Merchants were setting out their wares for the day, food and cloth and trinkets, and as the avenues began to buzz with activity, she hid herself away in an abandoned stall. There she pulled out her mother's journal from where it had been hiding in her jacket and cracked it open.

Clearly Mia had not been able to quell *all* her emotions, and she was grateful for it. Dark ink stretched across the page.

Duj katt. Griffin knows. I feel it in my blood, the clatter of his heart. In the way he looks at me.

Or does he? It is not always easy to distinguish the feelings of love from the feelings of anger. They are both forms of passion, though we tend to qualify love as good, a lofty pursuit we should all aspire to, and anger as bad, a twisted malformation of the heart.

Sometimes, when I am with your father, I have trouble reading the sensations of his body. The heightened pulse, the ripples of warmth when he touches me, our hearts twining in a symphony of sound—these could be the symptoms of love, but they could just as easily be the symptoms of rage.

Does he know I've betrayed him? Or does he love me?

I wonder: Is it possible for a human heart to hold both?

The truth is, I do not know which I deserve. I have crept inside your father's heart and made it mine. I have enchanted him and styled this enchantment as love. I have done it for the good of Dujia everywhere, but that does not make it right.

I feel his heart beat most strongly when he rocks you to sleep, or teaches you to climb a tree, or feeds your intellect with books acquired on his travels. Is it possible the murmurings of his heart are not rage at all, but love for you, his little girl?

*

Mia.

I must warn you against enthrallment. A Dujia is not immune to the pull of magic. Griffin makes victims out of all of us, but he has been my victim, too—and now I have fallen victim to my own crimes.

335

I have fallen in love with your father. I love him for how well he loves you.

Mia swiped at the heat behind her eyes. So her mother had loved her father after all, in a twisted sort of way. She was ashamed how fervently she wanted to believe her parents had loved each other—or *found* a way to love each other, carved a path through the deception and the lies. Why did she want this? Love only led to pain. *The people you love are the ones who hurt you most.*

The remaining pages in the book were blank; Mia snapped it shut and tucked it back into her jacket. She had promised Quin she would join him, and she would be true to her word. She forced one foot in front of the other until she was standing outside the Blue Phoenix. Hoots and cheers erupted from inside.

She was in no way prepared for what she saw.

Five boys stood atop the bar. Despite the early hour, they were in varying degrees of inebriation, holding assorted bottles and tankards and, by all appearances, *dancing*—or making a valiant go of it, anyway—to a chorus of whistles from the girls below. Not a single boy was wearing a shirt. All the shirts in Refúj had apparently taken refuge someplace else.

Domeniq was one of the five, his rugged brown torso chiseled into eight discrete sections.

She gulped. Make that ten.

If what he'd said were true, this was a decent percentage of the male population of the island (not counting the grandfathers). But then she realized boy number five wasn't actually a resident of Refúj.

He was Quin, Son of Clan Killian. Maker of Breakfasts, Discarder of Shirts.

The well-defined planes of Quin's stomach glistened with sweat as he tipped back a flask, chugged the murky liquid inside, and wiped his mouth on his arm.

"I just drank a sqorpion!" he yelled. "And glass!" The crowd cheered.

Mia was astonished. How long had she been lost in her mother's book? Surely not long enough for Quin to get *this* intoxicated. Her eyes combed his smooth golden body, which until now she had seen only in snips and slivers, peeking through his shirt or masked by sulfyric bubbles. He was more perfect than any of her anatomy plates, flawless symmetry and long, lean lines.

She hardly recognized him. How was this the same boy with whom she had fled the Kaer? To say Quin's transformation was complete would be an understatement: the curmudgeonly ice prince was now charming a pack of lusty Dujia, slugging back glass-and-sqorpion liquor, and dancing on a bar. He wasn't a very good dancer, but she was impressed by the effort.

She was also furious.

They'd been in Refúj one day, which as it turned out was plenty of time to have her whole life smashed to powder. Her mother had magic. Her parents had never been in love, or if they had, it was twisted, built on lies and secrets. Everything Mia had ever learned or studied about the Gwyrach had been a lie—and she still hadn't found her mother's murderer.

Couldn't Quin see how much she was hurting? Why didn't he care?

You didn't let him, said a nagging little voice. You shut him out. You wanted him to leave you alone, so he did.

One of the girls shouted something, and Domeniq threw back his head and laughed. He whispered something into the prince's ear. Quin blushed.

The boys were easy with one another. Comfortable. Like friends, but with a touch of something more. Mia could feel it: the crackling energy in the air. How had she failed to notice? She thought of the heat when she was standing between them in the Biqhotz, or the way Quin had looked longingly into the pub— the first place they had seen men in Refúj.

Suddenly she was encased in a loneliness so deep it surprised her. Was she really that naive? Had Quin ever been interested in her at all? Perhaps he was interested in boys, just like Dom. Which was fine. Of course it was fine. But she had begun to open her heart to someone, only to have him open his heart to another. Once again, she had proven she knew nothing, absolutely nothing about the human heart.

The heart as a bodily organ, she understood perfectly. Chordae tendineae, atrioventricular valves, papillary muscles: check, check, check. What she couldn't grasp were the mechanics of desire, of love. What was it made of? Did it coagulate in the bloodstream? Get pumped through the arteries? Love, passion, desire—they all seemed readily available to other people but continued to evade her. Just when she thought she'd grabbed hold of them, they wriggled away, swam just out of reach.

The human heart held four hollow chambers inside it. Anatomists had once believed the spirit of the gods flowed freely between the four hollows. It was only by careful, patient scrutiny that scientists had debunked these myths, reducing the body to a collection of rules and theorems, pieces and parts. There were no gods inside the human heart. Only suffering. Loss. Loneliness. And sometimes nothing at all.

In her darker moments, Mia wondered if she'd been mismade. Did her heart hold more than four empty chambers? Was it more hollow than full?

"Mia!" Quin saw her and clambered down from the bar, pulling his shirt back over his head as he approached. His face was flushed, his hair appealingly mussed. Mia fought the urge to reach out and run her fingers through his curls. "I didn't see you come in."

"I think maybe we should talk," she said.

Chapter 48

EVERYTHING YOU THOUGHT YOU KNEW

DUJIA MILLED ABOUT THE merqad as Mia led Quin down the avenues, searching for a quiet place to talk. The prince wasn't stumbling in the slightest, which meant he wasn't nearly as drunk as he'd appeared in the tavern. Why would he pretend? They passed the abandoned stall where Mia had been sitting minutes earlier, now filled with two older women in an amorous embrace.

"Not here," Mia said, taking Quin by the arm. She barreled past the tents and stalls until she found herself on the narrow footpath winding out of the merqad. Had it only been a day since she and Quin arrived in Refúj? It was hard to believe. She marched past the gnarled, spotted trees, and she was almost to where they'd landed in the red balloon when Quin stopped her.

"Mia," he said, "what is going on?"

She didn't understand all the emotions teeming inside her, so she reached for the one she recognized.

"I can't stay here. My sister is in danger, and I'm going back."

"Like I said, I'm happy to go with you. I just needed—"

"To drink and dance?" Her words were laced with anger. "My entire life is going up in flames, but I'm glad you've found time to throw back some sqorpion liquor. Is it just Dom's company you prefer over mine, or boys in general?"

"I prefer whom I prefer. Girls. Boys." Quin set his jaw. "What are we really talking about here? It seems to me we're pretending to have one conversation but really having another."

"You would know. Prince Quin, Master of the Pretending Arts."

He studied her, a swarm of complicated emotions flickering across his face. Behind him, she thought she saw the red balloon in the distance, descending slowly toward Refúj.

"You feel like I betrayed you," Quin said.

"It's not about being betrayed! Or maybe it is." She let out a huff of breath. "Look, I don't mean to blame you. I'm trying to stay clear in my head. It's just . . . I can't tell what's real and what's pretend anymore. I don't know if you care about me . . ."

"I care about you, Mia."

". . . or if you're just pretending. I don't want to be lied to any- more. Everything I've ever been told was a lie. For the past three years I have had only one ambition: to find the Gwyrach who killed my mother. I came here to Refúj, thinking I would find her, but I found Dujia, not Gwyrach. Instead of demons, I found angels. I don't know anything anymore. I don't know who hurt her, Quin."

She blinked back tears. "If I could find who did it . . . if I could put this to rest . . ."

"Perhaps there's something you're missing. Something that happened the night she died. She had no wounds when your father brought her to the Kaer. She looked like she was sleeping. But perhaps he—"

"What did you just say?"

Mia had gone as still and quiet as a tomb. A worm of an epiphany slithered across her neck.

"I only meant," Quin said, "that perhaps there's something you're missing."

"You said she looked like she was sleeping."

He held her gaze. All the cold she'd once felt oozing off him came rushing back, coating her skin in frostbite. The sun bathed her shoulders in balmy warmth, and yet she felt as if she were buried under frozen earth.

"You saw my mother."

He yanked a nervous hand through his curls. "I don't see why that should concern you. I was there in the crypt when the guards brought her body, yes. But it isn't as if I—"

"You didn't think to mention you were in the crypt that night?"

"I didn't want to upset you."

He was lying. His blood somersaulted through his veins.

342

"Why are you lying to me?"

Fear poured off him in a cold draft, but it was mingled with something else. Mia felt a buckling in her sternum, as if her lungs were folding in on themselves, and then a tremendous heaviness. The weight was so crushing she staggered forward, her chest a block of iron and ice. She knew intuitively what it was. *Shame.*

"What are you ashamed of, Quin?"

He stared at her intently. His lips were parted, his eyes wide, and for a moment she thought she could see the color of his shame: red, then gray, like a cauterized wound. He let out a long, low breath.

"That was the worst night of my life," he said.

Mine too, she thought. Mine too.

For three years she had refused to let it in, but memories were like water: they trickled under doors, seeped through cracks and holes, and pooled into pockets you never knew you had. They churned and grew stronger, strong enough to slam into you, to break the dam of everything you thought you knew.

The memory came in a flood, spilling out of her like a torrent.

The day her mother died.

Chapter 49

DESERVE IT

MIA WAS FOURTEEN, STUBBORN and precocious. She knew she was smart, obnoxiously so; she used her intellect to strike down anyone who didn't agree with her particular point of view. She felt big by making others feel small.

"An ogre," Angie called her, with affection. "A very brilliant ogre."

Mia prided herself on being an excellent student. There was good and there was evil, and the lines were clearly drawn. For her, the world was a clementine sliced neatly in two: one half sweet, the other half rotten.

Her mother thought the world was a dappled sparrow's egg in lovely hues of gray.

The day it happened, Wynna was packing a basket of provisions for a woman in a nearby village who had fallen ill. She had just lost her daughter; the girl had been delivered to King Ronan by one of his spies. The woman herself was rumored to be a Gwyrach, so the Hunters set up watch outside her house, scrutinizing her every move. "The poor dear," Wynna said. "They've taken everything from her. Even her grief."

Griffin and Angelyne had gone to the market, so Mia sat alone at the kitchen table, sketching the cranial nerves of a brain, while Wynna discarded her lambskin gloves. She rolled up her sleeves and set to work packing the basket with stone fruits, a loaf of bread, slabs of fresh butter, sweet brown mustard, a flask of blackthorn wine, and fried salted skalt wrapped in crisp brown paper.

Mia was fuming. Domeniq's father had been murdered only days before. All the mountain villages and river towns were on edge; the Gwyrach who had killed him roamed free, her rampage of death and destruction unchecked. Tensions were high in Ilwysion—including in the Roses' cottage.

"I don't understand why you're going to see this woman," Mia said to her mother. "She might be a Gwyrach."

"And what if she is?"

"She'll kill you without a second thought!"

"Or perhaps she won't. Perhaps she'll help me."

"That isn't the way magic works."

"And what do *you* know about the way magic works?"

"I know my best friend lost his father to a Gwyrach," Mia spat, "and that this woman might be the one who killed him. And you want to reward her with bread and wine?"

"It's not so simple. The world is far more nuanced than you think. There will always be a place for compassion and for love. Sometimes love is the stronger choice."

"How can you talk of love when they thrive on hate? The Gwyrach hurt and kill people. You talk about them as if they're human, Mother. I hate them for what they did to Dom."

"Hatred will only lead you astray. I've watched it change your father."

"Father has far more sense than you do. You would hand out loaves of bread and invite the Gwyrach to murder us in our sleep!"

"Mia, please." Her mother grabbed her hands. "You are so very talented. So smart, so gifted. But you must promise me this. You must learn to quiet your mind so you can listen to your heart. This is the most important thing. Whatever you're feeling—fear, anger, love—let yourself feel it. And then use those feelings for good. Use them to know and heal others; to ease their suffering, not cause them more. You must not let your feelings become warped by hate."

Her mother brushed a stray curl off Mia's cheek.

"You're just like me. I fought it, too. For years I fought my feelings. They are frightening, treacherous things. But they are the *only* things. In the end, love is all that matters. *Fidacteu zeu biqhotz limarya eu naj.* Trust your heart, even if it kills you."

Her hands were as sickly soft as the rest of her. Mia grabbed her by the wrists.

"I'm *not* like you. You say listening to the heart makes you strong, but I think it's made you weak. Father keeps us safe by hunting Gwyrach, while you rush care baskets to them, feeding them like ducks. They're not ducks, Mother. They're demons. If a demon killed Dom's father, what makes you think a demon won't kill you?"

She saw the hurt in her mother's hazel eyes, but she plunged ahead, fueled by righteousness and rage. "Maybe it's only *your* heart that will kill you. And maybe you deserve it."

Mia stormed out of the house, the door slamming behind her. She didn't look back.

Mia walked the forest on a bed of spruce and pine needles, waiting for her hands to stop shaking. She couldn't remember the last time she'd been so angry, and never at her mother. But this was different. After his father's death, Dom went numb, the twins cried for hours on end, and Lauriel walked the cottage like a ghost. The du Zols were decimated by their loss. And now Wynna was bringing treats to a woman who might be the Gwyrach who killed him? Mia couldn't forgive her for it. There was a place and time for gentleness, but it was neither here nor now.

She came to a small clearing where she heard a strange sound. A songbird was fluttering and thrashing on the ground, its wing broken. It warbled a long, melancholy note, eyes darting in their sockets. The little wren knew it was going to die.

Before she could attempt to rescue it, the bird twitched and went still.

Mia observed a moment of respectful silence, then drew a knife from her pocket. She sliced the bird's breast open, poking at its bones and tendons, marveling at the fragile anatomy that made it fly. She carried the wren to her secret cave, where she stored all the exotic treasures her father brought home from his adventures; she dipped the songbird's wings into a pot of chinchilla dust from Fojo, fluffing the feathers until they were glossy. She buffed two tiny pieces of Pembuka black schorl for the eyes. Then she stuffed the body with dry kindling and sewed the torn skin back together with needle and twine.

Though her thumbs were stippled with pinpricks by the time she was done, it was worth it. She threaded a filament of bronze through the songbird's feet and wrapped the wire around a forked twig. The wren looked like it might burst into song at any minute. She'd brought it back to life.

By the time she finished, night had slunk into the forest. Mia felt calmer now, penitent. Angelyne was right; she'd acted like an ogre. Even if her mother was misguided, she was only trying to be kind. Mia resolved to apologize as soon as she got home.

But something was wrong. She sensed it the minute she saw the cottage: the light inside was strange, the shadows long and ghoulish.

Then she heard her sister scream.

Mia flung the door open. She saw her father first—at the kitchen table with his head in his hands. Angelyne was sprawled facedown on the floor, weeping. Only after Mia stepped inside did she realize Angie had thrown herself on top of their mother's lifeless body.

In her shock, Mia defaulted to logic. She knelt and ran her hands over her mother's unbroken skin—her throat, her chest, her wrists. It was Mia who found the moonstone clutched in Wynna's fist, the talisman that had failed to protect her. "No wounds," she said, over and over. "She's not bleeding. She can't be dead, Father."

Her father's grief was so thick she could breathe it, a cloak of acrid smoke that burned her throat. "Gwyrach don't need swords or arrows," he said. "They can stop a human heart."

The king sent a royal summons that Griffin accompany his wife's body to the castle, and a few hours later, eight guards came and lowered her mother into an alabaster box. Even in her shock, Mia thought the number excessive. Eight men for one dead woman.

Mia begged to go with them.

"Stay with Angelyne," her father said. "Keep her safe."

She sat in speechless horror as the Hunters stalked the woods, looking for her mother's killer. The sick woman from the neighboring village was no longer a suspect: Mia would later discover the Hunters had taken her to the Kaer early that morning, long before Wynna was killed. Her Hand already graced the king's Hall of Hands.

It was Angie who had found their mother's corpse. She had run into the cottage, proudly holding an astrolabe she'd bought for Mia at the market, when she saw her mother lying on the floor. Poor Ange was only twelve, and she screamed and shook as Mia stroked her strawberry hair.

But all Mia could hear were the cruel words she'd said to her mother. They took on the air of augury, a malicious prophecy dancing across her eyelids every time she tried to sleep.

Maybe it's only your heart that will kill you. And maybe you deserve it.

Chapter 50

HOME

"MY FATHER'S MEN BROUGHT her to the castle," Quin said. "Eight guards."

Mia dragged herself back to the present. Her whole body was trembling, the blood howling in her ears. "I remember."

"They took her to the crypt and left her there."

It hurt imagining her mother's body abandoned on a cold stone.

"What were you doing there, Quin? Tell me the truth."

He stared at her a long moment. Then the words tumbled out quickly, as if he wanted to be rid of them.

"I was meeting someone. We needed a place where we wouldn't be discovered."

"Who were you meeting?"

"My music teacher."

"The boy who taught you piano?"

He nodded. "I told you he was my first friend, and that was true. I was smitten by his sister—she was beautiful—but before long I was smitten by him, too. Our friendship blossomed into something else. But in the Kaer, people were always watching: the servants, the guards, my father himself. We couldn't even touch each other. All we could do was play each other songs to express the way we felt."

"Like 'Under the Snow Plum Tree,'" Mia said. "The song you were playing in the library."

"It was the first song Tobin ever taught me. That haunting melody . . ." For a moment Quin's voice slipped away. Then he recovered it. "We wanted to meet somewhere we wouldn't be watched. And then we realized: the crypt was under the grove of plum trees! *Under the snow plums, if it's meant to be, you'll come to me.* The song had told us exactly where to go. So we made plans to rendezvous in the crypt once darkness fell."

He frowned. "But the night didn't go as planned. We'd only been in the crypt a few minutes when we heard the guards. We hid behind the tombs as they carried in the body. My father was with them, as was yours. They were quarreling. My father wanted to keep your mother's body in the Kaer—to study it, he said. They suspected she had magic, that the famed leader of the Hunters was harboring a Gwyrach in his home."

Mia's stomach sank. They had been right.

"My father won the argument, of course," Quin said. "He always does. Though he did let your father choose the burial stone—which is why your mother's vault is the only one in the crypt that isn't a grotesque parody, in my opinion. The moon and the bird."

The breath caught in her throat. The king hadn't merely used her as collateral to ensure Griffin fulfilled his quota of Hands. The truth was darker. Ronan had accused him of harboring a Gwyrach.

Mia's chest ached. Her father's only hope of saving his daughters' lives was to give the king whatever he wanted.

"This is why we were forced into marriage," she said.

"That wasn't the only reason." A pall passed over Quin's face. "My father discovered us lurking behind the tombs. I have never seen him so angry. When he gets angry, my father is . . . severe."

He exhaled. "He didn't hurt me—not physically, at least. But he hurt Tobin. And he made me watch."

A chill dripped down Mia's spine. "What did he do?"

"You tell me. You've seen Tobin yourself."

"What do you mean? How could I . . ."

The boy in the village.

It struck her like a thunderclap. Quin's music teacher was the boy in Killian Village who'd handed them bread and a pouch of snow plums. She remembered the hitch in the boy's gait, the two fingers missing on his right hand.

"He threw Tobin out of the Kaer," Quin said quietly, "and banished him to the village. But not before he made sure he would never play music again."

Mia paled. It was too horrible.

"I'm sorry, Quin. I can't imagine what that must have been like."

He straightened, scrubbing the emotion from his face.

"Like I said, worst night of my life."

For the first time, Mia understood why Quin had been cold and withdrawn every time she spoke of her mother. The fear and shame from that night mingled in his blood like a blizzard.

Something sparked in Mia's memory. "Is that why you told your father I was dangerous the night before our wedding?"

"Actually, he told me. Since they suspected your mother was a Gwyrach, they suspected you, too. Though to be honest, I had long suspected you might have magic. The circumstances of your mother's death were too odd. It was easy to blame your father, the great magic Hunter, but I had seen her body, and there were no wounds. In my darker moments, when that awful night played relentlessly in my head, I wondered if *you'd* done it."

"So you stuck a knife in your boot at the wedding."

He smiled, rueful. "You weren't very fond of me—that was readily apparent. I think it gave Father great pleasure, the idea of marrying me off to a girl who might actually kill me."

"You never did seem particularly surprised I had magic."

"And now you know why." He cleared his throat. "But I'm not afraid of you anymore, Mia. I know what kind of woman you are, and I've seen how much you grieve the loss of your mother. There was a while in the forest when I wondered if you'd killed her by mistake. But I don't think you can kill someone by mistake, even if you *do* have magic. I've only seen you use your magic for good."

Mia couldn't speak. A hole had opened up inside her. He'd meant the words to be a comfort, but they landed like an arrow in her heart. *I wondered if you'd killed her by mistake.*

She heard Zaga rasping: *If you want to kill a Dujia, touch her wrist when you are angry. The veins in our wrist are delicate but direct. They make beautiful vessels for rage.*

Mia had gripped her mother by the wrists, seething with rage.

"Quin." The words were fire in her throat. "I think I killed my mother."

He didn't have time to answer—a shout pierced the air. It was close, just around the corner. Through the trees Mia saw a flash of red in the distance. The hot air balloon.

More panicked shouts filled the air. She couldn't move. She was pinioned to the earth. But women were pouring out of the merqad, brushing past them and barreling toward the balloon. Whoever had arrived, they certainly weren't receiving the same dispassionate welcome Mia and Quin had received the day before.

I killed her. I killed my mother.

Quin took her by the hand. "Come on."

At the landing pad, an eerie hush descended on the crowd. The balloon bobbed gently, not yet secured, and the dark-skinned woman in the brilliant purple scarf—the one who seemed to be in charge—stood very still by the edge of the bronze bucket.

"They have found us," she said.

Mia stood beside Quin, dazed, as the woman pointed a long, accusing finger.

"Because of *you*."

Mia's heart constricted. Had the Hunters tracked her to the island, exposing the Dujia? How many angels would she unwittingly kill?

The woman in purple beckoned her closer. Mia loosed her stiff fingers from Quin's and moved slowly, as if walking to her doom.

There were no humans in the balloon. But when she peered into the bucket, her stomach sank. She wished she could erase what she'd seen.

A bird floated in a bath of blood. A slender, elegant white swan, its throat slit. As Mia stared at its mangled feathers, all she could think of was her sister. *Angie, my little swan.*

Written in blood on the inside of the bucket was a glistening red message.

Mia,
Come home.

PART FOUR

Blood

Chapter 51

THE THREAT OF VIOLENCE, OR THE PROMISE

THE DUJIA BOATS WERE sturdy, albeit small. The fleet was banked in a spacious cove an easy swim from the waterfall. "Fleet" was generous: there were only a dozen, each fitted with two oars and carved from a tough, fibrous wood varnished black. Unlike the *Sunbeam*'s walnut shape, the boats were long, pointed at one end and bulbous on the other. Like tears, Mia thought. Or drops of blood.

The arrival of the swan in Refúj had sent everyone into a panic. Their refuge, their safe haven, their sanctuary against the rest of the world—gone. Never before had the balloon arrived with a dead animal and a warning. Little girls cried while their mothers tried to calm them, but the women were just as frightened. They had been exposed.

Mia, come home.

The message was crystalline: if she ever wanted to see Angelyne alive again, she would return to Kaer Killian.

There had been no discussion. From the moment she saw the swan with its severed throat, she knew she would go back.

What she hadn't accounted for—and had fiercely protested— was that Zaga would insist on going with her. Zaga promised her Dujia sisters she would assess the threat herself. If only a few people knew, she would take care of them; if the Glasddirans were launching a full-scale attack, they would prepare to fight.

She instructed Dom and Pilar to accompany her, and to everyone's surprise, Quin. He had never met Zaga, and Mia knew from the icy gusts peeling off him he was afraid. Zaga cut a formidable figure, and when she ordered the prince to join them, he didn't argue.

They took only two boats, Quin and Domeniq rowing one; Pilar and Mia helmed the other, with Zaga hunched in the stern, her back deeply bowed. Two lone teardrops hugging Glas Ddir's eastern coast: one tear for the boys, and one for the Dujia.

I killed my mother.

Every few seconds the horror ripped through her anew. Mia's mother was dead because of her. Her sister would soon follow . . . if she wasn't dead already.

The boat rolled and listed on the waves. Mia's seasickness blended seamlessly into her guilt, muddying her grief. She tried to distract herself by postulating who had sent the bird. Was it Tristan? It seemed unlikely he had made it all the way back to the Kaer—they'd left him in the woods less than two days ago. King Ronan? Slitting a bird's throat seemed like just the sort of thing the king would do.

Or was it the Circle? The Hunters had spent enough time around the Roses' cottage to hear Wynna call Angelyne her little swan. Did Angie have unbloomed magic, too? The thought sent fear shrieking through Mia's heart. If the other Hunters had discovered the truth about Mia and her mother being Gwyrach, they would kill Angie in a heartbeat, eliminating any risk. And if they'd already killed her father for treason, he wouldn't be able to protect her.

"Do you wish to learn more about your magic?" Zaga asked from the stern, her voice smoky.

"No," Mia said. Then after a moment, "Yes."

All those senseless hours, poring over anatomy books, thinking she could have saved her mother if she'd only understood the way arterial blood circulated through the heart. She had been such a child. Mia's magic had killed her mother, but if she had known about it—if she'd been able to harness and control it—she could have saved her mother's life.

She thought she saw a flicker of softness behind Zaga's hard eyes.

"Did you know I was the one who taught your mother the art of the enthrall?"

She did know, from her mother's journal.

"I already know how to enthrall."

Pilar jumped in. "You know a simplified version. My mother can enthrall ten men at once."

Zaga nodded. "It is possible to enchant a roomful of men with desire."

A seed of dread settled in Mia's stomach. "Without touching anyone?"

"Yes. It requires great focus, but it can be done."

The ocean slapped against the boat in white-capped waves. Every time Mia closed her eyes, she saw Angie floating in a bath of blood. She gripped the oar more tightly. If she had failed to keep her mother safe, now was her opportunity to make it up to her by saving her sister. Mia had never meant to wield her anger like a blade, but perhaps now she would learn how to—a lesson learned three years too late.

"Why does nobody talk about the Three Laws?" she asked.

Zaga shifted. "There is nothing to discuss. The Laws have been passed down from one generation of Dujia to the next, simplified and codified over hundreds of years. The First Law: we do not use magic to hurt our fellow sisters. The Second Law: we do not use magic to hurt ourselves. The Third Law: we do not use magic to hurt those without magic—unless we have just cause to do so."

"And what qualifies as 'just cause'?"

A smile warped the edges of Zaga's lips. It was the first time Mia had seen her smile, and she was rusty, as if her mouth had forgotten the shape. "The Laws have always been somewhat open to interpretation."

If that's true, Mia thought, then what's the good of having laws?

"My mother said you were toying with a darker magic. Something about breaking the Second Law."

Mia watched the softness evaporate from Zaga's face. "There are certain things I do not care to remember." She snapped herself shut like a box. "Do you wish to learn the craft of enthrallment or no?"

As Zaga droned on, Mia tried to focus, but her mind roamed back to her father. *To enthrall someone is to enslave them, little rose. You've stripped them of consent, robbed them of their choice. And without choice, what are we?*

Had he known his wife had been enthralling him for years?

A tiny flame of hope glimmered. Her father had not wanted to marry her to the prince. If Griffin had in fact been disloyal to the crown, did it mean he'd found out about her mother . . . and tried to help her?

The flame grew bolder. Mia's father had given her the journal. Down in the crypt, he'd quizzed her on the fojuen stone, said it was the most important test she'd ever take. He might as well have handed her a custom-made map to Fojo. In a way, he had. She felt for the journal, tucked safely into the jacket Pilar had loaned her.

Her father knew. He *must* have known.

Your mother loved you more than anything. A love like that has power. You, too, bear this love.

What if he was using the word *love* in place of magic?

And if he knew she had magic, did he know she'd killed her own mother?

Mia could still feel his hand on her back as he escorted her to the Royal Chapel. Firm and solid, more book than hand. It was almost certainly her father who had slipped the journal into her wedding train as he walked her to the altar. Had he *wanted* her to run away, after pretending that he didn't? And why would he knowingly subject Angelyne to a royal wedding and the same cruel fate?

"Have you heard a word my mother said?" Pilar said, startling her.

"Of course," Mia said, though they both knew she was lying.

The journey back to the castle was faster by sea than by land. High above them she could see a smudge of blue swyn needles, the mountains slumping into hills before they sank into the river.

As their two boats cut swiftly up the coast, day blurred into night, then day, then night as they sailed into the Opalen Sea.

Mia's father had spoken fondly of the Opalen Sea, but she had never seen it. Now she hardly registered the water's opalescent glister, the silver starlight spilling onto the waves. She'd read that the ocean derived its distinctive color from animalcules banded together just beneath the surface, creating an otherworldly sheen. She didn't care. All she could think was: *Angie. Angie. Angie.*

"Won't there be an army waiting?" Mia murmured. "Whoever sent the swan is no doubt expecting us."

"If you had been listening," Pilar said, "you would know the enthrall makes us much more powerful than they are. If we can control the hearts of men, we control the men. Ronan could send a legion of ten thousand and they'd be no match for us."

Pilar seemed a trifle overconfident, Mia thought. If that were true, she highly doubted the Dujia would have spent so many centuries oppressed.

She gazed out at the other boat, where Quin and Dom were talking quietly. Every so often, a laugh rolled across the waves. She was jealous of their ease with one another, the innate trust. With Domeniq, Quin would never have to wonder if he were being enthralled. He could trust his own wants. His own desire.

They rowed for hours, fighting the waves slurping and sucking at their oars, stopping only briefly to eat the food they had packed. Mia's lips were chapped, burned by salt and sun. After two days of rowing, the cliff tapered off and the Opalen Sea spat them sharply into the mouth of the Natha. From there the path to Kaer Killian was swift: a clean, black line.

Mia's shoulders ached; the blisters on her fingers stung. Overhead, the moon broke into a thousand silver knives and danced upon the river. In the dark, the water simmered with the threat of violence, or the promise.

Mia recognized them first: the tall trees of Ilwysion. She inhaled the scent of pine. After three days of rowing, they had arrived.

"Quietly," Zaga instructed as they dragged the boats onto the riverbank, their feet sinking into the spongy black sand. They were a short distance outside Kaer Killian, far enough that the forest was deserted, close enough to see a dusky orange haze where the brothel torches burned bright.

Pilar helped her mother out of the boat. Considering how stiff Mia's limbs were, she could only imagine how Zaga had weathered the waves. She had required surprisingly little care on the boat; if the rocky trip had aggravated her injuries, she didn't show it.

Now Zaga leaned on her knotted white cane. "We will make camp here, sleep a few hours to recover our strength. Our magic is of no use if we are too weak to wield it. Then, when the night is at its darkest, we will descend into the quarry and follow the tunnels into the castle's underbelly."

Mia resented Zaga for taking control of what was meant to be a rescue operation. She wanted to go to the castle and find Angelyne immediately. But she knew she needed sleep. Zaga had indeed given her magic lessons on the boat, guiding her in a series of rudimentary exercises that had left her feeling exhausted.

They made camp. Zaga rested on a mossy rock while Mia busied herself building a fire. Pilar disappeared into the woods to hunt for supper, and Quin and Domeniq strung up a crude tarp for shelter. She hated how they were tiptoeing around her, speaking in hushed voices. She would rather they screamed.

Mia was jittery, nervous. Every twig crack or leaf crunch made her whirl around, half expecting to see Tristan or the king's guards come stumbling through the trees. If she'd done the math right—and she rarely did math *wrong*—the duke would be closing in on the castle right as they did.

She blew on the smoking branches until they sizzled pink. She heard a sound and pivoted, but it was only Pilar, marching proudly into camp with a wild boar slung over her shoulder. Whether she'd killed it with magic or arrow, Mia didn't ask. They roasted the meat over the fire, shredding tender hunks off the bone.

They spoke in hushed tones until Quin asked pointedly, "What am I doing here?" and the others fell silent. His eyes flicked from Zaga to Pilar to Mia. "It's clear you three are perfectly capable of laying siege to the castle yourselves."

Mia expected Zaga to answer his question with a question. But for once she spoke plainly.

"You will stay with Dom in the woods outside the Kaer. If we encounter any trouble, I am sure the king will be happy to know his son is just beyond the castle walls, whole and undamaged."

Mia's stomach slid over an inch. She heard the unspoken threat behind Zaga's words: whole and undamaged, *for now.*

Quin was collateral.

My blackmail groom.

She looked at Dom, who was feverishly rubbing his head. He didn't like it, either. Pilar wouldn't meet her eyes.

"Take what sleep you can." Zaga reached for her cane. "I will wake you when it is time."

She limped to a tall oak tree and sat on the mossy earth, back against the wide trunk, and shut her eyes.

Mia could feel Quin's fear, a veil of cold prickling her skin. She also felt his sadness, a bone-thick weariness in her hands and feet. Once again she wasn't sure how much his feelings were tangled up in her own; she, too, felt frightened. She, too, felt sad. Hadn't they hurt Quin enough? In the Royal Chapel, he'd nearly died, all because he'd been standing a little too close to her. Wrong place, wrong time, wrong wife.

How many people would die because of her?

Quin left the campfire. They were all being overly careful with one another as they silently buried the bones of their meal. Mia fluffed spruce needles into a makeshift pallet and nested the journal in the middle like a soft leather egg. Then she sculpted a protective mound of leaves and pinecones. She curled her body around it, but she was too anxious to sleep. She thought of waiting until the others drifted off and stealing into the castle by herself—she could spirit away Angie and take her somewhere safe.

But where would that be? Refúj was no longer a haven. Nowhere was safe.

She heard someone plop down a few feet away. The prince.

To her shame, she pretended to be asleep. Out of the corner of her eye she saw him lying stiffly on the cold ground, nowhere near the tarp he and Dom had erected, fists clenched tightly as he stared up at the sky. His curls seemed to breathe in the gentle wind, his face kissed by moonlight. In another world, she thought, in another life, I could love him.

Then his terror was a tent spike in her skull. If something went wrong tomorrow, would Zaga kill him?

Mia should have never brought him to Refúj. Dancing and drinking at the Blue Phoenix seemed a world away, the harmless diversions of children. Zaga was no child. She wouldn't hesitate to hurt Quin to protect her own.

Perhaps all mothers were that way.

"Mia?" Quin's voice was soft. "Are you awake?"

She said nothing. She hated herself for her silence. Did she really have so little left to give?

I'm keeping him safe, she told herself. She would keep Quin at a distance to protect him. Love was not something that could exist between them. Not now, not ever.

A cloud passed overhead. The sky crackled midnight blue, pocked with stars. The air was too heavy to breathe. Mia was worn out, thin as paper, rubbed raw from trying.

No matter what she did tomorrow, someone would get hurt.

Chapter 52

THE PEOPLE YOU LOVE

MIA WOKE TO A rustling, then a hush. A twig snapped under a
boot.

Every nerve in her body arched. Was it Tristan? She listened.
Another snap.

Her eyes swept the camp. The others were sound asleep. Dom
lay under the tarp with two hands on his belly. Pilar was sprawled
across the earth, good at taking up space. Zaga was still sitting
against the tree, spine curved like a scythe.

Quin was gone.

She heard the branches being shoved aside, footfall, breathing.
Something heavy splashed into the river. No one else stirred as
she stood and slipped soundlessly between the trees.

The forest floor was caked in green mosses and white lichen blooms. She passed leaning towers of ivory shale, gneiss, and quartzite marked with glacial striations like a lady's pocket fan. Mia imagined the river goddess, banished from her three sisters and their volqanic paradise. She saw her roaming this strange, stony kingdom, tears rolling off her cheeks and sluicing down the rocks until they swelled into the Natha.

The earth grew pliant, sifting to fine granules. She'd made it to the river.

She heard a swash, then saw a blur of gold against the black. She took a breath and stepped out of the trees.

Quin was sitting on the riverbank, throwing rocks into the Natha. His shoes were lined up neatly on the sand and his feet were bare; they dangled in the water. He bristled when he saw her.

"It's all right." She held up hands in surrender. "Zaga didn't send me to spy on you. I'm here as a friend."

"Friend." He smiled sadly. "Since when have you and I ever been friends? Refugees, maybe. Partners in crime. Questionably married. But never friends."

"Can I sit?"

"You can do whatever you like. If there's one thing I've learned about you, it's that you will anyway."

She sank into the sand. Together they watched the water surge past their feet. The air was rife with all the things they did not say.

"It's funny," she said at last. "I used to find such comfort in the trees. My mother always loved trees, and I think I loved them because she did; these big friendly giants watching over me as a little girl. But I think that was a lie. So much of what I believed was a lie. Now the water seems truer. Black and murky and able to kill you in the blink of an eye—and far more honest."

Quin stared into the dark swirling river for a long time.

"I don't want to go back, Mia."

"I don't blame you."

"Let's say Zaga doesn't kill me. That I make it back to the Kaer in one piece. If I go back there—back to my father, to that world—they'll crush me. They'll make me into someone I don't recognize."

He dug his fists into the sand. "I know you want to save your sister. And I don't want anything to happen to Angelyne. But I can't shake the feeling I'll die if I go back."

The blackthorn blossoms clung sweetly to the cool night air. The scent had been a staple of her childhood, a simple pleasure. Now it smelled of loss.

"I'm sorry." She looked down at her hands. "I've brought nothing but fear and terror into your life."

"No. The fear and terror were always there. I was scared of you, yes, but I've spent most of my life afraid of my father. After what he did to Tobin . . ." He shook his head. "I don't know why it surprised me. For years I'd watched him string up the hands of the women he killed. Girls. Such little girls . . ."

He choked on the words, unable to finish.

"I've spent my whole life scared of my father. But I've also been scared of turning out like him. Scared that sitting on the river throne would make me ruthless and brutal, someone who built a kingdom on bigotry and hate."

"Quin. Look at me." She cupped his chin in her hand. "You could never be like your father. *Never.* You are good and kind and generous. You care about people. Back in the Kaer, I thought you were selfish—just another coddled prince. But I was wrong about you. I was wrong about a lot of things."

He pressed her hand to his cheek. "You broke me out, Mia. You took me places I'd never been and gave me a taste of freedom. You showed me what my life might have been like. What *I* might have been like."

"Your life isn't over."

"It might be, depending on what happens tomorrow." He dropped her hand, reaching for a pebble and smoothing it with his thumb. "I never expected to be here. I couldn't have imagined it in a million years, not in all my pretending and my make-believe. But I don't regret it. I don't regret a single minute of getting to know you."

Mia wondered why she had regrown a heart if just to break it.

"I'm not going to let anything happen to you," she whispered. "I swear it."

He smiled. "You're beautiful when you lie."

When she flushed, he quickly added, "Not to diminish you or suggest that beauty is an indicator of your worth."

She didn't understand what was happening in her body. It wasn't the honeyed melting of an enthrall, but a feeling of spinning in midair, weightless. She imagined this was what desire felt like.

"But what about Dom?" she said.

"He's beautiful, too." Quin tossed the stone across the water, where it glided like a crane. "More than one person can be beautiful, you know."

"But do you . . ."

"I'm in love with you, Mia. For all your magic, did you really not know?"

She leaned forward, raked her fingers through his curls, and pulled his lips to hers.

Desire licked her collarbone, curling through her limbs. She hadn't known she could want someone. Not like this. Quin's mouth was soft, his lips warm and salty. He cradled her face in his hands and ran his thumb down her jaw, her skin melting into his touch.

She pulled back. "I'm not enthralling you. I don't want you to think . . ."

"I know." He fished a chain out of his pocket. A piece of uzoolion swung from the end. "A parting gift from Lauriel," he said, and snapped the clasp around his neck.

She held her breath, terrified that the desire would seep out of his eyes, that maybe she was enthralling him after all. But she felt steady in her body, powerful in a way she never had during an enthrall. She wanted him. That wasn't her magic; that was her.

"I want this," he said. "I want you."

She felt it pouring through her, the spiced fire of his want. When she'd enthralled him, it was artifice dressed in a pretty gown. It was manipulation masquerading as desire, and from the outside, it was lovely, even bewitching. But the feelings were manufactured, born of magic, not need.

This—now—the heat she felt pulsing through her, quivering in her fingertips, pulsing in her hips—was *real*.

He dug his hands into her curls, transforming her hair into streaming sunlight. With his other hand he swept his fingers across the soft skin of her nape. Gently he tilted her head back and pressed his lips to her cheek, her jaw, her neck. He traced the top of her shirt as he planted kisses on her collarbone like sparks. He was setting her aflame.

"Too warm," she murmured.

"What can I do?"

"Cool me off."

He peeled her shirt down at the neckline, just an inch, and blew cool air over her sweltering skin. Delicious sensations shivered down her spine.

"The river," she said.

They eased themselves into the Natha, the cool rush of water spilling over them. Their clothes clung to them like a second skin. Mia dug her fingers into his curls, mashed wet against his forehead, and tasted the plumpness of his bottom lip. She dragged her palms down his chest and stopped where the crest of his hip bones met the top of his trousers.

"Is this what drowning feels like?" he murmured. "Because I think I'd like to drown forever."

She laughed. "Sorry. I'm sorry. But I swear I read that exact line in one of my sister's novels."

She was scared she'd ruined the moment, but he laughed, too. "Needless to say," he whispered in her ear, "I read the same book."

His fingers were tangled up in the slick coils of her hair as he pulled her closer, his greedy lips exploring hers. She wrapped her legs around him, his body lean and taut, stronger than she expected. The cloth between them was dissolving in the river. Everything was dissolving. She felt like sugar sprinkled in the sea.

Quin's kisses were molten, incinerating her thoughts, her reason. She couldn't believe she'd ever thought the prince didn't have a red beating heart. She felt it now, crashing against her ribs.

Her body vibrated in a long, low hum. She lost track of time, seconds entwining into minutes, minutes to hours. There were no theorems to explain this. Why would she want to? What Quin was doing to her defied logic.

Mia ran her fingers over his wet skin, memorizing the map of his body. She was exploring the outer limits of his pleasure and her own, the boundary waters of desire. No science could describe the warmth extending outward from her center, sizzling spokes of fire and friction, like a sun-kissed star.

When they finally drew their bodies apart, they climbed out of the river and collapsed onto its banks, spent. Mia shivered warm, if such a thing were possible. All things seemed possible at the moment. She was wrapped in a dreamy, otherworldly haze.

Somewhere in the haze, she heard a distant whisper: *The people you love are the ones who hurt you most.* She shoved it away. She didn't want to hear it. Not now, not when the sorrows of the last week had finally given way to bliss.

"Lovely," Quin said, kissing her wrist. "Lovely." He kissed her collarbone. "Lovely." He got sidetracked by her lips.

She let out a low moan of pleasure, and the river moaned back.

Then a woman screamed.

Chapter 53

MOONLIGHT

THEY HEARD THE SCREAM again, pierced with fear.

Mia and Quin scrambled up from the riverbank and ran toward the sound.

There was no time to discuss a plan of action. They were flying through the forest, tripping over rocks and tree stumps. Seconds later they stumbled into a clearing where a stunning white mare was tethered to a tree. The horse nickered and stamped her hooves, clearly agitated.

A girl was pinned to the ground by two men. One had her by the thighs, the other by the wrists. Her hair stuck up in wild tufts, and her shirt was torn and gaping, one breast exposed.

"Karri!" Quin shouted.

Karri looked up at him, her eyes white with terror. She was fighting with all her might, writhing and kicking, but even the magnificent princess was no match for two men.

As Mia stared at the men, vitriol scalded her throat. Cousin Tristan and his lone surviving guardsman stared back.

The duke's hand hung limply at his side, his fingers shattered from where he had grabbed her ankle. He and his ginger-haired guard had been trekking back to Kaer Killian for days, thirsty, starving, their pale faces rough and unshaven and their bodies gaunt. They hadn't yet made it back to Mia's sister.

They had chanced upon Quin's sister instead.

The men should have been weakened by four days of snow and hunger, but lust had replenished their strength. They gulped down their power until they were glutted, drunk. They knew they could take what they wanted—and what Tristan wanted was his own cousin. For all she knew, the king had sanctioned it.

Mia felt sick. Not even Karri, Daughter of Clan Killian, Rightful Heir to the River Throne, was safe.

With a roar, the prince hurled himself at Tristan, hooking an arm around his cousin's throat. They fell to the ground, the duke yelling and clawing at Quin wildly.

Instead of retreat, the wiry guardsman thrust his whole weight onto Karri. He ran his dirty hand up the inside of her thigh.

"Fine with me, Princess," he growled. "I like 'em better when they fight."

Karri froze, and Mia felt fear, cold and deadly sharp. A lesson Zaga taught her in the boat ignited in her fingers; she knew exactly what to do. She wrapped her arms around the man from behind, digging the heels of her hands into his groin.

Her blood screeched through her hands. She felt the heat drain out of the man's groin as she channeled it down, down, down. She was unblooding him. Where his body had been rigid moments before, she could feel it deflating. She ground her palms in deeper, siphoning the blood to his feet where it couldn't hurt anyone. He let out a yelp and let go of Karri, grabbing at his toes, now engorged with excess blood.

The princess's face was wet with moonlight. Mia had never seen her cry.

"Mia," she whispered. "Thank the gods."

The rapist clambered out of the clearing, bellowing for his lord to follow. Tristan seized the moment of confusion, using his good hand to land a punch on Quin's shoulder that sent the prince spinning into the dirt. The duke and his guardsman crashed into the woods and vanished behind a copse of maples.

Karri was shaking. "I never thought . . . I didn't think he'd . . ."

The shock in her face twisted, turned into something else.

Mia heard a crunch behind her as a red arrow soared past her head and lodged deep in Karri's stomach.

She watched in horror as the princess sank to the forest floor.

Chapter 54

WEEPING BLOOD

"NO!" QUIN YELLED.

Instantly he was kneeling by his sister's side. She sputtered for breath, a halo of blood reaching outward, soaking her shirt, anointing Quin as he pressed his hands over the wound.

Mia couldn't move. She didn't have to; Pilar stepped out of the trees, the bowstring hot in her hands. She was trembling.

"My mother," she whispered. "My mother said . . ."

Zaga stepped out of the woods, white cane in hand.

"I said to wound her, Pilar. Not to kill."

The blood thickened in Mia's throat as the blood rose in Karri's. They were both choking. Karri's mouth moved around silent words. *Help. Please help me.*

Zaga bent over the fallen princess. She pressed her lips into a wan line.

"Heal her," she said to Mia.

"I don't know how."

"You do know how. You have done it before, with a similar fojuen arrow."

"You should do it, Zaga. I don't know if—"

"Every second you waste is precious. I will guide you so you do not fail."

She sensed Pilar backing away, shrinking into the forest, and she was dimly aware of Dom on the riverbank, a large but quiet presence. Mia was still dizzy from the unblooding, but she knelt and gently moved Quin's hands aside. He'd touched her with the same hands only minutes before, soft and warm; now they were blocks of ice, hardly human.

"Take this," Zaga said, and dropped a red stone into Mia's hands. Her mother's ruby wren, she realized with a jolt. Zaga must have retrieved it from the pallet in the forest.

"Keep it close to your heart," Zaga said, "so it will amplify your magic."

Mia nodded and tucked it into her blouse, then pressed her palms to Karri's stomach, her fingers stiff with fear.

"No," Zaga said sharply. "The heart."

She did as she was told. Every second mattered, and she couldn't risk any mistakes.

"Tell the blood to calm itself." Zaga's voice was low in Mia's ear. "You must quiet her raging heart."

Mia remembered healing Quin, the numbness in her fingers; the sensation of being a piece of wet cloth, wrung from both ends.

"You must slow her heartbeat. Send the blood away."

But wasn't that unblooding? To shunt the blood *away* from the heart? When she'd healed Quin, she'd put her hands directly over his wound, but then his wound had also been at his heart . . .

"You are distracted. You must wipe your mind clean."

Mia tried again. She closed her eyes and thought of quiet, steady things. The blue lake in Refúj. A pitcher of cream on a level table. A smooth white stone.

"Empty your mind of everything," Zaga rasped, and so Mia erased those images, too. She saw nothing. Only blankness.

Something was wrong.

Her hands weren't working. They were heavy and far too cold. Color and sound were all mashed up, the sound black, the color screaming.

"Stillness, Mia. A dark corridor. An empty room. You must keep her *still*."

She couldn't breathe. Her body was an avalanche. Cold. So cold.

The princess's eyes flew open as her body seized violently. She looked so betrayed. Then she went still.

"Karri?" Quin clutched his sister's hand. "Karri!"

Mia couldn't feel her heartbeat. She couldn't feel anything. The ruby wren was silent at her chest. The princess's large body seemed impossibly small, slumped across the forest floor. How had she never realized Karri was beautiful? Mia had been seduced by the river kingdom's idea of beauty: lithe waists, long hair, doe eyes. But in that moment Princess Karri was the most beautiful woman Mia had ever seen.

And now her heart was silent.

"You killed her." Quin's voice was so low she had to strain to hear it. "You killed my sister."

Karri's blue eyes stared up at the night sky, seeing nothing at all.

Quin wouldn't look at her. Moments before they had been twined together, two delicate instruments of desire. How easy it was for love to turn to hate.

Mia saw herself kneeling on the floor of their cottage, clutching her mother, desperate to call life back into a lifeless body.

"Mia," Zaga said coldly. "You have failed."

Men's shouts flooded the forest. Either King Ronan's guards had been waiting for them, or Tristan had returned and summoned them quickly. There was no time to react. The guards rode into the clearing, crushing delicate saplings and blackthorn blossoms beneath their horses' hooves.

Mia heard Dom bolt through the forest, but Pilar hesitated, torn. Zaga was rooted to the spot.

"Mother?" Pilar's voice was tight with panic. "We have to—"

The head guardsman charged toward her. Mia could feel the honeyed enthrall oozing off Pilar as the girl summoned every ounce of her magic, reaching her hands toward him.

He struck her hard across the face. His glove opened a seam in her cheek, her cheekbone weeping blood.

384

Mia saw what she hadn't before: his glove encrusted with blue stones. She scanned the other guards and saw they all wore armor studded with uzoolion. Someone had told them about the protective properties of the stone.

"Dirty little Gwyrach," snarled the guard, and Mia heard the word as if for the first time. *Gwyrach*. It was harsh and biting, consonants carved from fear and hate. So different from the smooth, mellifluous vowels of *Dujia*.

"Bind them all." The head guardsman pointed to Mia. "But take her first."

She tried to catch Quin's eye, but he was lost in anguish, crouched over his sister like a feral animal. The ropes bit into Mia's wrists as the guards bound her arms together. They threw her over one of their horses as carelessly as a sack of grain, bruising her ribs.

The thunder of hooves swallowed every sound.

Chapter 55

A FAMILY OF MAGGOTS

THE STENCH IN THE dungeon was foul, like putrefying flesh. Mia was surrounded on all sides by the carcasses of prisoners decomposing in the dark. How long until she joined them?

She didn't know how many hours had passed—maybe two, maybe twenty—since the guards thrust her into a stale, lightless cell. There was no way to pass the time; unsurprisingly, the dungeons did not come furnished with a library.

She kept thinking of the journal. The last piece of her mother languished on a bed of needles on the forest floor. She clasped the little ruby wren to her chest. Four chambers in a wren's heart, just like a human's, but even four chambers were not enough for all the grief and love and losses of a life.

In the dark, she saw Karri, the light seeping out of her eyes. If Mia hadn't touched her, she might have lived. Before she laid her hands over her heart, the princess was still conscious, still fighting.

Zaga had trusted Mia, and Mia had failed.

It was the worst failure of her life.

Where was Quin? Did he accompany Karri's body back to the castle? Had he taken her home?

When she thought of him kneeling by his sister in the forest, her heart cleaved in two. He'd been right to be afraid of her. She'd tried to save his sister and failed miserably. Mia was a killer, and that would never change.

She had no appetite, but her throat was parched. She knew a jailer sat at the top of the stairs, even if she couldn't see him.

"Please," she begged. "Can I have some water?"

"If the queen wants you to have a drink, she'll have a carton of horse piss delivered special."

She wished she hadn't asked.

She assumed Ronan was the one who'd had her imprisoned, but perhaps Rowena had taken a more active role in their absence. If the queen thought Mia was responsible for her son going missing, of course she would want her under lock and key. And if Queen Rowena knew Mia was the reason her daughter was dead, then it was a wonder she hadn't asked for her head on a plate.

"Please." She clanged her shackles. "Just one sip of water. I'm dying of thirst."

The jailer laughed.

Her breathing was ragged and irregular; she tried to remember her mother's lesson. She pressed her back into the filthy wall and planted her feet on the ground, placing her left hand over her heart and her right over her belly. She tried to conjure the wind. But she couldn't remember the sound.

She didn't deserve comfort. She deserved to be thrown in a dungeon, to rot in a dark room. The thought of Quin's naked grief wrecked her. She hadn't intended to kill his sister, but what did intention matter when the deed was done? Mia was a danger to herself and others. Had she really thought she could keep her own sister safe when her very touch was fatal?

Quin would never forgive her. She couldn't forgive herself. Lauriel had called her an angel; now she scoffed at the idea. She was a demon. Death with auburn curls.

Her hands were stained brown with Karri's blood. She couldn't see it, but every time she raked her fingertips over her skin, she felt the dried grains. She drew her fingernail down the lines in her palms, tracing a bloodied map of If Onlys.

If only she'd leapt in front of Karri to shield her from the arrow.

If only Zaga hadn't forced her to feel instead of think.

If only she had never journeyed to Refúj.

If only Pilar hadn't shot the prince.

If only her mother were still alive.

If only Mia didn't have magic.

"You. Thirsty rat." The jailer clanked his stick against the iron bars of her cell. She hadn't heard him trundle down the stairs. "Got a gift for you."

She braced herself for a carton of horse piss. Instead he handed her a bundle wrapped in white crinkled paper.

"Looks like you got yourself a friend in high places. Don't eat too fast—I won't be moppin' up your sick if you spew bile all over your cell."

He had the decency to wedge a small torch into the wall, leaving Mia with a dribble of light to eat by. She tore open the paper. A hunk of bread tumbled onto her lap, followed by a flask of clear liquid that nearly slipped through her fingers and shattered on the hard stone floor. She caught it just in time. She uncorked the flask and sniffed, only to find the liquid odorless. Poisons were odorless.

She tipped back the flask and drained it dry.

It was only water. And what did it matter if someone were trying to poison her? She was doomed to die in this cell one way or another. She ripped off stale hunks of bread and devoured those, too, hungrier than she thought.

Only after she had consumed the bread and water did she realize the crinkled paper was not blank.

Mia's eyes strained against the dim torchlight. She gasped.

She was holding a page from her mother's journal.

That was impossible. The book was back in the forest, buried under a mound of pinecones.

Unless someone had retrieved it. Someone who wanted her to read her mother's words.

She stared, disbelieving, at the sangflur ink. It was a page Mia had never seen. Her mother's handwriting was different from the other entries—her neat, flowery script had sloped into sharp, jagged lines, as if the words had been written many years later, or far more quickly.

Sometimes I think Griffin doesn't believe the things he teaches. That he knows they are lies, but he doesn't know how to undo the damage he has done, so he says nothing. That he continues to kill Dujia because he is too cowardly to admit he was wrong.

Your father knows more than he pretends to. I hear him lying to me, his blood thrashing in my ears. I feel the enthrall weakening, whether by some force he is exerting or by my own failure, I do not know. The way he looks at me . . .

If something happens to me, at least you and Angelyne will have each other. This is a great comfort.

But if it comes to this—if there is no other way—then I know what I must do. I have been experimenting, probing the same dark magic I once chastised the woman I loved for using. She was right, and I was wrong. Desperate times call for desperate magic.

I know, when and if the time comes, I will be ready. I will break the Second Law.

*

My clever daughter, my red raven, my eldest child.

We fought today. I know you didn't mean the things you said. I see both your tender heart and the way you try to silence it, shore it up with logic, with rules. We mothers know our children better than they think.

You are angry. So angry. I have failed you in this, as in so many things; I have not taught you how to be angry, how to care for yourself in your rage. As Dujia we are taught rage is dangerous— that we must snuff it out. But I disagree. I think rage is most dangerous when it is snuffed out; this is when it grows.

How could a Dujia not feel anger? Ours is a life of shadow and pain, suffering and loss. I

391

believe anger is only frightening when it gets hidden away. Feeling anger is natural, good. But we must channel it toward good, not evil.

My wish for you, little one, is simple: bring your rage into the light, and love will heal it.

*

Mia, something has happened. I was wrong. About everything.

Your father knows. He says he's been trying to protect me. He says I am in danger, but not from whom I thought. If it is as I fear . . . if the king suspects . . . then these pages may be the last you ever read.

There is a song you and Angie used to sing. "Under the plums, if it's meant to be. You'll come to me, under the snow plum tree." Fly, my red raven. Fly fast and free.

And if I have one final truth to impart
Fidacteu zeu biqhotz limarya eu naj
promise you will always trust your heart
even if you have to stop

That was where the words ended. Beneath them, her mother had drawn a hasty sketch of a snow plum tree.

The world was spinning around her, taffied shapes and grotesque shadows creeping across the dungeon walls, her memory shifting with them.

Her father knew. He hadn't turned against her mother—he'd been trying to protect her. But from whom? The king? The other Hunters?

Who else was there that night?

Mia had all the puzzle pieces, but she couldn't make them fit.

Even if you have to stop . . . what?

A new thought shuddered through her. Her mother had said she was ready to break the Second Law. *Magic shall never be used by a Dujia to consciously inflict pain, suffering, or death on herself.*

Had Wynna chosen to hurt herself? She wouldn't need knife or arrow, not when she could use magic to stop her own heart.

Had she taken her own life?

Mia bolted up off the ground. Someone was talking to the jailer upstairs in soft, syrupy tones. Then silence, followed by footsteps, light and quick.

A torch was bobbing in the darkness. If Mia squinted, she could just make out the white cap of one of the kitchen servants. Then a scullery maid stepped into the light, chin-length black hair pinned up under her frilly cap.

"Pilar?"

She looked exactly like she had the night of the final feast, clumsy hands and dark flashing eyes. With two notable differences:

the slash of dried blood on her cheek and the heavy ring of metal keys swinging from her hand.

"How did you get out?"

"I have my ways. Not *all* the guards were wearing uzool."

"You enthralled the jailer!"

"Naturally." Pilar wedged the torch into a rift in the wall, rifling through the keys until she found the one she wanted. She sniffed the air. "What died in here?"

"I think you mean who . . ."

"Well it's not going to be you. Not today."

The shackles dropped from Mia's wrists with a pleasing iron clunk. Instinctively she rubbed her wrists.

"Where are the others? Are they safe?"

"Don't worry about us. You're here to save your sister. So save her."

"And Quin's sister?"

They were both silent. Then Pilar said, "Truth be told, I'm not a very good shot."

Mia saw the crack in her bravado.

"You were just doing what your mother said."

"So were you. We both failed."

Pilar sighed. "You tried, Rose. That's the important thing. It's not your fault you don't know about magic. You didn't grow up with it like I did. I couldn't escape it, even if I wanted to." She darkened. "Sometimes I want to."

"I tried to heal her. I really tried."

"I know. You tried to quiet her heart, but you didn't know your own power, so you silenced it instead. When you stop a heart, you think of stillness. An empty room."

Pilar shifted her weight. "The kitchens are buzzing with activity. They say the queen is hosting a wedding feast."

A wedding feast. The words were a white-hot poker searing her flesh. Tristan was back at Kaer Killian, fresh from his rape attempt. Quin was home, too. While Mia didn't know which boy would be the groom, she knew exactly who would be the bride.

"Go get your sister," Pilar said. "We'll worry about the rest."

Mia had misjudged her. Pil's heart was true.

She held the torch high as they walked toward the stone stairs. In the winking light, Mia saw a strange shape in the corner of the dungeon. Her heart beat faster. Someone huddled under a thin blanket in the farthest cell.

"Wait."

Winter whipped across her neck, turning her blood to sludge. She saw a wisp of fair hair peeking out from under the blanket. The shape was much too still.

"Come on, Rose. Let's go."

"I need to see who's under there."

"They're not moving."

"I need to see."

"Fine. Then see." She thrust the torch into Mia's hands. "Find your sister and meet us in the quarry." With that she vanished up the stairs.

Mia inched forward. She couldn't hear heartbeats or any blood moving but her own. The stench was overpowering.

"Angie?" Her voice hardly broke the air.

Mia was deadly cold, her fear a manacle of ice around her throat. She could think of nothing more horrible than finding her sister under this blanket, rotting in the dungeons of Kaer Killian. But she had to know.

She gripped a corner of the blanket and ripped it back.

Two bodies decomposed on the dungeon floor, the smaller one trapped in a mass of honeyed blond hair. A family of maggots feasted on the eye sockets of a thin, dead face.

But it wasn't Angelyne. It was Queen Rowena.

Beside her lay King Ronan.

Chapter 56

DIAPHANOUS

MIA GROPED HER WAY out of the dungeons, past the enthralled jailer and back into the light. She was nauseous, disoriented; she stumbled out into the castle corridors where she collided with a wall of polished stone. All she could see were maggots crawling through the space where Rowena's violet eyes had been. She stared at the black onyx and tried to focus. Even her reflection unmoored her.

A gaggle of whispering servant girls spun past. They didn't treat her presence as anything out of the ordinary. One even curtsied. What in four hells was going on? The king and queen rotted on the dungeon floor, and no one seemed to notice.

She leaned against the wall and gulped down air that didn't

smell like decaying flesh. King Ronan had tortured and murdered thousands of innocent women. His fate did not seem unwarranted. But Queen Rowena had not committed these atrocious acts, though she had looked the other way, pretending not to notice. Did that mean she deserved to die, too?

Mia closed her eyes, trying to will away the image, but the maggots crawled through her mind. Karri was there, too, the look of betrayal in her eyes as she bled out on the ground. Quin's whole family: gone. He was alone in the world.

If she let that in, the truth of it, it would destroy her. She couldn't afford to be destroyed.

Mia rushed toward the part of the castle where her family had stayed. There were no guards outside the door to Angelyne's chambers; no one stopped her as she charged inside.

The room was empty. It smelled of lilacs and clean soap, and she saw necklaces and bracelets looped over knots of wood on the far wall, shimmering with stones; on the ivory dresser, hairpins, ribbons, and combs were neatly displayed. She could have kissed them for joy. Angie had been here, in these very chambers. There were no signs of distress.

"Little rose."

She whirled around to find her father standing in the doorway.

"Father!"

She had expected to feel a firestorm of emotions when she saw him again: grief, confusion, rage. But all her feelings boiled down to one. Relief.

Mia ran to him and threw her arms around his neck. He was

thinner than she remembered, his face drawn and his shoulders slumped, but oh so alive.

"Father," she said, her face buried in his jacket, tears pricking her eyes. "I know everything. I know you didn't want to give me away to the royal family . . . and I know why you had to. I know about Mother and how you tried to help her . . ."

He smiled faintly, but his eyes were no longer gray. They were black, glassy and distant.

"Your mind is dazzling, little rose."

But he said it without conviction, as if reading from a script. Mia frowned. Her father's black eyes made it seem as if he were staring right through her. Foreboding slunk down her spine.

"Where's Angelyne?"

He was silent. Mia's heart, so ecstatic a moment before, tripped on its own rhythm.

"Where is Angie, Father? Is she all right?"

Silence. The hairs on her arm began to rise.

"Yes," he said. His voice was a hollow bone with all the marrow sucked out.

He was lying.

Mia felt a clutch of terror. "Take me to her."

Her father turned and walked out of her chambers, his arms held stiffly at his sides. Mia's heart smashed through her ribs. She had a horrible sense of misgiving. Something wasn't right.

They hurried down the glittering black corridors, past the watching chamber and the gardens, and through the Hall of Hands. She winced when the hands twirled as they walked beneath them, morbid thoughts spinning through her mind. If the king had suspected Mia's mother was a Gwyrach, were her hands in the Hall? Had he collected them as trophies, sawed through the tendons and arteries and bones in her wrist?

The same wrist I touched, Mia thought, when I killed her.

She begged her knees to carry her forward, but her body felt broken, empty, a husk without a soul.

They stood outside the Grand Gallery. The air was laced with tantalizing aromas, savory meats and sweet puddings.

"We are expected," her father said, and nodded to the guards, who threw the doors open. She felt her father's hand, light and cool on her back, as he steered her into the Gallery. The heavy doors swung shut behind them, sealing them inside.

The room was full of people, and they were all perfectly still.

The long black feasting table had been set for a feast, steam curling off a lavish spread, as had the gray stone table across the gallery. Guests were dressed in silk gowns and tailored jackets, jewels on fingers, gems glinting around throats. Everyone held drinks or cutlery, their hands poised in midair, spines straight as books. The plates and platters were heaped high with food—cuts of roasted duck, smoked boar, trussed green goose, caramel courting cakes, gooseberry tarts, venison jellies, and candied fruits.

No one ate a morsel. No one made a sound.

The only noise was the cracking and popping of wood in the two giant stone hearths. Quin's yellow dogs lay by the nearest fireplace, legs stiffly extended, chests rising and falling. They appeared to be pinned down by an invisible force.

Mia's gaze swept the gray stone table like a lighthouse beam sweeping the sea. She knew every face. The Hunters sat in one long line, all facing the feasting table, though there were no longer thirteen: without Tuk, Lyman, or Domeniq, the Circle numbered ten. Mia had never seen the men so richly attired. The lone Huntress was nearly unrecognizable, dressed in a high-necked sable gown sleek as wet crow feathers in the firelight.

No one looked at Mia. Every pair of eyes was fixed on the feasting table.

The hierarchy among the royals had shifted. Queen Rowena's seat was conspicuously empty, with Tristan sitting stiffly to one side. And there were several new additions: Domeniq and Pilar, their eyes as glazed and black as schorl.

But it was Quin's face that rooted Mia to the spot. His eyes were as blank as the early days, back when she'd thought him an ice prince, and his uzoolion charm was no longer looped around his neck.

Her eyes swept to the left. When she saw who sat in King Ronan's gilded chair, she sucked in her breath.

No. It couldn't be.

Zaga presided over the Grand Gallery. Her face wasn't frozen; it was beaming bright. She lifted her goblet high and tipped it toward Mia.

She had betrayed them.

The walls were closing in. Mia stepped back and immediately felt the guards step behind her, barring the door. She was trapped.

She turned to ask her father what he had done, only to find his face transfixed, eyes blacker than before. He was watching someone over her shoulder.

"Beautifully done," came the lyrical voice.

A shape floated into her peripheral vision, a snowy-white gown richly embroidered with gold and green thread and emblazoned with the royal crest. Mia tried to make her eyes focus, but they could only absorb fragments: the slender waist, the heart-shaped face, the gloveless arms, the skin so pale it was almost diaphanous.

A golden crown kissed her sister's head, shimmering in the light.

"Oh, Mi," said Angelyne. "Welcome home."

Chapter 57

HEART FOR A HEART

ANGIE STEPPED FORWARD AND kissed her sweetly on both cheeks.

"Aren't you going to say hello? I suppose you're not. Well, I'm happy to see *you*."

Mia couldn't breathe.

Angelyne held out her hand. "My stone, please, Father."

Mia watched as her father fumbled with a chain around his neck. Only then did she realize he'd been wearing the moonstone pendant. He unlatched the clasp and placed the pearly gem in Angie's outstretched palm.

"Thank you. You've been very agreeable. You may sit."

Her father's eyes were thirsty gray again—and fresh with grief. He reached out a quavering hand.

"Sit, Father," Angie said, firmer this time. He turned on his heel and trudged to the feasting table, where he sank into his chair beside the others. Mia felt a cold so ferocious she staggered forward. It wasn't just her own fear she was sensing. Everyone in the Gallery was afraid.

Angie refastened the necklace, feeding the chain through the pendant until the jewel was centered at her throat. Their mother's moonstone shimmered like a knife above her heart.

"You're wondering about the stone. I thought you'd know all about that, since you've been off studying magic." Angie's words had an edge. "I've been experimenting with various gems, but the moonstone is unequivocally the best. There's no question why Mother used it—it can store an enthrall for days at a time. Particularly helpful when you're trying to, say, send someone out on an important errand. Such as a certain duke, sent to retrieve a certain Mia Rose."

She glared at Tristan. "Not that the stone ensures success. The duke did not bring you back to me."

Tristan was motionless. He stared blankly ahead, a thin line of sweat glistening at his scalp.

"You have magic," Mia said. Her voice was unrecognizable, an invasive species of vowels and consonants swarming her mouth.

Angie fixed her with a curious look. "Of course I do. You thought you were the only one? Just imagine the things we'll do together! A little raven and a little swan."

She laced her fingers through Mia's, but her skin felt coarse, foreign. Mia retracted her hand.

"It was you who sent the swan."

"Macabre, I know. But I didn't want you getting too comfortable out there. We have work to do here, in our own kingdom." She shot Zaga a withering glance. "Never mind that *I* was never invited to Refúj to study magic."

Mia kept her voice low. "If you had studied magic, you'd know to free the people in this room from whatever enchantment you've put them under. Someone is going to get hurt."

The smile slid off Angie's face. "You think I don't know that? I've been practicing magic for almost three years now. I'm self-taught. I'm far more powerful than you."

Angie's betrayal was a knife to the gut. Her sister had wanted this. She had orchestrated the whole thing.

"*You* were the castle spy."

Angelyne combed her fingers through a strand of long strawberry hair, then rubbed the moonstone's pearled surface.

"I don't care for that word. *Spy.* It sounds so nefarious. I serve the Dujia. I fight for our mother's true family. Not her family of origin—her family of choice."

"You told Pilar to put an arrow through my heart!"

"I told you to run! Remember? I sat in your chambers the night before the wedding and *begged* you to escape and leave me behind. You had the same kind of headaches I had when I bloomed."

She shook her head. "But then you practically ordered a massacre of Gwyrach as a dinner toast. Our own kind. Our *mother's* kind. You brought this on yourself, Mi. Pilar heard what you said at the final feast, which only confirmed what I'd been telling

Zaga for months. After that, it wasn't really up to me anymore. Things were already under way."

Mia's eyes found Pilar's. She thought she saw a trace of regret beneath the black glaze.

She turned back to Angelyne. "If you knew Mother had magic, why didn't you tell me?"

"You've always been so black-and-white. You know it's true. You fancied yourself a Huntress, a cool-headed scientist, but you were a bit of an ogre, weren't you? All you had was hate and fury in your heart. If I had told you I had magic, you would have killed me."

"I would never hurt you." Her hands were shaking. "You were all I cared about."

"That's what you told yourself. But you've never cared about me. Not really. You cared about the version of me you kept safe in your head, the fragile little sister who couldn't survive without you. You don't even know me. What's my favorite color?"

Mia paused. "Lavender."

"Wrong. Green. What's my favorite song?"

"I don't . . . 'Under the Snow Plum Tree'?"

"I can't stand that song. It's been stuck in my head for years, ever since you and I went dancing around the house pretending to be ladies." Her gaze was piercing. "What did I want to be when I grew up?"

Mia's palms were sticky with sweat. "An explorer."

"Wrong again. That was you. *You* wanted those things. I wanted to get married and have a family, and you thought those things made me weak. I dreamed of being a princess. A queen."

She touched her crown. "And here we are."

"You were willing to let me die for it."

"I never *wanted* that. You're my sister. Sisters do anything for each other." She twisted her hair into a rope and tossed it over her shoulder. "But the Dujia are my sisters, too, and I had to protect them. You know all about that, don't you? A sister who needs protecting?"

Mia had misinterpreted everything. She was so fixated on avenging their mother's death, her little sister had bloomed into someone else right beneath her nose. Angelyne was an equation she hadn't known she needed to solve.

No. That was just it. Angie wasn't an equation at all: she was a person. A hurt, sad, lost, angry girl. And somehow Mia had missed all of it.

Angie coughed, then smoothed her gown.

"My point is that we can put all that behind us now. You're a Dujia. That changes everything. I'm glad it happened this way—glad our archer was atrocious." She glowered at Pilar, then turned back to Mia. "I'm grateful you're alive. Zaga tells me you're talented."

Angie's eyes narrowed. "*Very* talented, I hear."

Mia felt bile burbling in her throat. She had to close her eyes to keep the Gallery from spinning. So this was jealousy. It had a taste, foul and putrid, like a slab of cheese gone moldy. It had a color, too, but that wasn't surprising. Envy was green.

Her gaze combed the feasting table, lighting on her father's face, then Quin's, then Domeniq's. Their eyes were all empty, wiped clean of agency. No one could help her. Standing in a roomful of people, she'd never been more alone.

"Impressive, isn't it?" Angie smiled.

"I don't understand. You're not even touching them."

"You're being very stubborn about this, Mi. Magic is not what we think it is. Our father lied to us." She gestured toward Zaga. "Even *she* lied to us. It's more powerful than we were ever taught. There are ways to test it—to push beyond the existing boundaries. While you've been daydreaming about exploring the four kingdoms, I've been exploring a far richer kingdom: the magic brewing under my own skin."

"What you're doing is wrong, Ange. You're taking away their choice. To enthrall someone is to—"

"Oh, this isn't an enthrall. What gave you that impression? Enthrallment is for juveniles. I told you: I've been practicing magic ever since Mother died. I've taught myself all sorts of wonderful things. I haven't enthralled these people. I've enkindled them."

Angie's mouth twisted into a smirk. "In the old language, *kindyl* means torch or flame. *Enkindyl* means to light something on fire. But for my purposes, it means to inspire or ignite. When I enkindle someone, I ignite a fervor in their heart. That fervor shifts the way the blood flows through their limbs, rewriting the messages their brain sends to their body. They desire something with every fiber of their being. They *yearn* for it. It replaces every other thought in their head."

"That's mind control."

"Wrong again. If anything, it's *heart* control." Angie smiled, pleased. "I know you like your logic and your theories, but a message forged in the brain will never carry the same weight as a feeling forged in the heart. Once that feeling has taken root, it's powerful. The brain has to accept it. Because, when all is said and done, the heart is the mind's master. Our minds can only accept the things our hearts tell us are true."

She smiled at the guests in the Grand Gallery, an indulgent smile, as if they were dogs waiting to have their ears scratched. "I'm not *hurting* them. Their bodies are intimately in tune with mine: they want what I want, feel what I feel."

She flourished a slender hand. "Speak!"

A cacophony of voices flooded the Gallery—screams, shouts, pleas for help, frantic words tumbling out in an ardent jumble.

"Be silent," Angie said.

Instantly they fell silent. The fires breathed and crackled in the hearth.

"Eat!"

The Grand Gallery clinked with the ding of cutlery on plates. Everyone in the room began to eat, chewing and grinding, gurgling and smacking, the sound of hundreds of teeth ripping into soft animal flesh.

Mia had never seen anything so horrific.

"This isn't what Dujia are meant to do. Magic is not about lording power over innocent people. It's meant to *correct* the imbalance of power."

"Who here is innocent?" Angie gestured first toward the

Hunters, then the royals. "Who among them hasn't hurt or raped or killed women like us?"

Mia shifted, uncomfortable. Her sister wasn't wrong.

"But you've taken over their bodies without their consent."

"Just like they've spent centuries taking over ours." Angie plucked an invisible speck from the bodice of her gown. "You're just not used to seeing me strong."

"If you were strong, you wouldn't need to enkindle people to make them follow you."

"You always do this!" Angie said, suddenly vicious. "My whole life you've treated me like a victim—your sick little sister. How could I ever survive without you? It's why I knew you'd come running back the minute I sent you that swan. Gods forbid sweet little Angie be without her big brave sister to save the day. You always wanted to fix me, but you were wrong. I was never broken."

Mia nodded toward Quin. "The prince has never hurt anyone. He's only tried to correct the wrongs of his father." She gestured toward the feasting table, where her friends moved their mouths and hands in sharp, manic motions. "Domeniq is innocent. So is Pilar. And yet you hold them hostage, too."

"An unfortunate consequence." She waved a hand. "Be still!" she shouted, and the Gallery grew quiet. She coughed again, this time more violently, and clutched the moonstone to her chest.

Mia had a new theory.

"I think you've warped the magic inside Mother's stone. She enthralled Father for years, and she struggled with the weight of that every day. But she also tried to use her magic for good. That moonstone was where she stored her magic—it helped her heal people who were sick or hurting. But you've taken the stone and twisted it into something else. And in return, it's twisted you. It's making you sick, Ange."

Mia summoned all her courage. "Let these people go. It's not too late."

Angelyne's smile was bent, her eyes bright with an emotion Mia couldn't place.

"But they haven't seen the entertainment."

Her gown whispered like a summer breeze as she paced the Hunters' table. Their weapons were all within reach—knives, daggers, bows—but their arms remained glued to their sides.

"Hunters, stand."

The ten remaining Hunters stood. Angelyne lifted a goblet of blackthorn wine. She held it high and beamed her beatific smile.

"To the heroes of this feast. You are the warriors who purge the four kingdoms of magic. You are the ones who live and die by the Hunters' Creed: *Heart for a heart, life for a life.* And so, for all the hearts you have destroyed, for all the lives you have taken, I give you: justice."

She let the goblet drop, the glass shattering on the floor, red wine puddling between the shards.

The Hunters fell.

Chapter 58

GRIEF AND SHAME AND MAGIC

THE HUNTERS COLLAPSED IN one solid line, some tipping forward and crashing into their dinner plates; others falling backward, smashing their heads against the hard stone. Except for the skulls that cracked open, no blood was spilled.

Mia was suffocating on air. She felt each death echo in her own heart, so many doors slamming shut, so much emptiness. The lone Huntress slumped forward, her face meeting an ignominious end in a pot of stew. Her white hair was thin and brittle at the scalp. She seemed so exposed, so achingly human.

Compassion welled in Mia's chest. If the Hunters believed Gwyrach were dangerous, it was only because that was the truth they had been taught. Theirs was a culture in which Gwyrach were demons who brought nothing but pain and suffering. Maybe the Hunters were evil heartless killers and murderers—or maybe they were simply misguided. After all, they, like Mia herself, had thought they were doing the right thing.

They were all victims of the river kingdom, she realized. Infected by centuries of living under Clan Killian—their lies, their cruelties, their hate.

"I showed compassion," Angelyne said. "I could have boiled their blood, burned them alive from the inside out. That's what I did to Tristan's little friend." A smile played at the corners of her mouth. "That rapist deserved it. But I showed mercy on the Hunters. Ten hearts ceasing to beat; a quick, painless death."

Mia's eyes alighted on her father at the feasting table, then Domeniq. At least Angie had not grouped them in with the Hunters. At least they were still alive.

This was all her fault. Angie's words echoed her own at the final feast, when she had evoked death and vengeance, a perverted sort of justice. Her sister was merely following her example—and giving that justice one final twist.

"I was wrong, Ange. I know I was. But you don't have to make the same mistakes I did. Whatever that stone has done to you . . . whatever lies Zaga has whispered in your ear . . . this is wrong."

"*Is* it? Are you sure? Because this was the Creed you lived by: hearts and lives for hearts and lives. You can't deny the Hunters have slaughtered hundreds of Dujia, maybe thousands. I am simply repaying the debt."

"There has to be another way. This isn't you, Ange. You're not a murderer. You're gentle. You love music and dancing and reading novels. Remember how we used to twirl through the cottage in Mother's gowns?"

"We were children, Mia! Real life is not about twirling. It's about shame and loss and painful choices. Choices that blur the line between what is lovely and what is foul." Angelyne let out her breath. "You think this has been easy for me? I've looked up to you since I was little. I thought you knew everything. But when I discovered I had magic, I was afraid of what you would do."

"I only wanted to protect you. There are so many things to be frightened of in this world. My whole life I've tried to keep you safe . . ."

"What if I told you I'm the reason Mother is dead?"

Mia willed herself calm.

"It isn't true. I killed Mother when we fought."

"No," Angie said. "You didn't. She was still alive."

The objection withered on her lips. Mia heard no whoosh of blood. Angelyne was telling the truth.

"She was there when we came home from the market," Angie said. "Father left to help the Hunters cart their latest trophy to the Kaer, so I went into the cottage alone and found a basket of food half packed on the kitchen table. And then, through the window, I looked out into the woods behind our house and saw Mother with Lauriel du Zol."

Tears were filling Mia's eyes. If what Angie was saying were true, it meant Mia hadn't killed her mother by touching her. As she had stomped through the woods that day, her rage slowly dimming, her mother was still alive.

"She wasn't wearing her gloves," Angelyne continued. "She had her hands on Lauriel's head—and Lauriel was sobbing, saying she wanted to die. I thought Mother was killing her."

"She was *healing* her! Lauriel had just lost her husband. Mother was calming her mind."

"I know that *now*. But at the time all I saw was our mother touching her best friend while she shook and screamed. In that moment I saw it all so clearly: Mother was the Gwyrach the Hunters were looking for. She had murdered Sach'a and Junay's father, and now she would murder their mother, too.

"But I was too much of a coward to stop her. I cowered in the kitchen, too frightened to go outside. I was weak—you were right about that part."

"I never meant—"

"I'm not finished. I didn't know what happened to Lauriel, only that one minute she was there and the next she wasn't. I was still trembling when Mother came back inside holding her moonstone, exhausted from whatever she'd just done. I said, 'You're a Gwyrach.' She was too tired to deny it.

"I thought she was going to hurt me. I started screaming for Father, for the Hunters—anyone. I was hysterical. She tried to calm me down, tried to touch me, but I wouldn't let her anywhere close."

Angelyne darkened. "My fear gave way to anger, as fear will often do. I'd just seen Junay and Sach'a ripped apart by grief. I was furious she would subject them to an even greater loss. Only Mother knew how volatile I could be when I was angry. You'd never seen my temper, nor had Father. But she knew.

"She begged me not to reveal her. She said she'd rather die a thousand deaths than have her hand grace the king's Hall. But I was too angry—and too afraid—to listen. I told her I would tell Father the truth as soon as he returned. Then I watched her wrap one hand around her wrist and press the other to her heart. She dropped to the floor."

Angelyne's blue eyes were dewed with tears. "Do you have any idea what that's like, Mi? Watching your own mother die in front of you?"

So it wasn't Mia's rage that had killed her mother. It was Angelyne's.

"I was wrong, of course. Terribly wrong. Not wrong about her having magic, but about her being wicked. Whatever inchoate magic I had inside me, Mother's moonstone summoned it to life. I bloomed within the week."

Angie brushed the moisture from her eyes. "Every morning I wake to shame and regret. Shame walks with me through the day, and each night I wrap my arms around regret before I sleep. All these years, I've borne the truth alone."

"Why didn't you tell me? I would have helped you. We could have helped each other."

Angelyne shook her head. "You think you're a cool-headed scientist, but you hold grudges, and you don't forget. The two things I could never tell you were my two biggest secrets: I had magic, and I was the reason Mother was dead."

Mia choked down her tears. She had been wrong about everything, everything but this: her mother had broken the Second Law. Faced with certain death at the hands of the Hunters, she had taken her own life.

And now Angelyne possessed the moonstone. She had warped their mother's healing gifts into a dark, powerful magic, one that no longer required touch. If Angie could enkindle a roomful of people—if one crushed goblet spawned ten instant deaths—what did the future hold?

Mia loved her sister, but she hadn't truly seen her, not for years. Angelyne, Daughter of Clan Rose, Keeper of Secrets. Grief and shame and magic had frayed the goodness in her heart.

And yet, in spite of everything—or maybe because of it—Mia loved her. Angie had struggled alone under the weight of these crushing secrets. Mia didn't feel hate or rage or disgust. She felt only grief.

"I'm sorry, Angie," she said. "I'm sorry I didn't see."

"Still obsessed with the seeing." Zaga spoke for the first time since Mia had arrived in the Gallery. She rose from the king's seat at the feasting table. "Your sister is able to do what you are not: to think with her heart and feel with her mind."

Zaga leaned into her cane as she came toward them. "She will make a fine queen."

Another puzzle piece clicked. What were the words Zaga had whispered to Mia as she knelt beside Princess Karri, trying desperately to save her? *Stillness. A dark corridor. An empty room.*

Mia ran her fingernails across her palms. Karri's blood was still caked into the creases.

"You never meant for me to heal Karri, did you? You wanted me to kill her."

"It is time Glas Ddir had a *new* queen. A powerful queen who can put aside personal passions and grievances for the good of her sisterhood."

Zaga stood beside Angelyne and curved an arm around her shoulders.

Mia sensed what was about to happen a split second too late: Zaga snatched the moonstone from her sister's throat. One quick yank was all it took to snap the fragile chain.

Chapter 59

WHO YOU ARE

MIA COULDN'T MOVE. HER feet had sprouted roots that moored her to the floor. She had never felt so powerless in her own body, her cranial nerves compromised, her brain unable to spur her muscles into action. She pooled all her concentration into her hands but couldn't move a single finger. Her blood was clumped sand, her bones a skeleton in an alabaster box.

"You are wondering why you cannot move," Zaga said, her voice razor calm. "You Glasddirans tell your children fairy tales about the Gwyrach. You say we steal into your chambers at night, bewitch your breath and blood and bone to do our bidding. In your stories, we are always cast as the demon or the witch. And sometimes you are right. We are demon, and we are witch. We are also human. This is what your fairy tales forget."

Mia watched, helpless, as Zaga folded the moonstone into her fist.

"No human is good or evil, black or white. We are all of us gradations. But we do have one thing in common: at heart we are creatures, and creatures do what they must do to survive."

In her peripheral vision, Mia could see Angelyne pinned in place where she had lurched toward the moonstone, her arms outstretched. Zaga held up a hand, and both Angie's arms fell limp at her sides.

"You will leave the stone in my care."

Angelyne's mouth went slack. Her eyes widened, though her body stayed immobile; Zaga must have released her face.

"Please," Angie whispered. "You swore you wouldn't take it from me."

"You have brought the Dujia a great gift with this 'enkindling,' as you call it. We have never seen the likes of it before. But you are self-taught. You have skipped over certain building blocks. For example: how to know when someone is lying."

She appraised the Rose sisters as if pleased with her handiwork.

"Your heart believes you cannot move, and so you cannot move. Your body does not *want* to move, because it wants what I want. Do you know why I can control you so completely? I am using your own magic against you. And your magic is stronger than you think."

Though her body was motionless, Mia's mind was wheeling. So this was what it felt like on the inside of enkindlement. It was terrifying. She'd spent her whole life feeling more connected to her brain than to her body, never realizing how much she took for granted having autonomy over her own anatomy, her own flesh.

Zaga waved a hand and the saliva began to seep back into Mia's mouth. She felt her jaw unhitch, her face loosen as blood flushed once again into her cheeks. She ran her tongue over her teeth, feeling a deep sense of unease at how strange the texture, how foreign. It was a hideous feeling, being invited by someone else to reenter your own body.

"You never wanted my sister or me, did you?" The words inched out of Mia slowly, painfully. "You wanted the moonstone."

Zaga walked to the nearest fireplace to warm her injured hand.

"Your mother was the best healer I knew. She was always far more talented than I was." She gestured toward Mia. "You have the same gift."

Mia felt a gentle tug in her neck, a slight easing of the muscles. She was able to swivel her head half an inch to catch Angelyne's eye. Her sister's face was a mix of fury and regret. So Zaga hadn't been honest with her, either. They had both been puppets in a grander scheme.

"I loved your mother," Zaga began, "but so did everyone. Wynna sparkled brighter than most. I wanted to steal her away to a place we would be safe, to make her mine and never have to share her with anyone. But I could feel I was losing her.

"My magic was my only hope. She knew I was a better Dujia, because I had spent so many years alone, honing my gifts. So I taught her. Then, when she started to lose interest, I began breaking the laws of magic. I thought if I could make her worry about me, she would love me more. But I could see in her eyes she loved me less.

"So I took drastic measures. Picked fights. I craved her attention, and her anger was better than her neglect. I poked at her, found the places of her private hurt and shame and exploited them. It drove me mad how distant she could be, so I hurt her. At least if there was hurt, I knew there was love.

"And then one night, I pushed her to the limit. She coiled and struck back. She was angry, and when she grabbed me by the wrist, her anger shunted through my veins."

Zaga touched her chest softly, as if the memory still lived in the flesh. "When she realized what she'd done, she brought me back from the brink of death. Wynna was always a gifted healer. But a part of my body died that she could not revive. She was consumed by guilt. She said she could no longer be with me, that we were poison to each other. I told her she could redeem herself in only one way."

"Marry my father," Mia said. She was unable to see him at the feasting table, but she thought she could detect the cold frost of his fear.

Zaga's faced was rimmed in shadow. "I have borne the wound of that night ever since, and not just on my skin. When she left me, she destroyed my heart. Love died inside me. I could not love anyone. Not even my own flesh and blood."

Mia was dimly aware of Pilar at the feasting table. A new

sensation drummed in her ears, neither hot nor cold. More like a resounding crack, a hard shatter, then a gust of thin, papery air. Mia wondered if this were the sound of a heart breaking.

"Why didn't you just come for the moonstone?" she said. It took great effort to work her mandible around the words. "Why did you embroil us in your petty jealousies and revenge? Pilar could have stolen the stone from around Angie's neck without ever having to aim an arrow at my heart."

Zaga let the pendant slip through her fingers, where it dangled off the chain.

"You are both your mother's daughters. Angelyne, you have a great gift. You can stop a heart without a single touch. You have taught yourself to channel your feelings, your sadness and your rage. You have used your heart to burnish your magic to a fine gleam."

She turned to Mia. "You have fought your magic, but it rises up in you still. You can enthrall, you can unblood, and you can heal as beautifully as your mother. Your mind tells you all the things you should never be, but your heart tells you who you *are*."

Zaga stood tall, majestic, the lloira stone gripped tightly in her fist. "Your mother's legacy is powerful, and it belongs to all Dujia. We are a sisterhood. But we demand allegiance from our sisters. Loyalty. Love. Sacrifice."

Mia could feel the magic trickling out of her marrow as the energy began to flow back into her fingers and toes. But as it trickled out, dread pooled in the cracks.

"You will have to make a choice," Zaga said. "But before you do, your mother owes me one final recompense." She beckoned to Angelyne and Mia. "Come."

She turned and faced the feasting table, pointing a long finger at Quin. "You will come with me as well."

As he rose from his chair, fresh terror bloomed in Mia's chest.

"Where are we going?" she asked, afraid of the answer.

Zaga smiled. "To pay your mother a visit."

Chapter 60

NOTHING

The crypt was quiet, as crypts are wont to be.

They filed in one after the other, Quin, then Mia, then Angelyne, with Zaga coming last. If she was worried about them running away, she needn't be. Most of the enkindle had burned off, and Mia's calf muscles were humming, aching to run. But where would she go? Her sister had betrayed her, and Zaga had betrayed them all. Every map Mia had ever clung to—even the one that promised safe haven—was now a blank page.

Mia's heart plummeted when she saw her mother's tomb. She wanted to kneel down and draw her fingers over the grooves of the snow plum tree, say hello to the tiny bird peering up at the moon.

Zaga gestured toward Wynna's tomb.

"Even in death, your mother is going to help me. But first, a test for you, Angelyne. You have done well. Very well. But I must know where your true loyalties lie."

She nodded toward Quin. "Enthrall him."

Mia stared at Quin. She tried to convey, in her eyes, how sorry she was for everything. His parents and sister were dead, and he himself had been wounded, controlled, and nearly killed. He didn't deserve that. The prince was gentle and good. She had been wrong—so wrong—about him.

Angie narrowed her eyes at Zaga, as if she were deep in thought.

"If I do this," she said, "if I enthrall the prince, will you give me the moonstone?"

"If you do not do this," Zaga said, "I will kill Mia while you watch."

Mia sensed the fear in her sister dancing with shame and regret. Surprising, since she had been ready to watch Pilar pierce her heart with an arrow.

"Don't do it, Ange," she said quietly. "Not because of me. Don't do it to *Quin*. Don't take away his choice. Remember how Father used to say magic relies on a cruel, unruly heart? He wasn't wrong; magic rises up when people commit cruel, unruly acts. But if we do the same—if we act out of cruelty—then we are no better."

It was the wrong thing to say, because Angie's face hardened. "Haven't you been listening? You don't get to tell me what to do. Not anymore."

Angelyne didn't even have to touch him. Without a word, Quin stood, scooped her face into his hands, and kissed her.

Mia wanted more than anything to look away, but she was transfixed. His long fingers roved through her sister's cascading tresses, fingertips pattering down her shoulders like a warm summer rain. The kiss started off sweet, then hungry, two bodies clasped together by desire. She knew it wasn't real, but it still hurt.

Mia closed her eyes and tried to conjure up the river, the feeling of his smooth, wet body pressed into hers. Whatever that was, it was real.

"There," her sister said, and Mia's eyes flew open. Quin's cheeks were rosy, his mouth too pink. Angie dabbed at her swollen lips.

"Good," Zaga said. "Your talents please me. I see they please your future husband as well. A beautiful, talented, powerful wife. What more could a king want?"

Husband? Wife? The final piece of the puzzle snapped into place: Angelyne was meant to take her place. Mia could practically see the news spreading through the kingdom: King Ronan, Queen Rowena, and Princess Karri had all been ruthlessly slaughtered, killed by Gwyrach Rebellion. With Zaga holding the puppet strings, Quin would become king of Glas Ddir, Angie his blushing bride.

Quin would be trapped in the very life he hated. And, in a strange way, history would repeat itself: Angelyne would lock herself into a farce of a marriage, enthralling a man she didn't love.

As for Mia Rose, she would be a footnote in her own story. If they didn't kill her, they would throw her back into the dungeons, or—worse—use her body as an instrument, a way for Dujia to hone their magical powers against one of their own. She would be sacrificed to the thing she had always loved: science. But she would no longer be the scientist. She would become the experiment.

Once again she searched herself for the fury she knew should be coursing through her. But all she felt was grief.

Mia's voice was low, desperate. "Angelyne, listen. I was wrong to belittle you for wanting the things I didn't want. There's nothing wrong with longing for a husband who loves you, or children, or a closetful of pretty gowns. But this isn't that life. This is a travesty of a marriage—a husband you must enthrall every hour of every day, just like our mother did. It's a mockery of the life you want. You deserve so much more."

Angelyne wavered. Mia saw it in her face—the wanting, the ache.

Then Zaga's voice sliced into them with deadly precision.

"It is as I suspected. As long as you two have each other, you will never choose anyone else. Your heart will belong to your sister over your sisterhood." She pressed her hands together. "There is only room in the river kingdom for one queen. The choice I leave up to you."

"I don't understand," Angelyne said.

"One of you lives. One of you dies."

Mia's skin was on fire. The heat of Zaga's gaze felt like being flayed alive. So this was what hatred felt like. She'd been wrong about that, too. Hatred wasn't cold. It was immolation.

She'd been wrong about everything.

Hate, love, anger—they intermingled in a person's blood, twining together, a symphony of fire and smoke and ashes. Why did it hurt so much, being human? It was astonishing anyone survived a life at all.

A sob rose in Mia's throat. She thought of her sister lying still, blue eyes gone blank forever. She saw Angie's pale face, trapped in this moment of death. No matter what Angelyne had done or what sins she had committed, the world without her was a world bled of its color. There was no music. No laughter. A piece of Mia's heart had died with her mother, and if she had to give up Angie, she knew she would lose the rest.

Hatred will only lead you astray. Love is the stronger choice.

Love is a lodestone, a force so powerful nothing can stop it. Not even death.

A chill perched on Mia's shoulder, birdlike. It nipped at her neck. Her father's words hummed beneath her skin, with one subtle but significant substitution.

Magic is a force so powerful nothing can stop it.

Not even death.

"Perhaps," Zaga said, "it will help you make your decision if I show you just how powerful magic can be."

She moved slowly toward Wynna's tomb, her injured leg hissing across the floor. She unclenched her fist, and the moonstone glinted in the palm of her hand.

"I gave this stone to your mother twenty years ago. One more way I tried to keep her: to shower her with gifts. Back then, the lloira was not strong enough to heal me."

She stroked the moonstone. "But it is much stronger now. Every time your mother healed someone, she grew stronger, as did the magic stored inside her stone. But a stone divorced from its owner is dangerous. If you take a lloira from the Dujia who owned it, the magic can become warped into something unrecognizable, promising only illness and suffering, even death."

Mia stole a glance at Angelyne, whose face was inscrutable.

An unnatural light gleamed in Zaga's eyes. "If the two are reunited, however, it will rekindle the magic in the stone."

She leaned forward, putting one hand on Wynna's name. With the other she held the lloira to the tomb. Her shadow fell over the carving so that Mia could no longer see the bird or the moon or the snow plum tree.

When Zaga stepped back, the moonstone was no longer in her hand.

Mia blinked. The stone was clinging to the tomb. She took a step closer and saw why: Zaga had placed the moonstone into the depression of the moon.

A perfect fit.

"The dust and bones of a Dujia can be powerful," Zaga said, a smile curling her lips. "Especially one as powerful as your mother." When she closed her eyes, she looked almost serene.

Suddenly Mia saw everything clearly. Zaga wanted to be healed. This was what she had always wanted: to reunite Wynna's stone with Wynna's body in the hopes that she could activate the healing magic of the stone. It made a kind of morbid sense: having the moonstone wasn't enough. Zaga had to steal into the

Kaer herself and press the stone into Wynna's tomb, so she could finally watch her black clotted veins fade to a healthy eggshell blue, a gossamer river of life flowing from wrist to heart. *Precious bones. Precious dust.*

Mia was flooded with a compassion so searing it took her breath away. Zaga wanted what anyone wanted. To be whole.

There was only one hitch.

It wasn't working.

Zaga's eyes flew open. She was as gaunt as ever, her emaciated arm still hanging lifeless by her side. "I do not understand," she murmured. "I have brought them back together. Wynna lies in this very tomb." She closed her eyes, lips thin as she pressed them together, willing all her hopes into this one desire.

Mia shivered as another memory snaked through her. The night before the wedding, she'd found her father in the crypt. *Your mother isn't here,* he'd said.

Mia's thoughts moved quickly, an arrow arcing from one target to the next. Her eyes flew to the bird carved into her mother's tomb. It was a ruby wren. Of course it was. Mia scrolled through all the facts she'd memorized: The ruby wren lived in the snow kingdom; it was the only bird that hibernated in winter; it had four chambers in its heart, like a human being; unlike a human being, it could still its heart for months on end to survive the bitter winter. And of course, it was her mother's favorite bird.

Still its heart.

Months on end.

Mia nearly choked.

The ruby wren stopped its own heart to survive.

Instinctively she dropped to her knees in front of her mother's tomb.

She traced the carving of the snow plum tree, letting her fingers flutter down the deep grooves, the way she had done a dozen times since arriving at the Kaer. But this time she let her fingertips linger in the hollow of the little bird.

She rested her forehead against the stone, mere inches away from where Zaga was leaning heavily. Quietly, Mia dipped her fingers into her pocket, and closed her hand around the ruby wren.

Fojuen was a special stone. Vitreous, with brittle tenacity, and—as her mother had taught her—deadly sharp. But it was more than its mineral properties. Fojuen was born in the violent, unruly heart of a volqano. It made a Dujia's heart pump faster and the blood flow quicker, heightening her magic. A talisman carved from fojuen would make it far easier for a Dujia to stop a fellow Dujia's heart.

Or her own.

But what if fojuen were paired with another stone? A stone with healing properties? A stone that drew its power from the moon, storing up magic that might mend a broken body, heal a hurting mind . . . or revive a stilled heart?

Fojuen to stop your heart, and lloira to restore it. Perhaps, with these two stones, a Dujia might give the appearance of ending her own life, when in truth she was merely hibernating.

432

"That is enough." Zaga was angry her plan had not worked, that her body was still broken. "Get up off the floor. Make your choice. Only one of you will leave this crypt."

Mia hardly heard the words. Her heart thrummed against her ribs. The hypothesis ballooning in her chest was wild, forged of instinct and desperation, which in the end made it not much of a hypothesis. It was scientifically suspect, flawed, irrational—and simmering with hope.

"Very well," she said. "Good-bye, Mother." She touched the cold stone one last time, discreetly fitting the ruby wren into the depression of the bird, just long enough for her to prove her theory.

The bird was a perfect fit.

Mia let the wren drop back into her palm and closed her fist. As she did, she scooped the moonstone out of its nook and palmed it as well. Zaga failed to notice the two stones clenched in Mia's hand as she stood and turned her back on her mother.

But her mother wasn't there. She had stilled her own heart—but not to kill herself. She had stilled it to *save* herself. She had stopped her heart from beating . . . but only until it was safe for it to beat again.

Mia felt the truth in the core of her being. Her father had known. He had commissioned a mason to carve the clues on her mother's tombstone: a bird, a moon, a snow plum tree. No, not clues—*ingredients*.

A murderous wren.

A healing moonstone.

And a map.

Under the plums, if it's meant to be. You'll come to me, under the snow plum tree.

Wynna was alive. And she was hiding in the snow kingdom, waiting.

"Time is not infinite," Zaga snapped. "Will your sister die, or will you?"

Mia turned to Angie. "You have to stop my heart."

Her sister's eyes went wide. "Mi."

"You were willing to sacrifice me before, weren't you?"

"That was different. I wasn't the one holding the bow."

"This won't end unless we end it. We have to choose. And I have chosen."

Angelyne shook her head. "Please, Mi. Don't make me do this."

"You have to," Mia said. "It has to be me."

Only days had passed since she tried to flee the Kaer, but it felt like half a lifetime. That seemed another Mia Rose, the girl who filched the pouch of boar's blood from the kitchens, faking her own death to save her sister and herself. She had been ready to break whatever laws she had to. Now she would break another.

Magic shall never be used by Dujia to consciously inflict pain, suffering, or death on herself.

Not a law, per se. More of a suggestion.

But who would take her body out of the crypt? Who would carry her to safety in the snow kingdom, where the Dujia could help make her heart beat again? She imagined it was her father who had transported her mother, but now he sat in the Grand Gallery, unable to come to her aid.

434

She didn't have the answers. Mia Morwynna Rose, Knower of All Things, had to trust the *not* knowing. It was time she trusted the quiet pull of her gut over the blinding whir of her mind.

Mia took Angie's hands in hers. "You won't have to do anything," she whispered. "I'll do it for you." With the ruby wren and the moonstone tucked into her left fist, she dug her right thumb into the soft, translucent skin of her wrist. With Angie's trembling hands cupped around hers, Mia brought them to her chest and held them steady. She pressed her thumb tip into her antecubital vein, the blue river of life running from wrist to heart.

"I love you, Ange."

Veins made beautiful vessels for rage, but they also made beautiful vessels for love.

She let her blood drink up every morsel. As she did, she saw a tumble of shapes and colors. She saw her mother standing on a snow-kissed balcony, wind tousling her chestnut hair as she sketched a wild plum tree. She saw Angie in a green gown with a baby cradled in her arms. She saw Karri riding fiercely into battle, sweat satiny against her bare, sunburnt arms. She saw the Hall of Hands, empty. And she saw Quin, sitting at the edge of the river, pouring his heart out like a song.

How could she love the prince? She hardly knew him. But she wanted to. Her heart wanted what it wanted, and she could feel it swimming toward him: a swatch of gold on a distant shore.

She found Quin's gaze and held it, his eyes blazing green. She would come back for him. There was a map etched inside her she had only now discovered, and he was there, too, waiting where the sea poured into the stars.

Angelyne's fingers were cold, but Mia's hands were warm. She was feverish with hope.

And then something impossible happened. She felt a flutter in her palm.

In the warm nest of her hand, the bird twitched and shivered. Mia sucked in her breath and loosened her fingers, just enough to peek into the dark cave of her palms. Out of the corner of her eye, she saw the wren spread one tiny wing.

The bird was no longer made of stone. It was made of bone and feathers, blood and breath. Her mother's ruby wren had come to life.

Filaments of light threaded through her fingers, and Mia's heart felt like it might burst. Her head understood nothing. Her heart knew everything.

Even as it stopped.

Epilogue

THE BIRD FLEW QUIETLY, slipping unseen through the girl's still fingers. It knew how to move through spaces undetected, silent as a stone. It glided above a boy with golden curls and a girl with wavy red hair as they knelt over the body. The eyes were open, a calm, thirsty gray.

The fissure in the stone was slender, but the bird was small: it winged its way through the rift and out into a grove of plum trees, where it stopped to eat a spider. It would need nourishment for the long journey ahead.

For twenty days and nights the bird beat its wings, stopping only to sup on insects and the occasional small frog. It flew above the watery veins of the river kingdom, over the ice caves and the red salt mines in the south, past Dead Man's Strait and the White Lagoon, steam curling off the surface, the dark sky inked by green lights and a buried sun, until the bird arrived on a balcony where a woman in a snow fox cloak was waiting.

"My clever little raven," the woman murmured, the ax slung over her shoulder twinkling in the sunlight. "She has found me at last."

She cupped her hands, and the ruby wren came home.

Acknowledgments

THEY SAY BREVITY IS the soul of wit, but it is not the soul of acknowledgments—or at least not mine. A book is a journey of a thousand thanks. I will aim to keep mine under a hundred.

Sometimes, when two people love each other, they create a beautiful little bundle called a book. There would be no bundle without Melissa Miller, who, after helping me coax Mia Rose into the world, birthed an actual human child. She's prolific! Huge thanks to my publisher Katherine Tegen, our gracious matriarch, for championing this story, and to Kate Jackson and Suzanne Murphy for being the best surrogate moms. Alex Arnold, my brilliant editor: the heart of this tale bloomed during our epic phone calls. Thank you for helping me nurture HoT into the bouncing baby book it is today.

Have I used up all the midwife metaphors? Alas.

Thanks to Kirby Kim for opening the door to a world I've always dreamed of. Kelsey Horton, I owe you a drink—for all the hours you spent editing, but also for helping coordinate the Singing Shark Attack of 2016. Thank you to Rebecca Aronson for being excellent at everything, Emily Rader and Jill Amack for buffing out all my mistakes, and the whole artistic team for designing a cover that made me understand the expression "love at first sight." Everyone at KT and HarperCollins: you are exceptional. Please *don't* quit your day jobs!

To my early readers: each of you made this book staggeringly better by lending me your eyeballs and your brains. Thank you Hannah, Josh, and Shari for reading the first draft aloud, and Hannah for reading the fourth draft quietly. Sara Sligar gave me tough love when I needed it the most. Kosoko Jackson sent funny GIFs and then pointed to all the places he knew I could do better. Dhonielle Clayton threw open the windows in my mind and showed me what this story could be. Brianne Johnson shined a light on the future—Other Bri, I look forward to all the books dappling the road ahead. Morgan, what can I say? Your real-time reactions were Everything. I will never get sick of reading "YASSSSSSSS THIS GETS BETTER AND BETTER CGCTRWFUVUV."

Thanks are due to Dana L. Davis for gracing my life daily, even when her messages delete themselves; Rachel Hyde for flooding my life with magic; Emily Bain Murphy for sending otters—and writing the book that saved me; Anna Priemaza for brightening dark days with flowers; Tara Carter for pouring her lovely heart out in email form; Melissa Albert for her genius and generosity; Rachael Gross for saving the day so splendidly she *must* be a witch; and Stephanie Garber for sharing exactly the right words at exactly the right time.

I am fortunate to have a host of supportive artist friends: Anna Frazier, Aruni Futuronsky, Ashley Rideaux, Brianne Kohl, Bridget Morrissey, Cori Nelson, Denise Long, Elana K. Arnold, Elise Winn, Emma Jaster, Farrah Penn, Hillary Fields, Jeff Giles, Jenna Moreci, Jilly Gagnon, Kim Chance, Kyle Boatwright, Lauren Spieller, Leah Henderson, Lorna Partington, Martha Brockenbrough, Maura Milan, Michele Moss, Rebecca Gray, Rebecca Nison, Rob Walz, Shawn Ashley, Shruti Swamy, Terry J. Benton, Windy Lynn Harris, the Sassy Djerassis, and countless members of both the 2017 and 2018 debut groups. Thanks for reading my too-long emails, guys.

Tremendous gratitude to all my teachers and mentors who knew I could do this, even when I didn't. Nova Ren Suma, I am indescribably grateful for your generous and loving heart. Michael Levin taught me how to make a living with words. Nicola Yoon, Francesca Lia Block, Kevin Brockmeier, and Kelly Link modeled not just how to write the best kind of books, but how to live the best kind of life. And if we pan back twenty years or so, we'll find my third-grade teacher Winifred Mundinger helping me bind "The Snog-Pig-Mouse"—my first work of fantasy—in brightly colored cardboard. That, folks, was where it all began.

I am indebted to Sara Fraser for handing me my first young adult novel; Joy Malek for stoking the flames of my creative soul;

and Chris DeRosa and Evangelene Strauss for cheering me on through so many long and difficult years. I finally made it!

Bill Posley, thanks for knowing I had one more take inside me. Honora Talbott, what is life without our lunches, your sketches, or four-hour pedicures? I want to be you when I grow up. Teresa Spencer, our text thread has sustained me for over a decade. From COGnates to Kauai, you are a gift in my life. Not just because you called this book a page-turner. #WeAreHankSorros.

To my brother: from the minute you tumbled into the world on that blustery April night, my life changed forever. Thanks for being my baby bro.

To my sister: I never imagined the raven-haired beauty I held in my arms would grow into my fierce, funny, courageous friend. You are the reason I write YA. I truly can't imagine my life without you in it!

To my mom: all those nights of Narnia at bedtime paid off. I wouldn't love words if you hadn't loved them first. I wouldn't know how to dream, fight, or persevere without you. Thank you for giving me life.

To Chris: you have cradled my delicate artsy heart in ways only you could do. Your love, patience, and compassion are not slight in the slightest. Finley Fergus is lucky to have you, but I am luckier. I love you.

And to all the book bloggers and reviewers and readers (yes, you!): this book ceases to be mine the minute the words are inked and stitched to a spine. Now it lives and breathes inside *your* hearts and minds. You are the real magicians. Thank you for sharing your magic with me.